continued

W9-BUL-572

continued . . .

Berkley titles by Nalini Singh

Psy-Changeling Series

SLAVE TO SENSATION
VISIONS OF HEAT
CARESSED BY ICE
MINE TO POSSESS
HOSTAGE TO PLEASURE
BRANDED BY FIRE

BLAZE OF MEMORY
BONDS OF JUSTICE
PLAY OF PASSION
KISS OF SNOW
TANGLE OF NEED

Guild Hunter Series

ANGELS' BLOOD
ARCHANGEL'S KISS
ARCHANGEL'S CONSORT
ARCHANGEL'S BLADE
ARCHANGEL'S STORM

Anthologies

AN ENCHANTED SEASON
(with Maggie Shayne, Erin McCarthy, and Jean Johnson)
THE MAGICAL CHRISTMAS CAT
(with Lora Leigh, Erin McCarthy, and Linda Winstead Jones)
MUST LOVE HELLHOUNDS
(with Charlaine Harris, Ilona Andrews, and Meljean Brook)
BURNING UP
(with Angela Knight, Virginia Kantra, and Meljean Brook)
ANGELS OF DARKNESS
(with Ilona Andrews, Meljean Brook, and Sharon Shinn)
ANGELS' FLIGHT
WILD INVITATION

Specials

ANGELS' PAWN
ANGELS' DANCE

Wild Invitation

NALINI SINGH

BERKLEY SENSATION, NEW YORK

THE BERKLEY PUBLISHING GROUP
Published by the Penguin Group
Penguin Group (USA) Inc.
375 Hudson Street, New York, New York 10014, USA

USA / Canada / UK / Ireland / Australia / New Zealand / India / South Africa / China

Penguin Books Ltd., Registered Offices: 80 Strand, London WC2R 0RL, England
For more information about the Penguin Group visit penguin.com

WILD INVITATION

A Berkley Sensation Book / published by arrangement with the author

Berkley Sensation Books are published by The Berkley Publishing Group.
BERKLEY SENSATION® is a registered trademark of Penguin Group (USA) Inc.
The "B" design is a trademark of Penguin Group (USA) Inc.

For information, address: The Berkley Publishing Group,
a division of Penguin Group (USA) Inc.,
375 Hudson Street, New York, New York 10014.

ISBN: 978-0-425-25513-1

PUBLISHING HISTORY
Berkley Sensation mass-market paperback edition / March 2013

PRINTED IN THE UNITED STATES OF AMERICA

10 9 8 7 6 5 4 3 2 1

Cover art by Don Sipley. Hand lettering by Ron Zinn.
Cover design by George Long.

ALWAYS LEARNING   **PEARSON**

Table of Contents

Beat of
Temptation

Happiness

THE PSY COUNCIL tried to outlaw Christmas once.

It was in the year 2019, four long decades after the implementation of the Silence Protocol. The Protocol itself arose out of the overwhelming incidence of insanity and serial killing in the Psy populace. Driven to the edge, the Psy made a choice. They conditioned their young to feel nothing—not jealousy, not rage, and certainly not joy at the thought of Christmas morning.

So it was that by 2019, only ice ran in the veins of the Psy politicians who wanted to make Christmas illegal. Since the Psy race controlled government then as it does now, *Law 5198: Deletion of Christmas and Associated Holidays* was near certain to pass.

There were a few minor hiccups. Some elderly Psy—those who had been too old at the inception of Silence to allow for true conditioning—weren't certain they wanted the holiday outlawed. But the old ones were few; the last, unwanted vestiges of an emotion-filled past the Psy preferred to forget. They were ignored, their fading voices drowned out by the Silent majority.

Law 5198 was read into the statute books and life moved on.

Except that the humans and changelings, the other two parts of the triumvirate that is the world, took no notice. Christmas trees went up as usual, gifts were bought, and carols were sung. Human business owners did a roaring trade in mulled wine, fruit cake, and roasts with all the trimmings.

In comparison, Psy who owned interests in companies that usually profited from Christmas suffered a sharp drop in income—*Law 5198* meant they could no longer advertise their products in conjunction with the outlawed holiday.

The Psy Council found itself faced with both a mass revolt by the other races, and considerable opposition from the very businesses that backed up its regime. Psy might not feel, but they also did not appreciate their profit margins being compromised. The businesses weren't the only ones who felt the negative impact of *Law 5198*—Enforcement could find no way to prosecute everyone who violated the law against Christmas.

The churches simply acted as if the law didn't exist. But they, in their solemn dignity, weren't the worst offenders. The changelings, in particular the nonpredatory deer species, took great amusement in walking the streets in their animal forms, dressed up as Santa's reindeer.

Then the horse changelings decided it wouldn't hurt their pride to be harnessed two by two to large sleds in order to transport shoppers around the cities. Finally, the humans, the weakest of the three races—with neither the psychic powers of the Psy, nor the animal strength of the changelings—came up with the killing strike.

They changed the name of Christmas to the Day of Happiness.

It was unacceptable for Psy to feel happiness. Those who did had their minds wiped clean and their personalities destroyed in a horrifying process known as "rehabilitation." But it wasn't illegal for anyone else to celebrate happiness. And if they wanted to do it by singing songs, gathering with loved ones, and attending certain ceremonies dressed in their Sunday best, well, that wasn't illegal either.

The powerful, deadly Psy Council was used to instant obedience in all things. However, in the year 2021, the Councilors admitted that wasting Psy resources to ensure compliance with *Law 5198* made no financial or strategic sense. The law was quietly repealed.

Now, some forty years later, Christmas is a celebration unlike any other. Though the Day of Happiness was retired soon after the repeal of *Law 5198*, changelings and humans have always known that they are one and the same thing. Of course, happiness isn't guaranteed by the magic of Christmas. Sometimes, a woman has to fight with everything in her, with her pride and her fury, her love and her anger, with her very soul, in order to claim the joy . . . and the man, meant to be hers.

Chapter 1

TAMSYN LOOKED ACROSS the Pack Circle to the men and women who stood on the other side. Lachlan, their alpha, his hair going the white of wisdom and age, was saying something to Lucas, who was barely fifteen but carried the scent of a future alpha. The past and the future side by side. One day soon, Lucas would lead them. Everyone knew that. The boy had been drenched in blood, his parents murdered in front of his eyes. But he would lead. It didn't matter that even if they waited a decade, he'd still be far too young.

Just like Tamsyn was too young at nineteen to be the senior healer for the DarkRiver leopard pack. Her mentor had been Lucas's mother, Shayla. The attack on Lucas's family had not only stolen their healer, it had left DarkRiver in a state of constant alert. That didn't mean they had given up. No, they were quietly building their strength until the day they could destroy the ShadowWalkers—the pack that had murdered their own.

She knew Nate would be one of those who went after the rogue pack when the time came. He stood tall and strong beside Lachlan, his concentration on whatever it was they were discussing. At twenty-nine years of age, he was one of the pack's top soldiers and would soon be a sentinel, assuming Cian's position when the older man retired from active duty. The sentinels were the pack's first line of defense. They were the strongest, most intelligent, and most dangerous predators of them all.

"Tammy, you're back!"

Startled, she looked away from Nate and into Lysa's bright green eyes. "I only got in an hour ago." Even now, she didn't quite believe she was home—the six months she'd spent at the teaching hospital in New York had been the hardest of her life.

"So the course is over?"

"Yes. That part of it anyway." She could finish the rest of her medical training in nearby San Francisco. Most changeling healers relied on their inborn gifts, but Tamsyn had made the decision to study conventional medicine as well. It was one more way to compensate for her inexperience, for the healing gifts that hadn't yet matured to full strength. She refused to allow her youth to disadvantage her pack.

"Nothing went wrong while I was away?" She'd hated leaving DarkRiver in someone else's care, though she fully trusted the healer who'd stepped in to hold the fort during her absence. "Maria?"

"She left this morning. Itching to get back home exactly like you." Lysa smiled. "It was nice of Maria's pack to lend her to us and she was great, but damn, I'm glad to have you back."

Tamsyn returned her friend's fierce hug. "I'm glad to be back."

Lysa set her free. "Go on. I know you're wanting to catch up with Nate."

"No." She glanced over her shoulder. "He's busy with Lachlan."

"The man's your mate, girl. You can drag him away."

Mate. The word made her heart skip as it had since the day she'd turned fifteen. That was when the mating instinct had awakened, when she'd realized she was one of the lucky ones— she'd been born into the same pack as her mate, had known him since childhood. "It's not official yet."

Lysa rolled her eyes. "As if that matters. Everyone knows you two are meant for each other."

Maybe, but they were nowhere near to consummating the relationship. Nate was determined she get the chance to explore her freedom before settling down. What she had never been able to make him see was that he *was* her freedom. She didn't want to be apart from him. But Nate was stronger than her. And at ten years her senior, he was used to giving orders and having them followed.

"I should freshen up," she said, dragging her eyes away from him a second time. "I just dropped off my bags before coming here." Searching for him.

"All right. I'll see you after you've settled in." Lysa smiled. "I have to go talk to Lachlan about something."

Nodding good-bye, Tamsyn began to move away from the large clearing ringed by trees that was the pack's outdoor meeting place.

NATE had seen Tammy arrive, waited for her to come to him. And now she was walking away. "Excuse me," he said to Lachlan, no longer caring about the discussion at hand. Some Psy named Solias King was apparently making what he thought were discreet inquiries about DarkRiver's territorial reach and ability to defend itself. Lachlan was fairly certain the man wanted to steal their land.

"This is important—oh." The DarkRiver alpha looked up and followed the path of Nate's gaze. His frown turned into a grin. "No wonder you're distracted. Guess we won't be seeing you for a while. We'll have to track this idiot down ourselves."

Good-natured laughter followed Nate out of the Pack Circle as he tracked his mate's scent through the trees. He caught her in under a minute. The second his palm clasped the back of her neck, she froze. "Nathan."

Her skin was delicate under his hand and he was very aware of how easily he could damage her. With her hair swept up into a long tail, her neck appeared even more vulnerable. He rubbed his thumb over the softness of her. "When did you get back?"

"Around four."

It was now five thirty and winter-dark. "Where have you been?" The leopard who was his other half didn't like that she hadn't come to him first.

She turned her head, eyes narrowed. "It's not like you left a note as to your whereabouts."

His beast calmed. She'd gone looking for him. Gentling his hold, he slid his hand to the side of her neck and pulled her to him. She came but her body was stiff against his. "What's the matter?"

"Juanita was very happy to tell me where you were."

He heard the jealousy. "She's a friend and a fellow soldier."

"She was also your lover."

The beast wanted to growl. "Who told you that?"

"I'm a decade younger than you," she retorted. "Of course you've had women. I don't need anyone to paint me a sign."

The jagged edge of anger turned his next words razor-sharp. "I haven't taken a lover since your fifteenth birthday." He was a healthy leopard male in his prime. Sexual hunger did not sit well with him. But neither did cheating on his mate. "And if someone's telling you different, I'll tear out their throat."

She blinked. "No one's telling me different." Her voice was husky. "But I don't like knowing you've had other women in your bed, that they've touched you, pleasured you."

Her bluntness shocked him. Tamsyn did not talk to him like that. "What exactly did you do in New York?" The possessive fury that hit him was close to feral, a harsh thing with claws and teeth.

Her mouth dropped open. "I don't believe this!" Breaking his hold with a quick move of her head—a move he'd taught her—she faced him, hands on her hips. "You think I would—" She gave a little scream. "You know what, if I had, whose fault would that be?"

He folded his arms to keep them from hauling her back against his chest and proving to his beast that she still belonged to him. "Tamsyn."

"No. I've had it up to here!" She jerked the edge of her hand to below her chin. "All the other females my age are taking lovers left, right, and center, and the only thing I get is frustration!"

Her raw need was simple truth. Newly mature females were very sexual, their scent intoxicating to the young males. Then there was the fact that the mating heat had shifted Tammy's natural hunger into higher gear. He could taste the woman musk of her, the lush ripeness just waiting to be bitten into—it was an exhilarating blend, and one he alone had the right to crave. Even the idea of any other male lusting after her pushed his temperature into explosive range. "If I take you," he said quietly, "it'll be for life."

"I know that! And I accept it. I need to belong to you—in every way."

His cock wanted to take her up on it. But she was *nineteen*. She didn't understand what it was she was committing to. He wasn't some cub who'd follow her around with his tongue hanging out like the young males did with the females. He'd take her and he'd keep her. Sexually, he was far more mature than she was, and a leopard changeling's sexual needs only grew more intense with time. "You don't know what you're asking."

"Damn it, Nate, I'm sick of needing you so much I can't sleep." Her hands fisted by her sides, caramel-colored eyes rich with heat. "I'm sick of stroking myself to sleep."

Jesus. The images that hit him were hot and erotic and so detailed they threatened to drive his beast to madness. "We've had this discussion before," he reminded her. "You're carrying too much responsibility as it is." Shayla's murder had forced Tammy to step into the older woman's position—as DarkRiver's healer—at seventeen years of age. She'd never had a chance to be a juvenile, to mess about, to play and roam. "I've seen exactly how wrong things can go if leopards bond before they're ready."

"We are not your parents," she spit back.

He went silent. "I told you to never bring up my parents again."

"Why not?" She was trembling. "They're the reason you're being so stupid. Just because your mother was miserable after deciding to take a permanent partner at age eighteen doesn't mean I will be."

His mother had been more than miserable. "She committed suicide." If not in truth, then in effect. Her drinking had escalated to such an extent that even her tough changeling physiology hadn't been able to repair the damage.

"We are not your parents!" Tamsyn repeated, her voice breaking on the last word. "You're my *mate*. And I'm yours. Your mother and father didn't have that connection."

No, his parents had fallen in love the old-fashioned way, without being driven by the mating instincts of the leopard. It happened like that sometimes. Though mating wasn't uncommon, not every changeling found his or her true mate, the one with whom they could bond on a level that was almost psychic. "Mating will demand more from you than a nonbond relationship ever would," he told her, cognizant of the terrifying animal fury of his hunger for her. "I don't want you walking into that before you're ready."

"And you're the one who decides if and when I'm ready?"

"I'm older and more experienced." She had years to go before she caught up.

She seemed to be gritting her teeth. "Fine! Enjoy yourself in your perfect little world where everything goes according to your plans. Don't blame me if I get sick of waiting for you!" She turned and began to stalk through the trees.

"Tamsyn." He used the tone of voice that made even the rowdiest juvenile stop and pay attention.

She kept walking.

"What the hell?" Striding after her, he caught up just in time to see her clothes disintegrate off her body as she shifted into leopard form.

He froze, stunned as always by the beauty of her. Her pelt was glossy, the dark rosettes defined luxuriantly against the gold. Suddenly, she looked over her shoulder and gave him a look that could only be described as haughty. Her eyes were green-gold, not caramel, in this form, but they were very definitely all female.

He growled at the implied challenge. She snapped her teeth in response and took off. He almost went after her—his claws were already out by the time he brought himself back under control. If he ran her down in his current state . . . well, she wouldn't be complaining about stroking herself to sleep again.

Oh, hell.

Now his mind was so full of images of soft feminine flesh and long stroking fingers that he was in danger of bursting out of his pants. "Shit." Turning in the opposite direction from her, he ran toward a nearby waterfall. An ice-cold bath was exactly what he needed to knock some sense into his head.

He wondered if she moaned when she brought herself to orgasm.

Chapter 2

TAMSYN SHIFTED BACK into human form near her parents' home. They lived fairly close to the Pack Circle and it was where she was staying for the time being, her life in limbo—she should have been living with Nate by now. Eyes stinging at the reminder of his rejection, she went to retrieve some clothes she'd hidden for just such contingencies. Nudity was no big deal in the pack, but she was already going to be a crybaby. At least she could be a clothed crybaby.

Dressed, she walked to the front door. Her mother opened it before she could knock. With her dark hair and pale brown eyes, Sadie Mahaire was an older, smaller version of Tamsyn. It was Tamsyn's father who had given his daughter her height. Her mother took one look at her face and opened her arms. "Come here, my darling."

Sobbing, Tamsyn went into her mother's embrace. "I don't know what to do, Mom," she said, what felt like hours later. She was lying on the sofa, her head in her mother's lap and her legs curled up on the cushions. "This need I have for him, it's clawing me to pieces. But . . . but he doesn't seem to feel the same." That knowledge crushed her, made her feel as if she were bleeding inside.

"Oh, yes he does." Sadie stroked Tamsyn's hair off her face with gentle hands. "He's simply had longer to get used to it."

"Longer? How? The bond awakened at the same instant in both of us." He'd come to the door on her fifteenth birthday and she'd felt something in her snap taut, a connection so strong, it vibrated with how utterly *right* it was.

"Yes, but you were fifteen. Your sexuality was young, immature."

She remembered the wave of heavy warmth that had uncurled in her stomach whenever she'd been around Nathan, the soft ache in low places. "I wanted him even then."

"But as a girl wants, not as a woman." Sadie pressed a kiss to her brow. "He, on the other hand, had to have had a brutal time of it. You were a baby and he'd never have allowed himself to touch you, but he was a man and his beast knew you were his mate."

Tamsyn began to see what her mother was saying. "He had to learn to chain the mating urges of the leopard, wait until I was ready." For the first time, she understood the pain it must've caused him. "And he couldn't be with any other woman."

"Mates don't cheat." Sadie sighed. "That's a very good thing, but it's also a hard thing to bear when things don't work out perfectly. But you understand about Nate now, don't you? He's as hungry for you as you are for him—it's just that he's had years to build up his will against the need."

"He's going to be a sentinel, Mom," she said, proud but afraid. "You know the kind of men who become sentinels. His will was already as strong as steel before he found out about the bond. Now I'm pretty certain it's unbreakable." She rubbed a hand over her heart, where the bond was a savagely twisted knot. Though it was meant to be an instinctive link, Nate had somehow learned to block it. Her animal heart kept reaching out to him . . . only to slam up against a solid wall of resistance.

"Oh, my baby." Sadie squeezed her shoulder and Tamsyn sat up, wiping away the final evidence of her tears. "Now listen," her mother said, pure love in her expression. "The man's will might be unbreakable for some, but not for you. You're his mate. You have a direct line to his soul."

"But he won't listen. He's made up his mind that we're going to wait and wait and wait and—" She shook her head, shoulders hunching in defeat. "I know he's thinking in terms of years, not months." A wait that long would drive her insane. She wasn't being overly dramatic—the lack of tactile contact between her and Nate, the denial of what their beasts craved, it physically *hurt*. "And it's not like I'm some sexy little thing that can seduce him." It was out before she could feel embarrassed.

"You're beautiful." Sadie's voice was full of maternal pride. "You have courage and strength and such spirit."

Tamsyn didn't have the heart to tell her mom that while those qualities might be nice, they didn't exactly make her a knockout. Her hands were practical healer's hands, her hair a plain brown, and her eyes . . . well, her eyes were okay. Sometimes she thought they looked like dark amber. But what man would care about her eyes when women like Juanita with their seductive, curvy bodies were sashaying around? Tamsyn was all legs and strong bones. More horse than leopard, she thought morosely.

"If you give up," Sadie said, cupping Tamsyn's cheeks with soft hands, "you'll regret it for all the long, lonely years that follow. So will he. Nathan thinks he knows what he's doing, but starving the bond will destroy both of you."

"How do I reach him?"

"That's for you to figure out." Her mother smiled. "But I'll give you a hint—he's a man. Treat him like one."

TWO hours later, Tamsyn still hadn't a clue about what she was going to do. Frustrated in more ways than one, she stomped downstairs with the intention of finding something with which to take her mind off Nate. Maybe her mom was quilting and needed an assistant. But the house proved to be empty. Sadie had left a note tacked to the back of the front door.

Your father and I decided to go for a bit of a roam.

Translation: They were off feeding their animals' need for the wild and who knew when they would return. It could be days.

"Great," she muttered, feeling sorry for herself. Trudging into the living room, she had the beginnings of a good sulk going when she spied a box on the coffee table with her name on it.

Another note:

Tammy, darling, I thought you might like to do these while things are quiet (and you're sulking). We could do with some new ones. Love, Mom

Opening the box, she found it filled with homemade Christmas decorations. She smiled, unable to resist their magic. Every year until the horrible day when a bloody nightmare had forced her to step into the position of DarkRiver's healer, she had made these with her family. There were silver cardboard angels and beads strung on fishing wire and beautifully detailed paper dolls. But what held her attention were the round glass ornaments.

Each was meticulously painted with scenes from fairy tale and legend. Most had been done by Tamsyn and her mother as they sat side by side for hours, her father content to "supervise." She smiled. Every ornament held a memory of happiness, of love. Her hand found one decorated with the image of a running panther. She stilled.

Healing's not just about bones and cuts, Tammy, sweetheart.

Tears pricked her eyes at the memory of Shayla's patient voice. Lucas's mother had been a black panther like her son. She had also been Tamsyn's teacher, her friend—a friend whose advice and guidance Tamsyn missed desperately. But today, in this moment, it felt as if Shayla stood right beside her, telling her the truths she needed to hear.

This would be the second Christmas since the attack. No one had been in the mood to celebrate the first, but perhaps it was time to heal her family, her pack.

Even if she couldn't heal herself.

Her eyes narrowed at the self-pitying thought. "Snap out of it," she ordered herself. Sulking be damned—she would not let Nate's idiocy ruin this Christmas for her. And she was going to make sure he knew it.

Chapter 3

SOLIAS KING WAS a Tp-Psy, a telepath with a Gradient 8 ability. That meant he was strong enough to use mind control should he ever decide to. Solias had done so before—politics didn't allow for such niceties as high moral principles.

His current plans, too, would have been far easier to implement had he been able to utilize his telepathic abilities to coerce and persuade. Unfortunately, changelings had rock-solid natural shields. He *might* be able to turn one of them—and that with considerable effort—but he couldn't control the entire DarkRiver pack. "However, that shouldn't be necessary."

"What, sir?" his aide and son, Kinshasa Lhosa, asked.

"Nothing of note." Solias turned. "Do you have the details?"

"Yes." Kinshasa passed them over. Despite his youth, the eighteen-year-old was extremely efficient. Solias had made a good investment when he'd entered into a reproduction contract with the Gradient 7 Tp-Psy who was Kinshasa's mother. Both Kinshasa and the second child from the contract were high-Gradient minds, powerful in their respective abilities.

"Give me a précis."

Kinshasa spoke from memory, his dark skin unlined. "The land in question is perfect for your needs. You can locate a small comm station and office there, then use it as a base for further expansion."

"The leopard pack?" Solias didn't trust Kinshasa—he trusted no one, blood relative or not. But the boy was undoubtedly good at research. "Will they pose a problem?"

"No," Kinshasa said, his tone holding the cool emptiness of Silence. "DarkRiver is a small group with no real presence.

If we were going up against the SnowDancer wolves, it would be a different story. They're somewhat more aggressive."

That was why Solias hadn't looked into "acquiring" wolf land. "Begin preparations for development." The leopards—animals shackled by the choke of emotion—were clearly no threat.

"Yes, sir." Kinshasa paused. "There was another matter, sir."

"Yes?"

"The Psy Council has requested a meeting with you."

Solias nodded. "Forward me the details." The Council was likely interested in the details of his political aspirations—power never changed hands without the Council's approval. If Solias played his cards right, he might not only take over the leadership of San Francisco, he could rise to the Council itself.

The Councilors would appreciate his firm hand with the animals. And if it all ended with a few dead leopards thrown into the mix, so much the better.

Chapter 4

HAVING HALF–FROZEN HIMSELF in the icy chill of the water-fall, Nate finally hunted Tamsyn down well after sunset. It wasn't that he didn't know where she was. It was that he wasn't sure he could face her without doing something stupid. Like yelling, "What the hell are you doing up there?"

Her eyes were night glow as she stood on a tree limb several dangerous feet off the ground, in human form. It would have been another matter if he'd found her there in leopard form. That was normal. The same couldn't be said for a woman with a rope of Christmas lights slung over one shoulder. Now, that woman snorted and began to string the lights around and along the boughs above her head.

"Tamsyn, I swear to God," he grit out, tracking her so he could catch her if she lost her footing, "if you make me come up there, you won't be sitting without wincing for weeks."

"You won't lay a hand on me, Nathan Ryder," she said. "That's the problem, as I recall."

She was right, of course. He'd rather cut off his hand than hurt her. "Fine." Slicing out his claws, he prepared to scale the tree and drag her down to safety.

"Don't you dare mess up my Christmas tree."

He stopped. "Your *what*?" The fir was so tall it seemed to touch the night clouds. Only a crazy woman would attempt to decorate this. But instead of asking if she'd lost her mind and chance getting his head bitten off, he decided to point out another fact. "It's not Christmas for weeks."

"It's a big tree." She continued walking along the branch as she strung the lights. "If you're not going to leave, make yourself useful and string the other side. There are more lights at the bottom of the trunk. Don't insult my cat by playing catcher."

Knowing she was right about her leopard being agile enough to ensure she'd always land on her feet, he looked down, then wished he hadn't. "Where did you get this many lights?" He picked up the heaviest rope, shoved it over one arm, and started climbing.

"People liked the idea of a giant Christmas tree."

"It'll draw Psy to the area like magnets." The other race knew nothing of the pack's network of lairs and aeries. It was a form of protection against the Psy hunger for power. "You want to announce our Pack Circle?"

"I'm not an idiot." The words were blades. "The lights are special low-impact ones. They won't even show to the top of the tree, much less put out a detectable heat signature."

He wondered if insanity was catching. "I can't believe I'm having this conversation with you. It's ten o'clock at night."

"Feel free to leave if it's past your bedtime."

The bite of sarcasm made him grin. His cat liked being near Tamsyn, no matter her mood. And he was animal enough to appreciate her claws—no leopard wanted a weak mate. "So, what are you planning to do for an encore? A parade of giant jack o'lanterns? Maybe we can use them to scare off the wolves?"

"Good idea." He could hear her smirk. "Shouldn't you be out doing important sentinel stuff?"

"I'm not officially a sentinel yet." Though he was already being allocated most of Cian's work as the other man concentrated on his role as advisor to Lachlan and trainer to Lucas. "I have the night off."

"And you're here? What, Juanita was busy?"

He let her hear the angry rumble of his growl. "Are you really accusing me of cheating?"

"Not possible to cheat on something that doesn't exist."

"Tamsyn," he began, intending to tear into her. Then his beast suddenly realized something. "You're still jealous of a relationship that was over years ago." He couldn't understand why, not when he'd made it plain that he'd been celibate since the mating bond snapped into being.

Silence for several minutes. "It hurts me to know a woman who's been allowed full skin privileges with you—while I'm not even worth a simple kiss."

He froze at the amount of pain in that single statement. "Don't you *ever* compare yourself to any other woman," he said, his beast raging at the mere idea. The instant he'd realized she'd been born for him, it had blinded him to anyone else.

She didn't answer.

"Tammy."

"I don't want to talk anymore."

He was certain he heard tears in her voice. It shook him. His strong, beautiful mate never cried. "Tammy, don't."

"Don't what? Decorate my tree in peace?" The acerbic edge was back.

"I thought . . ." He shook his head, relieved. "What's next, after the lights?"

"Ornaments. They'll take a while. I'm going to get the kids to make one each."

He jumped easily to the ground and picked up the last rope. Stringing that took far too little time though he tried to stretch it out. Tamsyn was waiting for him when he jumped down the second time. "Thanks."

He fisted his hands to keep from stroking the delicate line of her profile. "You going to turn it on?"

"Not until it's ready." She shoved her own hands into the pockets of her jeans. "I'd better get inside. It's chilly."

He was one step from pulling her into a hug, would have done so for any other packmate who needed it—touch was the cornerstone of who they were. But if he touched Tamsyn, it wouldn't stop at a simple hug. He'd take all of her, claim proprietary skin privileges from head to toe, spending extra time on every seductive feminine curve in between. His voice was leopard-rough when he asked, "What are you doing tomorrow?"

"Working with the kids on the ornaments. Going over some study papers." She turned on her heel. "Good night, Nate."

He frowned. "You're still angry."

"No." She gave him a tight smile. "But I'm also not a sucker for punishment. You might have had years to get used to resisting the full brunt of the mating heat, but I haven't. So help me out and keep your distance."

• • •

"KEEP my distance." Nate paced across the length of his living room and back. "Keep my distance." He was her mate—she *belonged* to him—and she'd told him to keep his distance.

Something growled deep in the forests that surrounded his home and he wondered which one of his pack was running under the moon. If he'd had to bet, he'd have said either Lucas or Vaughn, or maybe both. The two were still juveniles, but both had already seen death firsthand, been scarred by their losses. Now they waited to grow up so they could claim vengeance.

He would go with them when it was time to destroy the ShadowWalkers. The younger males would be fighting their demons, but he would be fighting for his mate's right to be safe. Something dark and almost violent in him tightened at the thought of her, a sense of complete rightness filling his soul. She was his, wouldn't ever be anyone else's. The reminder calmed the visceral hunger of his beast.

He would never forget the moment when he'd realized what she was to him. Because of the disparity in their ages, they had had different friends, moved in different levels of the pack. But he had always known who she was, adored her in a way that was everything good—her laugh soothed the rough edges of his beast, her smile made him want to smile in turn.

On the night of her fifteenth birthday, she had hosted a small sleepover party at her parents' home. He'd dropped in to wish her a happy birthday. It had been no fleeting impulse—he'd become used to swinging by to check if she was okay, especially during the times when her parents were out. As soon as she had opened the door, he'd felt the bond snap taut. The knowledge had been in her eyes, too, shocked and bright.

He'd touched her then, cupped her cheek with his hand. She had leaned into him, soft and welcoming and everything he had ever wanted. He'd known that, at that moment, he could ask anything of her and she'd give it to him. That was what had made him draw back. "Not until you're ready," he'd said, ending the contact.

It was a promise he refused to break.

Tamsyn thought he was being cruel. She hadn't seen what

he had with his parents. His mother had been too young, his father too demanding. Within a decade, they had destroyed each other and themselves. The idea of doing that to Tamsyn was his worst nightmare. Because he knew he was too much like his father—he would not be an easy man to mate with. He'd expect total devotion, demand complete sexual surrender, take absolute possession.

Tonight, his body hungered for her with a fury that was more animal than man. The cat had wanted her from the first. To the leopard, she'd smelled mature at fifteen, but the man had known she was nowhere near ready. Now . . . now he could have her—if he was willing to look into her eyes for the rest of his life and know he'd stolen what little freedom she could have had.

"No." He would not do that to her. She might be frustrated and annoyed with him, but she'd forgive him. It was what mates did.

TAMSYN was never going to forgive Nathan for putting her through this! "I can't stand it!" Her skin was so sensitive even the sheets felt abrasive. The flesh between her legs was swollen with need and there was only one man she wanted to rub against, only one thing she wanted to do. Unfortunately, Nate didn't want to play.

Why had he turned up tonight? To torture her? Her beast had become drunk on his scent, addicted to the proud masculine taste of him. It wanted more. So much more. Maybe that was why he'd come over—because his beast was starving, too? She snorted. More likely he'd come to tell her off for daring to turn her back on him this afternoon.

Nate was used to obedience. Particularly from her. As a fifteen-year-old, she'd taken everything he said as gospel. At sixteen, she'd given him the occasional moment of lip but had always accepted his decisions in the end. And he'd never let her down. He'd been her rock . . . especially after that dark day two years ago when she had failed to save Lucas's father.

"Carlos wanted to die," Nate had whispered in her ear, *holding her tight as she sobbed over the loss. He'd still held her then. "He didn't want to live without Shayla."*

It hadn't taken away her sense of failure, but she'd understood. The bond between mates was beautiful, powerful. Separated mates could live without each other, but it hurt. As she knew too well. And she shouldn't! Unlike those whose mates had been lost to death, Nate was alive but wouldn't touch her.

That was so incredibly wrong. Changelings weren't Psy. Touch was as necessary to them as food and air. Tamsyn thought nothing of hugging and kissing a fellow packmate who needed reassurance. That her mate wouldn't even give her that . . .

"I don't care," she lied into the dark. "Hell, yes, I do." Shoving off the sheets and blankets, she slid off the bed and went to get a glass of water. Ice-cold water. God, even her skin ached.

Filling up the glass, she took it and herself to the front window. Her plan—to distract herself by admiring her tree—disappeared the second she saw the leopard asleep on one of the branches. She couldn't make out his markings but she already knew who it was. Nathan. The man wouldn't take her as his mate in truth, but he thought he had the right to protect her? Damn him. Slamming down the glass, she was halfway to the door when she looked down at herself.

All she wore was an old football jersey. It was Nate's. She'd stolen it from him in a blatant bit of thievery, needing his scent around her. But big as it was, it gaped over her full breasts and only hit her midthigh. Maybe she should change. And it was freezing outside.

Nate probably wouldn't appreciate her walking around half-naked any— She slapped her forehead. "Tamsyn, sometimes you're an idiot." Of course he wouldn't appreciate her walking around half-naked. The sight of so much skin might incite his beast, tempt it enough to overpower the man's will.

Her lips curved.

Chapter 5

SHOVING HER FEET into a pair of fluffy slippers, she stamped outside and to the tree, knowing he'd have woken the second she opened the door. "Nathan, you get out of here right now!" She hugged her arms around herself, well aware the move plumped up her breasts, creating a deep cleavage.

The leopard growled at her, its green eyes dangerously bright.

"Don't you growl at me," she said, and her breath turned the air to mist. "You don't get to pick and choose which parts of the mating deal you want. It's all or nothing. *Go away!*"

He padded along the tree limb and leaped to the ground by her feet, a stunning creature she could stroke for hours. Then he butted at her legs, urging her inside the house.

The touch of his fur against her skin made her shiver. "I'm not leaving until you're gone." She'd meant to tease him, but already, her own leopard was scraping at the insides of her skin, so darkly needy it scared her.

He bared his teeth and gave a short, husky roar meant to snap her to attention. His eyes told her to get her little butt back inside or he'd do it for her. She hoped he would. Because if he shifted now, he'd be naked. Skin to skin contact at last. Her thighs trembled, but she somehow found the strength to stamp her foot and point away from her home. "Out! Leave!"

He began walking toward the house. She frowned, wondering what he was up to. He got to the door and looked over his shoulder. She wasn't going to fall for that. Then he walked inside. Her eyes wide, she hotfooted it inside, closing the door behind her.

The leopard was sitting in front of the currently unlit laz-fire, the artificial heating system designed to resemble a live blaze—but one that had zero chance of getting out of control. He glanced at her, his eyes night-glow in the darkness.

"Good idea," she said, half-frozen. Kicking off the furry slippers, she turned on the laz-fire. The flames shot to instantaneous life. "Brr." Rubbing her hands together, she sat down beside Nathan. She couldn't quite think straight but that was okay. Nate was in her house. He was here. And they were alone.

He butted at her hand with his head and she began to stroke him, her body warming up from the inside out. "What were you doing out there, Nate?"

He laid his head on her thigh and growled softly in response.

"It's because my parents are gone, isn't it?" She sighed and tried not to tremble at the proximity of him. He was so lethally beautiful, his body pure muscle under her strokes. "When are you going to accept that I'm a grown-up? Huh?"

No response. The steady rhythm of his breathing told her he'd fallen asleep. She couldn't bear to wake him. Tears pricked her eyes. If she shifted, they would both be cat and . . . No, she thought. She wouldn't use the animals' driving need against Nate.

It was the man who wanted to give her "freedom" and it was the man she had to convince. The animal already knew what was right. If only Nate's human half hadn't gotten in the way. Except, of course, she loved that part of him, too. Sighing, she stroked her fingers through his fur over and over.

It was a long while later when she curled up beside him and went to sleep.

NATE waited to lift his head until he was absolutely sure Tamsyn was fast asleep. The last hour had been both pain and pleasure, torture and redemption. The animal couldn't understand why he didn't claim her. One thought, a split-second shift into human form, and he could take her right there on the softness of the rug.

The temptation was shockingly strong.

She was the most exquisite creature he had ever seen. A long, tall drink of woman. He could spend all night stroking his hand up and down the sleekness of her thighs—exposed by that jersey she'd stolen years ago.

He'd known, of course. It had given him pleasure to think of her covered in his scent. Since he hadn't seen her wearing it around, he had guessed, *had wanted*, it to be her nightwear of choice. His claws dug into the rug as he shifted his attention to the proud thrust of her breasts. There was no question about it—Tamsyn was every inch a woman. And so heartbreakingly young.

No one would think to look at her that she'd been their healer for two years already. Oh, the few packs they had trusted after Shayla's murder—packs with men and women seeded from DarkRiver—had sent senior healers to complete her education, but it was Tamsyn the pack looked to. She was their own and she was deeply trusted.

Because she had never let them down.

He remembered her at seventeen. Her mentor was dead and Shayla's mate, Carlos, lay critically injured. Their son, Lucas, remained missing. Tammy had been so slender back then, a fragile reed he'd thought would snap under the weight of the dying sentinel's wounds. But she hadn't broken. Instead, she'd put every inch of her abilities into healing Carlos.

She hadn't been able to save his life, but she had given him the strength to whisper his final words—ones that told them Lucas was still alive. Tammy had been completely drained by the effort to save Carlos, but when they had rescued a badly injured Lucas, she had somehow found impossibly more to give. And she'd kept doing it for weeks.

She had slept only when Nate forced her to, worried she'd collapse under the strain. Even then, she would crawl out of bed after a few hours at most. Finally, Nate had had to half kidnap her. He'd held her in his lap and told her to sleep. And she had, curled up trustingly in his arms.

The girl who had been that slender reed was gone. She'd grown into a woman of courage and beauty, but one who had never been given the chance to be a juvenile. Leopards valued their freedom to roam—many left the pack and came back after spending time in the wild. He, too, had left DarkRiver for several years in his late teens. Tammy had never had that choice, her wings clipped at fifteen.

Backing away from the lush temptation of her, he dragged an afghan off the couch using his teeth and pulled it over her. It would've been easier in his human form, but he didn't trust his willpower that much. One touch was all it would take. He'd crumble like so much dust.

He decided to keep watch over her from the outside.

TAMSYN woke up warm . . . and alone. It hurt. "I could hate you, Nathan." Getting up, she hugged the afghan around herself and stared into the laz-fire. Her internal clock told her it was morning, sometime around six. Despite the fact that she'd done all she could to entice Nate, he hadn't so much as kissed her.

Was she that disgusting to him?

A sob caught in her throat. It was the first time she'd considered that Nate's recalcitrance might spring, not from his overwhelming protectiveness, but because he didn't *want* to be tied to her. Her lower lip trembled. She hugged the afghan even tighter around her body in a vain effort to ward off hysteria.

Being unwanted by a mate was a nightmare beyond comprehension. Mating wasn't marriage, wasn't infatuation, wasn't a connection you ever broke. She was tied to Nate on the level of her soul. More than that, she loved him. Some people said that there was no difference between the bond and love, but she knew there was. It was one thing to be compelled toward Nate, another to adore him like she did. She loved everything about him, from his strength to his laugh to his unashamed masculinity.

But what if, for Nate, the bond was simply a compulsion? One he couldn't dissolve, but that he wouldn't have chosen if he'd been given the choice? She was hardly a prize, she knew that, had always known it. Added to that, Nate was older, more experienced. Maybe he'd expected and wanted to find a mate who could match him, a woman who'd seen far more of the world than just their small corner of it.

In contrast, Tamsyn had always been tied to DarkRiver. That didn't matter to her. She was a woman of home and hearth. It was the way of most healers. They liked to be near their people, their lands. Healers built permanent homes before most others, took in anyone who needed their help, and cherished those who were their own. The months in New York had almost torn out her heart, she'd been so homesick.

But Nate had roamed. He'd left the pack for years as a juvenile and come back a man, strong, loyal, and with wild horizons in his eyes. What did he see in hers? Home—calm, steady, enduring. But not very exciting. No wonder he didn't want her!

Tamsyn had worked herself into quite a state, something that would've flabbergasted those who knew her, when the comm console chimed. It was the emergency code. She blinked and snapped to attention, the healer in her taking over. "Talk to me."

Juanita's face appeared onscreen. "Dorian broke his arm while we were sparring near the Circle. It's pretty bad."

"Don't move him." Turning off the screen, she got up, changed at the speed of light, grabbed her emergency supplies, and headed out.

The cold air cut across her cheeks as she ran. If Dorian hadn't been so close by, she'd have taken a vehicle. But at this distance, her changeling speed was faster than the vehicle would have been on the rutted forest roads. The roads had been damaged on purpose. It was another line of defense, meant to bog down the unwary. DarkRiver was never going to be caught off-guard again.

She found Juanita crouched beside Dorian, who was sitting propped up against a tree. Though the woman looked concerned, Dorian's face betrayed nothing. Barely into double digits, the boy was better at hiding his feelings than most adults. "What were you two doing to break that arm?" she asked, going down beside him.

"Karate. Brown belt. San-kyu," Juanita answered.

Tamsyn didn't berate the other woman for using such advanced techniques against a boy. They all knew Dorian was no child. He'd been born latent and had no ability to shift into leopard form. Perhaps it was something that might have been held against him had he not made it his mission to become so dangerous, no one would dare treat him as anything but another cat.

"A single break. Clean," she told him. "You were lucky."

Pure blue eyes looked into hers. "How long till I can use it?"

"As long as I say." She put a pressure injector against his

arm before he could object that he didn't need the anesthetic. Then, using the portable deep-tissue viewer to double-check the conclusions of her healing gift, she set the break and encased it in a lightweight but durable cast. Dorian had normal changeling strength and healing capacity—he'd regain the use of his arm far sooner than a human or Psy would have in the same situation.

"Nita, can you give me a minute with Dorian?" She glanced at the beautiful woman.

Juanita nodded. "I have a perimeter watch to take over."

"I'll make sure he gets home."

Dorian scowled as they talked about him but didn't say anything until Juanita had disappeared into the trees. "What?"

Shaking her head at that stubborn male expression, Tamsyn moved to sit slightly behind him. Then she threw her arms around his neck and leaned down to press her cheek against his. "San-kyu, that's the third level, isn't it?" With the dominant males—or with the young ones who would one day be dominant—you had to tread carefully. Demanding would get her nothing from Dorian.

He softened a little. "Yep. I'm going for black next month."

"Impressive. When I left for New York, you were still on the first level of brown."

He let her tug him further into her embrace. Touch was at the heart of a healthy pack. It was what bound them together, what gave them their strength. Smiling, she raised her hand and began to brush her fingers through his incongruously silky blond hair as he lay against her.

"I'm going to be past Juanita's level soon." It was a small boast and it was perfectly normal. Whatever had happened to break his arm, it hadn't bruised his pride too much.

She grinned. "Then who are you going to beat up?"

He actually smiled. "You want I should do Nate for you?"

It seemed the whole pack knew how things were between her and Nathan. "Brat."

"Yeah, but you like me."

Laughing, she pressed a kiss to his cheek before rising. He followed, his bones showing the promise of a height that would top hers by several inches at least. "Look after yourself, Dorian.

If I see you one more time this year, I'm going to do something nasty like pull healer rank and ground you."

"Like you wish you could ground Nate—maybe in your bedroom?"

"Dorian!"

Mischief in his grin, he backed away from her before turning to run off through the trees. She kept her smile hidden until he was gone. Then she bent down and began to gather up her supplies and equipment. She was pleased. Her medical training had come in very handy today. Otherwise she'd have used up healing energy to no useful purpose. What she did came from inside her—she had to conserve her strength for the worst injuries . . . as had happened with Carlos.

Leaves rustled to her left and she looked up to see Juanita step out. "Did you see my—ah, there it is." Nita picked a slender black timepiece off the ground. "Took it off while we were sparring. That boy is dangerous when he gets going."

Nodding, Tamsyn continued to put away her things. Nita was the last person she wanted to chat with, especially after the horrible realization she'd had that morning. Then the other woman went down on her haunches beside Tamsyn.

"Hey, Tammy. I need some advice."

Her healer core came to the surface, consigning the sick ugliness of jealousy to one tiny corner. "Is something the matter?" She looked into that sensual, exotic face and no longer saw a rival, but a packmate who might need help.

"You could say that." Dark eyes twinkled. "I'm wondering how to bring up Nate without putting my foot in it."

Chapter 6

TAMSYN FROZE. "WHAT about Nate?" she forced herself to say.

"Look"—Juanita tapped a finger against her knee—"he's a wonderful guy and we had some fun together—"

Tamsyn shut her bag and prepared to get up.

Juanita stopped her by holding on to her upper arm. "But that's all it was. Fun. We were friends then and we're friends now. Nothing more."

"Okay. I have to go." She was so hungry for Nate's touch that even the idea of him with another woman bruised her raw.

Juanita didn't release her. "You're not listening, Tammy. I'm telling you that that man never looked at me with the kind of wild heat with which he looks at you. He never craved me, not like he craves you."

Tamsyn stared at the other woman. "He left me," she found herself saying. "I was all but offering myself to him on a silver platter and he left me. He doesn't crave me."

Juanita laughed. "The man wants you so much, he's driving all the juveniles crazy. You know how sensitive they are to sexual hunger, and right now, Nate is a six-feet-plus shot of pure animal need. And he's not interested in anyone but you."

"But—"

"But nothing." Juanita stood and waited until Tamsyn, too, was up before continuing. "Don't take this the wrong way but you're young."

How else could she take it? "I'm more mature than people years older."

"Yes, you are. I wouldn't hesitate to come to you for advice on a thousand things." Juanita's matter-of-fact words took the wind out of Tamsyn's sails. "But there's one area in which you are a babe in the woods."

"Men," Tamsyn whispered, embarrassment a blaze across her cheeks.

"Yep. You were one of the lucky ones—you found your mate early, but that came with a price." Juanita didn't need to spell it out. "So trust me when I tell you the man is dying for a taste of you."

Tamsyn ached to believe. "He's very good at hiding it."

"Of course he is. He's stubborn and he's dominant. He wants to do this *his* way. It's up to you to change his mind. Please do it before he drives everyone insane."

Taking a deep breath, Tamsyn swallowed her pride and put her faith in the bonds of Pack. "You have experience. Teach me what I need to know."

Juanita grinned. "I thought you'd never ask."

A day after he'd left Tammy sleeping by the fire, Nate returned from a meeting with Lachlan to find the area around her home crawling with children. Not all of them were exactly underage. "What are you doing?" he asked Cian, who was sitting on what looked like a bench and table set stolen from their alpha's backyard.

The older man grinned. "Making Christmas decorations, what does it look like?" He returned to painting the small glass ball in his hand.

"Why?" Nate insisted.

Cian scowled at him. "Because Tamsyn said I had to."

"She's less than half your age."

"Have you tried to argue with her when she wants to get her own way?" Shaking his head, Cian returned to his task. "Besides, it's kind of fun. And she's got the juveniles interested in something other than raising hell, which makes our job easier."

Now that Cian had mentioned it, Nate realized just how many of the older kids were present. Even arm-cast-laden Dorian appeared to be having fun. Nate watched as the boy bent down to help a five-year-old paint something on her globe. When she smiled, so did Dorian.

Turning his head, Nate found Lucas sitting with another group of young ones. Several cubs were trying to use his body as a climbing frame, but from the sharp grin on his face, he didn't seem to be worried. He called out to someone else and Nate's eyes followed his gaze to locate another unexpected addition to Tamsyn's gathering. Vaughn. He was an even worse loner than Dorian. But there he was, patiently helping several of the three-year-olds.

"They're happy," a feminine voice said from beside him.

He looked down. "You did good."

Astonishment was open on her face. "Oh." A pause. "Thank you."

He scowled. "What's wrong with me complimenting you?"

"Nothing." She shrugged, her breasts pushing out against the softness of her black cowl-neck sweater. "You just don't do it much."

He reached out to pinch a bit of her sweater with his fingertips. "What is this stuff?" It was so damn strokable he was having a hard time keeping himself from doing exactly that. Shaping his mate's body with his palms seemed like the best idea he'd had all day.

"Angora blend." She pulled away from his touch and took a step backward. "Do you want to paint an ornament? Or you can help the children."

He didn't like the distance she'd put between them. "What's the matter with you?"

Something flickered in her eyes before her lashes lowered to screen her expression. "I'm living my own life. It's what you want, right?" A small smile. "I'm finally beginning to appreciate what you've been trying to tell me." With that, she went off to check up on a group of giggling teenage girls.

Nate wondered if he looked as sucker-punched as he felt. She'd pulled that stunt out of nowhere. All these months of fighting him, of demanding he accept their bond, and she was suddenly going to fall in line? Right. He'd believe that when he saw it. Tamsyn had called him every day from New York—she couldn't shut him out if she tried.

Twelve hours of near-silence later, long after everyone else had left, he grit his teeth and handed her an ornament. "This is the last finished one." Many had taken theirs home to complete.

"Thanks." She hung it on her damn tree before jumping down from the branch on which she'd crouched. "I think it'll look fabulous when it's done, don't you?" Without waiting for an answer, she turned to walk up the path to her door.

"Where are you going?" He barely kept the growl out of his voice.

She threw him a confused look. "It's dark. I'm going to have a bath and dinner."

He waited for the invitation to join her. It didn't come. "Your parents aren't back."

"Oh, don't worry." A tight smile accompanied her words. "A few of my girlfriends are dropping by tonight."

"Who?"

"Friends. Actually, do you mind not coming by at all?" she asked. "We can hardly talk girl-talk if we know you're out here skulking."

His temper wasn't easily stoked. But it was smoking now. "Skulking?"

She gave him an airy wave. "You know what I mean. We'll be fine. I even asked some of the other soldiers to swing past during their night watches. You should go do your own thing." A few seconds later, her door shut behind her.

He didn't move, rooted to the spot by pure disbelief. She'd told him to get lost. Nobody told him to get lost. Especially not his mate. He'd taken the first step up the path to her home when he felt someone walk out of the woods behind him. He turned to find Juanita. "What?" It was the leopard speaking.

"This is part of my night route." She gave him a curious look. "What are you doing here?"

What kind of idiotic question was that? "Looking after my mate."

Juanita scowled. "You're on the eastern perimeter, Nate. If you wanted a change, you should've told Cian. We'll have a gap there otherwise and you know we can't afford to. Especially not with Solias King's men sniffing around."

He knew she was right. "Cian factors mates into the watch assignments."

"Yeah, but you haven't claimed Tammy. He probably thought you wanted some space from her—you're getting more and more irritable." Her tone was blunt. "Look, I'd take the eastern for you, but I'm pulling a double anyway and I'd prefer to stay close to home."

There was nothing he could say to that. He was one of the most experienced soldiers in the pack, and as such, he had a job to do. "Don't let anything happen to her." It was half warning, half threat.

Juanita's response was a raised eyebrow. "Tammy's no cub. She can handle herself."

TAMSYN put out the snacks with trembling hands. She couldn't believe she'd "ignored" Nate all day. The act had stretched her nerves to the screaming point, the compulsion to speak to him as powerful and as intrinsic as her heartbeat. She was obsessing over their parting words when the soft buzz of the doorbell sliced her thoughts in half.

Taking a deep breath, she opened the door. "Oh, it's you."

Juanita grinned. "I told you it would work."

"He's furious." She looked over the other woman's shoulder, hoping to see Nate. "I thought he was going to march up here and demand I—"

"Precisely." Juanita put her hands on her hips and shook her head. "He's used to demanding something from you and getting it."

"Isn't that what mates do?"

"Sure. But he's being an ass about it. He's not exactly meeting your demands, is he?"

Tamsyn scowled on Nate's behalf. "You don't—"

"Don't you dare defend him," Juanita ordered. "And don't you back down, either. You're just giving him a taste of his own medicine. This is what he's been doing to you for over a year. Let him see how he likes it."

It made sense, but Tamsyn wasn't a soldier, to think of love like strategy. Her heart was that of a healer—gentle and easy to forgive. "He hates it."

"Good." The other woman grinned. "If you don't allow him access to you anytime he wants to feed the animal's need to be close to you, he's going to get desperate sooner rather than later. Then he'll jump you and, bang, we'll all live happily ever after."

Tamsyn nodded. She liked the idea of being jumped by a sexually hungry Nate. "If he doesn't do it soon, I might attack him myself." Her sensitivity to his proximity was getting worse, the mere sound of his voice enough to melt her to damp readiness.

Juanita grinned. "I give him a week."

TWO nights later, Tamsyn decided Juanita was a genius. Nate was scowling at her from across the Pack Circle, such violent need in those midnight blue eyes that she could feel her stomach twist itself into a thousand knots.

"Stop staring at him," she muttered noiselessly to herself. She hadn't said much more than hello to him for the past forty-eight hours, but if she didn't keep her eyes to herself, he'd figure out just how hard it was for her to maintain her distant air. She ached for him and the ache was a pulsing beat in every inch of her skin . . . and worse in lower, hotter places.

Breaking the connection through sheer effort of will, she focused on the dancers in the middle of the Circle. They were part of an impromptu gathering sparked by the full yellow moon, a happy diversion from the general air of wary alertness that had gripped DarkRiver since the attack by the Shadow-Walkers. That wasn't to say that their defenses were compromised. Those on watch were being spelled by off-duty packmates so everyone could join in the fun.

And it *was* fun—warm, friendly, brilliantly alive. Several people had pulled out instruments and the music was energetic and strong. She clapped along with the players, and when Lucas came to offer her his hand, she took it with a smile. "Watch out, I've got two left feet."

He grinned, the savage markings on one side of his face—markings he'd been born with—making him look more panther than boy. "Good thing I don't scare easy."

Laughing, she let him swirl her around in an energetic dance that required enough of her concentration that she almost stopped thinking about Nate. When the tall juvenile snapped her back into his arms, she was breathless. "You're in a good mood," she said, glad to see him happy for once.

There was darkness in Lucas, such darkness. She knew it would be there until the day he took vengeance on those who had stolen his family from him. He was four years younger than her, but looking into those eyes, she saw not a child but a man. Lucas would one day be an alpha of incredible strength, of that she had no doubt.

He held her closer, touching her with the easy friendliness of Pack. She rested her cheek against his shoulder and swayed to the gentler beat that had replaced the pounding dance music. "So?"

"So I thought you needed to be held." The words were blunt, the tone affectionate.

"Thank you. I did." There was no need to lie. Not with Pack.

"Dorian said you don't want us to beat some sense into Nate." He sighed as if in disappointment. "Are you sure?"

She laughed at his teasing. "I like him in one piece, but thanks for the offer."

"Do you want to dance with him? 'Cause he's heading this way."

Chapter 7

SHE SMELLED THE rich earthiness of Nathan's distinctive scent before she could answer. It hit her system like a drug. An instant later, the heavy weight of his hand dropped on to her hip. "Luc. Go find a girl your own age."

Lucas released her. "I think I like sexy older women—why don't I keep Tammy and you find someone else?"

Nate's growl was met with unrepentant laughter as Lucas threw Tammy a wink and walked away. She paid little attention to the exchange, her entire body focused on Nate as he placed both his hands low on her hips and pulled her back against his chest. "What the hell are you wearing?" He spoke against her ear, his breath hot.

It was an effort to think. "Jeans and a sweater. Is that a crime?"

"The sweater is orange and anyone can see down your cleavage."

She forced herself to laugh. "Nate, the vee isn't that deep and the color is soft peach, not orange." It went beautifully with her hair and eyes, throwing up golden highlights she'd never have believed possible.

"It's fucking painted on your body, just like your jeans."

"Watch your mouth, Nathan Ryder." Firming up her tone, she put her hands over his and began to sway against him. It wasn't a calculated act—her body simply craved the contact. "I'm nineteen years old. This is what women my age wear."

His breath seemed to catch for an instant. "You don't."

No, she didn't. It had always seemed to her that she shouldn't aggravate the situation between them by being deliberately sexual. But tonight, she'd followed Juanita's advice again and gone wild. The jeans—bought on a whim in New York—shaped her butt, and from the good-natured whistles she'd inspired in male packmates, it wasn't a bad butt.

As for the long-forgotten sweater, baggy when she'd been a gangly thirteen, it was made of a soft, strokable material that did feel painted on over her now-womanly figure. That was the point. It was meant to make it hotly clear to Nate that she was a sexual young female, not a nun happy to wait for him to make up his mind.

"I decided it was time to change my personal style." She moved against him again, exquisitely aware of the unforgiving ridge of his erection. "Have some fun before we settle down, exactly like you wanted."

"Stop that." But he didn't do anything to halt her subtle erotic movements. "This kind of fun isn't good for the blood pressure of the other men." He pulled her even closer.

"They know I'm yours," she murmured, feeling her skin flush. "Only yours."

"Then why are you dressed like an invitation?"

For you, you idiot, she wanted to say. "I wanted to feel sexy." She shrugged. "I haven't had much of a chance to explore that side of me." That, at least, was true. Between Nate's pigheadedness and her responsibilities, she hadn't had much play in her life. She did so want to play with Nate—silly, intimate, affectionate games.

His hands tightened. "And what are you going to do after getting yourself all heated up like this?" It was a half-growled question, but she knew him well enough to know that that roughness was an indication of need, not anger.

She tilted her head, looking up at him as he looked down. "I bought a friend."

He seemed to choke for a second. "A friend?"

"Uh-huh. He vibrates." It was a whisper meant to carry to his ears alone. "I think I'll try him out tonight."

His fingers were pressing down so hard, he was probably going to leave bruises. She didn't care. Not when he was burning her up with the heat in his eyes. "Don't."

Raising her arms, she linked them behind his neck. "Why not?"

"Your first time shouldn't be with *that*."

She shrugged. "I'm getting older, Nathan. I have needs." Dark, clawing needs. Needs only he could fulfill.

"Promise me you won't use that stupid toy."

"It's not stupid." She rubbed against the hardness of him and heard him suck in a breath. "It's smaller than you, though."

"Christ." Pulling her arms off his neck, he spun her around so she faced him. "Don't. Use. That. *Thing*." It was an order.

"Why not?" She pressed into him, the leopard in her inciting a desire to taunt, to torment. "Lots of women do it."

Eyes going cat, he leaned down to speak against her ear, his lips teasing a suddenly sensitive portion of her anatomy. "If you promise not to use it on yourself tonight," he whispered, "I'll use it on you."

Her legs threatened to collapse. "When?"

"Promise first."

She was weak, so weak where he was concerned. "I promise I won't use it tonight."

He nipped at the shell of her ear and it was then she realized he'd danced them to the farthest edge of the Pack Circle, well away from the reach of the temporary lights. She whimpered and held on. "Nate."

"Shh. It won't be that long, baby." His hand stroked over her back, a rigid inflexibility to his body that hadn't been there before. "You need a little more time."

A nauseous feeling twisted through her. "Nate, you said you'd—"

"When the time is right." There it was again, that tense restraint . . . as if with her surrender, he had found control.

Anger and pain mixed a caustic brew inside her. "Well," she said, wrenching away from him, "I only promised not to use it tonight."

"Tamsyn."

"And," she continued, "I'm not going to fall for that dirty trick again." She began backing into the Circle. "I'm sick of being teased and left wanting. Tomorrow night, I'm taking care of business."

• • •

TAKING care of business.

Nate glared into his morning coffee and then at the duty roster he'd just received from Cian. Punching in the sentinel's code on the comm console, he waited for Cian's face to appear. "What the hell are you on? This roster is a joke!" He was so pissed, he consigned seniority and rank to Hades.

Cian blinked. "I heard you wanted to be on the perimeter, away from Tammy."

"I don't recall asking for that particular *favor.*"

The other man winced at his tone. "You do make a point of avoiding her whenever she comes after you." He frowned. "Though she seems to have stopped doing that lately."

That observation made Nate's incisors threaten to erupt. The leopard was not happy with Tamsyn right now. Neither was the man. They both wanted to bite. To dominate. To mark. "Switch me with Juanita."

"You sure?" Cian scowled. "You're not exactly in a good mood. Do you want to be around Tammy?"

It was an insult—as if he'd ever hurt her. "If I had wanted advice, I'd have asked for it. Switch."

"Fine." Cian threw up his hands. "I'll tell Nita."

"And mind your own damn business from now on." Turning off the comm, he finished his coffee and headed out. He was hungry, but he figured Tammy would have something—she was the best cook in DarkRiver.

His new watch area was in the immediate vicinity of the Pack Circle and included Tammy's home among a few others. On his first pass, it appeared she was still asleep, but he caught the sharp freshness of tea leaves on the second pass. Since he'd remained in human form, it was easy to walk up to her back door and knock.

He knew she had to have scented him, but she peered out suspiciously from the kitchen window before opening the door with a scowl. "What are you doing here?"

Okay, so she was still mad. His cock throbbed at the memory of the events that had led to their fight. He wanted to put his hands on the sweet curves of her bottom, crush her to him, and kiss the hell out of her bad mood.

"Good morning to you, too, sunshine," he managed to say through the chokehold of desire. It was torture being near her, but that was infinitely better than the distance she'd maintained over the past few days.

"You're just hungry." She snorted and turned away, leaving the door open.

He walked in to find her at the counter, cutting slices of bread from what looked like a home-baked loaf. He forced himself to stand to the side instead of going behind her and bending down to draw in the lusciously feminine scent along the line of her throat. "Only bread today?"

She lifted the knife and pointed it in his direction. "Do you want to get fed or not?"

"I love bread." He knew how to stroke his mate when she needed stroking. His mind immediately took the image and ran with it, ratcheting his hunger past explosive. "Why are you half-dressed?" She was wearing his old football shirt and those ridiculous pink fluffy slippers. Sexy and adorable. A killer combination.

"I was minding my own business in my own house. You're the one who decided to intrude." She slapped some butter onto a slice of bread and shoved it in his direction.

He decided not to ask for jam. "Bad night?"

"Nate," she said very quietly, gripping the edge of the counter with her hands. "Did you come here to gloat?"

He put down the half-eaten piece of bread. "What the hell are you talking about?"

"You know exactly what I'm talking about!" She turned and poked at his chest with a sharp finger. "Look, I can make stupid, virginal Tammy Mahaire so hot she doesn't know which way is up. I can leave her gasping for me and walk away as if it doesn't matter!"

"Hey." He grabbed at her hand, but she pulled away. "I didn't mean anything like that. I didn't have a good night's sleep, either."

"Oh, that makes it all right!" She threw up her arms. "We were both miserable. Whoop-de-frickin'-do!"

There was no missing the sarcasm. It dripped from every word. "What the hell is it with you lately?" He succeeded in trapping her against the counter.

"Nothing!" She shoved at him but he was far stronger. "Go away. Go away and leave me alone. Don't you get that? How many times do I have to tell you?"

"You don't get to do that—I'm your mate."

She stopped fighting, her chest heaving. "No, Nate, like I told you before, you don't get to pick and choose which parts of the mating bond you want to accept. As far as your treatment of me goes, I'm not your mate. I'm simply another young, uninteresting female."

"Don't be an idiot."

"I'm not. I'm sexually frustrated." She narrowed her eyes. "But as we discussed last night, that can be easily fixed."

He snapped. How could she possibly think to replace him with some mechanical object? Masculine pride, pure need, and raw heat made for a volatile combination. "Sex? That's really what this is about?" He pushed harder into her, crushing the softness of her thighs under his.

Instead of backing off, she pushed *into* him. "Yes! Yes! Yes! Clear enough for you?"

"Fine." Grabbing her waist, he lifted her onto the counter, spreading her knees wide in the same move. Something fell to the floor and shattered, but he didn't give a shit. "You want to fuck, we'll fuck."

A hint of uncertainty moved over her face. "Nate—"

He closed his hand over the bare skin of her upper thigh. "You're backing off? Don't want me now that you're faced with the reality?"

Her lower lip quivered. "Not like this," she whispered. "Why are you being so mean?"

The protective male core of him couldn't bear to see her looking so emotionally bruised, but they had to have this out. He couldn't handle being pushed the way she'd been pushing him since her return from New York. "I'm trying to give you something—I'm trying to love you the only way I know how, and you're rejecting it because you're hot for sex?" That hurt him. Her freedom was the biggest gift he could give her. Some days, the cost it demanded threatened to drive him to murder.

"No, Nathan, no." She cupped his face in her hands. "I just need you—all of you—so much that I'm going crazy. I need your laugh. I need your company. I need you to sleep beside me and I need you to wake when I wake. I need you with everything in me."

"Then stop with the sex talk. It's not you."

Her hands dropped to his shoulders. "It's not me?" A soft question.

"No. You're warm and practical and loyal. You don't go around flaunting yourself like a—" He caught himself before he said something unforgivable.

"Why don't I finish it for you—like a bitch in heat—that's what you were going to say, wasn't it?"

Chapter 8

"DAMN IT, TAMMY, don't look like that." He was the one who cupped her face this time—her spine was straight, but she couldn't hide the hurt in her eyes. "All this, the way you've been talking and dressing, it's not anything normal for you and you know it."

She looked at him through her lashes. "Yeah. Don't know what I was thinking."

His beast didn't like the flatness in her tone. Reacting instinctively, he bent until their foreheads touched. "Come on, where's my sweet Tammy?" He missed the woman who had become his closest friend over the years, the one with whom he could totally lower his guard. It was something he hadn't been able to do since the day she'd started pushing at him. "Tamsyn?"

"I'm fine and I'm also late." She gave him a shaky smile, then pressed her hands gently against his chest. "Some of the kids will be here soon to finish up their ornaments. I'd better get dressed. I'll talk to you later, okay?"

"You sure you're all right, baby?" His leopard was pacing inside his skull, growling that something was wrong.

"Just a headache. Lack of sleep, you know." She shrugged, making the former point of contention a joke. When her lips curved upward in a deeper smile, the leopard relaxed.

"Yeah, I do." Laughing, he helped her down from the counter, then lifted her over the mess of the broken jam jar on the floor. "Go get changed. I'll clean this up and head out to continue my watch."

"Here." She reached out, picked up a muffin from a tin, and gave it to him. "I made them for the kids."

He bit into it. "Good thing I got here first."

TAMSYN left the room to the sound of Nate's chuckle. The knives of pain inside her stabbed with brutal force, but she kept her composure until she heard him leave the house. Then she sat down on her bed and cried. The tears weren't of frustration or simple hurt. They were the shattered cries of a broken heart.

Juanita had been wrong. The mating heat might have forced Nate into wanting her, but he didn't actually see her as a sexual, desirable woman. He saw her as comfortable . . . practical. Warm, loyal Tamsyn. If the bond hadn't thrown them together, he'd probably never have looked at her twice, not as a man looks at a woman.

She might have lain there for hours, but she couldn't bear to disappoint the kids. So she got up and dressed. What she saw in the mirror simply reinforced her earlier conclusions. Dressed in a pair of old jeans and a thick white sweater, with her hair pulled back into a ponytail, she looked young and . . . ordinary.

She was no temptress. She was safe and sensible, the one that juveniles came to for help without judgment, and mature women for ideas about how to handle rambunctious infants. Even senior packmates didn't blink at asking her advice on Pack issues. Because she was trusted, both for her steady temperament and for her loyal heart. None of which was bad. Only she didn't want Nathan to see her as that—she wanted him to see her as she saw him. As a lover, a playmate in the most intimate of arenas.

But he didn't. And that blow cut so deep, she could barely think.

Something registered in her consciousness. A second later, she picked up the high-pitched sounds of children's voices. The healer in her took over—there was no time for self-pity. Wiping her eyes with the backs of her hands, she went to the bathroom and splashed cold water over her face. Then she used her healing abilities to get rid of the redness around her eyes.

The doorbell rang.

Pasting on a smile, she walked down and opened the door. The kids' bright and excited faces turned her faux smile real, but nothing could heal the open wound that was the jagged beat of her animal heart.

NATE saw Tamsyn again that day, but it was hours later and with several others as they sat around her kitchen table eating dinner. She'd chosen not to sit next to him, but he could understand why. The awareness between them had only gotten stronger since this morning, until he could scent nothing but the sensual promise of her. She was everything he had ever wanted—that smile, that acerbic wit she seemed to show him alone, and Lord help him, that body—and she was his. No other man had the right to her.

His beast wanted to roar its claim, but he fought the impulse. He'd wait. He'd wait . . . but maybe not as long as he'd initially planned. He'd give her another six months of freedom at least, let her live some of her dreams. She could go roaming if she liked, explore a bit of the wild. It might be dangerous, but Tamsyn was smarter and more mature than most of the other young leopards. She'd be fine.

The cat in him didn't like the idea, knew how badly it would hurt to be parted from her, but it had to be done. He never wanted her to turn to him—as his mother had turned to his father—and accuse him of stealing her life. That would destroy him. Because she *was* his life. The thought of crushing her spirit was his personal nightmare.

"Are you going to eat or do you plan on staring at Tammy the whole night?" Juanita passed him the potatoes.

"I can stare if I like." It was his right.

Rolling her eyes, she called out to Tammy. "Hey, where's that dress you were going to wear tonight?"

Tammy colored. "I changed my mind."

"You look fine to me." Dressed in black slacks and a pale blue cardigan, she appeared soft and touchable. Strokable. Shit. His mind was going off track again. Before long, he'd start thinking about unbuttoning that cardigan and kissing his way—

"Great," Juanita hissed, breaking into the taut eroticism of his newest daydream. "Tell your mate she looks fine."

"What the hell's wrong with that?" He took the peas she almost shoved into his chest. "She looks—" He cut himself off before he said what he wanted to say, which was "pretty enough to bite into."

Juanita shot him a disgusted glance before turning her attention to the packmate on her other side. Ignoring her, Nate went back to the pleasurable task of watching Tamsyn. The beast bucked to taste her. *Six months*, he told it. *Six more months and then you can have her. In every way. And over again.*

BUT a mere week later, his hunger for her had gotten so bad that he had Cian reassign him to the perimeter. Tammy was no longer trying to flaunt herself at him—if anything, she seemed to be going to great lengths to give him space. Paradoxically, that only amplified the building pressure to mate, to touch and taste and claim. Without the control provided by the vivid scars of memory, he'd have given in a hundred times already.

Still, he couldn't keep from going to her each morning, just to see her smile. "Hey, sweetheart, any muffins today?"

She gave him one, but there was no smile on her lips. "How's the Solias King situation? Any decisions?"

"We're planning to make a move in a few days." He'd already told her what they intended to do—she was his mate, and more than that, she was damn sharp, an integral part of the steel backbone of the pack. "You want to come along? Be a nice run." He wanted to feel her beside him, strong and hotly female.

She shook her head. "This isn't working, Nate."

The quick change in subject rattled him. He put down the food, belatedly aware of the bags under her eyes, the lack of light in her face. "We'll get past it."

"Not living so close." She shook her head. "One of us has to leave."

He'd thought about setting her free to roam, but now that it had come down to it, he found he couldn't let her go. "Don't make any impulsive decisions. It'll die down."

"No, it won't. Don't lie to me," she snapped, folding her arms. "We're experiencing the final stages of the mating dance and it's going to keep getting worse, especially if our beasts continuously sense each other's presence. I was thinking I should go to—"

"Just wait." He fisted his hands to keep from touching her. "I'll talk to some of the other mated pairs. Maybe there's something we can do to lessen the impact."

"I thought you wanted me to go out into the world?" Her voice was soft, her skin flushed with need. "Isn't that why you keep pushing me away?"

"Stay." That single word held his heart.

Chapter 9

STAY, HE'D SAID, but Tamsyn knew he didn't mean it the way she needed him to mean it. The mating instinct urged him to protect her and so he wanted her in sight. It didn't make him happy just to see her. Not like it made her heart bloom simply being in the same room as him.

If the mating urge died tomorrow, there would still be no other man for her. He was her one and only. But she wasn't his. Her throat feeling as if she'd gotten a rock stuck in it, she left the parking garage in the city and crossed the street.

She'd promised the kids she'd get more lights for the tree, but now that she was here, she decided to pop into the bookstore, too. Nate liked reading. She knew exactly what to get him for Christmas. That thought made her want to cry again. Her nose grew stuffy with withheld tears as she strolled through the small and expensive hard-copy section. Most people bought the downloads, but she wanted to give Nate something he could hold, something that made him think of her.

Her choice was sold out, so she went to one of the consoles and ordered in another copy. That done, she picked up her other purchases and began to make her way to the exit.

That was when she saw her.

The Psy woman—a stranger with eyes of darkest brown and skin the same rich shade—was occupying a booth near the door. Dressed in a black pantsuit teamed with a white shirt, she appeared a serious business professional. But then again, all Psy seemed to wear variations on the same theme. Tamsyn had never seen one of the psychic race in any color, excepting

white, that didn't fall in the range from deep gray to brown/
black.

On any other day, she would have kept walking. But today,
she didn't, her motive a mystery even to herself. "Excuse me,"
she said, coming to a standstill near the woman.

The Psy looked up. "Did you want the terminal? I'll be
finished in approximately one minute." She glanced over Tamsyn's shoulder. "There are several others that appear free."

"No, I don't want the terminal." Tamsyn looked at her, at
her human-seeming eyes, her clear skin, and her shining fall
of jet-black hair. There was nothing overt that marked this
woman as different, as Psy, part of a race that had eliminated
its emotions. "I wanted to ask you a question."

The stranger considered her request for a second. "Why are
you asking me?"

"I need to ask a Psy and you're the only one here."

"I can't fault your logic." She tapped her finger on the screen
to complete her purchase, then turned to give Tamsyn her full
attention. "Your question?"

"Do you ever cry?" It seemed imperative that she know the
answer.

The Psy didn't react to the oddness of the question—if she
had, she wouldn't be Psy. "Even those of my race have little to
no control over certain physiological reactions. If, for example,
a foreign object were to accidentally enter or touch my eye,
that eye would certainly produce fluid in an attempt to excrete
the intruding matter."

Tamsyn frowned at the clinical description of such a
wrenching, heartbreaking act. "No. I don't mean that. I mean,
do you *cry*?"

The stranger looked at her for several long moments. "As
you chose to approach a Psy, you must know the answer to that
question. However, I'll respond as I see no possible negative
repercussions from doing so." She picked up a slim electronic
pad from the desk near the terminal. "No. We do not cry out
of fear or sadness, anger or rage. We do not feel; therefore, we
do not shed tears."

"Don't you miss it?" Tamsyn asked.

The Psy ran her gaze over Tamsyn's face. "Judging from
the redness of the blood vessels in your eyes and your stuffy

nose, I believe I can say with certainty that crying is in no way a positive experience. Why would I miss it?"

"No. I meant . . . don't you miss feeling?" Love and hope, joy and need.

"I can't miss what I've never experienced," the other woman said, as if that should have been self-evident. "My race chose to eradicate emotion for a reason. Those with emotions are weak. We're not. It's why the Psy rule this planet." With that, she gave a curt nod and left.

Tamsyn stared after her, the words circling around and around in her head. *Those with emotions are weak.* She saw the reflection of her drawn, listless face in the terminal and found herself agreeing. For a frozen heartbeat, she wished she were like that Psy woman. Cool, controlled, focused. No attachments, no hopes, no dreams.

And no Nathan.

Her eyes, which had started to close, snapped open. "No," she whispered fiercely. She would not, could not, live in a world where Nathan didn't exist. He might make her cry as much as he made her laugh, but she couldn't imagine waking up one day and having emptiness where he was.

She didn't know much about how and why the Psy race had stopped feeling, but it had to have been a terrible thing that had driven them down this path. Her healer's soul ached for them—for the love they would never touch, but she knew she couldn't help them. Not when they barricaded themselves in their high-rises, their minds shut to the possibility of hope.

It's why the Psy rule this planet.

Tamsyn shook her head. The stranger was wrong. The Psy might rule, but their world was limited to towers of steel and glass. They knew nothing of the joy of running under a full moon and listening to the music played by the wind, of feeling the sensation of a packmate's fur against human skin, of the sheer life that existed in the forests that were *her* world.

But the woman had been right about one thing—how could you miss something you had never experienced? Nathan had never been hers. Their beasts might cry out for each other, but if the human half of Nathan chose to repudiate that bond, who was she to stop him?

• • •

SHE left the next day. There was no other way. If she remained
within reach, Nathan's beast would eventually push him over
the edge. And she couldn't bear to lie with him knowing their
intimacy was nothing more than the result of a physical compulsion. It would be a glimpse into her own personal vision of
hell.

Her friend, Finn, was more than happy to fly in on short
notice.

"The healer in our pack's not even forty, so I'm not going
to get to do anything serious for a while," he told her when she
met him at the airport and escorted him into their territory.
DarkRiver wasn't known for its friendliness toward unknown
males. They couldn't afford to be, not after the attack by the
ShadowWalkers.

"I know," she said. "That's why I asked you rather than
Maria."

He gave her a smile but his eyes were watchful. "I appreciate it."

She ignored the unasked question. "I'm going to introduce
you to the alpha. He knows you're coming, of course, but the
hierarchy has to be maintained." The laws of rank and hierarchy were there for a reason—they balanced the predatory
nature of their animal halves with order.

Finn nodded. "I'll feel better once he adopts me into Dark-
River. It wouldn't do for one of your pack to slice me up because
they figured me for an intruder."

Since she thought the same, she made sure to take him to
Lachlan first thing. Even with that delay, she was ready to be
on her way out of DarkRiver territory by late afternoon. "Take
care of my people, Finn."

The twenty-one-year-old healer didn't bother to conceal his
worry this time. "What about you, Tam? Who's looking after
you?"

"I'll be fine." She tightened her hands around the straps of
her bag. "It might be permanent, you know that, right?"

"Yes." He stroked his hand over her hair, offering comfort
in the changeling way. "But it shouldn't be. You were born to
be DarkRiver's healer."

"I can work with another leopard pack." But Nathan couldn't be replaced. Not when it was clear that Lachlan was preparing Lucas to step into his role as alpha sooner rather than later. When the time came, Lucas would need to rely on Nate's experience and rock-solid advice. "Try it here," she made herself say. "If everything works out . . ."

"No rush." Finn's tone was gentle. "I'll hold your place until you come to your senses. Then I'll happily return to the civilized world of our territory instead of this jungle."

She smiled at his joking, but as she walked away, she had the sick feeling she might never return. When she neared the fir she'd strung with Christmas decorations and lights, her eyes stung. "I'm sorry, Shayla," she whispered to the ghost that reproached her for leaving her pack when it still needed her.

They would be okay, she told herself. She'd started them on the road to healing. All they had to do was follow it. Tempting as it was to pass by quickly, she made herself look up. There was the ornament Vaughn had painted, right next to the one by Cian. Around them wove the string of lights Nate had hung after he'd growled at her for putting her fool neck in danger. And there was the star she'd almost thrown at him, she'd been so mad.

"Oh God." Blinking, she looked away . . . and kept walking.

Chapter 10

NATE RETURNED HOME close to dawn, coming from a night raid to "suggest" Solias King look elsewhere for his development. The damn, encroaching Psy would follow their advice, of that Nate was certain. Even in leopard form, he wanted to grin.

He'd stood watch for hours as Cian and a couple of others with tech training had methodically taken apart every piece of Psy equipment already onsite. While that might have been enough, Nate had gone a step further and buried several of the most expensive pieces in a section of DarkRiver land that bordered SnowDancer territory. No Psy would dare venture that close to wolf land. The feral pack had a reputation for ripping out intruders' throats and using the bleached-out bones as fence posts.

Just in case Solias King missed their point even after all that, they had also removed the semipermanent survey markers and disabled the rudimentary comm tower erected a few days ago. It was why DarkRiver had allowed the thing to go up in the first place—so they could destroy it, and in a fashion that made it clear they would brook no further trespass on their lands.

Nate was particularly proud of the crowning touch. Inspired by Tammy, he'd taken along a large Christmas ornament—an old-fashioned picture of the man in red and white—and hung it from the now useless comm tower. Then he'd wrapped a string of blinking multicolored lights around the metal skeleton.

He couldn't wait to tell Tammy—she'd bust a gut over it.

Taking on the Psy wasn't usually a laughing matter, as the cold psychic race didn't hesitate to kill. But from everything they had been able to unearth, it appeared that Solias King's darker impulses were currently being curbed by his political aspirations. He couldn't afford to come down hard on the changelings. Any violence and his own Council would turn against him.

Nate had no illusions that the Psy Council cared about changelings, but they damn well did care about their bottom line. And that would suffer massive depreciation if people thought the Psy were declaring a racial war. The Council would never allow such a panic to start over a small piece of land in the territory of what they considered a minor pack. Nate had a feeling DarkRiver wasn't going to stay minor for long, but until then, they could and would use the Council's sense of arrogance to their advantage.

Shifting the second he cleared the doorway to his home, he pulled on a pair of jeans and an old cable-knit sweater. He had to see Tamsyn, no matter the ridiculously early hour. The royal blue sweater had been a gift from her. Maybe it would thaw her mood—she'd been more than a little distant when he'd dropped by this morning.

But his hopeful frame of mind disappeared the instant he got near her house—the area was blanketed in the scent of an unfamiliar male.

Unbidden, scenes of the carnage that had taken their last healer from them filled his mind. "Tammy!" He pounded on the door. "Tammy!"

The door swung open to reveal a young male. "Hel—" His voice cut off as Nate gripped him around the neck and lifted him off the floor.

"What have you done to her?" He tried to ignore the fact that the male was dressed only in a pair of pajama bottoms, his hair mussed.

I'm sick of stroking myself to sleep.

No, she wouldn't do that to him. The agony he felt at the thought of Tammy, *his* Tammy, with anyone, much less this runt, was enough to call the beast to the surface. His eyes shifted to cat. He couldn't hear anything through the pounding roar of blood in his head, was dangerously close to killing.

The single reason he didn't do so was that his leopard

suddenly started scrambling to find Tammy. He threw aside
the other man and strode into the house, preparing himself
for what he would find. If she was in bed— Something tore
inside him.

He wouldn't hurt her. He could never hurt her.

But that boy was going to die a slow, cruel death.

He shoved open the bedroom door . . . and found the bed
made, with no signs of recent occupation.

"I slept on the couch," a raspy voice said from the
doorway.

He turned to find the stranger supporting himself against a
wall, one hand rubbing at his throat. "Didn't seem right to sleep
in Tam's bed."

Tam? The leopard growled, harsh and vocal. "Who are you
and what are you doing in my mate's house?"

The other man's eyes widened. "Mate? She never—" He
slapped up his hands, palms out, when Nate started advancing.
"I'm a healer. Name's Finn."

That stopped Nate midstep. Healers, even enemy healers,
had automatic protection. Only blood-hungry packs like the
ShadowWalkers broke that rule. "We already have a healer."
Claws raked his gut, twisted through his body like hard fire.

"She asked me to fly in and take over for a while." Finn
coughed a few times. "Said it might be permanent. Our pack's
got a senior healer and another apprentice, so they were happy
to let me go."

"I *said* we already have a healer." Nate glared.

Finn didn't back down. "Not anymore you don't. She left."

The beast wanted to lash out, to tear and scar. "Where did
she go?"

The healer held up his hands a second time and Nate wondered what the other man had seen in his eyes. "I swear I don't
know. I figured she'd talked it over with your alpha—maybe a
sabbatical or some extra training. She introduced me to him."

Nate left on a mission to find Lachlan, but it was Lucas he
ran into first. He would have pushed past except that Lucas
stepped into his path and said, "Looking for Tammy?"

Nate stilled. "You knew she left?" At that moment, the first
rays of the rising sun hit the tree line, throwing light across
Lucas's savage facial markings.

"Didn't you?"

"Damn it, Luc. Answer the damn question."

"Sure." The juvenile folded his arms. "I heard her ask Nita to drive her out of the territory."

The urge to grab Lucas and shake Tammy's location out of him was so strong, Nate looked away and took a deep breath before saying, "And neither of you tried to stop her from leaving?"

"Why would we?" Lucas's tone was hard. "You made her cry, Nathan. You made your mate cry and then you didn't hold her."

The blow hit him with bruising force. "Where is she, Lucas?"

"I don't know—you could ask Nita, but I don't think she's around." He glanced at the sun-touched trees. "I have to get to the Circle for training."

Nate didn't try to stop him from leaving, and was still standing there when Cian appeared out of the shadows. "Nate? You after Lachlan? I just left him—he's free for the next half hour or so."

"I'm trying to find Tammy."

Cian's face showed instant comprehension and not a little anger. "What the hell are you doing to that girl, Nate?"

"What's right for her." Cian didn't understand what it was to watch a woman fall out of love with her man, turn bitter and self-destructive . . . and finally, suicidal. He'd held his mother's dead body. He refused to hold Tamsyn's. "She's too young."

"She was too young when Shayla died. But did you hear her complain?" The sentinel's voice was a whip. "Seventeen years old and she took on a position most people don't touch until they've reached their third decade."

"Exactly!" He blew out a frustrated breath. "All that responsibility and then a mate, too? I'd demand things she has no conception of—"

Cian swore, low and pithy. "Isn't that your job as her mate? To demand but to let her demand as much in turn? You're supposed to fucking share the burden, not add to it like you've been doing with your self-pitying bullshit."

"You might be my senior," Nate said, the leopard in his voice, "but you are not my father." His father was long dead, having literally driven himself to an early grave after his wife's death—he'd wrapped his car around a tree. "You want to take me on, go ahead."

"Screw that." Cian shrugged. "If I damaged you, Tammy would have my head."

With that simple comment, the other man defused every bit of Nate's anger. "Tell me where she is. I have to make sure she's safe." The leopard's desperation grew by the minute.

"I don't know." Cian shoved up his sleeves. "To be honest, I don't think you deserve to know, either. And don't bother asking Nita—she has no idea where Tammy went after getting out of the car."

"What, none of you bothered to ask her?" He couldn't believe that, not with how protective they had become after what had happened to Shayla. As this inquisition clearly proved. "You let her go off on her own without a word of protest?"

Cian's eyes turned opaque. "She's an adult leopard. No one has the right to question her decisions."

And she'd made one to leave him. Nate leaned against a tree and stared up at the dawn sky. It promised to turn a pure, mocking blue. "Where did Nita drop her?" She wouldn't be hard to track—she was carrying his heart with her.

Cian snorted. "Sorry, you're on your own. You made the mess, you can damn well clean it up. But since you look like you've been gut-punched, I will tell you something she said to Lachlan when she made the request to leave and bring Finn in as cover."

Nate straightened. "What?"

"She said you were more important to the pack. Since one of you had to go, she decided it had better be her." The older male shook his head. "My Keelie is the most precious part of my life. How could you let your mate think she was less than you, Nate?"

Nate still hadn't found an answer to that question seven hours later when he finally located the first hint of a trail. He was certain that this was where she'd left Nita's car. He looked up and found himself close to Tahoe. Tamsyn had vanished somewhere in the lake city's streets. Nathan had every intention of hunting her down.

• • •

UNFORTUNATELY, when he returned home to pick up his gear, he found another surprise waiting for him, this time in his living room.

"Where's my daughter, Nathan?" was Sadie's first question.

He began to grab what he needed. "I'll find her."

"I don't know if I want you to find her." Tamsyn's mother scowled. "You didn't do a great job of keeping her this time around."

"I'll bring her home."

"Why? So you can make her miserable?" She moved to block the doorway, fierce in her maternal protectiveness. "Let her roam. That's what you've been telling her to do. Well, looks like she listened. Don't you dare go after her."

The blunt words brought him to a halt. "I can't do that."

"Why not? It's *exactly* what you wanted."

"She's mine to protect."

"You gave up that right when you decided you didn't want to be her mate." Sadie shook her head. "You've done enough. Let my baby go."

He stared at her, a sick feeling in his gut. "I never said I didn't want to be her mate. Where the hell did you get that idea?" And did Tammy think the same?

Chapter 11

"FROM YOU, NATHAN." Sadie gave him an arch look as she shook the foundations of his world. "Tammy was practically screaming for your love and you wouldn't so much as hold her. She got the message—she can't break the bond, but she might be able to mute it with distance."

"What damn message?" Impatience, anger, and a painful hunger for the scent of his mate combined to roughen his tone. "The only thing I wanted to give her was a taste of freedom before—"

"I've heard it all before." She lifted a hand. "If you really mean it, then you'll put down that pack and go sit down. After all, she's free now, isn't she?"

"That's not what I meant," he said between gritted teeth. "I wanted her—"

"You wanted her on your leash—close enough to watch over so you could satisfy your beast." Sadie's eyes went pure leopard. "It didn't matter to you that her need was turning into a kind of slow torture. You are not doing that to my baby again! You let her go. Let her find someone who'll love her for what she is."

Violent rage turned to lethal calm. "What the hell are you talking about? She's my *mate*. That is not negotiable."

"Not if you won't let it be. If you set her free, maybe she'll fall for someone who'll adore her like she's meant to be adored."

"*I* adore her!" he yelled in disbelief. "No one else has that right!"

"Do you?" Sadie's features settled into a resolute expression.

"Then show her, for goodness' sake. Otherwise, free her in reality instead of just giving lip service to the idea." She vacated the doorway.

Nate walked out without replying, but her words wouldn't leave his mind, no matter how far he went. Tammy thought he didn't want to be her mate? How could such an idiotic idea have ever entered her head? The second he saw her, he was going to growl the truth to her until she damn well listened.

Well . . . maybe he'd hold her first. He'd made her cry and he hadn't held her. Lucas was right. That was unforgivable. But Tammy was his mate. She had to forgive him. And she had to come home. He couldn't exist without her close to him. Those months she had spent in New York had almost killed him, but at least then he'd been able to tell himself that she was still a girl, not a woman.

But now that he'd felt the lush heat of her, he could no longer kid himself. Tammy had grown up. And she'd left him. "We'll see about that." The leopard snarled, mad as hell.

Not much later, he reached the point where he'd first picked up her trail—close to Tahoe. From there, he could try to track her by scent or . . . or he could do the one thing certain to lead him to her. No choice at all, really.

Taking a deep breath, he released the stranglehold of control he'd held over the mating bond since the day she'd turned fifteen and he'd realized what she was to him. It felt like the whiplash unfurling of a coiled spring—a burst of pure power that actually hurt as it boomeranged off his chest, driving him to his knees.

When his head finally stopped spinning, he felt for the bond and found it stretched out taut and clear, a vibrating cord of need, desire, and belonging. He could feel Tammy deep within his core, as if he had a homing beacon tuned only to her signal. It was perfection. And he wasn't sure he could ever block it again. But he'd think about that later.

Right now, he had to survive the intensity of the emotions shooting down the bond. It felt like he could reach out and touch her. She was sweetness and hope, woman and fire, erotic heat and gentle affection. And she was his. Not fucking negotiable.

· · ·

IT felt like getting broadsided with a baseball bat.

Tamsyn staggered under the point-blank surge of pure emotion, sliding down the wall to sit with her back braced against it.

Nate had opened the bond.

She rubbed a hand over her chest, then realized the usual persistent ache, the hard knot of dull hurt was simply . . . gone. In its place was the blazing glory of a fully functioning mating bond. She trembled. Why had he taken that step now—after she'd done what he wanted and put distance between them? Surely he wasn't trying to track her?

No, she thought, she wasn't going to believe in fairy tales anymore. Nate had probably done it by accident. Okay, no. That was stupid. No one who'd been as determined as Nate to block their mating would lose that much control by accident. Her eye fell on the small silver phone sitting on the table by the sofa.

Her mother had called soon after Tamsyn arrived at the cabin. Sadie had been distraught to return from her run in the wild and find her daughter gone. Tamsyn had assured her over and over that she was fine, but knowing Sadie, she'd probably ordered Nate to locate her daughter and provide a firsthand report. Tamsyn shuddered, trying to breathe past the impact of the fully flowing bond. She had to think, had to stabilize herself before Nathan arrived, so he'd go back and tell Sadie there was no reason to worry.

That done, he would *think* the bond shut again.

Her blood flushed hot as the vibrant male energy of him raced through her veins. Mates were joined on an incredibly deep level. To other changelings, the scent of one half of a mated pair became difficult to distinguish from the other the longer they were together. Nate's refusal to accept the bond had denied them that closeness, starving her. Now, her senses wanted to gorge.

"No," she said out loud, forcing calm on herself. All healers had to learn such discipline. It allowed them to work in the chaos of a fight or when attempting to heal those they loved—a pack healer didn't have the luxury of passing on the hard cases to another medic. Every one of their cases was hard, because Pack was family.

Finally, after ten long minutes, she could think despite the masculine strength of the emotional connection surging through her. Then, for the first time, she tried to close her end of the exquisite pleasure/pain that was her link to this man she adored beyond life . . . and discovered she couldn't. She fisted her hands. Forget the known wisdom that said the bond couldn't be blocked—if Nate could do it, why couldn't she?

It took her an hour to come up with some sort of answer. She remembered what her mother had said—that Nate had had to learn to suppress his needs in order to allow her the time she needed to come of age. That control seemed to have carried over into everything he did in relation to her. But now he'd thrown off the reins and let the cat out to play.

It might be impossible to put the lid back on that bottle.

Her eyes widened. Nate was not going to be pleased if that proved true. More importantly, she wasn't pleased. She didn't want him to want her because he'd been forced into it by the primal cravings of his beast—cravings her own beast understood far too well. She wanted him to love her.

It was a terribly impractical dream for a practical, sensible healer.

EVEN with the bond, it took Nate three days to track Tamsyn to an isolated cottage so far south of the lake, there was nothing else within shouting distance. "What the hell are you doing out in the middle of nowhere?" he said, the second she opened the door.

Her eyes narrowed. "Trying to get away from you." Turning her back, she walked into the house, her hips encased in those damn painted-on jeans.

He was tired, sweaty, and hungry. Not for food. For her. Every soft, curvy, bitable piece of her. His cat wanted to test the resilience of her butt, while his— He slammed the door shut behind himself. "Jesus, Tammy. DarkRiver's operating at red alert while we prepare to take on the ShadowWalkers and you choose this shack to hide in?"

"It's not a shack and I'm not hiding," she said, sitting back down to what appeared to be her breakfast. "It's Cian's place. He likes the water."

Cian had lied to him. Not exactly a surprise. "It's miles from the lake!"

"It's not that far. He likes privacy, too."

Nate dropped his stuff by the door and shoved a hand through his hair. "What, this was some silly little jaunt and no one bothered to tell me?" He saw red.

Then she raised an eyebrow and that red morphed into something darker, more intense, a blatantly sexual surge of dominance. "I'm leaving DarkRiver. Finn's agreed to stay on permanently. His agreement was what I was waiting for."

He didn't believe her. "You're leaving the pack."

"Yes." She put down her uneaten toast and stood. "There, you've seen me. I'm fine." Her smile was sharp enough to cut, her eyes sparking with anger that intrigued the leopard even more than the spicy/wild/hot woman scent of her. "You can leave the same way you came in." She began to clear the table.

"Put those dishes *down*."

She ignored him.

Covering the distance between them, he closed his hand over her wrist. She released the dishes softly to the table but didn't turn to face him. "What do you want, Nate?"

"I want you to talk to me." He found himself pressing against her. It took only a single move to enclose her in the circle of his arms and bury his face against her neck. He was ravenous for the scent of her, the feel of her. "Come on, baby."

Her body trembled so violently he felt her skin move against his caressing lips. "I can't do this anymore." Her voice was a whisper. "Please let me go."

Chapter 12

A GROWL ROLLED up from his throat. "For how long?"

"Why are you asking me that?"

He didn't like the tremor in her voice. "Don't you dare cry, Tammy. That's not fair."

"I won't." But there was a wet kind of pain in her words. "I know you don't really want me. I know it's the cat pushing for mating. That's okay. If I go far enough away, maybe you—"

"What?" He couldn't believe his ears. "You really believe that load of shit?"

"You made it very clear."

Everything went quiet inside him. Lifting his head, he turned her in his arms. Her head stayed down—she wouldn't look at him. Keeping one arm around her, not sure she wasn't getting ready to bolt, he used the fingers of his other hand to tip up her chin. Her eyes were shiny-wet, but she met his gaze without flinching.

God, she was so proud. Proud and strong and stubborn. And she'd decided he didn't want her. He intended to teach her the error of her ways once and for all. Holding her gaze, he slid his hand down her neck, over her shoulder, and along her arm until he cupped the back of her hand with his. Then he lifted that feminine hand and placed it on his erection. She jerked in shock. The reflexive tightening of her fingers almost made him cry out.

"Does this feel like I don't want you?" he grit out.

"It's—" She paused, her breath hitching. "It's a result of the mating dance. You don't want me, not really." She pulled away her hand, curling it up to her chest as if it hurt.

Oh Jesus. She was not doing this to him. "Or is it that you don't want *me*?" he asked softly. "Is that it, Tamsyn? Am I too old for you?"

Her head snapped up. "Don't you put this on me!" The first hint of fire entered her tone. "I begged you, *begged* you, to make the bond real, to be my mate in truth. But you said no. You always say no! Well, you know what, I'm through with begging. I'm through with not being good enough for you!"

It felt like she'd stabbed him. "You are the best thing that's ever happened to me," he said, the leopard alive in his voice. "I've spent every day of the past four years thinking of myself as the luckiest man on the planet—frustrated as hell, but damn lucky."

She shook her head. "Don't. Don't lie."

It was all he could do not to crush his lips to hers and kiss her into accepting his words. "I watch you work and feel such pride, sometimes I think my heart will explode. I look at your body and have to fight the urge to bare my teeth and warn off anyone else from doing the same. You want to know why I lost it when you wore those tight, sexy clothes?"

"It was because others could see what was *mine*." It was a possessive, animal reaction, one he usually tempered with human civility. But Tamsyn needed to see the real man, claws and all. "I don't like to share."

Finally a reaction. "You didn't think I looked stupid?"

"I wanted to peel you out of those damn come-to-bed jeans" —something he was definitely going to do today—"and mount you right there in the Pack Circle."

"Nate!"

"I wanted to show everyone that you were mine. I wanted to put my hands on your breasts and my lips on yours and my co—"

She squeaked, slapping a hand over his mouth. "Nate!" The scandalized expression on her face was very Tamsyn. His mate had come back to him.

He pulled away the restraint, using his other hand to manacle her free hand, too. "Where was I? I have wanted you so damn long, my balls are permanently blue. As—"

"I believe you!" A hint of desperation.

"I don't want any mistakes about this." And her time was

up. The things he wanted to do to her were probably illegal in some countries. Too bad.

He backed her into a wall with slow deliberation, not stopping until her breasts were crushed warm and tempting against him, her stomach muscles clenching at the granite-hard thrust of his erection. "The sex—hell, yes, I want the sex. I want it so much I could devour you right this second, take little bites out of all those soft, delicate places."

Her breasts rose and fell in a jagged rhythm as she watched him through her lashes.

"But baby, I fell in love with you long before the mating heat kicked in this bad. Do you know why I came to wish you happy birthday when you were fifteen?"

She shook her head, mute.

"Because I adored everything about you as much then as I do now," he whispered, giving her words because she needed them, and because he'd made her cry. There was no excuse for that. "It wasn't sexual—you were too young. It was just this tightness inside my chest. Every time you smiled, my world lit up. All I wanted to do was keep giving you reasons to smile. The day I realized you were my mate, the happiness almost killed me. So don't you *ever* say I don't love or want you. I chose you, Tamsyn Mahaire. I chose you."

Tamsyn wanted to burst out crying. "Oh, Nate." She buried her face against his chest and, when he let go of her hands, wrapped her arms around him as he wrapped his around hers. She had never heard him speak in that impassioned, romantic way, never imagined he would. And to her? To his practical, sensible mate?

"You are not leaving me," he ordered, his voice predator deep. "If you want to go roaming, I'll take you. But you are not leaving me."

She wondered if he expected them to go back to the way things were. If so, he was about to get a surprise. Half of the mess that was their relationship had been her fault. She'd let him think he was the boss. Well, he wasn't. They were a partnership. Breaking the embrace, she pushed off his jacket. He was so surprised, he let her. Then she began undoing his rough wool-blend shirt.

"Tammy." He grabbed at her wrist.

"Forget it, Nathan," she snapped, tearing the shirt down the middle. Buttons went flying every which way. "I'm ready to lose my virginity and you're going to help me do it. I don't care if I have to kidnap you and tie you to the bed."

He opened his mouth as if to speak, but then she flattened her palms on his wonderful, hard chest and he shuddered instead. The same head-spinning rush hit her, powered by the skin-to-skin contact. *Skin privileges.* She had the most intimate kind.

"What about your freedom?" he whispered in her ear over a minute later, bracing his hands palms down on the wall beside her head. He made no move to stop her as she stroked and petted every inch of that sinfully gorgeous chest, all hard muscle and gleaming skin overlaid with silky-rough strands of dark hair.

"Idiot." She nipped at his jaw with her teeth. "The only freedom I ever wanted was the right to love you."

One of his hands stroked down to slip under her sweater. It was her turn to tremble.

"You're a stubborn woman."

"Yes." The roughness of his skin felt delicious on her.

"You're set on making this real."

"Try and stop me."

He smiled and it was beautiful and strong and quintessentially male. "What, and give up the chance to finally see your pretty breasts? Not a chance."

"Nathan!" And then his hand was squeezing her sensitive flesh and she was drowning in the rush of sensation.

"Why aren't you wearing a bra?" he asked before kissing the wits half out of her.

By the time she could gasp in enough air to breathe, her sweater was in shreds on the floor. Nate had used his claws to slice it to bits. His hand returned to massage and mold flesh that had never known a man's touch. She pushed into the caress. "Um . . . I forgot," she whispered. "I was nervous about you— Oh!"

He'd lifted her up so her legs wrapped around his waist. "You were right to be nervous." He kissed her again, then ran his lips down her neck to nibble on the tender upper slopes of her breasts.

She held on to his shoulders, trying hard to find a sensible thought. "Nervous?"

"I hope you've been exercising." His mouth closed over her nipple.

It might've been hours before she spoke again. "Exercising?" Single words seemed to be all her brain could manage.

He released her sensitive flesh . . . after gripping it lightly between his teeth for a heart-pounding instant. "Because you're going to be indulging in a lot of creative physical activity over the next few days."

Had he said *days*?

Then she lost even that thought and simply felt. Nate didn't ravage her as she'd half expected, given their combined hunger. He was excruciatingly tender and she knew how much that control had to be costing him.

"It's okay," she said several times.

"It's your first time. I'll say when it's okay."

She might have taken that order badly if he hadn't already brought her to orgasm twice by then. His tone may have been rough, but his hands were gentle and his mouth was pure magic. When he did finally decide she'd been pleasured enough, he took her with care that brought tears to her eyes.

The second time, she took him.

Chapter 13

SOLIAS KING DID not like to lose. "How much damage?" he asked.

Kinshasa repeated the number. "The missing parts will take weeks to reacquire."

"I thought you said they were a minor pack?" He pinned his aide to the spot with his eyes. "Your risk analysis was faulty."

"My variables were based on the known parameters of changeling intellect."

Solias couldn't fault Kinshasa. The general consensus among the Psy was that the animals weren't that smart. "Find me another site."

As Kinshasa left the suite, Solias wondered which one of his enemies had orchestrated the attack—covert Psy involvement had to be how the changelings had pulled this off. It was preposterous to think he'd been beaten by a pack of animals.

Arrogant in his belief of the Psy race's genetic and intellectual superiority, he never once considered that he might be blind to the truth. The truth that things were changing . . . that the Psy no longer ruled every corner of the planet. And that this minor pack had shown the first signs of the lethal danger it would one day become.

Chapter 14

A WEEK LATER, Nate watched Tamsyn bandage up a juvenile's arm and give the kid a stern warning about rock climbing without gear. She was firm and practical, her hands strong, her body tall. And she had breasts to make a man's mouth water, sweet feminine curves his palms itched to shape.

Then she looked up and smiled and he felt it deep, deep in his core. He wanted to pick her up and kiss her silly, but since the juvenile's eyes were already going wide, he decided to make himself scarce. "I'll see you tonight. I have to make that run into San Francisco."

Another smile. "Don't forget to pick up the things I asked for."

He nodded and left, recalling the list he'd shoved into his pocket. Tammy wanted a few healing supplies, a number of grocery items, and some paint to complete the Christmas decorations. He had the list in hand when he reached the city. It was easy to fill, as she'd included instructions about where to go and had called her suppliers ahead of time to let them know he was coming by.

"For Tammy?" a wizened old man asked as soon as Nate stepped into his tiny store in one of the older parts of Chinatown.

"Yes." His beast picked up a thousand intermingled traces—herbs and spices, medicines and incense, but the mix was strangely soothing. "I'm her mate, Nathan."

The man's smile was fond as he bent under the counter and lifted up a box. "She's a good soul, Tammy. You will protect her, love her. That is your destiny."

Nate looked at the shopkeeper, startled. "Do you see the future?"

"No." The man laughed. "I'm not Psy. Only human."

Only human, and yet there was such ageless wisdom in those dark button eyes. Nate wondered if the Psy, for all their gifts, would ever be able to achieve that look of utter peace. "You're right. About the loving and the protecting."

Wrinkled hands picked up a leather-bound book and consulted something written in a strange, unknown language. "The stars say you'll have a long and happy life."

"I'll take that." Nate grinned.

A hint of mischief entered the old man's eyes. "The women, they don't know what they do to us. It is our secret."

Laughing, Nate exited the shop with Tammy's things and began to walk back to the vehicle. He was putting the box into the trunk when he realized he'd parked in front of a florist's, though he didn't recall seeing it the first time around. Shrugging, he closed the trunk and wandered over to the shop, Tammy on his mind.

There was no stock displayed outside, probably because of the cold, so he pushed open the door. Hothouse air greeted him. The interior was a jungle of flowers, the air thick with their competing perfumes. "Some shop," he muttered, trying to separate out the mingled scents.

"I do try," said a gentle voice.

He turned to find a tiny Chinese woman beside him, her smile beatific. There was a twinkle in her eye that reminded him of someone. "I don't suppose you know the healer down the road."

"My husband."

Somehow, that seemed right. "Oh." He shifted his feet, slightly uncomfortable in a place that was so intrinsically female. "I want to buy flowers for my mate."

The woman slid her small hands into the front pockets of her apron. "Does she like roses? I just received a new batch."

"She's a healer, too," he found himself saying, never having thought to ask Tammy if she liked roses.

"Ah, a sensible woman." The florist waved him to follow as she weaved through the wild tangle of her shop. "Here." She pointed to a sturdy green potted plant with a few white flowers. "This will last for years with a little water. Doesn't need much care or attention. Practical. It will suit your healer."

Nathan scowled. "No."

She shrugged and moved to another area of the shop, to point at a bunch of daisies. "Sunny, easy to enjoy, but there will be no sadness when they fade."

"No." All of him—man and leopard—was getting angry and he couldn't understand why. "That's not what I want."

Unperturbed, the florist took him around another corner in this shop that was far larger than it appeared from the outside. "Ah, I think this must be what you are searching for." She touched the edges of a rough bouquet. "These flowers will survive no matter what. Very cheap," she said with a shop-keeper's smile. "Common, you know."

"No." The leopard's claws pricked the insides of his skin, a growl building in his throat. "Show me something beautiful, something extraordinary."

"Well . . ." The woman seemed to think for a while before nodding. She took him to the back of the shop, to a small glass case tucked away under special lights. "I have these. They aren't very strong and, as you can see, require much care. But if you love them right, they will reward you with great beauty. They're precious and rare, not easy to find or replace."

"Yes," man and beast said together, fascinated by the delicacy of the blooms he could see beyond the glass. "Give them to me."

"For a healer?" The florist raised a skeptical eyebrow.

"She's not a healer to me. She's my lover, my mate." Unlike these hothouse flowers, she was strong. But just like these rare blooms, she was both irreplaceable and beautiful enough to break his heart. "She's mine to cherish."

This time, the florist's smile was pure brightness. "It is as it should be."

TAMSYN had cooked the meal, set the table, and shimmied into a pretty knee-length dress. She bit her lip and looked in the mirror. The dress was an autumn red-orange that brought out the copper strands in her unbound hair. Shaping her body to the waist, it then flared out in a playful swirl. She'd paired it with heels and a fine gold bracelet.

"I look okay," she told herself, knowing Nate probably wouldn't even notice. It wasn't as if the dress changed who she was. But it made her feel good.

Taking a deep breath, she went into the front room, ready to fluff the cushions for the tenth time. She delighted in living with Nate and wanted to make a good home for him, but had to admit she might be going a bit overboard. The man loved her. He couldn't care less if the pillows were skewed or dinner was late.

She smelled Nathan's wild masculine scent before he knocked. Her heart tripped a beat. Thinking he must have his hands full, she pulled the door open. "Nathan, what—" Her eyes dropped to the flowers in his arms. They were a sumptuous cream color, with gold streaks that shimmered with an almost otherworldly iridescence.

"I thought you'd like these," he said, the cat in his voice.

She touched a hesitant finger to one perfect petal. "For me?"

"Of course they're for you." It was more growl than anything close to human. "Do you think I go around giving other women flowers?"

Shaking her head, she looked up into the velvet blue of his eyes. "You think I'm an orchid kind of girl?"

"Hell yes." He put them into her arms and wiped away the tear she hadn't been aware of shedding. "Stop that."

She sniffed, staring at those precious flowers. *Orchids.* Nathan had given her orchids. Rare and precious and beautiful . . . the kind of flowers a man gave to a girl who was all those things. "Thank you."

"You can thank me later," he murmured against her ear. "When I peel this sexy dress off you." He was behind her now, his hands caressing her hips as he pulled her back against his body. "Or maybe I'll leave the dress on and only take off the underwear."

"You're making me blush." It was a playful rejoinder—she loved his earthy sensuality.

"A dress gives a man ideas." He nibbled at her earlobe.

Her smile turned into a full-fledged grin as her heart filled with so much love she thought it would burst. "What if I took off everything but the heels?"

He groaned. "Put the damn orchids in water."

"They need tender care," she murmured, touching another petal.

"Yes." He kissed the curve of her neck. "But I want to take care of you. Let me."

She blinked. No one had ever offered to take care of her. She was the pack healer—she took care of everyone else. But Nate thought she was an orchid kind of girl. She had the wondrous realization that, to him, that was who she'd always been. He saw the woman behind the healer. Another tear streaked down her cheek. "Always."

His arms came around her tight.

BY the time Christmas rolled around, Solias King was a dim memory. The Psy had removed all his equipment from their land, leaving behind only the ornament and Christmas lights. Tamsyn had been more than happy to use them on her tree, though the chosen fir had no lack of decorations—every one of her packmates had added a piece or ten, so that by Christmas Day, that tree was truly the pack's Christmas tree.

Tamsyn thought Shayla would have been pleased. So many in DarkRiver remained damaged by what had happened, but at least this silly extravagant tree had brought some joy back into their lives. They held the Christmas party under its snow-dusted branches and it was there that Lachlan formally acknowledged her and Nate's mating.

"For me, our anniversary will always be the day you gave me orchids," she said to Nathan as they danced under sparkling tinsel.

He slid his hands down to her lower back. "I vote for the cabin in Tahoe."

She laughed. "What are we going to tell our children when they ask about our mating if we pick Tahoe? Hmm?"

"That DarkRiver looks after its own." Sadie's, Cian's, and even Nita's interference had been born of the ties of Pack, and Nate accepted it. "And that their daddy was a stupid idiot, but one who came to his senses in time." Nate wondered what their cubs would look like. Not that he was going to ask Tammy to have children anytime soon. She was only nineteen . . . and part of him still wasn't sure she wouldn't regret having mated so young. But on this magical Christmas night, he decided to believe in happy endings. "Want a replay?"

"Of the orchids?"

It was such an innocent question he almost missed the mischief in her eyes. "I'll make you pay for that." He stroked his hand over her bottom.

"Behave," she whispered with a blush. "The others will see."

"So?" He turned her until her back was to the tree. "I'm just playing with my mate."

This time, she cuddled into him, her hands sliding up under his sweater. "I want the replay with cream on top."

He grinned. "Why do you think I bought those cans of whipped cream?"

Eyes wide, she licked her lips. "Me first."

Epilogue

Eighteen Years Later: Year 2079

"WHERE'S THE WHIPPED cream?" Nate kissed his way down the naked line of his mate's back.

She glanced over her shoulder, beautiful enough to steal his breath. "Have you forgotten we have guests?"

"They can entertain themselves," he said, referring to the houseful of packmates who'd dropped by for a family dinner.

"They've already been doing that for an hour." She moaned. "Oooh, again."

He complied, kissing the dip at the base of her spine. "I suppose I have to go play host."

"Poor baby," she teased.

He bit the curve of her buttock. "Don't get smart with me, Tamsyn Ryder. I know all your secrets." And after eighteen years together, he knew she was his, body and soul. It had taken him almost two years to really believe that truth—but when she'd only gotten happier and happier as time passed, it had become impossible not to.

She nuzzled at his neck. "Stop seducing me. I need to go finish making dinner."

Rising halfway, he found his gaze caught by a golden envelope on the bureau. "What's that?"

"Card from Nita," she said, referring to the former packmate who'd mated with an outside-Pack male not long after his and Tamsyn's mating. "Her cubs are growing up so fast."

"So are ours." He stroked his hand over the curve where her

waist flared into her hip. "God, I'll have to teach them about women soon."

She laughed. "And what do you know about women?"

His reply was a kiss that stole her breath.

THE house was strangely quiet when they went down. Tamsyn soon found out why. Lucas and Vaughn were outside playing ball. They'd roped in their own mates and a couple of other sentinels, as well as the kids and several older juveniles.

"See, I told you they'd take care of themselves." Nate kissed the pulse in her neck as they stood on the back doorstep.

She smiled. "More like the women decided we needed privacy." They had been in the kitchen with her when Nate had walked in with the orchids. He did that every year, and every year, she turned to putty in his arms. It was hard not to melt for a man who still saw her as an orchid kind of girl after all these years together.

Her mate's teasing reply was lost in the gleeful cries of their cubs as they spotted their parents. Nate walked out and intercepted the pair, scooping them up and hanging them over his shoulders. In spite of Nate's worries, Roman and Julian were still babies, not even three years old. "Mommy! Help!" they cried now, between giggles.

Nate threw her a grin and something went hot and tight in her stomach. God, she loved him. Walking over, she tilted her head to peer at her babies. That knot in her stomach grew tighter. "I think you look good in that position."

"Mommy!"

Laughing, she freed a wriggling Roman. He peppered her face with kisses before asking to be put down so he could rejoin the game. Julian was playing with his daddy, but waited to give his mom a kiss before chasing off after his twin. "They're so tiny," she whispered, standing in the curve of Nate's arm. "I can't believe they're ours."

"My little pistons," Nate said proudly, watching as Vaughn threw Roman a soft pass. Instead of running, Roman threw a sneaky pass to his twin, who shot off down the field. "See that—a few more years and they'll be pummeling everyone else on the field. So, what about the Christmas tree?"

"I drove out there yesterday." A living Christmas tree had become a tradition, a happy memory that had survived the turmoil of the bleak years after the ShadowWalkers' attack. "Our tree is still going strong."

"Just like the pack," Nate said, echoing her thoughts.

She wrapped her arm around his waist. "Just like us."

He glanced down, a tenderness in his gaze that would have surprised those who saw him only as the most experienced of DarkRiver's dangerous sentinels. "As if I'd ever let you go."

"Sweet talker." She leaned up and kissed him, thinking that her mate was simply getting sexier with age. He now had the darkly sensual beauty of a leopard in the prime of his life, pure hard muscle and a finely honed sexuality that demanded everything she had. She found him irresistible. "I love you."

He nibbled at her lower lip and there was smug male pride in his eyes as he said, "I know."

She laughed. It had taken her years to get him to that point, where he believed she truly was happy with their life. Never once had she regretted mating at nineteen. She'd been one of the lucky ones—she'd found her mate early.

And then he whispered, "Always," and she fell in love with him all over again.

Stroke of
Enticement

Wishes

Dear Santa Claus,

I'm not sure I believe in you anymore, but I don't know who else to ask, so I hope you're not just imajinary like Daddy says. I'm in the hospital, but don't worry, I don't want you to use up your majick to make me better. The M-Psy came and looked at my leg and said I'd walk again. You know the Psy don't have feelings. I think that means they can't tell lies. And the nice changeling nurse—the one that can shapeshift into a deer—she told me with ~~rebalit~~ rehab, I'd be o.k.

The reason I'm writing to you is because I'm lonely. Don't tell my mom, o.k.? She comes to see me but she's always so sad. She looks at me like I'm broken, like I'm not her strong little girl anymore. And my daddy doesn't visit me. He never paid any ~~atent~~ attention to me anyways, but it still makes my heart hurt.

I know you can't make my daddy come see me, but I was wondering, since you're majick, do you think you could send me a friend? Someone fun who wanted to be with me and who didn't care that my leg was all mangled up. The kids here are nice, but they all go home after a little while. It would be wonderful to have someone who was mine, someone who didn't have to leave.

My friend can be human or Psy or changeling. I won't mind. Maybe you could find someone who was lonely, too, and then we could be unlonely together? I promise I'll share all my things, and I'll let her (or even a boy) choose the games we play.

I think that's all. Thanks for lisening.

Annie
p.s. I don't mind if you don't give me any other presents at all.
p.p.s. I'm sorry about the speling mistakes. I had to miss a lot of school but now I'm trying really hard to catch up with the hospital's computer tutor.

Chapter 1

ANNIE LOOKED UP and met the angry eyes of the seven-year-old sitting at the child-sized desk in front of her own, arms crossed and lip jutting out. Bryan glared at her, the fury of his leopard apparent in every line of his body. Annie was used to teaching changeling children—a lot of DarkRiver kids came to this school, close as it was to their territory. She was used to their affectionate natures, their occasional accidental shifts into leopard form, and even their shorter tempers when compared with those of human children. What she was not used to was such blatant disobedience.

"Bryan," she began, intending, once again, to try to get to the bottom of this.

He shook his head, stuck out his chin. "I'm not talking to anyone but Uncle Zach."

Annie glanced at her watch. She'd called Bryan's uncle twenty minutes ago, not long after last bell. "I left a message. But he might not check it straightaway."

"Then we wait."

She almost smiled at the stubbornness of him, but knew that that would only make matters worse. "Are you sure you don't want to tell me why you hit Morgan?"

"No."

Annie tucked back a strand of hair that had escaped the bun she'd anchored with a pair of lacquered chopsticks in a vain attempt at style. "Perhaps we could talk to your mom together—would you feel more comfortable discussing things with her?"

She'd already called Mrs. Nicholson to tell her that Bryan would be late getting home. The woman had taken it in her

stride—she had three boys. "And one of them's always in detention," she'd said with a laugh, love in every syllable. "Since
you're waiting on Zach, he can drive this misbehaving baby
home."

"Bryan?" she prompted, when her little mischief-maker
remained silent.

"No. You promised I could wait for Uncle Zach." He
scowled. "Promises are for keeping, that's what Uncle Zach
always says."

"That's true." Giving in, she smiled. "Let's hope your uncle
makes it here soon."

"Hot date?" The voice was rich, dark, and completely out
of place in her classroom.

Startled, she stood to face the man leaning in the doorway.
"Uncle Zach?"

A smile that cut her off at the knees. "Just Zach's fine." Vivid
aqua-colored eyes, straight black hair cut in a careless way,
copper-gold skin and bones that spoke of an ancestor from one
of the native tribes. "You called."

And he'd come.

She felt her cheeks blaze as the thought passed through her
head. "I'm Annie Kildaire, Bryan's teacher."

When Zach accepted the hand she'd extended in a gesture
of automatic politeness, the heat of him seared through her
skin to burn her on the inside. She felt her breath catch and
knew she was going even redder. Dear God, she was useless
around beautiful men. And "Uncle" Zach was the most beautiful man she'd ever seen.

He was also staring at her. Probably at her always messy
knot of hair, her bright red cheeks, her mortified brown eyes.
Tugging at her hand, she tried to extract it. He held on as he
glanced at Bryan. His nephew continued to sit there with a
mutinous expression on his face. Seeing their clasped hands,
he favored his uncle with a look that shouted "traitor."

Zach returned his attention to Annie. "Tell me what
happened."

"Could you—" She tugged at her hand again.

He looked down, seemed to consider it, then finally let go.
Fingers tingling in sensory memory, she quickly moved to busy
herself tidying the stack of book reports on her desk. "If you'd

like to take a seat?" He towered over her. That wasn't particularly difficult, but he was big in a very intimidating way. Solid shoulders, pure hard muscle, and lean strength. A soldier, she thought, aware of some of the ranks within the DarkRiver pack, Zach had to carry the rank of soldier.

"I'd rather stand."

"All right." She didn't sit either. It didn't give her much of an advantage—or any advantage if she was being honest—but if she sat down with him looming all big and intense over her, she'd probably lose the power of speech. "Bryan punched a classmate during last period. He refuses to tell me what caused the incident."

"I see." Zach frowned. "Why isn't the other boy here?"

She wondered if he thought she was playing favorites. "Morgan is in the sick bay. He's rather . . . delicate."

Zach raised an eyebrow. "Delicate?"

She wanted to glare at him herself. He knew perfectly well what she was talking about. "Morgan gets sick very easily." And had a mother who treated him as if he was made of spun glass. Given that the same thing had driven Annie insane as a child, she might've tried to talk to Mrs. Ainslow about it, except that it was obvious Morgan *liked* the fussing. "He was too upset to stay near Bryan, though I would've preferred to talk to them together."

"Human?" Zach asked.

"No," she said, trying not to feel *too* satisfied by his look of surprise. "Swan."

"Swans aren't predators"—which, Annie knew, was why Morgan's family had been allowed to stay in DarkRiver territory—"but they're not exactly weak."

"While all humans are?" she was irritated enough to say.

He raised an eyebrow. "Did I say that, sweetheart?"

Her face heated from the inside out. "I am Bryan's teacher."

"Not mine." A grin. "You could be though. Wanna play classroom, Teach?"

She dealt with DarkRiver cats throughout the year, but for the most part, they were mated pairs or couples in long-term relationships. She had no clue how to handle a teasing male who was clearly not only aware of the effect he had on her but confident enough to take advantage. Focus on the facts, she told herself, just focus. "Bryan is normally very good." He was, in truth, one of her best students. "He's kind, intelligent, and before today, he's never once hurt a classmate."

Zach's expression turned serious. "Strength is for protecting, not hurting. Bryan knows that as well as anybody in the pack."

Annie's heart clutched at the absolute way he said that, as if it was simply a fact of life. That core of unflinching honor was one of the things she most admired about the DarkRiver males she'd met. The other was the way they didn't make even the slightest attempt to hide the adoration they felt for their mates. It was . . . nice.

It was also yet another point of contention between her and her mother. Professor Kimberly Kildaire had very determined views on what men should be like. The word "civilized" appeared often in the description, along with generous helpings of "rational"—a man who teased with sensual ease was far too wild to ever make the professor's cut.

However, Annie knew her own mind, and her reaction to Zach was anything but rational. "That's why," she said, forcing herself to think past the nerves that threatened to turn her mute, "I was so surprised by what he did. Frankly, I have no idea what could've caused it. Morgan and Bryan don't even tend to play together."

"Give me a couple of minutes with him." With a nod, he walked to his nephew. "Come on, Jumping Bean, let's talk."

"Over there." Bryan got up and led his uncle to the back of the classroom. Annie looked away out of politeness, knowing she wouldn't have been able to hear the conversation even if they hadn't moved—changeling hearing was generally far more acute than a human's. But, and though she tried to keep her eyes on the book reports, her curiosity got the better of her.

She looked up to see Zach crouched in front of Bryan, his arms braced loosely on his knees. The position had raised the sleeve of his T-shirt to expose part of a tattoo on his right biceps. She squinted. It was something exotic and curved, something that beckoned her to stroke. Thankfully, before she could surrender to the urge to get closer, Bryan began to gesture so earnestly, she wondered what on earth he was saying.

• • •

"I didn't even hit him that hard, Uncle Zach." Bryan blew out a breath that made his dark brown bangs dance. "He's a sissy."

"Bryan."

"I mean he's 'delicate,' " Bryan said, proving he had very big ears. "He's always crying, even when nobody does anything on purpose. He cried yesterday when Holly elbowed him by accident."

"Oh?"

"Yeah—Holly's a *girl*. And she's human."

Zach knew exactly what Bryan meant. No matter their animal, changelings were physically tougher than humans. Their bones were stronger, their bodies healed faster, and in the case of predatory changelings, they could do a hell of a lot more damage. "Which doesn't explain why you hit him." He knew and liked his nephew. The boy had been born with a solid code of honor, a code that had been strengthened by the rules Dark-River men lived by. "You know we don't bully weaker people."

A shamefaced expression. "I know."

"Did the cat get angry?" The leopard was part of who they were. But for the younger ones, the wilder side of their nature was sometimes difficult to control.

Right then, Bryan's curvy temptation of a teacher shifted up front. Her delectable scent whispered over on disturbed air currents, ruffling the leopard's fur in the most enticing way. He barely bit back a responsive groan. Sometimes, adults had trouble with the cat, too. "Come on, JB. You know I'm not going to get mad at you if you lost control."

"Yeah, I guess I kinda got mad." Bryan shuffled his feet. "I wanted to growl and bite, but I hit him instead."

"That's good." A leopard's jaws could do a lot of damage.

"And it wasn't just the cat," his nephew elaborated. "It was all of me."

Zach understood. They weren't human, and they weren't animal. They were both. "What made you angry?"

"Morgan said something mean."

Zach knew that sometimes it was those who appeared

weakest who bore the nastiest of streaks. At least Ms. Kildaire seemed well aware of that—he hadn't missed the fact that she hadn't automatically blamed Bryan. "Tell me what it was."

Bryan darted a glance toward his teacher, then leaned closer. "I didn't want to say anything to Miss Kildaire, 'cause she's nice, and I like her."

"I like her, too." A truer statement had never been said. There was something about the little teacher with her jet-black hair and dark brown eyes that had the cat purring in interest. He wondered if she realized she had one hell of a sexy mouth, then wondered if she'd let him do all sorts of wicked things to that mouth. *Later,* he promised himself. Right now, Bryan needed him. "What does this have to do with Ms. Kildaire?"

"Morgan said that his mother said that Miss Kildaire is sitting on a shelf."

Zach had to think about that one for a few seconds. "He said she's on the shelf?"

"Uh-huh." An emphatic nod. "I don't know why Miss Kildaire would sit on a shelf, but that's what Morgan said."

"I'm guessing there's more."

"And *then* Morgan said that his mother said that Miss Kildaire was too fat to get a man."

What a load of horseshit, Zach thought. Morgan's mother was probably some shriveled-up jealous twit. "I see."

"And then Morgan said she was a cripple."

Zach had a sudden urge to punch out the little rat himself. "Go on."

"I told him to take it back. Miss Kildaire is the nicest teacher at the school, and she's not a cripple just 'cause she has a sore leg sometimes and has to use a cane." Temper flared in Bryan's eyes, the irises shifting to the jagged green of the leopard.

"Hold the cat, Bryan," Zach said, forcing a choke hold on his own anger. Cubs had to be taught control. Once, a long time ago, the animal fury of changelings had run unchecked, and it had led to the carnage of the Territorial Wars.

The other races might've forgotten those tormented years, but changelings never would. And they'd never allow it to happen again. "Hold it." He put his hand on Bryan's arm and allowed a low growl to rise from his throat. It was a gesture of dominance, and it worked to bring Bryan's leopard back under control.

"Sorry."

Zach felt his own cat pacing inside him before it became distracted by the exquisite scent of the luscious Ms. Kildaire. "It's okay. We all had to learn."

"Yeah." Bryan blew out a breath. "Anyway, Morgan kept saying she was a cripple, and I got mad and hit him."

Zach found himself in a quandary. He really couldn't disagree with his nephew's actions, but punching out another kid was against the rules. He looked into Bryan's intelligent face and made the only decision he could. "JB, you know we don't condone this kind of violence."

Bryan nodded.

"But I understand the provocation." Lying wasn't how the pack worked. And Bryan was old enough to know that understanding didn't mean approval.

His nephew's face melted into a smile. "I knew you would." He threw his arms around Zach's neck.

Zach hugged that small, sturdy body and waited until Bryan drew back before asking, "Why didn't you call your dad? He would've understood, too." Joe ran a bar that was a favorite gathering place for the pack, but he was also a fellow soldier.

"He's watching Liam's soccer game today. I didn't want to mess that up—Liam's been practicing his kicks for like a month."

Zach ruffled his nephew's hair. "You're a good kid, JB." Standing, he nodded at the cubbyholes that lined the back of the classroom. "Grab your stuff while I go sort this out with Ms. Kildaire."

Bryan grabbed his hand. "You won't—"

"I won't say anything. Promise."

Relaxing, Bryan went to a cubby to their right and began to gather his things.

Zach watched Annie rise from her chair as he walked over and had to fight the urge to growl that she sit back down. He'd noticed her shakiness earlier—her left leg was bothering her. But if he said what he wanted to, he'd be as bad as that runt, Morgan. Annie Kildaire had to be perfectly capable if she was running a classroom of seven-year-olds.

"Did he tell you?" she asked in that husky voice that brushed like black velvet over his skin. The cat stretched out, asking for more. Being stroked by Ms. Kildaire, he thought, both sides of him in agreement, might just be the best Christmas present ever.

"Yes, he gave up the goods."

She waited. "And?"

"And I can't tell you." He watched her brow furrow, her lips purse. He couldn't decide if he wanted to bite down on that full lower lip or lick the upper one.

"Mr. . . . Zach."

"Quinn," he supplied. "Zach Quinn."

Her cheeks flared with little red spots of temper. "Mr. Quinn, Bryan is a child. I expect you to act like an adult."

Oh, he had plenty of plans to act like an adult around Ms. Kildaire. "I promised JB."

She stared at him, then blew out a breath. "And promises are to be kept."

"Yes."

"What do you suggest I do?" She folded her arms. "I have to punish him, and I can't do that without knowing why he did what he did."

"I'll take care of it." Bryan had hit someone, and his nephew knew he'd be disciplined for it, provocation or not. But some things, Zach knew, were worth fighting over. "I'll make sure the punishment fits the crime."

"It's a school matter."

"It's a leopard matter."

Chapter 2

UNDERSTANDING FILTERED INTO those pretty melted-chocolate eyes. "He's usually so well controlled, I forget he's only seven."

"Boy'll grow up to be one of the dominants, probably a soldier." He glanced behind him. "Ready?"

Bryan nodded, backpack slung over his shoulder. "Yep."

Zach watched as his nephew walked up to the desk and said, "I'm sorry I dis—"—a frown of concentration—"disrupted the classroom. But I'm not sorry I hit Morgan."

Zach was looking at Annie and saw her struggle to hide a smile. "That's not a very good attitude, Bryan."

"I know. And I'm ready for the punishment. But I'm still not sorry."

Brown eyes flicked to him. "Is stubbornness a family trait?" Her lips curved just a little, just enough to make everything in him sit up in attention.

"Now that, sweetheart," he said, a stunning realization taking form in his chest, "is something you'll have to decide for yourself." *Well, hell.*

She colored again. "Thank you for coming in, Mr. Quinn. I'll look forward to seeing Bryan in class on Monday."

He didn't move, tasting the realization that had him by the throat. It was hot, wild, *right*. Utterly, absolutely right. The knowledge made his smile slow and seductive. "Why don't you walk out with us?" The corridors had been close to empty when he arrived, and he couldn't hear any movement now. No way was he leaving sweet Annie Kildaire alone in a building with winter darkness only an hour away at most.

"I'll be out in a moment." She began to gather the papers on her desk.

"We'll wait." He glanced at Bryan. "Can you wait?"

"Yep." A sunny smile. "But I'm hungry."

Reaching into the back pocket of his jeans, he pulled out a muesli bar he'd grabbed on his way here. "I got you this for the ride home."

Bryan caught it with cat-quick reflexes and happily went off to scramble into a seat, backpack at his feet. Meanwhile, Ms. Kildaire was giving him a guarded kind of look. "Really Mr. Quinn—"

"Zach. You can only call me Mr. Quinn when you're angry."

"Mr.—"

"Zach."

Her hand fisted. "Fine. Zach."

He smiled, liking that she was already comfortable enough to argue with him. Some women found him a little too dangerous to play with. And he very much wanted to play with Annie. "Yes, Teach?"

He could hear her gritting her teeth. "I'll be perfectly fine walking out alone. I do it every day of the week."

He shrugged, enjoying the verbal sparring. "I'm here today."

"And what you says goes?" Looking down, she shoved her papers into an untidy pile.

"Unless you can talk me out of it." He saw her jaw set and knew she was gritting those human teeth again. All that beautiful passion, he thought in pleasure, hidden behind the shyness that had first stained her cheeks.

"And why should I be talking you out of anything?" She grabbed what looked like a black leather-synth satchel and put the papers inside. "You're nobody to me."

The cat didn't like that. The man didn't either. "That wasn't very nice."

She turned to shoot him a glare, then recommenced packing her satchel. He could almost see her trying to figure out if he was being serious or if he was teasing her. That it took her that much focus told him she hadn't been teased much. That was a shame. Because when Annie got mad, she forgot to be shy.

Now, she slapped her satchel closed and swung it over her

shoulder. Or tried to. Zach slid it out of her hand and brought the strap over his head, settling it diagonally across his body.

"Mr. Quinn!" She looked like she wanted to bite him.

His cat purred in interest, even as Bryan giggled. "Nobody calls Uncle Zach that."

"Yeah, nobody does," Zach added. "Come on, Jumping Bean. We're moving out." He nodded at the coat thrown carelessly over the back of Annie's chair. "Don't forget that. It's cold out." He began to walk to the door, knowing she'd have no choice but to follow.

After a taut second, she did. He heard her clothing rustle as she put the coat on over her stern gray pants and tailored white shirt, his mind obliging him with a fantasy slide show of the feminine softness he knew lurked underneath. Pity it was all covered up now. "After you, Teach." Letting Bryan scamper a few feet ahead, he held the door open and watched Annie Kildaire walk toward him.

Her limp was very slight, but even that meant the injury had to have been horrendous. Either that, or the impairment was a natural one surgeons hadn't been able to repair fully. And there wasn't much surgeons couldn't repair these days. "What happened to your leg?" he asked once they were out in the hallway.

She faltered for a second before her shoulders squared. "There was a freak bullet-train derailment when I was seven. My leg was crushed so badly, it was pretty much unrecognizable as anything other than meat with a few fragments of bone."

He heard the simmering pride in her, had the sense that she was bracing herself for a blow. "They did a good job of reconstructing it. Titanium?"

He could tell from her expression that that wasn't the response she'd expected. "No. Some kind of new plassteel. Very high-tech. It 'grew' as I grew, so I only needed a couple of extra surgeries over the years."

"And now?"

"I shouldn't need any work done on it unless I injure the leg in some way."

Zach knew that couldn't be all of it. "Still hurt?"

She hesitated. "Sometimes." She indicated a corridor to their left. "I want to make sure Morgan's been picked up."

"JB, hold up." Knowing he could trust the boy not to dart outside, he followed Annie the short distance to the sick bay. Looking over her shoulder, he saw the darkened interior. "He's gone."

She jumped. "You walk like a cat!"

"I am a cat, sweetheart." He wanted to tease her again, so he let a low growl rumble up from his chest. "See?"

Streaks of vibrant color stained her cheeks once more. But she didn't back down. "Are you planning to move?"

"No." He drew in a deep breath, fighting the urge to nuzzle at her throat. "You smell good. Can I taste you?" It was a half-serious question. "Just a little?"

"Mr. Quinn!" She took a step around him and headed off.

But he'd already caught the tart bite of arousal in her scent. Satisfied, he followed, on his best behavior now. It wouldn't do to scare Annie away. *Not when he planned to keep her.*

A moment later, they reached the front door, where Bryan was waiting. Zach pulled it open. "Stay with me," he told his nephew. The boy was leopard fast, but he was still a boy. Sometimes, he didn't look where he was going, and cars could hurt him as easily as they could a human or Psy child.

The outside air was cold, but it made Zach sigh in exhilaration. Being outdoors was in his blood, the reason why he loved his day job as a ranger in Yosemite. The work fitted naturally into his duties as a DarkRiver soldier—he could run patrols and check up on his wild charges at the same time.

"Where's your car?" he asked Annie, noticing that her face had brightened, too. Sexy, kissable Annie Kildaire liked being outside as much as he did. It pleased the cat, soothed the man.

"Over there." Giving him a look still colored with the tart kiss of temper, she pointed to a little compact that would cut his legs in half if he was ever insane enough to try to fold himself inside. But she was on the small side, he thought, wondering if she'd mind tussling with a taller man. The idea of the games he wanted to play with Annie made him grin. "JB and I will walk you over."

She didn't argue with him this time, simply asked about his vehicle. He jerked a thumb in the direction of the rugged all-wheel-drive parked a few spaces away.

"I suppose you need that in the forest?" Her voice held a touch of wistfulness.

"Yeah." DarkRiver's territory covered a lot of beautiful but harsh land. And now that they had allied with the SnowDancer wolves, that territory included the Sierra Nevada mountains. "Have you ever been out in Yosemite?" The nearest edge of the massive forest was only about an hour from here, the reason why this school was so popular with the pack. Many of them lived on the fringes of Yosemite.

"Just the public areas." She pressed her thumb to the door of her car, deactivating the security lock. "I guess those sections only make up a tiny fraction of your territory?"

Zach nodded. In the past, DarkRiver had been relaxed about offering access to other parts of the forest—so long as people obeyed the rules that protected the land and its wild inhabitants. However, right now, with the Psy Council looking for any weakness in their defenses, they'd become more stringent. Nobody but Pack went in past what DarkRiver considered the public boundary. Of course, members of the pack could bring guests in. "Want to see more?"

Her expression was startled. "I—" She snapped her mouth shut, and he saw her gaze dip to her leg. The movement was so quick, he would've missed it if he hadn't been watching her so closely.

Someone, he thought, a growl building inside him, had done a number on her confidence. "I can drive you up tomorrow," he said, clamping down on the anger, "show you some of the sights most people never get to see."

"I shouldn't." But temptation whispered through her eyes. "I have to prepare for the class's contribution to the Christmas pageant." A fond look directed at Bryan.

His nephew jumped up and down. "We're going to do the story of how the Psy once tried to cancel Christmas. It's gonna be so funny!"

"Make sure you get me a ticket," Zach said, but his mind was on how to secure Annie's company for tomorrow. Challenge might work. Or perhaps . . . "Once-in-a-lifetime offer," he said with a smile that he tried to keep from being ravenous. If she caught even a hint of what he truly wanted from her, she'd never get into a car with him, much less let him drive her into the lush privacy of the forest. "Pack's getting strict about who we allow in."

She bit down on that full lower lip of hers, arousing his jealousy. He wanted to do the biting.

"Well," she said, clearly torn.

Then Bryan clinched the deal for him. "You should come, Miss Kildaire! Then after, you can come to the picnic."

"Picnic?" She looked at Zach. "It's winter."

"Winter picnic," he said, as if that was normal. It was, for DarkRiver. "It's informal, just a chance for people to get together before the Christmas madness."

"Please come, Miss Kildaire," Bryan pleaded. "*Please.*"

He saw Annie melt at that childish plea and knew he had her.

"All right," she said, and looked up. Her smile faded . . . because he'd let the cat seep into his eyes, let her see the dark hunger pumping through his blood.

"I'll pick you up at nine." He leaned closer, drawing in the scent of her. "Be ready for me, sweetheart."

ANNIE closed the door to her apartment and asked herself if she'd lost her mind. Not half an hour ago, she'd agreed to spend an entire day with a man so dangerous, a sane woman would've run in the opposite direction . . . instead of fantasizing about kissing him on those should-be-illegal lips. Her entire body went hot as she remembered the look in his eyes as he'd asked her to be ready for him. Dear God, the man was lethal.

"Calm down, Annie," she told herself. "It's not like he's really going to do anything." Because while Zach Quinn might've flirted with her, might even have looked at her as a man looks at a woman he wants, she was pragmatic enough to know that it had probably been nothing more than a momentary diversion on his part. A man that good-looking had to have women begging to crawl into his bed.

The idea of Zach sprawled in bed, all gleaming skin and liquid muscle, made her stomach flutter. Then she imagined him crooking a finger, that teasing smile playing over his lips. "If he ever looks at me like that," she whispered, pulling the chopsticks out of her hair as she walked into the bedroom, "I'm a goner." Her black hair tumbled around her face in a mass of soft curls.

Zach's hair had looked heavier than hers, sleeker.

Her thoughts went from his hair to what he might look like in leopard form. A predator, all muscle and power covered with a gold-and-black coat. Would he allow a woman to stroke him? Her fingers tingled in awareness, and standing as she was in front of the vanity mirror, she saw her lips part, her eyes widen. The ache between her thighs turned into an erotic pulse.

Her cell phone beeped.

She ignored it, shocked by the raw intensity of the hunger surging through her. She'd never before reacted this passionately to a man, until her entire body trembled with the force of it. "Lord have mercy." Because if this was what simply thinking about him did to her, how in the world was she going to survive being alone with him for an entire day?

Beep. Beep. Beep.

She answered the cell just to shut off the sound. "Yes?"

Chapter 3

"ANGELICA, WHAT'S THE matter? You're snapping."

She took a deep breath. "Nothing, Mom. I just got home."

"Well, it's Friday, so you can relax a little. Drink that chamomile tea I got you."

Annie hated chamomile tea. "You know I don't like it."

"It's good for you."

She'd heard that so many times it no longer made any impact. "I think I want to be bad, today." And it wasn't herbal tea on her mind. "Very, very bad."

"Honestly, Angelica!" Kimberly blew out a frustrated breath. "Forget the tea. I wanted to tell you to dress nicely for dinner tomorrow night."

Dinner? Annie's stomach sunk to the bottom of her toes as she realized she'd blanked the event from her mind. "Mom, you said you wouldn't—"

"He's a nice young professor from London. Over here on a sabbatical."

"When you say young . . ."

"He's only forty-three, dear."

Annie was twenty-eight. "Oh." She rubbed her forehead. "The thing is—"

"No arguments. Your father and I want you settled. We won't be around to look after you forever."

"I can look after myself." She felt her hand fist, released it with effort. There was no point in getting angry, not when this was a conversation they'd been having for more years than she could remember. "I'm not a child."

"Well you can't spend the rest of your life alone." Her mother's tone was harsh, but it held an edge of desperation—Kimberly really was worried by the thought of her daughter living a solitary life. She'd never bothered to wonder if Annie was single by choice. "Professor Markson is a lovely man. You could do a lot worse."

What her mother actually meant, Annie thought with a stab of old resentment, was that it wasn't as if she had any other options. To Kimberly, Annie was a damaged and fragile creature most men would bypass. "Is Caro coming?"

"Of course not." Her mother made a sound of annoyance. "We want the professor's attention on you. Much as I like her, your cousin tends to steal the limelight, even now that she's married."

Annie's headache intensified—Caro was usually the only point of sanity at these ritual humiliations. "Right."

"I'll expect you at seven for cocktails."

"I might be a little late."

"Work?"

"No." How did she say this? "I, er, arranged an in-depth tour of Yosemite." Though she didn't live far from the forest, her parents were closer to San Francisco. Even in a high-speed vehicle, it would take her over an hour to make the trip.

"Really, Annie. You knew we were having this dinner."

"I said I didn't want to be set up on any more dates." Especially when she had no intention of marrying or entering into a long-term relationship. *Ever.* And most certainly not when the men came in expecting someone like Caro and got Annie instead. "I'll try to be there as soon as I can, but I can't promise anything."

Her mother hung up after a few more sharp words. Rubbing her forehead, Annie walked out of the bedroom and to the bathroom, cell phone still in hand. After that call, she definitely needed the soothing properties of a bath liberally laced with mineral salts. Stripping off, she sat on the edge of the tub while it filled, taking the chance to massage some of the stiffness out of her thigh.

Does it hurt?

Such a simple question, without judgment or pity. It had undone her just a little. Not only that, but Zach had continued to flirt with her even after discovering that she was less than perfect. It might not have meant much to him, but it had meant something to her.

No, Angelica, you can't do that. Your leg's too weak.

Too often, it felt as if her mother had been born into the wrong race. She would've made a good Psy, with her analytical mind and need for perfection in all things.

The only place Kimberly had failed was with Annie.

Her mood might've dimmed again, but she was too busy daydreaming about kissing Zach on those beautiful lips of his. The man was too sinful to be real. And the way he flirted . . . wow. It would've been nice to be confident enough to flirt back. "Instead of blushing and going tongue-tied," she muttered.

She'd seen enough DarkRiver couples to identify the kind of women dominant changeling men found attractive—and Zach was definitely a dominant. Those women were all striking in some way, but it was their self-assurance that really shone through. Vividly intelligent, they didn't hesitate to speak their minds or give back as good as they got. Feminine strength didn't scare men of Zach Quinn's ilk, it enticed them.

And that was exactly what attracted her to him. She knew after having met him only once that he'd never tell her she couldn't do something. Zach would simply expect her to match him. And that was a seduction all on its own.

The bath pinged to alert her it was full. She was about to step in when her eye fell on the cell phone she'd left on top of her discarded clothes. She grabbed it, deciding to give Caro a call. Her cousin was an expert on men, and it was advice on that subject that Annie needed right now.

Putting it within reach, she sank into the hot water with a moan. After ten minutes of just lying there soaking in the heat, she reached out to get the phone. It beeped an incoming call as her fingers brushed the case. Rolling her eyes because it was probably her mother again, she flipped it open without checking the display and answered audio only.

"It's me," she said, dropping her head back against the wall and pressing her feet flat against the end of the bath.

"Hello, me."

Her breath stuck in her throat at the sound of that sensually amused voice. "Zach . . . Mr. Quinn—" She'd have jerked upright except that she was frozen in place.

"Zach," he corrected. "I hope I'm not disturbing you."

"No, I"—water dripped as she raised a hand to push streamers of hair off her face—"I was just relaxing."

"In the bath?"

She blinked, mortified that she'd left the visual feed on by accident. But no, it was switched off.

"Leopards have good ears."

Her cheeks colored. "Of course." She stayed very still, not wanting him to hear her splashing about.

"I didn't mean to intrude into your relaxation time." An apology made in a voice that was close to a purr.

Annie told herself to breathe. "That's okay." Realizing he couldn't see her, she stopped fighting herself and allowed her face to suffuse with the pleasure she got from simply listening to him. She'd never before met a man with a voice like Zach's—so masculine, but with that delectable hint of play. As if while he might be a honed blade of a soldier, he knew how to laugh, too. "Was there a problem with Bryan?"

"No, JB's fine. No runs with the other kids for a week for him."

Annie frowned. "I thought he'd have entertainment privileges suspended."

Zach chuckled, and it rippled through her like living fire. "That *is* his favorite form of entertainment. Leopard changelings, especially boys his age, hate being trapped inside."

"Of course." She remembered one of the other parents saying something along those lines during a parent-teacher conference. "Was that what you called to tell me?"

"That, and I wanted to warn you about the cold up in the higher elevations. We might even hit some snow. Dress in layers."

"Okay." She bit down on her lower lip, wanting to keep him on the phone but not knowing what to say to achieve that goal. "So, nine a.m. tomorrow?"

"Hmm." He sounded distracted to her ears.

"I should let you go," she began.

"Tired of me already?"

She really didn't know how to deal with him. "No."

Another male chuckle. "Tell me something about you, Annie."

"What do you want to know?" *Why* did he want to know?

"How long have you been a teacher?"

"Five years," she said with a smile. "I started teaching new entrants, but for the past couple of years, it's been kids Bryan's age."

"You like it."

"I love it." She found she'd relaxed again, soothed by the timbre of his voice, so easy, so deliciously male. "What do you do?"

"I'm a forest ranger, specializing in the predatory species that call Yosemite home."

The work fitted him better than anything she could've imagined. "Do you like what you do?"

"It's in my blood." He paused. "Someone's at the door. I'll pick you up at nine on the dot. Sweet dreams." The last was a husky murmur laced with temptation.

"Bye." She ended the call and just sat there, flushing alternately hot and cold. Surely she was reading too much into the conversation. He'd called to make sure she dressed right. The way his voice had felt like a caress over her most sensitive skin . . . that was the result of her pulse-pounding susceptibility to him. It didn't mean he wanted her, too.

But she couldn't quite stop herself from hoping.

ZACH pulled open the door to his small home, already aware of his visitor's identity. He'd picked up the scent the instant the other changeling stepped out of his vehicle.

"Luc." He welcomed his alpha inside. "What's up?"

Lucas walked in, dressed in a dark gray suit that said he'd come straight from DarkRiver's business HQ. "Nice place."

"Nice suit." Opening the cooler, he threw Lucas a sleek glass bottle before taking one for himself.

"What the hell is this?" Lucas scowled at the pale blue liquid inside. "And the suit's camouflage."

"It's some new energy drink Joe's come up with." He twisted off the top. "We're supposed to give him feedback."

Lucas took a pull. "Not bad—for something that looks like it glows in the dark."

Zach grinned. "So, why the camouflage?"

"I had a meeting with a Psy group today."

"New deal?" DarkRiver had recently completed its second major construction project for Psy Councilor Nikita Duncan. The success of the venture had been so dramatic, they'd attracted considerable interest from other Psy businesses.

"Signed and sealed." Lucas's grin was very feline in its satisfaction. "I wanted to talk to you about some of the land you cover during your duties as ranger."

Zach nodded. "Is there a problem?"

"Shouldn't be, but I want you to keep an extra-sharp eye out. Psy don't usually venture anywhere near our territory, but they've been changing the rules recently."

"You think they might be trying to use the land to familiarize themselves with the forest," Zach guessed. Psy weren't, as a rule, comfortable in wide-open spaces. They preferred the cities, with their towers of glass and steel. But as Lucas's mate, Sascha, showed, the psychic race was supremely adaptable.

"I don't think it's happened yet, but there's a possibility it might—we'd be fools if we didn't prepare for the unexpected."

"I'll keep you updated." He put down his empty bottle beside the one Lucas had just finished. "You didn't really come here for that." Lucas's caution was something Zach was a senior-enough soldier to figure out for himself.

Lucas shrugged, the clawlike markings on the right side of his face standing out in vivid relief. "I was passing through to talk to Tammy about the Christmas celebrations, decided to drop in, touch base."

Since Tammy and Nate were Zach's closest neighbors, that made sense. "Tell Nate I saw his cubs chasing a dog yesterday."

Lucas grinned. "Sounds about right."

"Can I ask you a question?"

Lucas raised an eyebrow and waited.

"How fragile are humans?" He'd had human lovers before, but he'd never wanted any woman, human or changeling, with the raw fury that colored his hunger for Annie. It worried him that he might hurt her in passion. "How much do I have to hold back?"

"They're not as breakable as we tend to think," Lucas said,

and Zach knew he was speaking from experience. Physically, Psy were even weaker than humans, yet Lucas was very happily mated to Sascha. "Just don't use the same force on her that you'd use on me or one of the other males, and you'll be fine."

"Who said there's a 'her'?"

"There's always a her."

"Her name is Annie, and I'm bringing her to the picnic tomorrow."

Lucas's eyes gleamed cat green. "You're introducing her to the pack? When did you meet her?"

"Today."

"Well, hell." Lucas rocked back on his heels. "She have any idea what that means?"

"She's a little wary, but she likes me," he said, thinking of how her eyes had drunk him up. A man could get used to being looked at that way. Especially when the woman doing the looking was someone he'd like to eat up in small, delicious bites. "I'm going to court her first." But he already considered her his—because not only did Annie Kildaire arouse his most primal instincts, she was his mate . . . and he was a possessive kind of cat.

Chapter 4

ANNIE WAS READY by eight the next morning. Feeling jumpy and overexcited, she checked her clothing in the mirror one more time. She'd taken Zach's advice and layered it up, beginning with a plain white tee and a thin V-necked cashmere-blend sweater that felt divine on her skin. On the bottom, she'd worn her favorite jeans, along with a pair of hiking boots, in case the drive turned into a walk. Completing her outfit was an insulated puffy jacket.

"I look like an egg." Caroline had made her buy the cheerful yellow garment, insisting it brightened her face. Annie had agreed because it looked sunny. But it wasn't exactly flattering. Oh well, she thought, peeling it off and putting it on the little backpack that held her camera and water, it wasn't as if this was a date.

Sweet dreams.

The memory of Zach's voice sent desire skittering through her veins. All she could think about was what it would be like to have that voice whisper in her ear while those strong hands touched her with bold confidence. "Oh, man." She pressed a hand flat to her stomach. "Calm, Annie. Calm." It was difficult to listen to her own advice when she'd spent the whole night dreaming about him. The tattoo she'd glimpsed on his biceps fascinated her—in her dreams, she'd stroked her fingers over the exotic lines of it, pressed her lips to that muscled flesh . . . and then touched another, harder part of his body.

"A whole *day*," she almost moaned, and went to shove a hand through her hair before realizing she'd pulled it back into a ponytail. Now she glanced into the mirror and made a face. She'd eschewed makeup—who went to a forest with makeup on?—but had given in to the urge to slick on some gloss. It plumped up her lips . . . except that her lips were already plump. "Argh." Too late, she remembered why she never used gloss. She was searching for a tissue to wipe it off when the doorbell rang. "Who on earth?" Running to the door, she pulled it open.

A leopard in human skin stood on the other side. "I was hoping to wake you," he drawled, leaning against the doorjamb. "But you're all dressed." He tried to look sad, but the wicked lights dancing in his eyes made that impossible.

"You're early," she said, unable to stop staring at him. He was wearing a pair of faded blue jeans, hiking boots, and a soft gray sweatshirt stamped with the San Francisco Giants emblem. Casual clothes, but his hair was still damp from the shower and his jaw freshly shaven.

It was all she could do not to run her fingertips over that smooth skin and nuzzle the masculine scent of him into her lungs.

"I woke up early—had somewhere I wanted to be." He smiled at her, slow and persuasive. "Are you going to invite me in?" Raising a hand, he showed her a brown paper bag bearing the logo of a nearby bakery. "I brought breakfast."

She knew she shouldn't let him get his own way so very easily, but stepped aside in welcome. "What did you bring?"

"Come and see." He waited for her to close the door, then followed as she led the way into the kitchen through the living room of her apartment. "You like to read."

She saw him glance at the paperbacks on the shelves, stacked on the coffee table, placed facedown on the arm of her sofa. "Yes."

"Me, too." He put the bag on the counter and slid onto a stool. "Why are you standing over there?"

She looked at him from the other side of the counter. "I thought I'd make coffee."

"Okay." He kept the bag closed. "But you're not seeing what's in here until you come around to this side."

He was definitely flirting. And she was definitely playing with fire by allowing it to go on. Because if there was one thing she knew about predatory changeling men, it was that they were quite ferally possessive—and belonging to anyone was simply not on her agenda. Of course, she was also getting *way* ahead of herself. He was only flirting. It wasn't as if he planned to drag her off to the chapel. "What do you read?" she asked, telling herself it was okay to try to flirt back, that this pull she felt toward him was nothing more than sexual attraction.

"Thrillers, some nonfiction." He looked around her open-plan kitchen and living room. "It's a small place."

"For you, maybe." He was so big, so unashamedly male, he took over the space . . . threatened to take her over, too.

He glanced at her, expression shifting to something darker and infinitely more dangerous. "Hmm, you're right. You're a bit smaller than me."

She tried to control her erratic breathing as she finished putting on the coffee. He just sat there and watched her with a feline patience that had her nerves sparking in reaction.

"How long have you lived here?"

"Last five years. I moved in after I got the teaching job."

"Did you live at home before that?"

She laughed through the thudding beat of her pulse. "Lord, no. I was outta there at eighteen."

"You ever get lonely, Annie?" he asked, his tone liquid heat over her skin.

"I like living alone. I intend to keep it that way." She thought she'd surprised him with that, but instead of replying, he lifted up the bag and raised an eyebrow. It was a dare. Annie had never considered herself particularly courageous, but she walked around the counter. He nodded at her to take the stool beside his.

Knowing it would be silly to refuse, she sat, rubbing her thigh with one hand. He noticed. "It hurt today?"

"What?" She looked down. "Oh, no, not really. It's habit." It was always a little achy in the mornings. "So, breakfast?"

His eyes went cat on her between one instant and the next. She sucked in a breath at the intensity of that green-gold gaze. "Wow."

He smiled. "Let's play a game."

She had a feeling that playing with this big kitty cat was a very bad idea, but since she'd already given in to her insanity, she said, "What're the rules?"

"Close your eyes. Eat what I give you, and tell me what it is."

The notion of having him feed her had her heart racing at the speed of light. "What do I get if I guess correctly?"

"Mystery prize." His lashes lowered, and she thought she caught a glimpse of something edgy, something that blazed with raw male heat, but when he looked back up, there was nothing but amusement in those leopard eyes. "Yes?"

"Yes." She watched mesmerized as he opened the paper bag with those hands she wanted to have all over her.

"Close your eyes, sweetheart."

She swallowed hunger of a far different sort and let her lashes flutter down. It made her even more aware of the scent of him, the warmth of him, the sheer presence of him. When he shifted position to put one of his feet on the outside of her stool, effectively trapping her, she opened her mouth to tell him . . . something.

But his finger brushed over her lips. "Taste."

He was all around her, in her blood, in her breath. Losing her train of thought, she closed her teeth over the pastry he put to her lips. The flaky stuff just about melted in her mouth, and she licked her lips without thinking about it.

Zach seemed to go very still, but when he spoke, his words were light. "Guess?"

"Danish."

"Wrong." She went to open her eyes, but he said, "No, keep them shut."

"Why?"

"I'm going to give you another shot. Right now, you owe a single forfeit. Let's see if we can even the decks."

"Forfeit?" She wondered why the thought sent excitement arcing through her. "You never said anything about a forfeit."

"You never asked."

As she'd thought—playing with this cat was an invitation to trouble. "Now I am."

"Later. First, taste this." He put something else to her mouth, and she bit down, determined to get it this time—he sounded far too delighted by the idea of having her owe him a forfeit.

She smiled. "Blueberry muffin."

A finger brushed over her lips, making her eyes snap open. "A crumb," he said.

"Oh."

He didn't smile this time, watching her with an intensity that reminded her that for all his playfulness, he was a Dark-River soldier. And DarkRiver controlled the greater San Francisco area. More than that, they were allied with the bloodthirsty SnowDancer wolves.

"What're you thinking?" he asked her.

"That you're dangerous."

"Not to you," he said. "I wouldn't bite unless you asked very nicely."

Heat flooded her cheeks at the teasing promise, and she was more than glad to hear the coffeemaker ping. "Coffee's done, I'll grab it."

He let her go, but she had a feeling the game had only just begun. And that she was the prey.

ZACH wanted to groan in frustration as he watched Annie move about the kitchen. He'd come within an inch of kissing the life out of her when she'd licked her lips. Perfect, luscious, bitable lips. He'd resisted the temptation for two reasons. One, the cat liked the chase. And two, the man liked the idea of having Annie melt at his touch. He planned to seduce her until she purred for him.

"Coffee." She put a cup in front of him, and he took a sip, attempting to behave when what he really wanted to do was haul her close and just *take*. Patience, he told himself. The last thing he wanted to do was scare Annie with the wild fury of his hunger.

"It's good." Sighing in appreciation, he passed her the muffin and a flaky croissant with a chocolate center. "The reason for your forfeit."

She scowled at the pain au chocolat. "So do the win and loss cancel each other out?"

"No. I'll collect my forfeit." His eyes drifted to her lips and lingered there. "A kiss, Annie. You owe me a kiss."

Her lips parted, her breath whispering out in a soft gasp. "And"—she coughed—"my winnings?"

"I'll give them to you later today." He wanted to drink up the scent of her, spiced as it was by the seduction of her growing arousal. However that arousal was nowhere near enough to satiate the savagery of his own need. But the cat was a patient hunter. By the time this day was through, he planned to have coaxed and tempted Annie Kildaire until she was as desperate for him as he was for her. "Now eat, or we'll be late."

She nibbled at her croissant, shooting him quick glances as

he finished off the bagel he'd bought for himself. "When are you going to . . . collect?" she asked afterward, clearing away the cups with feminine efficiency that failed to mask her responsive awareness.

"I've got all day." He slid off the stool and smiled. "Ready?"

"You look very much the cat when you smile that way," she said. "You're enjoying teasing me."

He walked over and took the basket she'd picked up from the small table in one corner. "What's this?"

"I packed a couple of things for the picnic, and some snacks for the ride."

He peeked in. "Chocolate cake?"

"Chocolate *mud* cake," she said, with an adorable note of pride that made him want to claim his forfeit then and there. "I made it last night, gave it time to settle."

"You'll be Sascha's new best friend." Leaning in, he brushed his lips over her ear. "And yes, Teach, I like teasing you."

ANNIE still hadn't gotten over the sensation of his lips on her skin as Zach pulled away from her ground-floor apartment and out into the street. Open sexual heat laced his teasing, but she wasn't sure quite how far he'd take it. If he pushed, would she surrender?

The temptation was blindingly strong. Not only was he beautiful in the most masculine way, she flat out liked him. Being with Zach, if only for a night, would be, she already knew, a delight. He wouldn't be the least bit selfish, she thought. His partner's pleasure would matter to him. And, given his nature, he wasn't likely to want any kind of a commitment.

It was perfect.

Yet Annie found herself hesitating. Already, she reacted to him more deeply than she had to any other man her entire life. What would it do to her to sleep with him, to know him that intimately . . . then watch him walk away? Her mind flicked to a slide show of images. They were all of one woman. A woman with years of disappointment in her eyes.

"Look."

She jerked up at the sound of his voice. "What?"

"There." He pointed out the windshield.

Her eyes widened at the parade of old-fashioned automobiles on the other side of the road, all huge bodies and gleaming paint. They were so old they had no hover capacity, but there was something very sexy about them. "They look amazing. I wonder where they're going?"

"I read something about a vintage-car show about a twenty-minute drive from here. We could swing by after the picnic today."

Despite her fear at how quickly he'd gotten under her skin, she couldn't help but be delighted that he wanted to spend more time with her. Hard on its heels came disappointment. "I have to be back by six," she said. "Family dinner."

Zach shot her a quick glance. "You don't sound too enthusiastic."

She understood the surprise in his voice. All the DarkRiver cats she knew had one thing in common—family was the bedrock of their world. And Pack was one big extended family as far as they were concerned—she'd had senior pack members turn up to parent-teacher conferences more than once when the parent was ill or unavoidably delayed. "My mom keeps trying to set me up with men."

Zach's expression changed and, for the first time, she saw the ruthless soldier in him. "What kind of men?"

"Academics." She shrugged. "Mom and Dad are both professors at Berkeley—math and physics respectively."

"Are academics your type?"

"No."

He glanced at her again, and those eyes had gone leopard on her. "Are you sure?"

"Quite." She found herself refusing to be intimidated by the sense of incipient danger in the air. If she gave an inch, Zach would take a mile. And while she might not be a dominant female, it was important that he respect her. She frowned. Of course it was important, but that thought, it had been so vivid, so strong, so *visceral*—as if her mind knew something it wasn't yet ready to share.

Then Zach spoke again, breaking her train of thought. "So you'll be skipping the dinner." It was an order plain and simple.

Annie opened her mouth. What came out was, "No, I'll take you."

Chapter 5

ZACH'S GRIN WAS openly pleased. "What's the blind date going to say?"

She couldn't believe she'd just done that, ordered him to do something. More, she couldn't believe he'd agreed. "Probably, 'Thank God.'"

"Huh?"

"My cousin Caroline works at the university, too. The men come in expecting a statuesque, intellectual, blond beauty and get me."

"So?"

She scowled, wondering if he was teasing her again. "So, I'm about as opposite Caro as you can get."

"If they ignored you, that's their loss. Too damn bad for them." He shrugged. "Do you want to put on some music?"

She blinked at the way he'd swept aside the disappointments of the past with that simple statement. If she hadn't already liked him, that would've done it. "No, I need to tell you something about my mom." She swallowed, realizing she'd made a mess of things. If she hadn't mentioned the dinner, she could've avoided this altogether.

Zach groaned. "Don't tell me, she's a vegetarian?" he said, as if that was the worst thing possible.

She supposed for a leopard changeling, it was. "No." For once, he couldn't make her smile despite herself. "My mum is a little"—she tried to find an easy way to say this and failed—"biased against changelings."

"Ah. Let me guess—she thinks we're only one step up from animals?"

She felt very, very awkward discussing this, but she had to warn him about what he might face if he went to dinner with her. "It's not so blunt. She has no problem with other humans, and she admires the Psy, but she's never wanted me dating, or getting friendly with"—she raised her fingers in quotation marks—"'the rough changeling element.'"

"What about you?" A deceptively soft question.

"That's an insult, Zach," she said as softly. "If that's what you really think of me—"

He swore. "Sorry, Annie, you're right, I'm being an ass. My only excuse is that you hit a hot button."

"I know." She couldn't blame him for his reaction. "It makes me really uncomfortable, but I've tried to change her mind, and it's never worked."

"What does she think of you teaching in a school with such a big changeling population?"

"That it's my version of acting out." She laughed at his expression, awkwardness dissipating. "No, she doesn't seem to realize I'm a grown-up, as the kids would say."

"Why do you let her get away with it?"

She was beginning to expect the straight-up questions from him. "My mom was on that train with me. She tried and tried and *tried* to get me out even though I was pinned under so much wreckage, she didn't have a hope of shifting anything." Her throat choked with the force of memory. "Her arm was broken at the time, but she didn't cry a single tear. She just kept trying to get me out."

Zach reached out to run his knuckles over her cheek. "She loves you."

She found comfort in the touch, and when he returned his hand to the steering wheel, she realized he'd somehow given her strength. "Yes. That's why I let her get away with so much." She leaned her head against the seat. "This thing she has for the Psy, the way she almost deifies them, it has its roots in the accident, too."

"How?"

"There was this boy—I don't know where he came from, but he was small, my age or younger. Cardinal eyes." She shivered at the memory of the chill in those extraordinary white-stars-on-black-velvet eyes. Psy lived lives devoid of emotion, but she'd never seen a child that utterly cold. "He lifted the wreckage off me."

"Telekinetic." Zach whistled. "You got lucky."

"Yeah." The Council didn't release its telekinetics for mundane rescue work—especially not when an incident affected mainly humans and changelings. "The medics told me he'd saved my life. My internal organs were close to collapse—a few more minutes, and I wouldn't have made it."

"Did you ever find out who he was?"

She shook her head. "He disappeared in the chaos. I've always thought that he teleported in from another location, after somehow seeing me in the live coverage. I remember there was a remote media chopper flying overhead, and if he was strong enough to lift the amount of wreckage that he did, he was strong enough to teleport." She couldn't imagine the strength of will it took to harness that much power. "He can't have been on the train—his clothes were spotless, and he didn't have so much as a smudge on his face."

"Psy aren't born lacking emotions," Zach told her, "they're conditioned to it. So it could be that he was still human enough to feel the need to help when he saw what had happened."

"How do you know about the conditioning?" She answered her own question a second later. "Your alpha's mated to a cardinal Psy." The news of that mating had sent shockwaves throughout the country.

"Sascha," he said, nodding. "Vaughn, one of the sentinels, is also mated to a Psy."

She couldn't imagine a member of the cold Psy race embracing emotion. But changeling leopards mated for life, and the bond between mates was a dazzling beacon apparent even to a human observer. If these women had mated with DarkRiver cats, they were undoubtedly as radiant and as strong as the other women she'd seen. "Will I meet them today?"

"I know Luc and Sascha are coming. Likely Faith and Vaughn will, too." He turned down a quiet road lined with trees. "I'll try to get you back by six so you can get ready for dinner, but we might cut it fine."

She bit the inside of her cheek. "I think I should cancel. I really don't want my mom to . . . I would hate for you to feel that—"

"Hey," he said, shooting her a glance that spoke of the soldier within, "I'm a big boy. I can handle it. Promise."

Promises are for keeping.

Deciding to trust him, she dug out her phone from the pocket of her jeans. "I'll tell Mom I'm bringing someone and that we'll be late."

"Yeah. It'll give your date time to find another partner." That lethal edge was back in his voice.

Her stomach muscles tightened. "Zach?"

"Might as well get this out in the open." He pulled the car into a small layby and turned to brace his hand against the top edge of her seat. "I'm not real good at sharing."

She swallowed. "Oh."

Zach could've kicked himself. He'd gone to all this trouble to lull her into a relaxed mood, then the cat had struck out in a burst of primitive jealousy. "Scared?"

Wary caution crept into her eyes, but she shook her head. "You said you wouldn't bite unless I asked . . . very nicely."

Surprise had the cat freezing. He'd forgotten that beneath the blushes and big brown eyes was a woman quite capable of calling him on his behavior. "That's true," he drawled, letting the cat out to play. "Come closer and ask me."

She shook her head again.

"Please."

Her cheeks colored, but he knew the heat wasn't because of embarrassment. Her arousal was a decadent whisper in the confines of the car, a drug his cat could lap at for hours. But what he really wanted to do was lap at her. He moved a little closer.

She held up the phone. "I need to make this call." Her voice was breathless, her tone jagged.

Instinct urged him to keep pushing, but he didn't want to make her feel cornered. No, he thought, shifting back into his seat, he'd do his teasing out in the open arms of the forest. "Go on, sweetheart." He smiled. "I've got all day to play with you."

She sucked in a breath. "Is that what this is? Play?"

"Sure." He drove them back onto the road, knowing she was talking about more than his teasing promise—pretty, sexy Annie Kildaire thought they were heading for a quick, hot fling. He grinned inwardly. Poor baby was going to get one hell of a surprise when he told her the truth, but she wasn't ready for that yet. "The best kind of play."

She was silent for a few minutes, then he heard her coding in the call. With her being so close, he could hear both sides of the conversation. Most humans who lived with changelings tended to get earpieces, so they could have private conversations. He'd have to get Annie one, he thought absently.

"Mom, it's Annie. About tonight," she began.

"Don't you dare cancel, Angelica Kildaire."

Angelica?

"I'm not," Annie said, obviously attempting to keep her temper in the face of the sharp response. "I'll be late, and—"

"We're doing this for you," her mother interrupted. "The least you can do is turn up on time."

Annie pressed her fingers to her forehead and seemed to mentally count to five. "I'm bringing a guest," she said without any lead-in. "His name is Zach."

Complete silence from the other end. Then, "Well good grief, Annie. Now you tell me. I'll have to find another woman to balance out the table. Who is he?"

"A DarkRiver soldier."

The silence was longer and deeper this time. Zach could feel Annie's distress at the reaction, but he was proud of her for sticking to her guns.

"Mom?"

"Aren't you a little too old for childish games?" her mother asked. "I know some women find those rough types attractive, but you have a brain. How long do you think he'll be able to keep that engaged?"

Zach's cat smiled in feral amusement. He was used to the preconceptions some humans, and most Psy, had about changelings. The majority of the time, it rolled off his back. But this time, it mattered. Because this was Annie's mother.

"I am not having this discussion with you," Annie said, tone final. "We'll be there for dinner. If you'd rather we didn't come, just say so."

"No, bring him," was the immediate response. "I want to meet this Zach who's got you ordering your own mother around." She hung up.

Annie stared at the phone for several seconds before thrusting it back into her pocket. "How much did you hear?"

"All of it."

She shifted uncomfortably. "Sorry—"

"Annie, sweetheart, leave your mom to me." He shot her a grin brimming with deliberate wickedness. "Today, I want to lead you astray."

Her returning smile was a little shy but full of a quiet mischief he figured most people never saw. "Are you sure I'm not already beyond redemption?"

He chuckled. "How could you be with a name like Angelica?"

She made a face. "I'm an Annie, not an Angelica."

"I prefer Angel."

"Do you like your women angelic?"

He chuckled. "No, baby, I like my woman exactly as she is." He knew he'd surprised her, waited to see what she'd do.

"So, this thing . . . you want more than just a day?"

He wasn't going to lie to her. "Are you going to run if I say yes?" He pulled into the forest proper, taking a narrow track that would lead them to one of the smaller waterfalls. It was only a trickle right now because of the cold, but it was still a sight to be seen.

"I'm here today, aren't I?" A question with a slight acerbic bite.

Tasting the piquancy of it on his tongue, he decided he liked it. "All alone with a big, bad cat who's rethinking his policy on biting."

Arousal colored the air again, and he sucked in a breath to contain his most primal instincts. "Look ahead," he said, voice husky.

"Oh!" Her eyes went huge. "It's a buck," she whispered, as if afraid the animal would hear her. "His antlers are huge."

Zach slowed the vehicle to a crawl, but the buck caught his scent and shot off into the trees. "Sorry. They tend to scatter the instant they smell leopard. It's why I look after the predators—it's hard for me to check data on the nonpredatories."

"They know they're prey." She looked at him. "Do you hunt them?"

"When the cat needs it, yes." He glanced at her. "Can you handle knowing that?"

"I teach a lot of little cats," she reminded him in a prim, schoolteacher voice. "I might not be an expert on changeling behavior, but I've picked up enough to know that when in animal form, you behave according to the needs of the animal."

He couldn't help himself. He turned and snapped his teeth at her, making her jump. When he began to chuckle, her eyes narrowed. "You're as bad as Bryan. He does that to Katie all the time."

"Odds on, he has a crush on her."

Her lips twitched. "That's what I think, too. Was the fight about Katie?"

"Sneaky, Ms. Kildaire, but I'm sworn to secrecy." Laughing at the face she made, he reached over to tug at her ponytail. "You up to a small hike?"

Shadows swept across her face. "You don't think I can do it?"

He parked the vehicle off to the side of the track and turned. "I don't know your limits yet," he told her honestly. "That's why I'm asking."

She colored. "Sorry. I'm a bit touchy on the whole subject."

He shrugged. "If I think you can't do something, I'll make sure you're not doing it." Protecting the vulnerable was instinct. Protecting Annie would probably become an obsession.

"You'll *make* sure I'm not doing it?" The arch sound of a human female metaphorically flexing her claws.

"Definitely." He held her gaze. "I'm flexible, little cat, but I'm not a pushover."

Her arousal spiked at his words, but so did her anger. "As if I ever believed that."

"Annie, you're used to academic types who probably let you walk all over them."

"Hold on," she began, eyes snapping with temper.

God, she was pretty. He reached forward while she was distracted, gripped her chin. And kissed her.

Chapter 6

SHE WAS SOFTER than he'd imagined, more luscious than anything he'd ever experienced. Cat and man both purred inwardly, and when her lips parted on a gasp, he swept inside to taste her. Sweet and tart, innocent and woman, she was his own personal brand of intoxication.

He bit her lower lip, sucked on it, let her gasp in another breath before kissing her again. "Mmm." It was a sound of sheer pleasure as he indulged his need to touch this woman. Leopard changelings were tactile as a rule—something that translated into sensual affection in a relationship. It didn't always have to lead to sex. Sometimes it was just about the pleasure of skin-to-skin contact.

When he drew back, her lips were a little swollen, her pupils dilated. He rubbed his thumb over her lower lip and tried to temper his escalating need. She wasn't ready, not yet. As he'd learned this morning, her soft exterior hid a fierce core of independence—the instant she learned what he really wanted, she'd stop playing with him.

And that was simply not acceptable. "You know how to kiss a man, Angel." He dropped his gaze to the rise and fall of her generous breasts. The temptation to caress them was so wrenching, he took his hand off her chin and thrust it through his hair. "About that hike . . . ?"

She gave a jerky nod. "I can walk."

"Tell me if it hurts."

"It won't."

Frowning, he grabbed her chin again and this time, he

wasn't playing. "I mean it, Annie. I need to be able to trust you. I'm giving you that. You give me honesty. That's fair."

Her expression shifted again, a true smile curving over her lips. "I will, I promise. It'll probably ache some, but that's normal. If it gets any worse, I'll tell you."

He wanted to kiss her again but knew full well that if he didn't get them out of the car quick smart, he'd end up taking her right here—like some randy juvenile in his parents' car. "Let's go." Grabbing her little pack, he thrust his own bottle of water inside and opened the door.

She met him a few feet from the vehicle, her fluffy yellow jacket a dash of pure summer. "I know," she said, when his eyes landed on her, "I look like a baby duck."

Not bothering with a coat himself, he took her hand. "No. I like it." Her hand was small but not weak in his. "It suits you." Pretty and bright and sunny, that was his Annie.

They walked in silence for a while, and he felt his beast sigh in pleasure. The forest was home, and it called to both parts of his soul. But today, he had a new reason for happiness—Annie. "You're in shape," he said after a while.

"Nowhere close to you." She made a rueful face. "I know you're keeping your stride shorter for me."

He hadn't even noticed, the act had been so natural. "Of course," he said matter-of-factly. "How would I have my wicked way with you if I left you in my dust?"

Her smile was startled, but it grew until the leopard batted at its warmth, utterly captivated. "I exercise," she said. "I have to, or the leg will freeze up."

"Every day?"

She nodded. "It's a habit now." Looking up at the trail as it wound its way into the forest she took a deep breath. "It's so beautiful here."

"Yeah." He watched her face suffuse with joy and felt the razor-sharp bite of envy. The cat really wasn't good at sharing. Neither was the man—he wanted to be the one to put that look of delight on her face. Soon, he promised himself.

She glanced at him, smile changing into a very feminine look of realization. "Zach." Her lips parted.

It was all the invitation he needed. Dipping his head, he claimed another bold kiss, curving his hand around the silken warmth of her neck. When her hands came to rest on his chest, the cat stretched out in pleasure within him. He wanted those hands on his bare skin, his hunger for her so extreme it would make her bolt if she knew about it.

That thought in mind, he pulled on the reins. Even so, he couldn't keep from nipping at her lip.

Her eyes widened even as her hands clenched on his chest. "You only had one forfeit."

He felt his mouth curve. "Put it on my account," he said without an ounce of repentance.

She laughed, and he knew that today was going to be one of the best days of his life.

SEVERAL hours later, Annie sighed and rested her head back against the seat as Zach drove them to the Pack Circle. "That was wonderful. Thank you."

"You fit here," he said quietly, his voice lacking its usual playfulness. "The age of the trees, the immensity of the forest, it doesn't scare you."

"It makes me feel free," she admitted. "Out here, no one's watching, waiting for me to stumble." She wondered how she'd come to trust him so quickly—quickly enough to reveal a vulnerability she kept hidden from even her closest friends.

It scared her a little, the intensity of the emotions growing in her heart. She tried to tell herself it was nothing but a silly crush, but all she could think of was the way his kisses had tugged at her soul. All day long he'd stolen them, until her lips remembered the shape of his, and her breasts ached for his touch. Swallowing, she attempted to redirect her thoughts. "The Pack Circle's usually kept secret."

"We don't take strangers there," he acknowledged. "Only those we trust to honor our faith."

Her heart warmed from the inside out. "Thank you."

"Don't thank me just yet. Wait till you meet the pack—they're a nosy bunch."

Nerves snapped to full wakefulness as Zach parked his vehicle behind several others and turned to run his knuckles over her cheek. "Don't be nervous."

"How do you know—"

"I can smell the change in your scent."

She was still sitting there, mind awash with the implications of what he'd said, when he walked around and opened her door. "Come on, Angel. Let's go face the masses."

She got out but didn't take his hand. "You can smell the changes in my body?" She watched him reach in back for the picnic basket.

"Yes." Basket in hand, he tugged her hand from where she'd wrapped her arms around herself. "Does that bother you?" A direct gaze.

She saw no flirtation in those eyes for the first time in hours. "A little," she admitted.

"You'll get used to it." He said that as if it was inevitable.

She wasn't sure. Privacy was a big deal for her—she'd spent almost a year in the hospital, only to go home to her mother's constant hovering. Those experiences had combined to make her zealous about guarding her personal space, and what was more personal, more private, than her body itself?

Zach glanced at her as they walked past the other cars. "It's natural to us," he said. "We don't tend to notice a particular scent unless it's something that matters."

"But other people will know," she said, her stomach in knots. She could accept her hunger for Zach, accept that he knew, but to have everyone else be aware of it, too?

Zach raised her hand to his lips and kissed her knuckles, the tenderness undoing her. He was, she realized, far more a threat to her than she'd initially thought. If she wasn't careful, Zach Quinn would steal her heart and leave her with nothing, her worst nightmare come to life. But even knowing that, she couldn't help moving closer when he tugged at her.

"Your arousal is a vibrant thread to me," he whispered, voice husky, "but for the others, it'll simply be background noise. They'll be focused on their mates, lovers, children—different threads. There are millions of them in any one instant."

His explanation made sense, enough to release some of the tension in her stomach. However, she couldn't help but be a little wary as they entered the Circle. Then several people cried out hellos, and, to her shock, she realized that though they weren't all parents, she knew a good number of them from various school events. The friendliness washed over her in an effervescent wave.

"Miss Kildaire, you came!" Bryan skidded to a stop by her feet. "Did Uncle Zach show you the forest?"

Conscious of several interested adult gazes, she nodded. "What have you been up to?"

"I'm playing hide-and-seek with Priyanka." With that, he ran off. She was still smiling after him when she felt Zach's hand on her lower back.

"Come on, I want to introduce you to someone."

She walked with him, cognizant of the possessiveness implied by his touch. A warning bell rang in her head, but she silenced it. His dominant nature wasn't going to be a problem—it wasn't as if she was his mate. He'd be gone as soon as he'd satisfied his curiosity about her. "Where's the picnic basket?" she asked, trying to ignore the stab of pain provoked by that last thought. After all, she had no desire to tie herself to a man—even a man as enticing as Zach.

"I gave it to one of the juveniles," Zach answered with a smile so bright, she couldn't help but smile in return. "Cory will stick it with the other food so everyone can grab what they want." He stopped beside an older woman with snow-white hair and a face that echoed his own so strongly, Annie knew they were related. Not only that, it was clear where Zach had inherited his sun-kissed skin and bones.

As he leaned forward to kiss the woman's cheek, she said, "Zach, my dear." Her eyes went to Annie, and they were as sharp as her body was toned. Given the way she stood, her supple strength, Annie guessed her to be a soldier, too. It wasn't surprising—changelings didn't really slow down until well into their eighth or ninth decade. "And who have you brought me?"

"Grandma, this is Annie," Zach said, his love for his grandmother a shining light in his eyes. It hit her right in the gut, making her wonder what it would be like to have that open and powerful love directed at her. "My grandmother, Cerise."

Cerise held out both hands, her smile so welcoming that Annie accepted the touch without hesitation. "Don't let this boy talk you into anything wicked," Cerise said. "He's been getting his own way since the day he first looked at his mother and batted those pretty eyelashes."

Annie felt her lips curve, but before she could answer, Zach was set upon by a pair of identical teenage girls. "Zach!" they screamed, wrapping their arms around him from either side. "We haven't seen you in ages!"

"You saw me three days ago." Laughing, he hugged them to his sides.

Sparkling eyes landed on Annie. "Oooooooh," one of them said, "you brought a giiiiirrrrrrrrrrrrrl."

"Who is she?" her twin whispered, brushing aside a waterfall of sleek black hair. "Where did you meet? How long have you been dating?"

Cerise frowned. "Girls, manners!"

The girls dimpled. "Sorry, Grandma."

Zach looked at her. "Annie, meet my baby sisters, Silly and Giggly."

"Hey!" They both slapped his chest. "I'm Lissa, and that's Noelle," the one on the left said.

Annie was beginning to be able to tell them apart. They were both confident and cheerful, but Lissa had more mischief in her eyes, while Noelle's smile was wide enough to light up any room she entered. "Nice to meet you."

Cerise squeezed her hands before letting go. "Where are your sisters?" she asked the twins.

Annie felt her eyes widen. More sisters? Zach saw her look and began to laugh. "Four of them," he said. "*Four.* Jess—she's Bryan's mom—and Poppy are older than these two brats."

"Aw, you know you love us, big brother." Lissa reached up to press a kiss to his jaw. "I'll go look for them. They'll want to meet your girl."

"Talk to you later, Annie." Wiggling her fingers, Noelle ran off with her twin.

Annie didn't know whether to laugh or shake her head in amazement. "Four younger sisters?"

He wrapped an arm around her shoulders and cuddled her to his side. "They're the reason for my gray hairs. See?" He dipped his head.

The dark silk of his hair made her want to stroke it. "You big liar. You don't have a single gray hair." Held against him, she'd never felt safer or more protected. Fear ignited. Okay, she thought, quashing the emotion, this relationship was becoming more important than she'd originally believed it would, but it wasn't as if she was going to do something stupid—like begin to rely on Zach.

Cerise laughed. "She's on to you, boyo. I bet she gets along with Jess like a house on fire."

"Speaking of Jess"—Annie frowned—"doesn't Bryan have an older brother? When did Jess get married? Mated," she corrected herself.

Cerise was the one who answered. "At twenty. She's thirty now, only a year younger than Zachary here. Her oldest is nine."

"Twenty's so young," she murmured.

"She found her mate early," Zach said, a shimmering joy in his tone, the love of a brother for his sister. "And that was that. She always wanted a big family, so the kids came soon afterward. She's happy." A simple statement, and yet it spoke of such love, such trust. Annie couldn't imagine taking that big a leap of faith, putting that much of herself into a man's hands.

"Yes, she's very happy," Cerise agreed. "But enough of family talk—why don't you two grab some food before the juveniles inhale it all. I swear, I don't know where it goes."

"Into the hollow leg every teenage boy possesses, of course." The voice was male and familiar.

"Lucas." Cerise hugged the tall man with green eyes, as Annie pegged him for the DarkRiver alpha. "Oh dear." Zach's grandmother drew back, her attention on something over Lucas's shoulder. "I think I need to go rescue a cub that's climbed a bit too high. And if that's not one of Tammy's boys, I'll eat my boot." She headed off in the direction of an ancient fir, from where Annie could hear the pleading strains of an adorable growl.

"Hello, Annie, isn't it?" Lucas held out a hand.

As she took it, she had the strangest sensation that everyone was watching her. "Good memory. You only met me once, at last year's Christmas pageant."

He grinned. "Let's just say I had some advance intel. So, how was the tour?"

"Perfect," Zach said, arm tightening around her. "But for some unfathomable reason, Annie's still deciding if she wants to date me."

"Zach!" She glared up at him.

He grinned and dropped a fast kiss on her lips. Blushing, she wondered if such public affection was normal within the pack. She got her answer a few seconds later as an exotically beautiful woman wrapped her arms around Lucas's neck from behind and pressed a kiss to his jaw. Her eyes, when they met Annie's, were the night sky of a cardinal Psy. White stars on black velvet.

"Hello, you must be Annie." Her voice was summer breezes and open fires, welcoming and gentle. "Lissa and Noelle," she explained, at Annie's surprised look. "They've been telling everyone they covet your jacket. They're planning to charm it off you before you leave. Be careful."

Annie couldn't do anything but smile in response to the warmth in that voice. "Thanks for the warning."

"Sascha," Zach said, "Annie made chocolate mud cake."

Sascha's face lit up like a child's. "Really?" She moved to grab Lucas's hand. "Come on, or the juveniles will eat it all. Talk to you later, Annie!"

Annie watched the pair leave and breathed out a sigh. "Your pack's . . . overwhelming."

"You'll get used to them." He rubbed the back of her neck. "They're just curious about you."

She felt another warning flicker in her mind, but then someone else was calling out Zach's name, and she was being introduced to more people, and then Zach was feeding her with the teasing smile of the cat flirting on his lips, and she forgot what it was that she'd worried about.

Chapter 7

THEY ARRIVED AT her apartment a few minutes after six. "I'll shower and change quickly," she told him as she unlocked the door and entered.

"Can I use your shower after?" He lifted up the suit bag he'd carried inside. "I got a packmate to drop by my house and bring this to the picnic. Want to make a good first impression on your folks."

Her stomach sank. "It probably won't make any difference."

"I told you, don't worry." Draping the suit bag over the back of her sofa, he prowled over. "Go, shower." It was a whisper that implied all sorts of sinful things. "I'll just sit out here and imagine the droplets racing over your skin, touching you . . . stroking you."

She felt her legs tremble. "Come in with me." It was the boldest invitation she'd ever made.

He smiled. "I plan to. But not today." He brushed his lips over hers. "When I shower with you, I don't want a time limit."

"Oh." Her mind bombarded her with images of the undoubtedly delicious things he'd do to her in the shower. "I should go . . ."

He rubbed a thumb over her bottom lip before shaking his head and pulling back. "Go, before I forget my good intentions. We'd never make it to the dinner then."

She hesitated.

He tapped her lightly on the bottom. "Don't even try it. I'm meeting your parents." So he could look them in the eye and let them know that regardless of what they thought of him, he was now in their daughter's life, and they had to deal with it. No more blind dates.

"Bossy." Annie shot him a scowl but went into the bedroom to grab her stuff.

She was going to be all hot and wet and naked soon.

"Christ." Shoving his hands through his hair, he tried to get the hard thrust of his cock to settle down. It refused. Especially since he could hear the rustle of cloth sliding over skin, of boots hitting tile, of lace being peeled off . . . or maybe that was his imagination.

But he definitely heard the shower come on. Groaning, he began to pace around the room, distracting himself by looking at Annie's things. Aside from books, she had several holoframes on the walls. Family photos, he guessed, noting her resemblance to the older woman in the central portrait. The man in the photo—her father, he assumed—was smiling genially, but there was something about him that struck the cat as distant.

The shower shut off.

"Shower's free!" came the call a few minutes later.

He gave her another couple of minutes to close herself in the bedroom, not sure he'd be able to resist if he saw her swathed in the tempting impermanence of an easily removable towel. When he entered the small, tiled enclosure at last, it was to find it steamy with the lavish scent of some feminine lotion. But the soap, he was glad to see, was nothing too girly. A man had to have standards, he thought, and programmed the shower to freezing.

It finally succeeded in cooling down his body.

ANNIE sat in Zach's car in her parents' drive and twisted her fingers in her lap. "I've never brought a man home," she blurted out. "It didn't seem worth the fuss."

"I'm flattered."

She frowned at him. "Don't tease me now." But she felt her nerves loosen a fraction. "Come on, we might as well get this over with." Opening the door, she stepped out.

They met at the front of the vehicle. "At least it's a nice night," she said.

Zach put an arm around her with the lazy grace of the leopard he was. "I like your dress," he murmured, playing his fingertips over her hip.

"Oh." Her nerves frayed again, for a different reason. She'd chosen the black crossover dress because it would give her mother nothing to complain about. But Zach's words made her realize it might actually qualify as sexy. "You don't think I'm not thin enough for it?"

"I'll tell you tonight . . . after I unwrap you." He made her sound like a present.

She felt her eyes widen, her pulse jump. "Behave."

"Do I still get to unwrap you?"

A moment of silence, the night sky cut with shards of glittering diamond.

"Yes." She wanted to dance with the wildness in him, wanted to feel what it was to be treated like a beautiful, sensual woman. But more, she wanted to lie with this man who'd already made a place for himself in her heart.

She knew she was about to break one of her most fundamental rules in deepening this relationship, in putting her heart on the line, but she also knew that if she didn't love Zach, she'd regret it for the rest of her life. Perhaps, she thought for the first time, perhaps her mother's choices hadn't been as simple as the child in Annie had always believed. Perhaps with that one man who mattered, there *was* no choice, no protecting yourself against the inevitable end of the dream. "Yes," she said again. "You get to unwrap me."

"Then I'll be on my best behavior." He pressed a kiss to her temple. "Let's go, Angel."

She was already used to the nickname. Strange as it was, it felt as if he'd been calling her that forever . . . as if it was *right*. Walking up to the door, she held that sense of rightness to her like a talisman. "Here we go." She pressed the doorbell.

Her mother opened it a couple of seconds later. Dressed in a severe black dress accented with a discreet string of pearls, her dark hair twisted into a sleek knot, Kimberly Kildaire looked what she was—a successful, sophisticated professional. No one could've guessed at the deep vulnerability that Annie knew lay beneath the polished surface.

"Angelica." Her mother leaned forward to allow Annie to peck her on the cheek.

After drawing back, she said, "Mom, this is Zach Quinn."

Her mother's expression didn't change, but Annie knew that Kimberly would have noted everything about the man by her side, from his black suit, to his sleek silver belt buckle, to his crisp white shirt. Open at the collar, it looked both formal and relaxed. She'd about swallowed her tongue when she'd walked out of the bedroom and seen him waiting for her by the door. Zach wild was enough to blow her mind, but Zach playing at being tame . . . wow.

"Mr. Quinn," her mother now said, holding out her hand—Professor Kildaire might not think particularly highly of changelings, but no one would ever criticize her manners.

"Professor Kildaire."

Releasing his hand, Kimberly stepped back. "Do come in." She led them through the hallway and into the sunken living room off to the right.

There were far more people mingling below than Annie had expected. "I thought this was supposed to be a small dinner?"

Her mother's smile did nothing to warm the cool disapproval in her eyes. "I invited some university people. I thought your . . . friend would feel more comfortable if it wasn't just family."

It was a very subtle insult. Professor Markson was worthy of a family dinner. Zach wasn't. Temper spiked, not so much at the slight against Zach—he was tough enough to take care of himself—but because Annie couldn't believe her mother would try to sabotage her and Zach's relationship with such calculated rudeness.

But before she could say something she might not have been able to take back, Zach squeezed her hip lightly, and said, "I'm honored you went to so much trouble to put me at ease." His voice was smooth whiskey and effortless warmth. "I know how close Annie is to you, so I'm delighted by the welcome."

Annie saw her mother's expression falter for a second, but Kimberly Kildaire was nothing if not quick on her feet. "Of course. Come, I'll introduce you." She led them into the knot of curious people below.

Caroline was the first to come over. Though she told herself not to, Annie found herself tensing up as she waited to see Zach's reaction to her cousin. Caro was one of her favorite people in the world. She was also quite impossibly stunning. Annie had never before been jealous of the way her cousin drew men to her like moths to a flame—no man had ever mattered enough. But Zach did.

She saw him smile at Caroline's exuberant welcome . . . but it was the same kind of smile he'd shared with his sisters. "Congratulations on your baby," he said, his voice gentle.

Caroline beamed. "Can you tell? I'm not showing yet. I can't wait to get big and Madonna-like! Oh, and I want the glow everyone talks about—I so want the glow!"

Zach's lips quirked. "I don't think you need to worry. You already glow."

Caroline laughed. "You're a charmer, aren't you?" She looked to Annie. "I like him, Annie. He'll give you beautiful babies."

"Caro!" Annie didn't know whether to blush or thank her cousin for breaking the ice so completely. Several people laughed, and Zach sent her a teasing smile, his eyes heating in a way they hadn't for Caro.

"How did you know?" her mother asked pointedly. "Caroline is right—she's barely showing. Even most women don't notice."

"Her scent, Professor Kildaire," Zach replied with open candor. "Changelings always know when a woman has a life within her."

"A breach of privacy, wouldn't you say?" Kimberly raised an eyebrow.

Zach shrugged. "It's simply another sense. Ours just happens to be keener in that area—no different from an M-Psy being able to see inside the body, or you yourself being able to tell her condition because you know the subtle physical signs."

Annie bit the inside of her cheek to keep from interfering. Caro took the chance to whisper, "Oh, he's good. Wherever did you find Mr. Scrumptious?"

Annie threw her a quelling look. "Where's Aman?"

"My darling husband is driving back from a meeting in Tahoe. He'll probably make it in time for dessert." She smiled. "I know what *you're* having for dessert."

Annie felt Zach's hand move on her waist. It was obvious he'd heard Caro's outrageous prediction, and that he liked the idea. However, when she looked up, it was to find his attention not on her, but on someone else—a stranger her mother had just waved over.

"This is Professor Jeremy Markson," she was saying. "This is Annie's . . . friend, Zach Quinn."

Given that her own temper was close to igniting, Annie figured Zach would blow this time—he'd been blunt in saying he didn't share. But, to her surprise, he remained completely relaxed.

"Markson." Zach inclined his head in masculine acknowledgment. "What's your field, professor?"

"Molecular physics," Markson said. "It's a fascinating subject. Do you know anything about it?"

Arrogant twerp, Annie thought. "No, I don't, Professor," she said before Zach could respond. "Perhaps you'd care to enlighten me."

The professor blinked, as if he hadn't expected her to speak. "Well, I—"

"Tell them about your latest project," her mother encouraged, shooting daggers at Annie.

Markson nodded, and off he went. Annie's eyes began to glaze over after the first few minutes. "That's so interesting," she said, when he paused for breath. "Do you work with my father?"

"Yes." He beamed.

"Where *is* Dad?" Annie asked, deliberately changing the focus of the conversation.

Her mother waved a hand. "You know your father. He's probably lost in research." The words were light, but Annie heard the hurt Kimberly had never quite stopped feeling. "He promised he'd try to be here by the time dinner was served."

Which meant, Annie knew, that they'd be lucky if they saw him tonight. "What's on the menu?" she asked with a smile, hating that bruised pain in her mother's eyes.

Kimberly brightened. "I made your favorite vegetable dish for an entrée." Her words were sincere, her love open. "Don't start, Caro," she said, when Caroline opened her mouth. "I made your favorite pie, too."

"That's why you're my bestest aunt."

Thankfully, the conversation stayed light and easy from then on. They were about to move into the dining room when wonder of wonders, her father walked in. Erik Kildaire was dressed in the rumpled clothing of a man for whom looks mattered little, but he seemed to be with them today, rather than in his head.

Her mother's face lit up from within, and Annie smiled. "It's good to see you, Dad," she said, accepting her father's enthusiastic kiss on the cheek. Love swelled in her heart, but it was a love that had learned to be cautious. She'd never had the tangled relationship with her father that she had with her mother, but that was probably because he'd never been around to argue with her. A different kind of hurt altogether.

"And who's this?" he asked, looking Zach up and down while sliding one arm around her mother's waist.

Annie made the introductions, but her father's reaction was not what she'd expected.

"Zach Quinn," he muttered. "That's familiar. Zach Quinn. Zach—" The fog cleared. "The same Zachary Quinn who published a study on the wildcat population of Yosemite last year?"

Beside her, Zach nodded. "I'm surprised you recognized my name."

"Not my department," her father acknowledged, "but my good friend Ted—Professor Ingram—was very excited by it. Said it was the best doctoral thesis he'd seen his entire tenure."

Zach had a *Ph.D.*?

Annie could've kicked him for keeping that from her, especially when her mother shot her a look of accusation. Thankfully, her dad said something at that moment and drew her mom away, leaving Zach and Annie alone for the first time since their arrival. She raised an eyebrow. "Keeping secrets?"

He had the grace to look a little sheepish. "To be honest, I didn't think anyone would realize or even care. You told me they were math and physics people."

"My father knows everything about everyone. And a Ph.D. is a Ph.D.." She rapped a fist gently against his chest. "If you'd told me you had one, I wouldn't have worried so much about my mother's reaction—even she can't argue against a doctorate."

"Your mother's not the one whose opinion I care about. Does the Ph.D. matter to you, Annie?" The look in his eyes was guarded.

The hint of unfamiliar vulnerability caught her unawares. "Zach, if degrees mattered to me," she said honestly, "I'd have married the triple-Ph.D.'d physicist my mother picked out for me when I was twenty-two. Or the MD with more letters after his name than the alphabet. Or the multipublished grand pooh-bah who stared at nothing but my breasts for the entire meal."

His smile creased his cheeks. "The man had excellent taste."

"Stop making me blush." But she wasn't, not any longer—somehow, Zach Quinn had earned the trust of her vulnerable feminine heart.

It startled her, made her afraid.

But before the dark emotion could grow, Zach bent to brush his lips gently over hers, acting in the way of changelings, not caring that they had an audience. When he drew away, she leaned into him, fear—if not forgotten—then at least temporarily caged.

Chapter 8

TWO AND A half hours later, Zach found himself on the balcony sipping coffee while Annie stood inside, chatting with her cousin. God, but she was beautiful to him—all he wanted was to take her home, hold her safe, and keep her just for himself.

It was an unalterable part of him, this possessiveness, coming from the cat and man both. But no matter his primitive instincts, he wouldn't do that to Annie, wouldn't contain her that way. Still, he needed to mark her—to take her until his scent was embedded so deep into her skin, no one would dare question his right to her. An animal desire. Yet often, the animal's heart was far more pure, far more honest, than the thinking man's.

"Mr. Quinn."

He glanced at Kimberly Kildaire. "Please call me Zach."

"Zach." A regal nod. "Let me get straight to the point—from the instant Angelica told me about you, I was prepared to dislike you."

"I guessed."

"I've changed my mind."

Zach raised an eyebrow. "The Ph.D.?"

"No. In certain departments, any monkey can get a Ph.D." It was a gauntlet.

He picked it up. "Good thing I'm a leopard, then."

Her lips threatened to smile. "I've always pushed Annie toward men who are more cerebral than physical."

Zach waited with a predator's quiet patience.

"It was a conscious choice," Kimberly said without apology, "my way of ensuring she would never again be put in harm's way. I even rejected a brilliant engineer as a possible match because he frequently goes off to work on projects in remote locations. His humanity mattered less than the danger he might've exposed Annie to."

Her eyes met his. "To be quite blunt, changelings take that possible danger to the nth degree. Your very nature is one filled with the violence of the wild."

He was floored by her candor. "You're very aware."

"I know others might say I'm intellectualizing away prejudice, but I'm no bigot." She held his gaze with a strength he suspected had been honed by surviving a lifetime of hurt. "I simply want my daughter safe. I saw her almost die once—it's not something I want to witness ever again."

His cat detected no lies in her. "I'll keep her safe."

"I have a feeling you will. It seems I made a critical error— in thinking about how you could lead her into danger, I forgot that predatory changelings are also known for their willingness to protect to the death." Her eyes—Annie's eyes—clashed with his. "But that's not why I've decided for you."

"Oh?"

"It's because of the way you look at her, Zach. As if she's your sunshine." Her voice caught. "I want that for my daughter. Don't you ever stop looking at her that way."

Zach reached out and touched her lightly on the arm, sensing how very brittle her composure was at that moment. "I give you my promise."

A sharp nod. "Excuse me, I should go mingle."

As she walked away, Zach blew out a slow breath. It was becoming clear to him that he'd have a far harder road to travel with Annie than he'd initially thought. She'd grown up watching her mother love a man who, quite bluntly, didn't love her the same way. After only one meeting, Zach knew that Erik Kildaire was devoted to his work, while Kimberly was devoted to him. The insouciance with which Erik had crushed his wife's heart an hour ago—bussing her on the cheek and telling her he had something important to do at the lab—had angered Zach enough that he'd had to fight the urge to say something.

Annie would never have to worry about that kind of hurt with him. Once the cat decided on a woman, it didn't flinch. Devotion was almost obsession with those of his kind, and he was at peace with that. But words wouldn't convince Annie—she'd have to be stroked into trusting him, into relying on him. Because not only was she wary of loving, she'd become almost mutinously independent in her desire to avoid opening herself up to pain.

I like living alone. I intend to keep it that way.

That, he thought, the cat rising to a hunting crouch, was just too damn bad. But even as the predator in him prepared for the hunt, a vicious vulnerability grew in his heart. He *needed* Annie's trust, needed the surety of knowing she'd come to him no matter what. If she didn't . . . No, he thought, jaw setting, that simply wasn't an option. Annie was his. End of story.

"WHAT magic did you do with my mother?" Annie asked, letting them into her apartment.

"That's my secret." He closed the door and prowled along behind her.

Her heart went into hyperdrive.

She was going to go to bed with him, with this man she'd met only yesterday. But it felt as if they'd never been strangers, it was so very easy being with him.

Careful, Annie.

Fear rose up in an insidious wave, showing her image after image of Kimberly's face as she watched Erik walk away. Was that what awaited her? Did the question matter now that she'd decided to take the chance and weather the hurt when it came?

"Hey." Zach brought her to a halt, nuzzling at her neck from behind as his hands closed over her hips. "Stop thinking so hard."

"I can't help it," she whispered. "I'm not . . ." She bit her lip, trying to think of a way to say this without betraying how incredibly important he'd become to her in such a short time.

"You're not the kind to kiss and walk away as if it meant nothing," he said, running his lips lightly over her skin, inducing a shiver. "Neither am I. This is no one-night stand."

"Changelings live by different rules."

He licked at her, and she felt her purse slip from her hand to drop to the floor. "Zach." A whisper, perhaps a plea.

He hugged her tighter against him. "We might be more

tactile than humans, but it's nothing casual. It's about friendship, about pleasure, about trust."

"It sounds wonderful."

"It is." Another kiss pressed to the sensitive skin of her neck.
"Trust me, Annie. I won't hurt you."

At that moment, she almost believed him. Closing her hands
over his, she let her body melt into the hard masculine heat of
his. "You make me feel beautiful."

"You're more than beautiful," he whispered, "you're sexier
than sin."

"You're complaining?" She dropped her hands as he moved
his to the side of her dress and tugged at the tie that held it up.

The tie came loose. "I didn't like the way Markson was
undressing you with his eyes."

"He was not." Feeling the dress fall open at the front, she
shifted so he could pull the tie out of the inner loop. He did . . .
and the fabric dropped.

"Mmm." It was a murmur of utter pleasure as he began to
pull the dress down over her arms. "I'm the only one allowed
to undress you"—a kiss on her bare shoulder—"to pet you."

Pet.

The word reminded her that he wasn't human, wasn't anything tame. "You're very possessive." Air hit her back, her
breasts. Then the dress was falling over her fingertips to pool
on the floor.

Behind her, he made a sound strikingly close to a growl,
one hand caressing the curve of her waist. "You already knew
that, Annie."

Of course she had. A predatory changeling male, no matter
how playful, had possessiveness built into his soul. For as long
as she kept his interest, he would demand everything from her.
She knew she'd give him what he wanted—everything but her
faith. That, she thought, she no longer had to give. Her parents'
marriage had shattered her belief in forever a long time ago.
Sadness might've beckoned, but then Zach slid his hand up to
lie flat over her stomach, big, hot, and darkly possessive, and
her thoughts fractured. "Zach?"

"Shh. I'm looking."

The husky statement made her body clench inside, her
thighs tremble. She was wearing black lace . . . for him.

"*Annie.*" He groaned and reached up to unhook her bra. "I want to see."

An instant later, she found herself standing there in nothing but her panties and a pair of strappy sandals. She was in no way ready for the boldness with which he moved to cup her breast. "Oh!" She trembled at the touch, at the erotic sight of his hand on her. His skin was tanned, rawly masculine against her creamy flesh. When he squeezed, it was all she could do not to collapse.

"You're so pretty, Annie"—he spread the fingers of his other hand on her stomach—"I could lap you right up."

Completely in his thrall, she raised her hand to reach back and touch his face. He nipped at her with his teeth, chuckling when she jumped. "I want to be in bed. This is going to take some time."

Her brain turned to mush right then and there, and when he shifted to scoop her into his arms, she was so startled, she squeaked and grabbed on to his neck. "I'm too heavy, Zach. Put me down."

"Questioning my muscles?" A wicked smile. "Kiss me."

Unable to resist, she obeyed, not stopping until he laid her down on the bed and rose. His eyes glittered the green-gold of the cat, hunger in every stark line of his face. She watched, heart in her throat, as he stripped off his jacket, then removed his shirt. He was built sleek and powerful, a predator in human form.

She sighed in unashamed pleasure and saw his eyes gleam as he bent down to get rid of his shoes and socks. "Now yours," he said, moving to the bottom of the bed and tugging off her sandals one by one, following each removal with a long, slow look up her body.

By the time he finally got on the bed beside her, she was so aroused that she rose to claim a kiss of her own. When he nipped at her lips as he seemed to like doing, she nipped back. He raised his head, his hand closing possessively over her breast. "Do that again."

Eyes wide, she did. He purred into her mouth. She broke the kiss to stare at him. "What was that?"

A feline smile. "Nothing." He reclaimed her lips, and a second later she felt that vibration again, that sign that he was something other, changeling to her human. It made her shudder with the need to crush her breasts against him.

"You purr," she accused when they parted.

"So do you." Coming over her, he began to kiss his way down the line of her neck. He seemed to get distracted between the curves of her breasts, leaving her to clutch at the sheets in unadulterated pleasure as he sucked and kissed. When teeth became involved, she cried out, feeling her body tighten into a fist so tight, a single touch would send her over.

He blew his breath deliberately across one wet nipple.

She shattered, and the pleasure was a tidal wave that demanded everything she had. When she finally resurfaced, Zach had recommenced his sensual exploration of her body, the dark strands of his hair sweeping over her like a thousand stroking fingers. She ran her hands through the rough silk of it, feeling sated and content. And happy.

He looked up, a lazy smile in his eyes. "Yes?"

"Come kiss me." She'd never imagined she would one day make such a brazen demand, but Zach listened to her. Even if he didn't always give her what she wanted.

He shook his head. "After."

"After what?"

His answer was to keep on kissing her, going steadily lower. When his lips pressed over black lace, she trembled. He did it again. Then she felt the whisper of something on her outer thighs—glancing down, she saw her panties being thrown off the side of the bed. "How?"

The eyes that met hers were wild, exotic. "I used a claw to cut them off."

"Oh." She looked at his human hand. "Like a very small shift?"

"Hmm." He wasn't paying attention, more concerned with pushing apart her thighs and raising her legs to put them over his shoulders. She'd never felt so exposed, so vulnerable. She waited, stomach tight.

But nothing could've prepared her for the ecstasy of his touch. Zach liked to take his time—he pushed her to insanity over and over. It might've terrified her except that he made no effort to hide his own arousal, murmuring his pleasure with every slow lick. "Sweet, pretty, Annie," he said. "My Annie."

She discovered she was raising her body to his mouth, moving with a sensual bliss that was scandalous in its eroticism. He liked it. She knew, because he told her so, his voice close to a growl.

"I am definitely going to bite," he whispered. And then he did.

By the time she could think again, he was getting off the bed. She exhaled in pleasure as he stripped off to reveal a body hard with arousal.

"Look what you do to me," he whispered, moving to kneel between her legs. He stroked his hands under her thighs. "Come here."

She swallowed at what he was asking, knowing it had far more to do with trust than sex. But she couldn't refuse, had the strangest feeling that any hint of rejection from her would wound him incredibly deeply. Rising, she held on to his shoulders and let him support her bottom as her body brushed over the tip of his erection. "Zach," she whispered, drowning in the intimacy of his eyes, "you undo me."

His eyes flickered from cat back to human. "Hold on to me, baby. I won't let go."

Breath coming in jagged bursts, she lowered herself onto him. He stretched her to the limit. But she wanted him inside her, wanted to possess him as absolutely as he'd possessed her. She drove down and shuddered. "It's too much." The angle was deep, the penetration intense.

He kissed her. "We'll practice until you get used to it." It was a husky promise as he laid her back down, bracing his body over hers using his hands.

"How much practice?" She wrapped her legs around the lean beauty of his hips, no longer shy with this man who treated her as if she was a goddess.

He groaned, pulled out a little, then thrust, as if he couldn't help himself. "Lots." Though sweat-damp hair hung over his forehead, and sexual need was an inferno in his eyes, he waited to give her time to adjust.

She felt a violent tenderness grab hold of her heart. He was, quite simply, *wonderful*. Raising her arms, she pulled him down and kissed him, telling him without words that it was okay to let go.

He groaned. And began to move.

• • •

ANNIE looked down at the male sprawled by her side the next morning and felt her body sigh. He was fast asleep and gilded dark gold by the sunlight sneaking in through the blinds. He'd kept her up half the night, loving her so thoroughly that she felt possessed. Taken. Branded.

Refusing to surrender to panic, to give him up to protect herself, she reached out to trace the tattoo she'd discovered on his back sometime during the night.

It linked to the one on his biceps, which was actually the stylized tail of a dragon. That dragon's front claws rested on his left shoulder, the mythical creature's sinuous body stretching across his back. It was a stunning design . . . and another example of the wildness in him.

That wildness brought her alive, made joy sear her blood.

It also frightened her—the depth of what she felt. Finally, she truly understood why her mother had stayed with her father all these years. Her mind filled with the echo of Kimberly's voice from a rainy night more than fifteen years ago.

Your father used to call me his heaven.

That time had passed long ago, as would Zach's interest in her. Yet even after the spark faded, Annie now knew that the temptation to stay, to hope for another moment when he might look at her as he once used to, would be overwhelming. It was that futile hope that kept her mother tied to her father, but though she understood it, it wasn't a path Annie would ever allow herself to follow.

It would break her heart to see Zach look at her with disinterest in his eyes. She'd leave before that, at the first insidious signs of fading passion. It was bound to happen . . . but not yet, she prayed. *Please not yet.* Heart tight with a mixture of joy and pain, she lay down beside him, content to trail her fingertips over his tattoo and watch him sleep.

That was when she noticed his lips were curved.

"Zach." A whisper.

Cat eyes looking into hers. "Mmm?"

"How long have you been awake?"

Chapter 9

"LONG ENOUGH TO enjoy you petting me." Unrepentant mischief in his eyes. And desire. The desire was still there.

Relief made her melt from the inside out. "You're such a cat."

"Want to see?" he asked.

"See what?"

"My cat."

Her eyes went wide. "Really?"

He yawned, every inch the indolent feline. "Hmm." Without warning, color shimmered all around him, sparkles of light and shadow, beauty and eternity.

She held her breath until it ended. The leopard lying on her bed looked at her with familiar eyes. Swallowing at her proximity to such a dangerous creature, she struggled up into a sitting position, sheet held to her breasts. The temptation to touch was blinding. She lifted a hesitant hand—it was one thing to know intellectually that this was Zach, quite another to believe it.

When she didn't touch, the leopard raised its head to butt at her hand. Shuddering, she gave in to temptation and stroked him. He relaxed, closing his eyes in bliss. It made her awe morph into delight. "I think I just got conned." But stroking him, adoring him, was no hardship.

When the shimmer came again, she went utterly still. A few moments later, her hand lay on the muscular back of a man so sexy, he made her heart trip simply looking at him.

"So?" he asked.

She snuggled up to him, positioning her body so that they

lay face-to-face, her hand now on his shoulder. "You're gorgeous, and you know that."

For once, he didn't smile. "Is it too much to handle?"

"No." She frowned. "Did I give that impression?"

"Just checking." She got a smile this time, a slow, lazy thing that tugged at things low and deep in her. "Some women like the idea of being with a changeling but find the reality harder to accept."

"Some women?" A prickly flare of jealousy.

His smile widened. "Not that I would know."

She felt her lips twitch. "Of course not, Mr. Innocent."

"Hey, you're the one who led me off the straight and narrow." He ran his hand down to her bottom in a possessive caress. "I seem to recall you demanding I do 'the licking thing' one more time."

Her body ignited to sensual life. Deciding to fight fire with fire, she said, "You never gave me my winnings yesterday."

Sensual mischief in his eyes. "Yes, I did. With interest. And then again."

"Cat." Wrapping her arms around him, she rubbed her nose affectionately against his. It felt natural, easy. He made a sound of contentment and shifted until she was under him, skin-to-skin contact all over. It was sexual, but it was also something more. Touch for the sake of touch, cuddling because it felt good.

"How long does the affection last?" she asked half seriously. Making love with him was so stunningly beautiful, but this kind of simple contact . . . it was somehow deeper, going beyond pleasure and into a kind of trust that left her breathless.

Zach kissed her cheek, her jaw, her chin. "Always. *Not* touching is abnormal for us."

She remembered the easy affection she'd witnessed at the picnic. "I'm guessing that doesn't apply to strangers."

"No."

"That's good," she said, swallowing an unexpected pulse of hurt at the idea of being outside the circle of his pack. If she'd been his mate— She cut off that thought at once, more than a little panicked at the idea of being locked into a relationship that offered no escape . . . no matter if the love died. "I'm not easy with people I don't know well," she said to cover the sudden burst of fear.

"You're in charge of skin privileges, baby." He traced circles on her shoulder. "The pack will pick up the cues."

"'Skin privileges'?"

"The right to touch." He kissed the corner of her mouth.

She wondered if she'd ever get enough of this play. "I guess you have total skin privileges then."

A sound of smug male pleasure. It made her laugh, he was so shameless about it. And that was when she knew. She was too much her mother's daughter. She'd love only once. And she'd love forever.

Zach was it.

For him, she'd break every rule, allow him into her home, into her very soul. For him, she'd jump into the abyss and worry about the bruises later. Because sometimes, there were no choices.

"Hey." His voice was a husky murmur. "What's the matter, Angel?"

She shook her head, glad that he wasn't Psy, that he couldn't read her mind. "Love me, Zach."

"Always."

But she knew he hadn't understood what she'd asked, hadn't promised what she needed. It didn't matter. He was hers, if only for now, and she would treasure every moment of that joy. The pain could wait until after he was gone.

Chapter 10

A MONTH AFTER he'd first met Annie, Zach sat on one of the car-sized boulders scattered around Yosemite and wondered what the hell he was doing wrong. He'd spent every night since the day of the picnic with her. She was fire in his arms, warm, beautiful, and loving . . . but she continued to withhold a part of herself.

Most men wouldn't have noticed. But he wasn't most men. Every time she waved off his offer to help her in some way, every time she pulled her independence around her like a shield, he noticed. It wounded the cat, confused the man. "Mercy, I can hear you."

A tall redhead jumped down from a branch a few feet in front of him. "Only because I let you."

He snorted. "You were making enough noise for a herd of elephants." He threw the sentinel a spare bottle of water.

"I didn't want to bruise your masculine ego by sneaking up," Mercy said, perching on a boulder opposite him. "Not when you already looked so pathetic."

"Gee, so thoughtful of you."

"I can be a right peach." She drank some water. "Let me guess—you've mated with the little teacher?"

He raised an eyebrow.

"Oh, puhleese," Mercy drawled. "As if you'd bring anyone but your mate to the Pack Circle."

"She's fighting the bond," he found himself saying.

"Why?"

"You're the female. You tell me."

"Hmm." Mercy capped the bottle and tapped it against her leg. "Did she say why?"

He stared at her.

Mercy rolled her eyes. "You did *tell* her that she's your mate, didn't you?"

"She's a bit resistant to the idea of commitment." That resistance frustrated the hell out of him, but he was trying to be patient. Not only did he care about her happiness, he wanted her to trust him enough to make the choice—even though there was only one answer he'd accept. "I don't think she'd react well to the whole 'till death *really* does us part' bit."

"So you're making the choice for her?" She raised an eyebrow. "Arrogant."

Anger flared. "I want to give her time to become comfortable with me."

"Is it working?"

"I thought so, but the bond hasn't snapped into being." The mating bond was an instinctive thing, but the female usually had to accept it in some way for it to go from possibility to truth. "It's tearing me up, Mercy." The leopard was lost, hurt. What was wrong with him that Annie didn't want him?

"Talk to her, you idiot." Mercy shook her head. "Has it crossed your little male mind that maybe she's protecting herself in case you decide to indulge in some hot sex, then flick her off?"

He growled. "She knows I'd never do that. It's about the commitment—she's scared of trusting someone with her heart." He couldn't blame her, not after what he'd seen of her parents' marriage.

"Correct me if I'm wrong," Mercy said, "but haven't you two been joined at the hip for the past month? Pack grapevine says you've all but moved into her place."

"Yeah, so?"

"Geez, Zach, I thought you were smart." Trapping the bottle between her knees, she raised her hands to redo her ponytail. "Sounds to me like she's already committed to you."

She'd given him a key to her apartment, to the place that was her bolt-hole. His heart slammed against his ribs. No, he thought, he couldn't have made that big a mistake. "But the bond—"

"Okay," Mercy interrupted. "Maybe you're right, and your Annie's going to freak about the mating, but let's say your amazing Psy mind-reading abilities are wrong—"

He growled.

"—and she's ready to risk everything for you. What would keep her from taking the final step?" She raised an eyebrow. "You know the rep we have. Humans tend to think of leopard changelings as affectionate but casual."

"That's not it," he insisted. "I told her this was serious right at the start."

"Let me share a secret with you, Zach. Men have been telling women things for centuries. Then they've been breaking our hearts."

Zach's mind filled with the memory of Kimberly Kildaire's shattered face as Erik Kildaire walked away. Promises, he thought, lots and lots of broken promises.

"Only way," Mercy continued, "for you to gain her trust might be to forget the pride that seems to come embedded in the Y chromosome. You ready to wear your heart on your sleeve and hope she doesn't crush the life out of it?"

He met her gaze. "You got a streak of mean in you, Mercy."

"Thank you very much." Finishing off the water, she threw him the bottle. "I'd better head off—have to meet Lucas."

He watched her climb back up into the trees, her words beating at him. Had he really been that much of an idiot, thinking he knew what was going on in Annie's head while being so very wrong? More importantly, was he willing to swallow his need for dominance, for control, and put the most important decision of his life into her hands? What if she rejected him? The pain of the thought was paralyzing.

ANNIE finished putting away her things with eager hands. It was five on Friday, which meant she had the entire weekend to spend with Zach. He'd promised to show her some of the secret treasures of his forest, and she couldn't wait. Of course, she thought with a smile, even if he'd told her he wanted to watch the entertainment network all weekend, she'd have had the same reaction. She flat out adored being with him, wicked teasing and all. Especially since she'd gotten pretty good at teasing him back.

"Hey, Teach."

"Zach!" She walked over to hug him. "What're you doing here?"

His expression was solemn. "I need to talk to you."

Her stomach knotted. "Oh." She stepped back, trying to appear calm.

"Mercy was right," he said.

Annie knew who Mercy was, having met the sentinel at the picnic. "About what?"

"You're waiting for me to leave you."

The world fell out from under her feet. She trembled, unable to move, as he closed the door and walked to her. "I will never leave you, Annie." Cupping her cheeks in his hands, he bent so his forehead pressed against hers. "Not unless you ask me to." He frowned. "Actually, I won't leave you then, either. Just so you know."

"Wh-what?"

"You're my mate," he said simply. "You're in my blood, in my heart, in my soul. To walk away from you would cut me to pieces."

The room spun around her. "I need to sit down."

He let her go, let her lean against her desk.

"Mate?" she whispered.

"Yes." His face grew bleak. "It's a lifetime commitment. Mercy was right about one thing, but I'm right about this—you're not too keen on that, are you?"

She didn't answer his question, her mind spinning. "Are you sure that I'm . . . ?"

"Baby, I was sure the first day we met. You fit me."

It brought tears to her eyes, because he fit her, too. Perfectly. "Zach, I . . ." She blinked, trying to think past the rushing thunder of emotion. "I never thought I'd marry," she admitted. "But it's not the commitment I have a problem with. It's what comes after." A confession made in a voice that threatened to break. "It's this cold terror that the promise, the love, will one day turn into a trap."

"I know."

"She still waits," Annie found herself saying. "For a Valentine or a birthday present or just a loving word. *She still waits.*"

"Oh, sweetheart." He tried to come closer, but she held up her hand, fighting to think, to understand.

"I could survive you leaving me," she said, "but I couldn't survive you stopping to 'see' me." And the mating bond would leave her with no way out. It truly was forever.

"That's something you never have to fear," Zach said, the declaration resolute. "It's not possible for mates to ignore each other."

"But—"

"No buts," he said, slashing out a hand. "I will never stop seeing you, never stop loving you. Mates *can't* shut each other out."

Part of her wanted to grab that promise and never let go. But another part of her, the part that had been trapped first by injury, then a mother's fear, was hesitant. Was she ready to take this chance on the faith of a man's promise? Was she ready to give up the freedom she'd fought a lifetime to attain? "I'm so afraid, Zach."

"Ah, Annie. Don't you know? My cat is devoted to you. If you asked me to crawl, I'd crawl."

It shattered her, the way he'd just ripped open his heart and laid it at her feet. Trembling, she placed two fingers against his lips. "I would never ask that."

"Neither would I." His lips moved against her touch. "Trust me."

There it was, the crux of it. She adored him, loved him beyond reason, but trust . . . trust was a harder thing. Then she looked into that proud face, into the wild heart of the leopard within, and knew there could be only one answer. She refused to let fear cheat her out of the promise of glory.

"I do," she said, cutting the last safety rope that had held her suspended above the fathomless depths of the abyss. "I trust you more than I've ever trusted anyone." Something tightened in her chest at that second and then snapped, leaving her breathless. She clung instinctively to Zach, and he held her tight, burying his face in the curve of her neck. When she could breathe again, she tangled her fingers gently in his hair. "Zach?"

He shuddered. "God, I was so scared you were going to say no."

She felt it then—his terror, his love, his devotion. It was as if she had a direct line to his soul. The beauty of it staggered. "Oh my God." There was no way this bond would ever let either of them ignore each other. "Zach, I adore you." She could finally admit that, needed to admit it, needed to tell him that he wasn't alone.

"I know." He squeezed her even as a wave of love flavored with the primal fury of the cat came down the bond between them. "I can feel you inside me."

So could she, she thought in mute wonder, so could she.

A week later, Annie sat down in Zach's lap, blocking his view of the football game. He reached up to kiss her. "Want to play, Teach?"

She always wanted to play with him. But they had things to discuss. "No, this is business."

He turned off the game. "So?"

"So we have to have a wedding."

"We're mated." A growl poured out of his mouth. "Why the hell do we need to have a wedding? Those things drive everyone crazy—last year, I saw a grown man cry during the buildup."

Once, she would've wondered how on earth changeling women dared stand up to their mates when the men got all growly. Now she knew—just like her, those women knew that heaven might fall and the earth might crumble, but their mates would never hurt them. "Didn't you say we were going to have a mating ceremony?"

"It's not really a ceremony." He scowled. "More a celebration of our being together."

She couldn't help it. She reached out to stroke her fingers through his hair. "It's getting stronger," she said.

"It'll keep doing that." His scowl turned into a smile that hit her right in the heart. "Even when we're a hundred and twenty, I'll still want to crawl all over you."

"Zach, you're a menace." And she loved him for it. Was starting to truly see what she'd gotten when she accepted the mating. It was a powerful, almost vicious need, but it was also a bond of the deepest, most unflinching love. Even when he wasn't with her, she felt him loving her deep inside. "We need to have a wedding," she said, coaxing him with a slow kiss, "because my parents need to see me married, and Caro's already picked out a matron of honor dress." Then she dealt what she knew would be the deathblow to any further objections. "Their happiness is important to me."

He blew out a breath. "Fine. When?"

"I was thinking spring for both ceremonies."

"That's a while away." He slid his hands under her sweater, touching skin. "We could do it at Christmas. A present for both of us."

"No," she said, stroking his nape with her fingertips. "It has to be spring. I want everything alive and growing." As she felt she was growing, opening, becoming. "And I already have my present."

Eyes the color of the deepest ocean gleamed with feline curiosity. "Yeah?"

"A long time ago, during the Christmas I lay in hospital," she told him, retrieving a memory that had once been painful, but was now full of wonder, "I wished for someone who would be mine, someone I could play with and share all my secrets." Never could she have imagined the astonishing final outcome of that long-ago wish.

He moved his hands down to close over her thighs. "Are you calling me your gift?"

"Yes." She smiled. "How do you feel about that?"

"Like it's my turn to be unwrapped." He nibbled at her mouth. "Do it slow."

Her laughter mingled with his and the sound felt like starlight on her skin, like the promise of forever . . . like a lick of "majick."

❖

Declaration of
Courtship

Chapter 1

COOPER HAD BEEN good.

Very good.

More good than he'd ever before been in his life.

He'd stayed away from his sexy new systems-maintenance engineer for over six months. *Six* months. It might as well have been a decade, as far as he was concerned. A dominant predatory changeling male did not do patient when he decided on a woman, but circumstances had forced patience on him, and it was a patience that had worn his wolf's temper to a feral edge.

With her curvy body and that soft ebony hair he wanted to fist in his hands while he used his mouth, his teeth, to mark her creamy skin, she spoke to his every male instinct. The wolf who was his other half was in full agreement. Both sides of him wanted to claim her until no one had any doubts that she belonged to him.

He'd gritted his teeth and fought the primal urge, however, aware that as the lieutenant in charge of the satellite Snow-Dancer den located on the northern edge of the San Gabriel Mountains, Grace was under his protection. His status wouldn't have put the brakes on his pursuit had she been even a moderately strong dominant, but Grace was one of the most submissive wolves in SnowDancer. Cooper knew damn well submissives didn't automatically obey dominants, but the impulse was a visceral one.

Added to that, Grace had been deeply vulnerable immediately after shifting into a new den. Cooper had known he couldn't go after her until she'd formed new friendships, created a support system that would give her the strength to reject him if his courtship was unwelcome.

His claws pricked the insides of his skin at the thought, but man and wolf both knew that if she said no, he had to back off. At once. Because where a dominant female might run to incite a man to chase her in a challenge that came from the wild heart of his wolf, if a submissive ran and it wasn't open play, she was trying to escape.

Don't run from me, sweetheart, he thought as he took the final steps to her. *I only bite a little.* Not quite true, but he was planning to be on his best behavior until she trusted him enough to handle the aggressive sensuality that was an integral aspect of his nature. "Grace."

GRACE felt her heart kick against her ribs at the sound of that deep masculine voice as darkly delicious as it was dangerous to her senses.

Get a grip, Grace. You're being ridiculous.

It was the same thing she'd been telling herself over and over since her first day in the San Gabriel den, when Cooper had welcomed her to the region. Big and deadly and gorgeous as he was, it wasn't hard to see why he'd knocked the breath out of her at first sight. The man was a living, breathing aphrodisiac. If they'd been alone, she wasn't sure she'd have survived that meeting without doing something very stupid.

Like attempting to claim skin privileges from a male she was certain no one dared touch without his explicit permission.

Yet even in her stunned state, she'd known the attraction to be a wild impossibility. While dominants mated or bonded with submissives often enough that it wasn't considered unusual, the dominance gap between her and Cooper was *too* wide. They were literally at opposite ends of the hierarchy—her wolf knew Cooper could chew her up and spit her out without noticing.

And still, every time he came near her, her entire body went taut with expectation.

"Hi," she said, without looking up from her kneeling position in a corner, beside a heating conduit that needed a minor refit.

Akin to the den in the San Rafael Mountains where she'd

spent her teenage years, and on a smaller scale than the central den in the Sierra Nevada mountains, this den had literally been carved into and below a mountain, then reinforced with stone walls. The tunnels were wide and spacious, the rooms generous, but underneath the raw natural beauty of the stone pierced with threads of glittering mineral lay a highly complex technological heartbeat, one that Grace helped maintain.

"Has there been a malfunction in one of the critical systems?" she asked, guessing that was why Cooper had taken the time to personally track her down. With both the chief and deputy chief of her department away at different tech conferences, Grace was currently the one in charge. "I can look at it straight away—this isn't urgent."

"No, everything's fine." He crouched down beside her, immediately taking up all available air in the vicinity.

Concentrate on the job, she ordered herself, attempting to focus on the digital wrench she was using to remove a fried tube . . . but her entire body was attuned to his every breath, her muscles strung tight.

"How's it going in this section?" he asked, his voice pitched at a level she recognized as "careful."

She fought the suicidal urge to throw a tool at his head. Her place in the hierarchy didn't determine her entire personality. As with every other dominance level, submissives could be shy or exuberant, cheerful or moody, sensual or reserved. Grace might be quiet and a little shy in comparison to the majority of her packmates, but she could handle loud voices just fine— growing up with two older adoptive siblings, dominants who'd inherited a hair-trigger temper from their father, she'd heard more than her share.

"We're about halfway through the overhaul," she said, wishing he'd forget her place in the hierarchy and see her simply as a woman . . . a woman he wanted.

If he did, what would you do?

Probably run very fast in the other direction.

She twisted the wrench a fraction too hard and almost broke the tube. "Damn." Cheeks burning, she flexed her fingers, took a deep breath, and completed the extraction with care, hotly conscious of Cooper's watchful gaze. "There. We can recycle the components."

"Removed without a scratch. Impressive." He picked up the burned-out tube. "Did you get the new shipment you wanted?"

She tore her eyes away from his hands, face heating even further at the raw images that had formed unbidden in her mind—of those big hands on her body, on her breasts, his skin exquisitely rough against her own. Never had she responded to a man in such a way, and that it was a man whose mere presence made her wolf acutely uncomfortable? Surely, fate was having a good laugh at Grace's expense.

"Yes," she managed to say in response to his question, "I did. They were high quality, as promised." Hearing a gentle click as he returned the tube to the floor, she put down the wrench and went to pick up a—

"Grace." Fingers curling around her wrist.

Her pulse spiked as she stared at that strong, dark-skinned hand so warm and gentle, the calluses on his palm a sensual abrasion. She couldn't speak, the rush of noise inside her head too loud, drowning out all else.

"Grace." Softer this time. Coaxing. "Look at me."

Swallowing, she chanced a peek, her wolf at rigid attention. If he'd commanded, she would've obeyed at once, her nature such that defiance of an order from a lieutenant stressed her on a primal level. The fact that she was a changeling rather than a wild wolf meant she *had* the capacity for such defiance, but it would require bone-deep disagreement on her part, enough for the human side of her nature to override the powerful instincts of her wolf.

But Cooper hadn't commanded. He'd requested . . . in a way that made everything female in Grace come to trembling attention. Now, her eyes met the intense near black of his and skated away. When he did nothing but wait with a patience she'd never expected from him, she lifted her lashes again, her gaze locking with his.

It sent a thrill through her wolf. To hold the gaze of a lieutenant was a bold move for any wolf, but for a submissive, it went far beyond that. In any other circumstance, it could've been dangerous—just as she had her instincts, dominants had theirs. If one interpreted the eye contact as a challenge, it could end badly. The fact that in the majority of cases where such a thing had happened both parties had been in wolf form did nothing to negate the danger of triggering an inadvertent violent response.

Because a submissive would *never* come out the winner.

Cooper's thumb brushed over the skittering pulse in her wrist. "There you are." The low murmur touched her in a caress so intimate, it felt as if she was bare to the skin, exposed and vulnerable.

Inhaling a jerky breath, she broke the shocking eye contact, tugged gently at her wrist. When Cooper's fingers tightened for an instant, her heart stuttered. He released her before the next beat. Not certain of anything, she fell back on what she knew, picking up another one of her tools to do . . . something. Except her thoughts were jumbled, a burn of lingering heat around her wrist. She began working on a random nonessential section of the duct, where she could easily fix any errors later.

Beside her, Cooper shifted a fraction, the single inch he closed between them enough to have her wolf quivering and alert, with anticipation, desire, and a good dose of panic all mixed in.

"You don't ever have to fear anything from me, Grace." It was a rough murmur, a verbal pet of her senses. "If you want me to stop anytime, anywhere, the only word you ever need to use is 'No.' Okay?"

She jerked her head up and down, her throat as dry as the shimmering sands of the Mojave.

"But," he continued, "I don't intend to go away until you tell me to do so. I'm planning to court you."

The tool fell from her nerveless fingers to clatter to the floor. Reaching over, Cooper picked it up, put it back into her toolbox. "I'll leave you to your work . . . but Grace? I'll be seeing you again soon." With that promise, he rose and was gone, his powerful body moving with a wild strength kept in fierce check as he strode down the relatively narrow access corridor and out into the den proper.

Heart crashing against her ribs hard enough to hurt, her breath jagged in her throat, Grace collapsed against the smooth stone of the wall. "Oh, God. Oh, God. Oh, *God*." Her chest rose and fell in a harsh, uneven rhythm as she attempted to take in air, clear her head.

The effort failed.

Reaching blindly for her water bottle, she swallowed.

The cool liquid wet her throat but did nothing to calm the fever in her blood.

"I'm planning to court you."

Never in her wildest imaginings had she thought Cooper would speak those words to her. The furthest she'd dared had been improbable erotic fantasies that left her sweat-soaked and aching for completion, fantasies in which they lay skin to skin, her lips on his throat, his hands gripping her hips as he pinned her under him in readiness for his possession. In real life, she'd almost certainly panic if she was ever in that position, her wolf seizing her mind to present quiescent submission to the predator in bed with her, but the hard reality of the hierarchy didn't matter in her fantasies.

Had Cooper invited her to his bed, those fantasies may have given her some kind of a foundation in which to ground herself, ephemeral though it would've been. However a changeling male like Cooper didn't use the word "court" when he was welcoming a woman to share his body and his bed, whether for the night or longer. No, he was *serious*.

Big, dangerous, beautiful Cooper wanted her as his.

Chapter 2

ALMOST READY TO believe she'd imagined the whole thing, Grace lifted the inside of her wrist to her face, drew in the wild earth and dark amber of Cooper's scent from her skin. The complex notes made her want to nuzzle her nose into his throat and breathe deep, until she could separate out the elements that made up the decadent whole.

Even now, the lingering whisper of it caused her skin to prickle, her mind cascading with sensory memories of the dark heat of his muscled body, the deep bronze of his skin, the black hair he'd taken to shaving so close to his skull that she had to constantly fight the urge to reach up and brush her hand over the bristles. Like those on his jaw.

What would that jaw feel like rubbing against skin she bared only in the privacy of her bedroom?

Groaning, she took another drink of water. It didn't do much good, adrenaline continuing to pump hard and urgent through her veins until it felt as if her skin was going to burst from the frenetic energy ricocheting within her body, her wolf as dazed as the human side of herself. So when she heard someone else enter the access corridor, her brain seized on the distraction. And when she scented Vivienne a second before the tall, slender woman appeared around the corner, she wanted to sob with joy.

Ice-cold beauty, that's the initial impression Grace had had of her fellow engineer with her ruler-straight black hair pulled back into a sleek ponytail and almond-shaped eyes of brown, cool against flawless white skin. Then Vivienne had smiled—as she did now—with infectious warmth, revealing the joyous reality of her spirit. "Hey, boss. I'm on my way to begin the rehaul of the comm system in this grid—the issue with the 7B comm line was nothing but a slight glitch."

Grace touched the space beside her. "Have a break." Critically for both their working relationship and friendship, while Vivienne was a dominant—albeit on the lower end of the power scale—she had no problem taking orders from a submissive supervisor. The level of such flexibility possessed by each individual, no matter his or her place in the hierarchy, was a fact the "civilian" chiefs in the pack had to keep constantly in mind when they created work teams.

Because when it came down to it, they weren't human; they were changeling, they were wolf.

"Was Coop here? I love the depth of his scent." It was a cheerful comment as Vivienne took the seat Grace had offered. "It's so quintessentially male, you know? If my wolf wasn't half terrified of him, I'd be tempted to serve myself up to him on a platter." She sighed. "That scar of his should detract from his looks, but it only adds to his sex appeal. God, can you imagine what he'd be like in bed?"

Grace opened her mouth and the words just fell out, sounding as surreal as the first time she'd heard them. "He says he's going to court me."

Vivienne's head snapped toward her. "I *knew* it!" Rampant glee. "I told Todd not to flirt with you, but would my dumbass twin listen? No! Hah! I can't wait to see the look on his face when I tell him he was attempting to make time with the lieutenant's woman."

Grace blinked at the unexpected response. "You did not know. And I'm not his woman." It sounded so strange to say those words, to even consider the idea outside of her fantasies.

Vivienne waved away the qualification. "Okay, fine, I didn't *know* know, but I suspected. I grew up in this den, was seventeen when Coop took over, and let me tell you: the man might've kept his distance since you arrived, but he's never looked at a woman the way he looks at you. All kind of intense and protective and ravenous"—a shiver—"like he's waiting to take a bite."

The idea of Cooper's mouth on her skin made Grace squeeze

her thighs together, even as another part of her yelled that she'd lost her mind. She did not have the tools to handle a man like that—strong, raw, demanding—in bed. "You're not helping."

"I'm sorry." Voice solicitous, Vivienne patted her thigh. "It's just that he's so hot, I lost my marbles for a second."

Grace snorted a surprised laugh and it was a needed release. "You're an idiot."

Vivienne winked, asked, "You don't like him?"

"Like's not the word I'd use," Grace said, her voice husky with remembered emotion. "I . . . he *is* hot. Extremely." The kind of hot that could ruin her for other men even as it burned her to a cinder. "But, he's a lieutenant."

"Is he using his position to pressure you?" A frown. "I can't see Coop—"

"No! No, he'd never do that." He might be rough around the edges, bad in a way her sensible side warned her put him way out of her sexual league, and definitely dangerous, but he was also honorable to the core.

"If you want me to stop anytime, anywhere, the only word you ever need to use is 'No.'"

Vivienne nudged her shoulder, one long leg bent at the knee, the foot of the other pressing against the opposite wall. "Then what?"

"I'm a submissive." An obvious, unalterable fact. "Always have been—and I'm happy with my place in the hierarchy." She was needed, her role in SnowDancer no less important than any other. For one, the pups were utterly unafraid of her. In an emergency, she could grab any child and run, knowing that child would cling to her rather than fight.

On a day-to-day basis, and without throwing the dynamite of passion into the mix, Grace and those like her helped their stronger brethren maintain control of their aggressive natures by inciting an intense and often unconscious protectiveness.

Though, from the submissive end, the effect wasn't always by chance.

More than once, Grace had asked an angry and frustrated dominant to assist her in some task she could just as well do herself, aware the influence of her wolf would calm theirs. Such things were part of the rhythm of a healthy pack. Those packs that lost their natural complement of submissives—whether through accidents or a lack of care and respect—and didn't redress the imbalance eventually splintered, the energy in the den turning violent.

"Always remember"—*a warm hand stroking over her hair*—*"as we need their strength to make us feel safe deep inside, the soldiers and other dominants need us to retain their humanity. That's why SnowDancer is such a powerful pack. Because one is not considered more or less than the other."*

"But," she continued, heart clenching at the echo of her lost father's gentle voice, "wolves like me don't date packmates as strong as Cooper." Desire altered the rules on a fundamental level, changed the effect her wolf had on his, his on hers, until she could no longer predict how either one of them might react in any given situation.

Vivienne's next words were solemn. "He makes you uncomfortable, doesn't he?"

On the most basic female level. "He's just so overwhelming." So masculine, so primal, so harshly beautiful. Just . . . *so.*

"I get that. Coop's not a man who'd ever be an easy kind of lover."

Grace's throat went dry again at the thought of calling Cooper her lover. "It's not only that," she rasped, having to take a sip of water before she could continue. "You remember what I told you? About how part of the reason I accepted the promotion and moved here was because of how overprotective my family was being?" Until wolf and woman both knew it wasn't good for her.

Though she loved her adoptive parents and siblings with all her heart, and knew she was cherished in turn, at times such as this she missed her long-gone "Papa" and "Mama" so much it hurt. Her father had been a submissive, had understood her on a fundamental level, her mother a dominant soldier who'd mated and loved a submissive long enough to have gained an inherent understanding of what her daughter needed to flourish. They'd both recognized that Grace's need to feel safe and secure didn't equal a rigid wall of protection.

"I see your point." Vivienne's voice penetrated the bittersweet memories of the happy, content child she'd been before the pack was drenched bloodred. "As a lieutenant, Coop's pretty much built to protect." Twisting her body, she faced Grace. "If you tell him to back off, he will. I guess everything else aside, the question is—is that what you want?"

"No." An instant and categorical repudiation. Grace couldn't bear the thought of never again feeling the abrasive warmth of Cooper's touch, hearing that caressing note of promise in his voice.

Vivienne's lips curved in a wicked smile. "Then you'd better find a way to deal with the big, bad wolf who wants to have you for his own *very* personal snack."

A thousand butterflies took flight in Grace's stomach.

HE'D scared her.

The soldier in front of Cooper paled under the tanned gold of his skin. "Sir?"

And now he was scaring everyone else. Rubbing a hand over his face in an attempt to dislodge his scowl, his thumb brushing over the jagged scar along his left cheek, he said, "The perimeter incursion, you're certain it was just a couple of human kids necking?" Wolf territory was clearly marked, but juveniles the world over had a mysterious ability to see only what they wanted to see.

Daniel nodded, his sandy hair sliding over his forehead. "I caught them myself. Made sure they knew they were trespassing on SnowDancer land, and told them it was the single warning they'd get before we took action." A flash of teeth. "They couldn't get out fast enough."

"Good." Cooper didn't enjoy putting fear in the eyes of teenagers with more hormones than brains, but it had to be done.

SnowDancer's vicious reputation was its first line of defense.

The pack hadn't always been so outwardly aggressive. Their discipline and focus on family, however, had made their enemies believe SnowDancer weak; the ensuing bloodshed had devastated the pack. So many had been lost in the carnage— including Grace's parents.

Never again, thought Cooper.

"Keep an eye out for them," he said to Daniel. "Sometimes kids like to play chicken." Youthful stupidity knew no boundaries, regardless of whether the young were changeling or human.

"I'll alert the other sentries. What should we do if one of us catches them again?"

"Disable their vehicle and call me." SnowDancer had sole jurisdiction on its land. Maybe Enforcement would've challenged that claim once upon a time, but not anymore—not with the world shuddering under the violent weight of a change that was redefining power itself. "I'll walk them out personally."

If the human pups were old enough to neck, they were old enough to know better than to dare a predatory changeling pack. Cooper intended to give the two misbehaving teens the same dressing-down he'd give one of the juveniles under his command should they pull a stupid stunt. "No one's ever come back a third time."

Daniel grinned.

Shoving his hands over the bristling roughness of his scalp after the soldier left, Cooper stared moodily at the view outside his window. While the majority of the den was underground, his office was located on the highest level, tucked into a natural curve of the mountain. The glass was treated so as not to reflect, but it afforded him a good view of the main path up to the den. Bathed in sunshine today, the land beyond was verdant with trees, until you'd never know the Mojave desert sprawled just beyond the distant ridgeline.

He liked being able to keep an eye on things from here, but the lack of windows in the main den didn't bother his wolves—they loved coming home to a snug den, a place where their pups were always protected. Added to that, the tunnels were wide and bathed in simulated daylight and moonlight depending on the time of day, the air-filtration and temperature-control mechanisms fine-tuned to create an effortless transition between the outside and inside.

SnowDancer's scientific arm had been responsible for the original development of the technology, but it was the highly trained systems engineers who maintained and calibrated the interconnected systems on a day-to-day basis. Each could handle most of the minor issues that cropped up from time to time, but they all had their specialties. Grace's expertise was in the simulated natural light so important to the pack's well-being.

His hand fisted, his scowl returning at the reminder of how she'd trembled under his touch. Yes, he could be scary—hell, it was an asset when it came to protecting the pack—but he didn't want to scare Grace. He wanted to pet her, hold her, learn the intricacies of the smart, sexy woman who handled her high-tech tools with the care and elegance of a surgeon . . . and made him wonder how she'd use those same hands on him. Because he most definitely wanted to coax her to strip off the workman-like coveralls that drove him wild, and breathe his fill of her scent as he explored those incredible, dangerous feminine curves with his body, his mouth.

A curl of wood falling to the floor.

He realized his claws had shot out, carved grooves into the wood of his desk. "Great," he muttered, retracting them into his skin. "If you're trying not to scare a woman, learn to keep your fucking claws in, Cooper." Shoving back from his desk, he strode out of his office, taking the steps that led down into the main core of the den two at a time.

Chapter 3

BETHANY CAUGHT HIM just as he reached the bottom. "Coop, I need to talk to you about the juveniles."

"Whatever they've done," he growled, continuing on toward the exit, "handcuff the lot of them and put them in the brig. I'll spring them in a few years when they're full-grown adults."

"Funny." The short, curly-haired maternal female, her mouth bracketed by laugh lines that told of a life well lived, said, "Some of us remember when you were the worst of the lot. Wasn't it a pink ribbon? Or did you sport the purple and Riaz the pink?"

Wincing, he halted. "You have the memory of an elephant, Aunt Beth."

"It comes in handy when I need blackmail material." Dimples dented her round cheeks, a mischievous expression in the dark, dark eyes that marked them as kin. "Which, in this case, is unnecessary. The juveniles have been good."

"Did you drug their soup?"

She threatened to pull his ear—probably would have if he didn't top her by over a foot. "About fifteen of them joined up to clear that invasive weed that somehow made its way into one of the streams. Spent the whole weekend at it, and as of today, the weed is history. It'd be nice if you could swing by."

"I'll do it now." He glanced at the small comm screen set into the den wall, saw it was almost midday. "Kids had lunch?"

"I took them a couple of baskets." Bethany patted him on the chest. "With enough for a big, strong lieutenant."

"Sometimes I think you take me for granted." Leaning

down, he kissed her cheek, the scent of her inciting a keen protectiveness.

It was Bethany who'd taken him in as a grieving, angry sixteen-year-old, enfolding him in love. What she hadn't done was attempt to reverse the sudden adulthood that had been shoved on him that cold, rainy night—because some things couldn't be changed, and the loss of his childhood had been a permanent one.

"However," he added when she stood on tiptoe to smooth his T-shirt across his shoulders, "I'll fall in with your cunning plans."

"You always were a good boy, Cooper, even during your hellion juvenile years." Her smile was an echo of his mother's, caused a familiar ache in his chest. "Now go, before they inhale lunch. You'll be lucky to find a few bones to gnaw on."

The teenagers had in fact resisted the lure of the sandwiches, cake, and fruit, and were checking the final section of the stream with industrious eyes when he arrived. Visibly perking up at his presence, they clustered around to show him what they'd done.

"I'm proud of you," he said after listening to their explanations of the project, his wolf in pleased agreement.

The juveniles beamed, tugged him to another part of the stream.

When two younger kids showed up in pup form a few minutes later, he scooped them up before they could poke their curious noses into the picnic baskets. "Behave or it's back to the nursery with you."

The miscreants pretended to claw him, growling and snarling. Laughing, he tapped their noses in a light reprimand and put them on their feet, where they leaned their small, warm bodies against his legs as he finished speaking to the teenagers. By the time the group sat down to lunch—the two pups shifting form to curl up against him and eat more cake than was good for them—the tension had left his muscles.

Nothing could alter the fact that he was an aggressive dominant, but as the pups and juveniles showed, he had the capacity to earn the trust of even the pack's most vulnerable. It would take time with Grace, the trust he asked of her a piercing intimacy, but Cooper had been called a stubborn bastard more than once. It wasn't an unfair accusation.

And he was determined to seduce, pet, and coax Grace into his arms.

Where he planned to keep her.

All night.

All day.

Always.

HALF relieved, half disappointed that she hadn't seen Cooper again since his declaration of courtship, Grace put her tools away in her office, then stripped off her black coveralls to reveal the jeans and sleek black tank she wore underneath. She was hungry after the long day, should've gone home. But pulling on her favorite blue sweater, the fabric fine rather than heavy, she checked her hair and face in the mirror, then turned in the direction of the indoor training arena where she'd heard Cooper was working with some of the novice soldiers.

Seeing the access door up ahead, she used her palm print to get through, then shut it behind her. The good thing about being in systems maintenance was that she knew all of the hidden nooks and crannies of the den. This particular access-way led to another door on the inner wall of the training arena, and that door had a window to ensure maintenance personnel didn't accidentally walk out into a dangerous training situation.

Grace made her way to that window with quick steps, happy to see that it was clean, as mandated by the safety regs. Beyond the glass, it appeared the novices had been split into two teams and were "at war," though she could see kicks being pulled and punches turned into light taps. Still, people occasionally went down—someone was calling points she realized, and a certain number equaled incapacitated or dead.

She saw a disappointed novice go to his knees before her attention was captured by the adult male who came over, hauled the lanky youth to his feet, and proceeded to show him where he'd gone wrong. Cooper's actions were powerful, his expression intent. The younger man nodded, copied the moves Cooper had demonstrated while compensating for his own lighter body mass, and grinned when his intelligence earned him a slap on the back.

Grace couldn't keep her eyes off the lieutenant, a problem she'd had since the day she moved into the den. It was amazing how many times she could find a fault that needed checking right next to where Cooper might be running a training session or working out on his own. Now, she saw him call the battle to a halt, and from the victorious cheer that thundered over the left side of the room, he'd declared a winner. A minute later, the novices cleared the floor to position themselves against the walls.

Into the open space walked a senior soldier who'd been helping to supervise the session. As she watched, Shamus stripped off his T-shirt and threw it aside. She wrenched her head toward Cooper to see if he was doing the same. He was. Rippling muscle under hot, dark silk, a fine pelt of black hair on his chest, his cheeks creased as he laughed at something Shamus had said; he was the most beautiful man she had ever seen.

Dressed only in cargo pants, their feet bare, the two dominants took position against one another and began to go through a combat routine even Grace could tell was in half time, a teaching aid for the novices. Shamus was well built—sexy, she supposed—but all Grace could see was Cooper, his fluid actions akin to rough music. How might that strong, trained body move in other, far more intimate situations?

Even as her teeth sank into her lower lip, even as her breath caught, her wolf paced, agitated and confused. It reminded her that Cooper's demands would be fierce, his need furious. The possibility that she might not be up to the task of satisfying him made her mood go dark, especially when she finally turned her awareness to the men and women who watched the bout—to see that three other adults had joined the group. All were female, and two of them had their eyes on Cooper.

Grace took careful mental note of their identities. Maybe she'd switch the air in their quarters to freezing, ensure they didn't have any hot water for good measure. The wicked thoughts were gratifying, but nothing came close to seeing Cooper's body flex with predatory grace as he and Shamus stepped it up a notch. It was breathtaking to witness, the dance as primal as it was violent.

Her heart was in her throat when they came to a sudden, unexpected halt . . . and Cooper's head whipped around, his eyes locking with Grace's.

COOPER shifted his attention back to Shamus after that instant's distraction. He was dead certain he'd caught the finest trace of Grace's scent—peaches, luscious and ripe, intertwined with a softness that was pure, sensual woman.

His woman.

Slamming up a hand to block a kick to the head, he twisted around with a kick of his own. "Full speed," he called, and the two of them went into the final stage of the display, its purpose to demonstrate to the novices how simple moves could be put together to lethal effect.

Afterward, he listened as Shamus questioned the group. They didn't do too badly, and Cooper released the class after pairing them up for a self-practice session the following day. As the novices left, he saw Shamus go over to his math teacher mate. Dark-eyed, black-haired "Ms. Lopez"—as the pups called her—had come in toward the end of the session and now hugged her mate hello, the couple nuzzling one another in wolfish affection.

"I thought you two had a room!" Cooper called out across the training arena.

The newly mated couple grinned before Shamus wrapped one arm around Emma and said, "Green is not a good color on you, Coop. And we're going to that room now, where I plan to do things to Teach you can only dream about in your cold, lonely bed."

Cooper saw Emma slap at Shamus's chest for that shameless boast as the two of them disappeared out the door.

Grinning, he met the laughing gazes of the two senior soldiers who'd come in with Emma. "What did you think?"

Margot was the one who answered, blue eyes dancing. "About Shamus's plans, or the novices?"

Vitoria blew a wild curl out of her eyes, her hair an explosion of bronze and black with the odd thread of unexpected red-blonde. "Scuttlebutt is that Emma was missing at lunch today and so was Shamus."

"I can do you one better." Margot paused for dramatic effect, the sun-golden skin of her face marked by a faint greenish bruise caused by a rogue baseball. "Apparently when Shamus stripped off to shift a couple of hours ago, it was pointed out that he might possibly have carpet burns on his butt."

Cooper's wolf huffed with laughter as both women cracked up, but damn it, he *was* jealous. He wanted to sneak a certain deliciously sexy engineer away for a lunchtime snack of his own, carpet burns optional. "Leaving aside Shamus's sex life," he said when the laughter subsided, "what about the novices?"

"I like how they listen but still ask questions," Margot said. "Shows they're thinking for themselves without getting cocky."

Vitoria nodded. "We were saying we could take the next class—we've taught that one before."

"Great." It'd give him more time to court Grace. "I'll let Shamus know."

When the women continued to look at him, he put down the water bottle he'd drained and raised an eyebrow.

Margot's responding smile was playful. "Aw, come on, Coop. You know."

"I know you two are best friends," he murmured, "but if you're offering what I think you're offering, I didn't know you were that close."

Vitoria snorted. "We're not. We just figured we'd play fair and give each other the same shot. So?" A warm invitation in eyes of jade green brilliant against skin the color of pure, unadulterated coffee. "We've noticed you've been abstaining."

Damn pack. Nosy as hell. "It's by choice," he said bluntly, knowing the women wouldn't take it as an insult, as he hadn't their affectionate offer to assuage his increasing touch hunger—a hunger focused on one woman and one woman only. He wanted Grace's hands on his body or no one's. "I'm taken."

Two pairs of eyes lit up in unholy delight.

"Do tell." Margot sidled closer. "We'll keep it a secret."

He was the one who snorted this time. "Wolves gossip like old women." It was the flip side to their incredible loyalty—everyone wanted to poke his or her nose into everyone else's business. "I'll tell when I'm ready to tell." Not that it wouldn't become obvious soon enough. He didn't plan to pursue Grace in secret; he wasn't the subtle type. Though since he was meant to be on his best behavior, he'd try to give her a fraction more breathing room to get accustomed to the idea of him.

"This should be fun." Vitoria actually rubbed her hands. "Who would dare give Coop the runaround?"

"None of your business." It was a growl.

Rising on her toes, Vitoria kissed him on the cheek, bracing her hand on his shoulder. "You know we only care because we love you."

Another kiss on his opposite cheek, this one from Margot, the soldier tall enough that she didn't have to reach like Vitoria. "Soooooo . . . her name starts with . . . ?"

Laughing at their playful teasing, he snapped his teeth. "Out. I have things to do." *A certain submissive wolf to catch.*

Vitoria and Margot made faces at him but obeyed the order. It left him alone in the training arena. The first thing he did was walk to the service door and pull it open. The luscious scent of ripe peaches warmed against a certain woman's creamy skin whispered into his lungs, strong enough that he knew she'd been here not long ago.

His lips curved.

His mood more cheerful than it had been for six long months, he shut the door and headed to his quarters to shower. Pulling on a pair of black cargo pants and an olive green T-shirt afterward, he ran a hand over his chin, felt the stubble, and decided to shave. That done, he slapped on some aftershave, figured it was the best he'd ever look. Pretty he wasn't.

What if Grace liked pretty?

Biting back a growl, he grabbed the little box he'd been hoarding for over seven weeks. He was about to walk out the door when he realized that the moment his packmates spotted the shimmery blue wrapping paper and silver bow, they'd stalk him with brazen relish. Digging out the small backpack he used to carry his water and food when he wanted to go into the forest in human form, he stowed the box inside and slung the pack over his shoulder.

Several people said hello as he walked through the den, and he returned the greeting but didn't stop. No one paid him much mind when he knocked on Grace's door—everyone was used to seeing him talk to people from different parts of the den, and in the absence of her two immediate superiors, Grace was the one in charge of her department.

"Just a second!" In spite of her words, it took Grace at least two minutes to open the door, and from her flustered expression and damp hair, she'd been in the shower.

The image of her creamy skin soap slick and slippery wasn't good for Cooper's self-control. *Patience*, he snarled at himself, wrenching so hard on the reins that his wolf yipped in protest and his voice came out a near growl. "Can I come in?"

Chapter 4

CONSCIOUS AT ONCE that he might just have screwed up his attempt at a gentle courtship, he said, "Or we can go outside." Where he could talk her into skin privileges of the sinful kind.

Cheeks flushed with soft color he wanted to lick up, she stepped back. "No, here's fine."

Not giving her time to change her mind, he slipped inside and nudged the door until it was almost closed, creating the privacy he craved. "Hey." Finally alone with her, her scent caressing his skin, he felt a fraction more in control.

Grace tucked the damp curls of her hair behind her ear, her smile shy. "Hey."

Pulling off his backpack, he unzipped it to retrieve the box. "I got this for you." He'd never courted anyone before, didn't know if he was supposed to work up to this, but he wanted to give her a present and didn't see the point in pretending otherwise.

A startled look out of chocolate brown eyes before her lashes shaded her expression again. He couldn't wait until she held his gaze anytime she felt like it, though he knew it would take staggering trust on her part—an acceptance that he'd *never* see any such eye contact as a challenge on the pack level, even were they in the midst of a blazing fight. It was a significant accommodation, but one his wolf was more than willing to make. Neither part of him wanted his woman to feel at any kind of a disadvantage in a relationship.

Of course, he thought as she accepted the gift with a husky "thank you," if she felt the urge to challenge him on the private male/female level, he'd pick up the gauntlet in a heartbeat. The thought of Grace trusting him enough to play with him on such an intimate level made his entire body tighten in need.

"Here." He held out his hand for the ribbon she'd untied.

When she handed it over with a deeper smile, he dared step an inch closer, his wolf brushing against his skin. She proved as impatient with presents as he was—the paper tore, and a few seconds later, she held the box in her hands.

Taking the paper, he watched as she removed the lid of the box. Nestled against the white satin within, the blue glass of the bracelet almost glowed, the tiny daisies captured in each of the square links appearing to have been picked but a moment ago.

"Oh!" A captivated gasp. "How did you know?"

He grinned, smug, and shoving the used paper and ribbon into his backpack, let it drop to the floor. "I have my ways." He'd seen daisies in the vase she kept in her office, had noticed she sometimes wore a dress patterned with the same flower—a floaty, summery thing that made him want to tumble her into his lap and demand a hundred laughing kisses. "You want me to do it up for you?"

"Thank you, Cooper."

He could listen to her lips shape his name forever. Muscles taut against the urge to cuddle her close, his own personal bundle of warm, trusting woman, he went to do up the clasp. His fingers appeared too big, too clumsy for the task—as they appeared too rough to touch Grace. He knew differently, knew he'd never hurt her. "There." Keeping hold of her hand, he brushed his thumb over her skin.

She shivered, but didn't pull away. "I shouldn't keep it. It's too much."

Her skin was so soft, so appealing to stroke that he did it again. "It's normal to give flowers during courtship."

"I can't lie," she admitted with a delighted smile that hit him straight in the heart, "I love it already. I'll wear it all the time."

God, but he wanted to cover that luscious mouth with his own, taste her long and deep. *Slow goddamnit, slow.* "Will you come for a walk with me?" he asked, keeping his eyes scrupulously off the bed he could glimpse behind a shoji screen patterned with shoots of green bamboo. "We can sneak out through the access tunnel to the back entrance." Though he wanted everyone, particularly the unmated males, to know she was off-limits, Grace wasn't the hard-ass he was, would find the attention difficult to deal with.

Smile turning a little shy, she said, "Let me tie back my hair and change."

The thought of her silky-skinned and naked beyond the thin barrier of a single doorway annihilated his attempt at good behavior. "I think you look edible." Since he'd already blown it, he surrendered to need and took a deep breath, barely resisting the urge to nuzzle at her throat. "Peaches. You smell like lush, ripe peaches. Can I take just a little bite?"

Grace's skin glowed with color, but instead of shying or backing off in fear, she pointed to the door. Grinning because his submissive wolf had just proven she could handle him fine even when he was bad, he went. "I'll be waiting."

GRACE leaned against the door after Cooper exited, taking jerky breath after jerky breath. God, he was dangerous—even more so when he turned on that rough charm.

"Can I take just a little bite?"

Swallowing her whimper, she put herself in motion, changing out of the sweats she'd thrown on at Cooper's knock and into jeans paired with a soft cashmere cardigan in a rich raspberry shade that felt exquisite against her skin. If she planned to play with a wolf as strong and aggressive as Cooper, she had to learn to cope with the fact that he was going to push. Hard. It was in his nature.

"I did cope," she muttered, tying the laces on her boots with jagged moves after quickly braiding her hair. "I didn't turn tail and run, did I?" No, she'd made her opinion plain . . . and he'd listened. The big, teasing wolf who outranked every single person in the den had obeyed her silent order without the least protest.

It was a gift as wonderful as the whimsical bracelet on her wrist.

Hope a rich spice in her blood, she walked out to discover he'd moved to the end of the corridor, was chatting with Shamus, who—from the container in his hand—had made a run to the kitchen to pick up a slice of key lime pie. While Grace didn't know the senior soldier well, she'd become close friends with his mate, Emma, after meeting the sweet maternal dominant at the book club Vivienne organized once a month. So she knew the pie was Emma's favorite, as was lipstick in a particular shade of vibrant red, a trace of which marked Shamus's jaw. It made Grace smile, seeing how crazy they were for one another.

"Off for a walk?" Shamus asked with an inquiring glance when she halted beside Cooper.

Cooper answered before she could become flustered. "I thought I'd point out one of the evacuation routes to Grace in case of emergency."

Shamus threw back his head in a belly laugh, his thick brown hair catching the light. "And I was about to say it was a romantic night. Have fun."

Waving good-bye, they waited until he was out of sight before entering the narrow access corridor that led to a rarely used exit. Though kissed by a cool wind that promised rain, the night was as lovely as Shamus had said, the satin black of the sky dotted with what appeared to be a million stars.

Cooper's hand closed over hers. "First, so I'm not a liar, there's the start of the evac route." He pointed northeast. "Okay?"

"I already know the routes," she said, heart thudding at the skin-to-skin contact. "It's part of the welcome-to-the-den module for submissives." Submissives were the ones charged with evacuating the pups should it ever become necessary to abandon the den because of hostilities, while the soldiers held the line of defense.

"Good thing Shamus doesn't know that," he said as he tugged her into the trees, stroking his thumb over her skin in that maddening, arousing way. "I think you'll like this."

Her wolf wide-eyed and watchful, she walked quietly beside him through a natural passageway created by two near-perfect rows of trees, their branches twining to form a lacy canopy, the stars visible in glittering glimpses. However, it wasn't the velvet night that held her attention, but the predator by her side. The one who'd claimed her hand, claimed skin privileges, in a way that shouted possession.

The thought of belonging to Cooper made her wolf pad

around her skin in a confusion of panic and delight once more. But neither part of her wanted to be anywhere but here, in this exhilarating, exquisite instant. Maybe this courtship was ridiculous and impossible and bound for failure, but she wasn't going to give up on it, give up on Cooper, without trying her damndest.

"Here." His body brushed hers as he brought her to a stop in what appeared to be a small clearing. "Do you smell it?"

"Yes." Ripe, juicy blackberries.

Reaching out to pluck a berry from one of the canes that surrounded them, he brushed it across her lips. "Open for me, beautiful, sexy Grace."

Her toes curled inside her boots at that low-voiced request, a liquid kind of heat in her abdomen. Parting her lips, she allowed him to feed her the plump fruit, the juices bursting inside her mouth. When he picked off more, fed her decadent berry by decadent berry, she didn't protest. And when he spread his legs and tugged her closer, she went, her wolf quivering at the risk.

He ran a berry across her lower lip, painting it with the juice as the masculine heat of his body seeped into her every cell, and his face blocked out the night. "I'm going to kiss you." His voice vibrated where her breasts pressed against the strength of his chest, making her nipples ache. "Don't say no."

Releasing her hand when she remained silent at the rough-voiced request, he tipped up her chin with his fingers and suckled on her juice-drenched lower lip. The sweet, hot sensation was over almost before she knew it, her eyes fluttering open. He returned for another suckling taste, coaxing her closer as he did so. "Mmm." It was a sound of deep male pleasure, his hand sliding from her chin to cup the side of her neck. "You taste delicious." This time, his lips covered hers, the kiss an intimate seduction.

She clenched her hands on his chest as she rose toward his sinful mouth, felt the flex of warm, tensile muscle beneath the cotton of his T-shirt. Groaning, he licked his tongue across the seam of her lips, one of his hands coming to lie against her lower back, the rigid heat of his erection pushing against her abdomen—

Claws pricking the insides of her skin, the wolf threatening to take control.

Jerking back, she gasped in the cool night air. Her breasts felt swollen, the place between her legs damp, and she had no doubt Cooper had scented the musk of her arousal. But that wasn't the sole emotion in play, her wolf's sudden, wrenching realization of the violent strength of the predator who held her a visceral punch to the gut.

The wolf didn't want to run. It knew such an action would never work, that it would only enrage the predator. Instead, it demanded she lie down, let Cooper do what he would, its deep-rooted survival instincts colliding against her human need to make a conscious choice. It was all she could do to hold back the impulse to bare her throat to the male whose scent lingered rich and wild in her mouth; to whimper in primal submission—a submission that would end this relationship before it began, because that kind of mindless surrender would humiliate her and horrify Cooper.

"This isn't going to work." The words came out ragged, regret a hollowness inside her chest that caused a true physical hurt. "I'm too submissive."

Cooper, having remained motionless thus far, shifted to pluck a berry off the plant near him and pop it into his mouth. She watched him swallow, wanted to trace the movement down the tendons of his neck with her lips, lick up the dark amber and rich earth of his scent. When she finally dragged her eyes back up to his face, his lips were curved. "It'll work," he murmured, eating another berry. "It might require lots and lots of foreplay, but it'll work."

"*Cooper.*" Turning away from the raw sexuality of him, she shoved a berry into her own mouth to give herself time to think. "If—"

"No ifs," he murmured in a tone that spoke of the dominant he was. "Not yet. Even if you can't trust me in any other way, trust me in this—the instant your wolf overwhelms you without your conscious volition, I'll stop."

She felt him come closer, but he didn't bury his face in her neck as she craved, even though she knew her wolf was in no state to accept the searing intimacy of having him near her jugular. Even now, it buried its head in its paws, sad and scared and wanting all at once. "How will you know?" she asked, unable to hide the tremor of hope in her voice.

"I guess it's part of what makes me a lieutenant—being able to sense when the wolf is close to a packmate's skin."

She shuddered in relief. "Always?"

"Always." The barest touch on her hip. "Have you eaten?"

"No." Her stomach had been too full of butterflies after that scorching instant of eye contact in the training arena. "I'm hungry." A hesitant invitation, should he want to take it.

Knuckles brushing down her cheek. "I can't wait to feed you." A low purr of a statement that made her breath catch, her heartbeat accelerate.

"You earned your reputation, didn't you?" It came out husky.

He tapped her lower lip with a finger. "Play with me and I'll teach you all sorts of bad, bad things . . . but you're only ever allowed to do them to me."

Grace knew she was in trouble. Big, sexy, dangerous trouble.

Chapter 5

AFTER DRIVING GRACE home from dinner in the pounding rain that was the leading edge of an unforeseen storm front, Cooper had expected to spend the night tossing and turning as a result of extended sexual frustration. And hey, he wasn't against some hot, erotic dreams featuring his favorite engineer. However pleasure wasn't what awaited him when he fell into bed.

At first, all he could hear was rain.

He was sitting under a lee of rock outside the den, sheltered and snug from the cold droplets, enjoying its music. He'd always liked rain until that night. Every so often, he'd twitch his tail to shoo away a suicidal crow he couldn't be bothered to snap his teeth at—

—and then he was in human form on a long, slick road, watching two huge lights bearing down on him. He wasn't afraid. He knew who they were, and that they'd stop.

They did.

Opening the door, he got into the backseat as if it was an ordinary thing to get into a car from the middle of the road. His mother turned, laughing at something his father had said as she reached out a hand toward Cooper, the pearl earrings she so loved flashing in the flickering firelight.

Except, there shouldn't be a fire. They were alone on the dark, twisting road—

He was outside the car, screaming at them to stop, but they were both still laughing, dressed in the clothes they'd worn to attend the wedding, and they didn't hear him, didn't even see him—

—fire! He was trapped inside the car and the flames were blistering his flesh. He cried out, reached for his parents . . . but they'd turned to bone, charred and black. "No! No!" he screamed as his flesh melted.

Cooper jerked awake on a scream, the echo of it hanging in the air. Shuddering, he thrust his hands through sweat-soaked hair and checked the status of the audio shield round his room. *Thank God,* he thought when he saw the switch flicked in the right direction. The last thing the den needed was to hear its lieutenant screaming in terror like a child.

Shoving off the sheets tangled around his legs, he walked into the shower. Scalding, that's how he wanted the water. To thaw the lump of ice that was his heart. Always, he woke from that nightmare chilled to the bone. He'd never understood it, not when the fire was so *hot.*

He stayed until the shower stall was so full of steam, he couldn't see the hands he'd braced on the wall. Wrenching off the tap, he stepped out, dried off, and—towel wrapped around his hips—stared into the mirror. His jaw was dark with stubble, so he focused on that, shaved. The task took a bare few minutes, and then he no longer had even that slim buffer against the echoes of nightmare.

It had been worse this time, because he hadn't expected it, hadn't prepared himself for the horror that awaited him in the dark of night. It had been so many years since he'd been trapped inside that phantom car, burning and burning and burning.

"Enough." It was a quiet command to himself.

Leaving the bathroom, he pulled on underwear, jeans, a black T-shirt, socks, and boots.

The den was quiet when he stepped out, not unexpected at five in the morning. He almost turned toward Grace's room, wanting desperately to ask her to let him hold her, just that. But he didn't have the right to push for those skin privileges, so he took himself up to his office and began to go through a number of financial reports Jem had forwarded.

His fellow lieutenant kept an eye on Los Angeles and the surrounding areas, was the one Sebastian in San Diego called first if he had a problem. Cooper, by contrast, looked outward to the border with Arizona, Joshua Tree, and the arid Mojave falling under his mandate.

His and Jem's geographic closeness—relatively speaking—meant they could get together in person every so often, but they did most of their work via the comm. Both having an aptitude for and training in finance, they were in charge of the pack's investments, working with a small, dedicated team to ensure SnowDancer stayed healthy on that level. Normally, Cooper found the intricacies of the work invigorating, a complex jungle of a different kind, but today it felt like wading through quicksand. Still, he got it done, then began to plow steadily through the other paperwork that had built up on his desk.

All the while, the rain continued to fall beyond the window, and no matter what he did, he couldn't forget the charred black of his parents' bodies.

GRACE returned to work on sector 4B the next morning, after a systems and tech meeting where it was revealed the previous night's storm had done major damage to the solar panels. Specifically designed to blend into the environment so as not to give away the den's location, the panels provided the main source of its power.

"We're switching to hydro-station power till the replacement panels come in," the lead power tech had said, referring to the ecologically sound system that harnessed the kinetic energy of the water as it thundered down the mountains. "Shouldn't cause any issues, but keep an eye out for power surges anyway."

As she worked, Grace couldn't help but replay the previous night in her mind. Every now and then, she'd push back the sleeve of her coverall and sneak a look at the bracelet Cooper had given her. Which led her to recall the callused skin of his palm against her neck, the wild, dark taste of him in her mouth as his tongue licked at her own. The things the lieutenant could coax her to do . . .

Her nipples rubbed against the supple fabric of her bra.

Glancing guiltily around, she saw she remained alone. But the moment was enough to have her snapping her attention back to work.

When lunch came and went—a lunch she had with her crew—without word from Cooper, her mood began to plummet. Dominant males never backed off during a courtship.

Perhaps Cooper had rethought things in light of her wolf's response by the blackberries, decided he didn't need the hassle of dealing with a timid submissive when he could have an enthusiastic dominant playmate anytime he wanted?

"Or maybe," she muttered, annoyed with herself, "he's a lieutenant in charge of a den and got caught up in work."

Putting down her tools, she closed the cover on the computronic junction she'd finished checking, then glanced at her watch. Three forty-five. Since she was well ahead of schedule after working like a fiend on the off-chance that Cooper would turn up for a visit, she decided it was time for a coffee break.

About to tag Vivienne, she hesitated. Neither side of her nature was comfortable pursuing a male, but this one had made his interest clear. Taking a deep breath, she stowed her tools in her office, then went looking for Cooper. He wasn't in his office, but Bethany saw her coming down the smooth stone stairs and said, "If you're trying to hunt down Coop, he's out with the crew handling a slip caused by last night's rain."

"I hadn't heard." It hadn't been mentioned in the daily den e-bulletin. "Was anyone hurt?"

Bethany shook her head. "But it's on an evacuation route, so it needs to be cleared, the land stabilized. At least the rain's stopped for now."

"I've been inside all day," Grace said, hoping Cooper's aunt would accept her words at face value. "I can take coffee out to the crew, stretch my legs."

"You're a doll." A beaming smile. "There's four of them— Cooper, Shamus, Vitoria, and one of the structural engineers. Todd, I think."

Not bothering to change out of her coveralls given the area was likely a muddy mess anyway, Grace popped into the large communal kitchen and prepared a big thermos of coffee, as well as a smaller one of tea, then added some plas cups. The cook had just baked several trays of blueberry muffins, so she appropriated a bunch of those as well, plus some fruit, putting it all in an insulated carrier.

It only took her ten minutes to walk to the site of the slip using the directions Bethany had provided. Cooper was standing with his back to her when she arrived, his T-shirt stuck to his skin, boots caked with mud. She saw they'd cleared a path, were working on a temporary retaining system until the storm-damaged trees could regain their hold on the soil, or new trees could be planted. As she watched, Cooper thrust his shovel down . . . and turned to look at her, eyes of near black intense with emotion so raw, it stabbed at her heart.

"Tell me you have tea!" Todd's voice shattered the piercing intensity of the silent connection.

"Pussy drink!" Shamus yelled in return. "Grace's smart enough to bring a manly drink like black coffee."

Vitoria, a colorful scarf holding her curls off her face, punched him on the arm. "Who're you calling manly?"

"Ouch." Shamus rubbed his arm as they ambled over to where Grace was setting out the food and drink on the flat surface provided by an old tree stump.

"Coffee," she said, tapping one thermos, then, "tea," tapping the other.

"I knew I could count on you." Todd kissed her on the cheek before going for the tea.

Only then, when the other three were occupied, did Cooper touch his fingers to her lower back in a fleeting but undeniably possessive caress. "You know Todd likes tea."

Yes, definitely possessive. "I've had meals with him and Vivienne lots of times." She poured Cooper a cup of coffee, added cream from the little bottle she'd slipped in. "I also know a certain lieutenant," she whispered, "doesn't particularly care for Shamus's manly black coffee."

His lips kicked up at the corners at the gentle tease as he accepted the cup, and it did something to her to know she'd made him smile. "Thank you, Grace."

Simple, everyday words, and yet they sounded akin to a caress. When Shamus asked him something, Grace chanced a look up, hungry to drink in the sight of him without worrying about matters of dominance. Except he looked back for a single electric second before returning his attention to the senior soldier.

In that instant, Grace felt her entire body come to life . . . even as she once again caught the shadows of pain in the midnight depths of his gaze. Unable to understand how no one else saw the hurt he carried within, she waited until the others had headed back to work, with Cooper remaining behind—ostensibly to talk to her about a maintenance issue—to say, "Cooper? Are you okay?"

An instant's stillness before he handed her an empty thermos to pack away. "Sure. Little stressed with this slip, I guess."

His refusal to admit to his hurt was no surprise. Grace was well aware that often, the only way a woman could get a dominant male to open up was to ram at his defenses. Only she wasn't the ramming kind, wasn't even sure she had that right, their relationship a nascent thing. "Will you walk me back a little ways?"

"Anytime." He slung the bag over his shoulder.

Grace stopped once they were around the corner and out of sight of the rest of the team. Then she did what came naturally to *her* in this situation and slipped her arms around the muscled heat of his body, the scent of clean, male sweat and Cooper in her lungs. "I'm sorry for whatever it is that's put that look in your eyes."

His arms came around her, his cheek rubbing against her temple as her wolf rubbed up against his in an effort to offer comfort. In that instant, she felt no fear at this strength, only the need to temper his pain.

"I'm fine," he murmured. "Especially now that I'm holding you."

Frustration clawed through her at his stonewalling, but Cooper wasn't a man who'd trust easily. That he'd accepted her need to care for him, accepted her affection when he had to be feeling vulnerable, it was a powerful step. So she just held him, stroking his back until she felt the final fragments of tension leave his body . . . and when he rubbed his nose playfully against her own, she shyly petted him with a slow dance of a kiss that made champagne bubble through her veins.

COOPER returned to the site of the slip feeling more himself than he had since waking from the nightmare. It wasn't the first time a submissive wolf had done or said something to heal an emotional wound in a dominant—in their own way, they were as fiercely protective as the soldiers. But it was the first time Grace had done the same for Cooper. More, it was the first time she'd initiated skin privileges, her kiss a luscious gift that gave him all sorts of ideas about winning another from her tonight at the dinner she'd promised to have with him.

"Everything okay in the den?" Shamus asked when Cooper got back, wiping his face on the sleeve of his T-shirt. "You were with Grace awhile."

"Nothing the systems and tech teams can't handle," he said, and gestured to a post they were planning to sink to anchor the temporary retaining mesh. It wasn't the best option, but with more rain on the horizon, they had to get something in place, at least for the next few days. "How're we going to get that in without causing vibrations that might further destabilize this area?"

"I have an idea. Spoke to Todd and he thinks it'll work."

As the two of them got down to work, Cooper thought again of Grace. So perceptive, his highly intelligent, intuitive engineer; seeing what no one else had, what he'd thought he'd successfully submerged. Part of him didn't want her to see, didn't want her to know, but another part of him howled in delight, seeing in her insight the promise of a bond that would make her his on the most elemental, most primal level.

Chapter 6

HAVING SPENT THE remainder of the afternoon in 4B, Grace headed home at close to six p.m. All she wanted was to wash off the grime from crawling around in access corridors and narrow ducts she knew full well had been cleaned a mere two weeks ago.

Too bad spiders only needed a day to build a sticky mansion, complete with multiple rooms and storage facilities. She shuddered at the reminder of the bugs she'd seen trapped in the webs. Yes, she was changeling, hunted when her wolf needed it. But there was something very creepy about keeping your food hanging around.

Her comm panel chimed an incoming call just as she was stepping out of the shower cubicle. Recognizing the caller's ID code, she wrapped a towel around herself and answered with a smile, picking up another towel to rub at her hair as the visual feed went live. "Hi, Mom." It was a choice she'd made as a child, to call Milena and James Mom and Dad. It gave them the beloved place they deserved in her life while differentiating them from her lost mama and papa.

"Hi, munchkin." Milena beamed, the natural deep honey of her skin caressed by a glow that said she'd spent several hours outside under bright sunshine. "How was your day?"

"Great." Unable to resist, Grace bragged a little about how her crew was ahead of schedule, then asked her mother about the rest of the family.

"I know you talk to Pia and Revel, too," Milena said after catching her up on a few things, "but I don't know how long

I'll be able to keep the two of them, not to mention your father, from paying a visit to check up on you."

"They turn up, I'll kick them back out." She cherished her family, but they continued to see her as the half-mute seven-year-old they'd taken in after her parents were killed in the catastrophic events that had overtaken the main Sierra Nevada den roughly two decades ago.

So many children had become orphans, but none had been left without support, without family. Milena and James, and their teenage children, Pia and Revel, had become hers. Old enough not to mind the tiny intruder in their home, the teenagers had thrown their protection over Grace. Hardly surprising, since both Pia and Rev were strong dominants who now held senior soldier status.

As a shocked child, she'd needed the comfort of their protective natures, needed the cage provided by falling asleep curled between her siblings, all of them in wolf form. It had made her feel safe when her world had splintered into so many pieces, she didn't know what to do, how to survive each painful hour.

But she hadn't been seven for a long time.

"I'll pass on the message," Milena said with a sigh, "but you know how stubborn they are." Then she laughed, hazel eyes shimmering. "Look who I'm talking to—you always were a stubborn thing. I remember trying to get you to release your blankie so I could wash it. You didn't scream, didn't cry, didn't claw out at me or growl, but would you let go? No. I had to resort to sneaking it away one night weeks later when you finally fell asleep without it clutched in your little fist."

The story was a favorite one of her mother's and still made Grace laugh. Now, she reached out and picked up the furry orange teddy bear Milena had made from the scraps of her blankie after it had finally fallen apart. He'd survived her childhood and these days sat cheerfully on her bookshelf, next to photos of her family. "I wash him, I swear."

"Cheeky girl." Blowing her a kiss, Milena said, "I better go. I promised your father I'd make his favorite quesadillas. I love you, baby."

"I love you, too, Mom."

As she ended the call, Grace thanked God that neither Pia nor Rev had been posted to this den—they'd have been appalled at the idea of their sister dating a lieutenant. Grace would have told the two of them to butt out, of course, but she much preferred to play with Cooper with no one looking over her shoulder.

"Tell me what bad-girl things you got up to as a juvenile."

Even as heat bloomed in her abdomen at the memory of that lazy, caressing voice asking her wicked, wicked things at dinner the previous night—while he fed her spoonfuls of decadent chocolate mousse—a message came in on her cell phone.

Storm-damaged tree found along main den route. Needs to be brought down. Rain check for dinner? Coop.

Disappointed, she went to say yes, paused. *Has your team eaten?*

No. Bethany's bringing it over in a half hour.

I'll do it.

xx

It made a goofy smile break out over her face that Cooper had signed off with kisses. Dressing quickly, she found Bethany in the kitchen, putting together the meal. When she offered to take it, the older woman raised an eyebrow. "Todd?"

Grace squirmed. "Er, no."

"Hmm. Who else is out there?" She continued to make the sandwiches. "Bill replaced Shamus and they're both mated, in any case. Which leaves my Cooper."

Having finished her own set of sandwiches, Grace wrapped them up so they'd stay soft. "I'll get some of the brownies."

"Grace."

She froze, bit her lip. "It's new. We're not ready for the pack to know."

Bethany didn't stop her again when she moved to grab the brownies. Since the site was at least a half hour away on foot, Grace headed to the garage, Bethany walking down with her. They saw Vitoria on the way, the other woman having had to return to the den in order to teach a novice class. "You have more hot drinks for everyone?" the senior soldier asked from the other side of the corridor. "It's chilly out tonight."

Grace's nod received a thumbs-up before Vitoria turned to continue on her way.

"He always was a law unto himself," Bethany mused as Grace got into the driver's seat of a sturdy four-wheel drive, "so all I'm going to say is—submissive or not, you make sure you don't just sit and take his care. You give back."

Grace's hands tightened on the steering wheel. "If you think only dominants know how to love, you don't know your pack-mates very well."

Bethany's response was startling. Laughing, she leaned in to kiss Grace on the cheek with open affection. "Just checking you've got spine—you'll need it with Coop. That boy likes to get his own way. Good luck."

AFTER helping to demolish the food Grace had brought, Cooper nixed her offer to stay and help with the tree, receiving unexpected support for his decision from Todd.

"Can't risk those hands," the engineer said. "You're a surgeon with the systems."

"Anyway," Bill added, shoving a hand through his blond mop, "this shouldn't take long. Now that we have it down, all we have to do is cut this baby up enough that we can clear the road. Rest of the cleanup can be done tomorrow by a novice team."

Grace folded her arms, expression mutinous. "Fine. But I'll wait and drive you all back to the den."

Todd burst out laughing, followed by Bill. When Grace scowled, Cooper tipped up her chin and kissed it off in a quick, light caress that wouldn't startle or scare her wolf. "You're with three dominants." He grinned, his lips brushing hers as he spoke. "All of us have a well-known and occasionally mocked tendency for wanting to control the vehicles we're in. What do you think your chances are of retaining the wheel?"

"Okay, I'll give you that one." An amused smile, but her eyes skated toward Todd and Bill, who weren't even pretending not to watch them, shit-eating grins on their faces.

Cupping her hip in a protective caress, Cooper pointed a finger at the two men. "Sworn to secrecy."

"Aw, come on, Coop!" was the joint refrain, but he glared them into agreement . . . and later that night, got another shy, sexy kiss from Grace for his trouble, her wolf rubbing up against her skin with an affection his own returned.

But even though he fell into bed bone tired, the exquisite taste of Grace in his mouth, he dreamed of horror. "No! *No!*"

THE next day was a crazy one. One of the major air conduits just up and died without warning, pulling Grace's entire team out of bed at six a.m. Paul, their air-systems expert, had them working nonstop until after five, when he decreed the job complete. Tired but pleased, they slapped one another on the back, then went their separate ways.

It was only after she'd showered that Grace realized Cooper hadn't said anything about seeing her tonight when he'd dropped by to check on the progress of the repair. Of course, it had hardly been a private moment—and Cooper was doing his best to give her time to get used to their relationship in private before it inevitably went public.

It wouldn't be too much longer, she knew that, especially after the kiss at the tree site. Predatory changeling males, regardless of their place in the hierarchy, were all openly possessive. The fact that Cooper had fought his instincts on the point this long . . . well, it simply made her melt for him even more.

"I like your kisses, bad girl."

Toes curling, she went to check her messages, only to discover one from her brother but nothing from Cooper. And she knew for a fact he was in the den, so he hadn't been pulled away.

Frowning, she sat down on her bed and thought things through. Given that Cooper had made it crystal clear he intended to have her . . . keep her, added to the reality that dominant males went after the women they wanted no holds barred, the fact that he'd expended no effort whatsoever to pin her down for tonight could only mean one thing—he was treating her as his, as if their spending time together was a given.

It was a very subtle form of dominance play, and no matter how much woman and wolf both adored Cooper, Grace had no intention of being led on a leash.

Chapter 7

COOPER'S BLOOD WENT ice-cold when no one seemed to know where Grace had gone. He pulled out his cell phone to call her, knowing she'd see it as a controlling move on his part, but he needed to know she was okay, was *safe*. The rain was only a drizzle for the moment, but that didn't mean the roads weren't dangerous.

"Hey, Coop." Shamus ran over before he could input the call. "Emma's abandoned me for dinner out with Grace and Vivienne. You want to grab a pizza?"

It took everything Cooper had to hide his relief. "I'm heading out," he managed to say. "Need to run. But I think a few of the others are hanging in the break room."

"We'll save you a slice." Shamus turned, ran backward for a few feet. "I was just outside. Still raining on and off, but the wind's gone flat and the moon's actually out—best view is past the twin waterfalls."

"Thanks." Cooper shoved his cell phone back into his pocket as the senior soldier disappeared around the corner, and bracing his palm against the stone wall of the den, he gave in to a shudder. He knew his response was extreme, would scare Grace, seeming to spring from a level of possessiveness that went far beyond what might be expected from a SnowDancer lieutenant. No woman wanted to be with a man who wouldn't permit her to breathe, whose care became a cage. Which was why he had to get a grip on himself before she saw him again.

Growling under his breath, he made his way outside and ran until he could think through the chaotic haze of his emotions. He wanted to go after Grace with every cell of his being, needed desperately to scent her alive and well, but he'd already miscalculated once. Making his way to the den instead, damp but not cold, he showered, then grabbed some dinner from the kitchen and spent the next couple of hours working in his office.

As was usual when he was alone in his office at this time of night, more than one member of the pack dropped by to talk or ask for advice. It kept him busy, and he was fine for the first half hour, okay for the second. The third and fourth were like having nails pounded into his flesh. The only thing that made it bearable was knowing Grace wasn't alone and that Shamus was surely in touch with Emma. Anything happened, Cooper would have the information within minutes.

Finally, he saw the women's vehicle come in, the lights cutting through the dark of the night outside before the SUV slid silently into the underground garage. He forced himself to give Grace fifteen minutes to change and settle in, then stalked down to knock on her door.

This time, he attracted a few interested glances from passing packmates. It was late for a man to be going to a woman's room, and as Grace's boss had returned that afternoon, Cooper couldn't excuse it on the grounds of a systems emergency. He knew they were close to busted. *Good.* He needed people to know she was his, that he should be told if she was ever in any trouble.

The lack of secrecy would also give him room to court her as outrageously as he liked.

When the door opened to reveal her clad in pajama pants of pale blue fleece featuring fluffy white sheep, along with a soft black T-shirt that caressed her with the finesse of a lover, her hair tumbling over her shoulders in a dark cloud, he had to take a deep, deep breath to restrain his instinctive response to thrust his hands into the luxuriant mass, tilt back her neck, and bite.

She'd scared him.

He *hated* the feeling, but he also knew his scars weren't Grace's fault. She'd acted as any female wolf would with a man who'd dared take her for granted; she could have no idea of the violent response she'd incited in him. And if he had his way, she never would. Cooper didn't want his nightmares to shadow the life he intended to build with her.

"Hello, Grace." He leaned against the doorjamb, doing nothing to hide his appraisal of her beautiful body. When her nipples pushed against the well-washed fabric of her tee as her breath hitched, he realized she wasn't wearing a bra, and self-control became one hell of a test. "I left my bag here the other day."

"What?" Pulse thudding in her throat, she swallowed. "Oh, yes, I put it right here." She went to get it, paused, turned back. "You did it on purpose."

Smile deepening, he let his gaze linger on her lips. "Did I?"

Chest rising and falling in an increasingly rapid rhythm, she swallowed. "You're being pushy." It was a husky accusation.

He shrugged, his wolf prowling to the surface of his mind. "It's who I am, you know that." His gentleness with her hadn't been feigned—he adored coaxing and petting Grace, but she needed to see and accept this side of him, too. He'd intended to ease her into it, but she'd changed his plans with her rebellion, aroused the primal core of his nature. "Your fault, you know."

Her hand clenched on the edge of the door. "Mine?"

"You did challenge me tonight." In her own way. "You know how wolf males react to a private challenge from a female."

Her cheeks colored that pretty color he wanted to lick up from every inch of her skin. "It wasn't a challenge."

"Don't be a liar now." A slow tease. "I got the message." He straightened from his leaning position to brace his hands on the top of the doorway, blocking her from the view of those in the corridor. This woman was his. He didn't want to share. Not tonight. "Invite me in, bad girl."

"If you got the message," she murmured, standing firm, "you know I'm a little mad at you."

Strong, sexy, beautiful woman. "I think I can coax you out of a little mad." Dropping one hand, letting her see it so she wouldn't startle, he ran a finger over her cheek. "All you need to do is open the door a fraction wider."

Grace shivered . . . and stepped back. Not bothering to see if they had an audience, he walked inside, and this time, he shut the door. But rather than blocking the exit, he shifted to lean against the wall beside her bed, the shoji screen sitting neatly folded in the opposite corner, and crooked a finger. "You know you want to."

Rather than scowling at his arrogance as he'd expected, Grace frowned, her eyes looking into his for a single, compelling instant. "Cooper, what's wrong?" she said, and he wondered what he'd betrayed, what she'd seen. "There's—"

Not giving her a chance to continue, he reached back and pulled off his T-shirt. Her gasp was a stroke to his ego, but he wanted more than that. Needed more than that, the irrational fear that had gripped him by the throat having left raw edges in its wake that hurt with every breath.

Dropping the T-shirt to the floor, he prowled across the space that separated them, hotly conscious of the way she watched him, her arousal an erotic musk in the air.

Thank God.

It was a heartfelt thought, because the fact was, his body was more than a bit beat up, had a number of scars—even changeling-quick healing couldn't fix everything. Added to that, he was a big man. Big enough to intimidate—which was the response he caught a faint hint of in Grace's eyes just as he reached her.

"Touch me," he said, stripping his need bare. "I promise I won't touch you in return until you ask." Make no demands that might force her wolf to react with throat-baring submission, savaging the fragile trust that had grown between them.

"That's not fair on you." Quiet words, her eyes continuing to eat him up in a way that had his cock at rigid attention.

"I'll never complain if you have your hands . . . or your mouth, on any part of my body." He might go insane, but it would be a glorious madness.

Her breasts caught his attention as she sucked in a breath, her nipples tight peaks against her T-shirt. Mouth watering, he put his hands behind his back and locked his arms by gripping one of his wrists with his other hand. "I," he murmured, "give you permission to punish me for my behavior tonight."

"It doesn't sound like you're dreading it," she said, placing her hands on his chest.

He bit back a growl of demand. "Trust me, it's torture."

Lips curved, she began to shape and pet him with a distinct feminine possessiveness in every stroke, that of a woman who considered him her personal property. God, it felt good. He couldn't hold back a groan when she skated her fingernails over his nipples. She paused . . . and repeated the caress.

"Christ, Grace." Shuddering, he dipped his head forward.

Not the least hesitant, she rose up on tiptoe and kissed him, her hands gripping his waist. He took full advantage, coaxing and seducing with his mouth, his tongue. She let him in, and when he sucked on her tongue, she echoed the intimate caress, her breasts pressed against his chest, her nipples hard little points he wanted to roll between his fingertips, tug and squeeze until he knew exactly what made her moan, what made her writhe and go molten around his cock.

Breath ragged, Grace broke the intimate contact to press an openmouthed kiss over his left nipple. Pleasure rocked his entire body, almost breaking him in two. When she repeated the caress on the other side of his chest, he had to use teeth-gritting control to keep from throwing her onto her bed, tugging off her pajama pants, and mounting her in the most primitive of matings. He wanted to see that curvy behind move against him, wanted to reach down and play with her heavy breasts as he slid his cock in and out of her in a pounding rhythm.

He just *wanted*.

And since he couldn't touch, he began to talk. "You know how I'd like to take you the first time we're together?" Too fast, he was moving too fast, being too aggressive for his sexy Grace, but he couldn't stop.

Nails pricking his chest. "How?"

"Face-to-face, you spread out under me, your legs locked around my hips, and my cock buried balls deep in you."

She swallowed at the raw sexuality of his words, but he wasn't finished.

"I'd kiss you over and over because I love the taste of you, but I'd have to play with those pretty, pretty breasts. I'd suck and lick and maybe even bite a little. You don't mind teeth, do you, Grace?"

A shake of her head, her skin flushed, the opulent scent of her arousal a drug.

"Good." He dropped his gaze to her breasts. "While I was fucking you slow and deep, so damn deep, I'd close my hand over one of your breasts, squeeze and pet. And you know what else?"

"What?" A near-soundless question.

"I'd look into your eyes the entire time."

GRACE was having trouble thinking. Serious trouble. But she knew one thing: the lieutenant was using the addictive pleasure of intimate skin privileges to distract her. And doing a brilliant job of it. Arousal gripped her by the throat, turned her skin so sensitive that her clothes felt abrasive, the delicate flesh between her thighs plump and wet.

So it was as well that her wolf danced away without warning, darkly conscious that the man she petted with such proprietary hands could overpower her in a heartbeat. How could she think of being naked in his arms when she couldn't guarantee her submission would be a conscious, voluntary response, rather than being born of primitive instinct?

"I'd look into your eyes the entire time."

What if all he saw was a submissive looking back at him, whimpering and quiescent, Grace's human personality overwhelmed into obedience?

Fear taking an icy hold on her heart, she stepped away. "Put on your T-shirt." So she could concentrate, could think.

Cooper growled.

Jumping, she lowered her head. "Please."

"Damn it, Grace." He wrenched on the tee, impatient and angry. "I wasn't growling because you gave me an order. I was growling because I wasn't done playing with you."

For some reason, that snarling response made her relax, chance a peek up. "Does sexual frustration always make you so bad tempered?"

Another growl that had her wolf clawing at her to shut up.

"Go on," he said in a low tone that was a dare. "Keep on poking the hungry wolf, see how naked it gets you."

Heat burned her cheeks, but she wasn't going to allow him to do this to her again. "Cooper, I'm not an idiot. I know something was bothering you when you knocked on the door."

He made a sound of teeth-gritting aggravation. "I was angry you took off without telling me, okay? Didn't think you'd like it if I pointed it out."

It made sense . . . yet what she'd glimpsed had been far more violent an emotion, somehow *old*. Akin to the hurt she'd seen in his eyes at the site of the slip. "You don't have to pretend around me," she said, uncomfortable with shoving at his defenses but frustrated enough by his refusal to even acknowledge he was in pain that she had to make the attempt.

"Grace, no male wants to further piss off an already pissed-off woman whom he has every intention of talking into bed as fast as possible." He ran his hands over his scalp. "Goddamnit, now I'm yelling."

"So? I don't want you to turn down the volume of your personality or your emotions," she said, dismayed at the idea. "That's not healthy on any level for you." It would drive him slowly insane. "If that's what you're having to do when we're together"—the thought *hurt,* so much—"you know it won't work."

His growl raised every hair on her body. "It damn well will work." The statement of a man used to getting what he wanted.

Stubborn, infuriating male.

She went to open her mouth to argue, but she'd pushed her wolf's limits long enough. It clawed to the surface, wrenching the reins from her hands, and doing what it deemed necessary in order to pacify an angry dominant.

A submissive whimper left her throat.

Cooper froze.

Chapter 8

GRACE COLLAPSED TO her knees as the door closed behind Cooper, tremors quaking her frame.

He'd cupped her cheek, rubbed his own against her temple with an affection that soothed some of her wolf's panic, before saying, "Good night, Grace," and leaving.

It had happened exactly as she'd feared, her nature unable to stand the sheer, unleashed force of Cooper's dominance. In her lupine form, she'd have tucked her tail between her legs, maybe even rolled over onto her back to expose the vulnerable flesh of her belly.

Sobs escaped her mouth, filled her chest until she could hardly breathe.

She was simply *not built* to handle the hot-blooded passions and brutal depth of emotion of a man of Cooper's strength. Nothing could change the very makeup of her being. What if the next time it happened, they were in bed? What if Cooper was inside her?

Then he'll stop.

The answer came from the tiny part of her that wasn't a complete mess. And it was true. Cooper would always stop—as he'd done today. But that didn't mean she had any right to put him in that position, any right to demand he muzzle the raw beauty of his sexuality, his personality. What she'd said, it was an absolute, unavoidable truth—for him to strangle his instincts would be a horribly damaging act.

It would kill him and destroy her.

"I don't want to let him go."

The whispered confession was a slap.

If she couldn't bear to set him free, couldn't bear to imagine another woman's hands on his skin, another woman's lips on his own, then she had to find a way to deal. But how?

It was as she was washing her tear-ravaged face that she realized she had to talk to someone who'd been through this. Except no one had. Yes, she knew—was friends with—any number of submissives who'd mated with or lived in permanent loving relationships with dominants. Not one of those relationships, however, mirrored the extreme power gulf that separated her and Cooper.

"There must be *someone*."

Determined to discover an answer, she was on her second cup of coffee when she remembered the woman who'd been her nursery school teacher while Grace lived in the Sierra Nevada den as a child. Twelve when her family shifted dens, she well remembered the lovely woman with the stunning indigo eyes who'd always had a hug and a word of praise for her long after she'd left the nursery.

Tarah was a submissive not much stronger than Grace. Her mate, Abel, by contrast, was a very strong dominant, a soldier who held a senior position in the pack. One of their daughters was a lieutenant, the other a submissive close to Grace in the hierarchy. If anyone would understand the forces tearing Grace apart, it was Tarah.

Not giving herself time to change her mind, she looked up Tarah's number in the internal pack directory and input the call, realizing too late that it was past ten at night.

Abel was the one who answered. "Almost threw me," he said after a short pause, "but I never forget one of Tarah's kids. How are you, Grace darling?"

The gentleness of the question told her he'd sensed her distress. "Good." She met the deep gray of his eyes for the barest second. "I know it's late. I'm sorry. I wanted to talk to Tarah and didn't think about the time."

"She's up. Hold on."

Tarah took a seat in front of the comm a second later, her eyes the same vivid hue Grace remembered from childhood, her voice brimming with joyful welcome. "It's so good to see you, Grace."

They chitchatted for a few minutes before Tarah turned

those perceptive eyes off-screen. "Darling, give us a few minutes, will you? Girl talk."

Abel snorted. "If I know you, it'll be more like an hour." Coming into view, he tipped up Tarah's head to claim a kiss, then glanced at Grace. "You make sure you drop by if you're ever in the area."

"Now," Tarah said once her mate was gone, her face holding a kindness that was innate, "what's the matter?"

Grace forced herself to describe what had happened, found herself on the brink of tears again by the end. "How can I be with him if I can't trust my wolf not to regress to instinctive behavior? As if I don't know him, don't have faith in him?" His lover's trust was integral to a dominant's sense of self. Steal that from Cooper and she might as well stab him in the heart.

Tarah's expression was sympathetic. "It'll take work, I won't lie about that. But it *is* doable, and when it works. . . . Abel is my rock and my heartbeat."

The haunting depth of love in that statement made Grace yearn. "Is there anything you can tell me that might help?"

"Compromise is the magic word, just as it is in most relationships." A wry smile crept over her face. "Though I should warn you, a dominant's idea of compromise is sometimes very 'flexible.'"

Grace's laugh was a watery sound. "I can imagine." Taking a shaky breath to settle herself, she said, "What worries me most is the level of control he has to keep over himself. It's constant. Does—" She halted, suddenly conscious of how intimate a question she was about to ask.

Tarah tapped the comm screen as if tapping the nose of a recalcitrant pup. "Ask what you need to—and to answer that last question, Abel doesn't hold back. He doesn't need to, because my wolf *knows* he never expects submission from me, even when I'm at my most defenseless." A penetrating gaze. "You can't rush the development of that trust, because it's not a conscious choice. It comes from the animal within—for the wolf, learning to judge a predator is a survival mechanism."

Tarah's words made too much sense. "Thank you for being so honest."

"You're welcome, sweetheart." Her long-ago teacher gave her a mischievous smile. "Tease him, Grace, play with him, give him the chase he needs, and take the time you need. There's something to be said for anticipation."

Later, considering everything Tarah had said, Grace stripped and shifted. It was agony and it was ecstasy, the shift separating her into a million particles of light and color before coalescing into the wolf that was her other half. She shook herself to settle her new skin, then hopped onto the bed and allowed the animal to rise to the surface of her mind, felt it sigh at the freedom, sigh, too, at the lingering scent of dark amber and wild earth.

Ours.

Yes, agreed the human part of her, *he's ours.*

COOPER decided he must hate himself as he walked into his bedroom at just past one a.m., after attempting to wear himself out in the gym. He knew Grace couldn't help her reaction—and that had been fine until the dreams. He'd had the strength to be patient, had actually been having an intoxicating kind of fun coaxing her to him kiss by kiss. Now, however, he had a hell of a time maintaining his hold on his more primitive emotions.

Showering under a cold spray in an effort to control his rebellious body, he shook himself off wolf fashion afterward and pulled on some sweatpants. Then he slumped on his back in bed. Sleep, of course, was a vain hope with his cock in a vise, and it wasn't as if he'd wake well rested.

Christ, what was he going to do when he and Grace did become lovers?

No way would he ever leave her alone afterward, but he couldn't fall asleep, didn't want her to hear him screaming like a child. "And how long do you think you can function without sleep, genius?"

Growling, he got up and decided to make someone else miserable, too, the comm his weapon of choice.

"Whoever you are," came the voice rough with the gravel of deep sleep, "I will hunt you down, tear out your spleen, and eat it fried with mushrooms."

"Creative," he said to Riaz.

His fellow lieutenant's sleep-mussed hair appeared on the

screen, followed by the rest of his face, as if he was levering up on his elbow in bed. "Coop? Is this an emergency?"

"Yes. My cock's about to break in half."

"If it was anyone but you . . ." Disappearing off-screen, Riaz returned with damp strands of hair around his face, eyes of dark gold no longer hazy with sleep. "Right, tell me what's up."

So Cooper did. He wasn't a big talker, especially when it came to something this important, but he and Riaz had been friends since childhood, knew each other inside out. The other man would understand what this meant.

"You're really gone for her," Riaz murmured when he paused. "Is she your mate?"

"Yeah." The mating dance hadn't begun, but that was a minor detail as far as Cooper was concerned—soon as her wolf was ready, it would. "Only, she doesn't know it yet."

"Uh-huh."

"I think I want to punch you." A good drag-down fight was what he needed, but in this mood, he'd slaughter anyone but another one of the lieutenants, or the alpha. "You don't know how lucky you are to be sitting pretty halfway across the state."

Riaz's grin was without remorse. "You'd laugh, too, if it was me gaga over a woman."

Cooper rubbed a hand over his cropped hair, wondered absently if he should just shave everything off like a few of the other guys. Then again, some of their women hadn't exactly been impressed by the look. So maybe he should check with Grace first. And if that made him pussy-whipped, he didn't give a shit. He *wanted* her to care about what he did with his body, wanted her to consider him her damn business.

"I need help, Riaz," he said to the man with whom he'd first strategized about how to attract female attention—they'd been gawky teens at the time. "How do I court her?"

"Didn't you say you were with her tonight?"

"Yes." He hadn't mentioned any specific details, just that he was frustrated in the aftermath.

"Well, it's been less than a week—if your submissive's allowing you close enough that you've got blue balls, I'd say you're already doing things right. We both know you're a bit much for even some of the dominant females."

Cooper winced because Riaz was right. He was demanding,

in bed and out. Even when he tried to tone it down, it only lasted so long. "Grace can handle me." She had to—because he'd been waiting for her for a lifetime. "Though maybe I should try a more subtle approach, at least for a while."

"I gotta ask, Coop. You sure about this?" His friend's eyes were night-glow in the dark of his bedroom. "Your Grace, she hasn't got any claws, not in comparison to you."

Cooper bristled. "It feels righter than anything else in my life; she's tougher than everyone thinks. She's already challenged me once. I know she'll go toe-to-toe with me once her wolf accepts I'll never use my dominance against her."

"In that case, balls to the wall, man." Riaz yawned. "No guts, no glory."

"Why are you spouting aphorisms at me?"

"Because it's two-fucking-thirty in the morning and I need to be up for a six a.m. shift."

"Wimp."

Riaz gave him the finger. "Get some sleep and chase your wolf tomorrow." Another yawn. "And Coop? Forget about subtle. That's not your style."

AT nine the next morning, Grace stared at the extravagant bunch of flowers that had been delivered to her office a few minutes ago, direct from the greenhouse attached to the den. Overflowing with color and texture and scent, though she saw he hadn't forgotten her favorite daisies, it was a blatant public declaration of intent.

Then there was the card. According to the grinning juvenile who'd delivered the flowers, Cooper had inserted it into the bouquet himself, promising a horrible death to anyone other than Grace who dared open it.

Like I said. Lots and lots of foreplay. xx Coop.

Blushing, even as relief coursed through her that he hadn't been scared off last night, she tucked the scandalous card into her pocket just as the comm panel chimed an incoming call.

"Indigo," she said, acknowledging the lieutenant with a split-second of eye contact. "Chief's with the healer—he twisted his ankle this morning. Said to tell you he'll get in touch later today."

"No problem," Indigo said in a distracted tone. "Those are some gorgeous flowers on your desk."

"Yes. From Cooper," Grace admitted, knowing the gossip would reach the Sierra Nevada den by the end of the day anyway.

She'd underestimated the speed of the pack grapevine.

"I figured." An open grin. "So . . . why do you look mortified?" Her tone cooled. "You don't share his interest?"

"Of course I do." Until her entire body ached for his touch. "God, what red-blooded woman would turn away from a man like Cooper?"

Indigo laughed. "Sorry about that," she said a little sheepishly. "I know it's none of my business, but he's my friend. I'd hate for him to be hurt." A pause before she added, "I can see he's made a good choice—you're smart, sexy . . . and without a doubt want to jump his bones."

Grace groaned at the sly tease. "Everyone is going to be watching us now."

She was right. And that was before Cooper stole her away for lunch since he had to be on night shift on a perimeter section and wouldn't see her for dinner. "Did you like the flowers?" he asked, bracing his arm above her head on the tree trunk on which she leaned.

He looked so pleased with himself that she felt a surge of wild affection. "Yes." And because there was no pain in his eyes today, she didn't bring up the worry that continued to simmer in her at whatever it was that was hurting him. Instead, she petted him with her words, her hands. "I'll miss you tonight."

"Tomorrow, you're all mine." The rough promise melted her bones.

Of course, her family wasn't so excited about the news of her relationship with Cooper. The only way Grace kept them from coming down to meddle in the situation was to threaten to never return home for a visit again. When she finally got off the comm with them, she fell into bed, her wolf exhausted by the aggression.

Chapter 9

TORMENTED BY EROTIC dreams in which she indulged in the
most delicious of sins with Cooper, Grace came into her office
the next day to find it filled with balloons and her workmates
hanging around with huge grins on their faces.

The part of her that had been forced into rebellion in an
effort to fight her family's overprotectiveness thought she
should be annoyed at the way Cooper was accelerating things,
but she looked beyond that, to the core of who she was and
knew she was charmed. This male, her wolf said, knew how
to make his woman feel good.

The truth was, she didn't need the reins of their courtship,
wouldn't be comfortable with them. And while it occasionally
made her blush, she could deal with the pack's good-natured
and gentle teasing. Of course, Cooper had to keep ratcheting
it up a notch—boxes of fine chocolates delivered to her home
and office, an honest-to-God gorilla love-gram that had her
entire crew in hysterics . . . and gifts far more private.

Like the exotic perfume he insisted on dabbing on her wrists
himself after making her a home-cooked dinner, and the midnight blue silk sheets she found on her bed one day when she
went home midmorning to pick up something she'd forgotten.
Her breath caught, her fingers unable to resist touching the
exquisite fabric, her mind supplying her with vivid images of
what Cooper would look like sprawled on those sheets, all
darkly bronzed skin and heavy muscle.

Her fingers curled into her palms, a needy whimper escaping her lips. Because in one area, Cooper wasn't pushing, the
skin privileges they shared limited to long, lazy kisses that had

addicted both sides of her nature. She knew it was on purpose, that he was seducing her one small, luscious bite at a time, taking care not to set off her wolf's survival instincts as he had that night in her bedroom, but she ached, sexual frustration a slow burning ember in her gut.

Until when Cooper tracked her down that afternoon, she said, "You're driving me insane."

He went motionless where he'd taken a seat in the access corridor beside her crouching form. "Want me to stop?"

No! "I . . ." And because he mattered, because she never wanted him to think he couldn't be who he was with her, she found the courage to say, "I like it when you're bad."

He reached out to run his hand over her thigh and the embers glowed a deep, hot red. "You have no idea how much I enjoy corrupting you." A squeeze. "It's going to make me crazy to think of you lying on those sheets, your skin creamy, your curves bitable. I'll have to stroke myself to sleep, and damn, it'll be a pale substitute."

His sexuality was so raw, so honest, far more earthy than her own . . . but she was starting to believe she might just be able to handle it. It aroused her to lush readiness when he talked that way—and he knew it. "I did," she murmured, deciding to torment him in turn.

"What?"

Putting down the tool she'd been using, she went to her knees, placed one hand on his shoulder and leaned in to whisper in his ear. "Stroke myself." She'd been a mess of need by the time he'd walked her home the previous night.

His growl echoed over the stone walls. "Witch."

She laughed, the sound soft, husky. He made her feel strong and wild and brave, her wolf daring to rub up against his own. She wanted, needed to take care of him in turn—it continued to frustrate her that he'd gone stubborn on her when it came to whatever it was that was putting increasing marks of strain on his face.

"Just tired from the late shifts. Don't worry about it."

She knew it was far more than that, but even a hint of confrontation on the issue made him shut down, and there was a point beyond which her wolf simply refused to push. It worried her on the innermost level, because their relationship could not survive if he wouldn't share his problems—it would savage her to see him hurting without being able to do anything about it, make her feel useless rather than a partner.

Grace had no intention of permitting that to happen, and if confronting him about it wasn't going to work, then she'd pet, adore, and persuade the truth from him. Submissives could be as relentlessly stubborn as any dominant—and this one was falling too hard for her man not to do everything in her power to rid the shadows that haunted him. "Vivienne told me there's a fair not far from us," she said. "Will you go with me?"

His eyes were ringed with a fine circle of yellow when he answered, and she knew the wolf was looking out at her. "If you promise to go necking with me afterward."

The idea of necking with Cooper made the embers turn molten. Which was how she ended up walking hand in hand with him through the happy chaos of the fair that had set up about a half hour's drive from the edge of den territory. He bought her cotton candy, and reminded of a childhood incident, she found herself telling him about her family, both the present and the past.

"I still miss my mama and papa," she admitted. "I feel disloyal to Milena and James for it, but I think they understand."

"Of course they do." He hugged her to his side. "Just because your parents are gone doesn't mean you'll ever forget the way they loved you and how you loved them back." Fingers playing with her hair.

"I didn't understand for a long time that they were never coming back. When I did . . . I cried all night, until I made myself sick." She reached up to link her hand with the one he had on her shoulder. "You understand." He'd lost his parents, too, though not in the violence that had taken her own.

"Yes." A rough agreement before he stole the last of her cotton candy and teased her into a smile, then led her to the dazzlingly lit up spokes of the old-fashioned Ferris wheel. "Having fun?" he asked as they slid into the gently swinging bench seat.

"Yes." She snuggled into the heat of him after he pulled down the safety bar and their seat moved forward a spot. "Are you?"

"Yes, but I'm really waiting for the necking." His fingers

brushed over the delicate fabric of the fitted sunshine yellow cardigan she wore buttoned up over a white tank. "You're cold."

"A little. I should've brought a jacket."

He held her closer as they slowly reached the top of the wheel, the view dazzling. Leaning down, he nuzzled a kiss above her ear. "Or we could make out right here, warm ourselves up."

His caresses felt good. Possessive. Regardless of all else, Grace loved that about Cooper, loved that she didn't have to wonder where she fit in his life. When he bit down on her lower lip, she bit back. His chest rumbled against her breasts. "Do that again."

The low-voiced request made her blush—and tip her face up for another kiss. He gave her that, more, before running his lips over her jaw and down her throat. Grace was so used to his kisses that she forgot he'd never gone for her neck before. It shocked her when fear overwhelmed her in a brutal wave, her wolf telling her not to move, not to incite the predator who had his teeth so close to her carotid, her jugular.

He heard the rapid stutter of her heart, sensed her incipient panic, because he raised his head at once. "I'm not demanding submission." It was an irritated growl. "When and if I ever do, it'll be because we're playing a bedroom game. Got it?"

Grace's wolf quivered at the anger in his voice . . . but it was also aware of the protective way he continued to hold her. "How would you like it if an alpha wolf went for your throat?" she said instead of backing down.

Cooper smiled, slow and wide, because there'd been no fear in those words, only feminine outrage. If he had to make Grace mad to get her to forget the dominance imbalance between them, he'd frustrate, aggravate, and annoy her as much as possible. "I'd tell Hawke he wasn't my type."

A feminine snarl as the wheel began to sweep around at full speed.

Delighted, he tipped up her chin and nipped playfully at her nose. "God, I hope you make that sound when we're naked."

She nipped back. Hard.

"Ouch." He rubbed his nose. "That wasn't nice."

Glaring at him, she tucked her head back against his chest. He allowed himself to grin, his wolf smug. Grace might not realize it, but they'd just taken one hell of a big step in their relationship. Pretty soon, he'd have his engineer snarling at him in bed while she raked her nails down his back.

Grumpy as she was with him, however, and given the failure of his earlier attempt, he wasn't expecting her to remind him he'd promised to take her necking. Instantly aroused, he drove them deep into a secluded part of the forested territory around the den. "Come here," he said once he'd brought the vehicle to a stop, his wolf in his voice.

Grace shivered and undid her safety belt, but instead of obeying his order, she slid back her door. "Outside." A whisper.

It was cold out, and he didn't like her being uncomfortable, but he had the sudden realization that his submissive lover was trying to set things up so she'd be far less likely to panic. Sliding back his own door, he walked out to meet her at the front of the car. Already, he could see nerves in her movements. Not giving her time to stew, he picked her up and perched her on the hood, moving to stand between her legs.

She gasped, went still, her hands on his shoulders. But then his sweet, sexy, incredibly strong Grace said, "Can I kiss your neck?"

He groaned. "Anytime."

Angling her head, one hand cupping his nape, she brushed her lips shyly along the column in an intimacy he rarely allowed. The majority of dominants were choosy about who they permitted that particular caress. He knew that was why she'd asked. If she'd attempted to touch him there without permission, implicit or explicit, he might've reacted in anger—except of course, it was Grace. He would've done exactly what he was doing now and held her to him with a gentle grip in her hair.

Shuddering at the pleasure of feeling her tongue flick out to taste him, he let the wolf rumble in his chest, felt her arousal scent the air. "I want to lick you up," he said, playing the fingers of his free hand over her hip. "Spread your thighs and suck and bite and taste until you come."

A tremor rippled over Grace's frame. "It wouldn't take long." The intimate whisper was a fist around his rigid erection.

Teeth grazed his throat an instant later.

"Grace." He fisted his hand more tightly in her hair. "You owe me two now."

He felt her thighs tense as she squeezed, hazy brown eyes meeting his for a blinding instant as she lifted her head from his neck . . . to lean back a little, arch her throat in an act of conscious trust that humbled him. Shuddering, he ran a finger down the slender column. "Such pretty skin, so easy to mark." He stroked again. "Should I suck hard, Grace? Leave a bruise no one will mistake?"

She whimpered but didn't change her position, and that sound, it wasn't one of fear-drenched submission.

"I think you like that idea." Leaning in, he flicked his tongue over her pulse, drawing the erotic musk of her into his lungs. "What if I did the same thing to these beautiful breasts, hmm?" A brush of his knuckles over one ripe mound. "Those particular marks would be for my eyes alone. I'd lick at each until it faded, suck another."

Her arms rose, one going around his shoulder, the hand of the other on the back of his head. "Stop talking."

The breathless command made his lips curve. "But you like it." Her arousal spiked with every one of his words. "When I have you open and wet under me, I'll make it a point to tell you—"

Her mouth closed over his. Groaning, he held her in place, devouring her lips, sucking on her tongue, drowning in the scent of her until she pushed at his shoulders. "Air," she gasped.

Flattening his hands on the cold metal of the hood, he heaved out breath after breath, his head hanging low. He wanted another kiss, wasn't sure he could control himself from going further. Not with her so aroused and soft around him. But he knew she wasn't ready, wasn't at the point where she'd trust him not only in front of her, but at her back. He wanted everything before he tumbled her into bed, because there was no way he was going to be able to resist fulfilling his fantasies about watching her move against him as he mounted her.

Warm fingers on his nape. "Why did you shave off most of your hair?"

"Don't you like it?" His wolf stretched out.

"I didn't say that." She continued to stroke him. "You look good either way."

He wasn't a vain man, but he enjoyed being petted by Grace. "For convenience."

"I like the way the bristles feel." Her cheek rubbing against his temple. "Did you really get this scar"—a single finger trailing over his cheek—"from fighting a rabid bear?"

"Yes," he admitted. "I was young, a bit of an idiot." A juvenile, he'd come upon the bear chasing two petrified young wolves. He'd thrown the pups onto a high branch and taken on the bear when it became clear the maddened animal wouldn't allow itself to be led away from the children. "I managed to avoid getting bitten, but it clawed me. This wound and the one on my back didn't heal right for some reason."

"They only make you sexier."

He arched his neck in a silent invitation, had the pleasure of feeling her suck hard enough to leave a mark. Possessive wolf.

"And," she said, licking over the mark that delighted him on every level, "there were pups' lives at stake." Nipping kisses along his throat, the scent of peaches warmed against skin a sensual caress. "You'd do it again if necessary, wouldn't you?"

"Yeah, I guess I'm still a bit of an idiot." He held her face against him, hissed out a breath as she bit down over his pulse. "That's three, bad girl."

Her thighs squeezed . . . and this time when she tipped back her head, there was only anticipation in the arch of her spine.

That was when he felt it, the wild howling from his wolf that sounded the start of the mating dance.

Chapter 10

GRACE STARED AT the mark on her throat the next morning.

"Now everyone will know you're mine."

Shivering at the memory of the way he'd run his finger over the spot when they finally got home after making out like teenagers, Grace decided not to cover it up with makeup. She was proud to be Cooper's. And it wasn't as if her packmates had any doubts about his intentions, she thought with a delighted laugh, her entire body humming with anticipation for the night to come. The fact her wolf had accepted him at her throat . . .

Happy and excited and a little bit terrified—in the breath-stealing way of a woman who knew a sexy, dangerous man would soon be in her bed—she went to work with a smile on her face, ready to handle the teasing.

What she was not ready for was for her brother and sister to turn up. The two took one look at the unmistakable mark on her throat and lost it, their eyes turning an identical wolf amber swirled with green.

"Are you insane, Grace?" Pia yelled, having dragged her out into the sunshine-drenched forest so they could talk without being overheard, her petite size no indication of her temperament. "The man is a lieutenant! Not only that, he's a lieutenant with a reputation for being a total hard-ass. He eats submissives like you for breakfast!"

Slender Rev was more elegant in his choice of words but no less violent in his repudiation. "You need someone gentle, someone who knows to treat your wolf with care. Thank God we talked Dad out of coming with us—he'd be ready to spill blood after seeing that bruise on your neck."

As she opened her mouth to point out that the "bruise" was a very welcome love bite and that she'd seen *plenty* like it on the throats of Revel's various lovers, her sister went off again, so she folded her arms and waited. Pia would eventually run out of steam, or pause to catch a breath. Meanwhile Rev would wait for Grace's reply to rebut her words. It was an aggravatingly familiar pattern—but she knew the doofuses were freaked out because they loved her.

Her wolf sighed in exasperation, put its head on its paws, and waited.

Except the pattern altered in a rush of fury as another man snarled into the clearing. "Are you all right?" was Cooper's first question, his irises ringed with that distinctive feral yellow that said his wolf was riding him.

"I'm fine." Shifting closer, she put her hand on his chest. "What's the matter?"

"What's the *matter*?" It was a snap of sound. "I get a report that two unfamiliar dominants hauled you bodily out of the den, and you ask me that?"

Suddenly infuriated, she narrowed her eyes. "Don't you use that tone of voice with me." She *would not* take it, not from anyone, and especially not from the man with whom she intended to share skin privileges both intimate and precious.

His response was to shove her behind the wall of muscle that was his body. "You"—his words were snapped out at Pia and Rev—"have three seconds to explain why you dared lay hands on her."

"She's our sister." All black hair and wolf eyes, Pia was magnificent in her anger—she would also be mincemeat if Cooper took offense at her aggression. "And you have no right to use your position to force her to share skin privileges."

Grace wanted to beat her head against a mountain of brick at that ugly statement from her generous-hearted, talk-before-she-thought sister. But she didn't have time, because Cooper's claws had shot out, a violent growl coloring the air. Slipping around his body and gripping at his arms with her own claws when he picked her up and attempted to put her back, she raised her voice to be heard over the cacophony of her siblings' cries for her to get away, to run.

"Cooper. *Cooper!*" Twisting her head when she felt Pia and Revel move, she said, *"No!"*

They halted, unvarnished shock in their expressions. Grace never yelled. Not at them.

Satisfied she'd bought a fraction more time, her feet still dangling off the ground, she leaned forward and did the bravest thing she'd ever done in her life. She bit Cooper hard on the jaw . . . and got no response aside from a slightly irritated snarl, his gaze locked on her siblings. "Cooper," she said, digging her claws deeper into his flesh, "you ignore me now and that's it. We're done."

Her desperate gamble worked, his gaze ricocheting to her, the yellow so bright, it was a shocking kind of beauty. "They challenged me. They said *I hurt you.*"

"I know." Allowing her own wolf to rise to the surface, to guide her, she held his gaze . . . and wasn't afraid, not of his anger. Because even though she'd bitten him, clawed him, he held her with a gentleness that was a silent rebuttal to any accusation of abuse. "And I know I'm asking a great deal, asking you to go against your every instinct, but please don't hurt them."

His lashes came down, thick and straight and inky black. Lifted again. Yellow eyes stared at her, and she knew the wolf was listening but wasn't convinced, especially when her siblings continued to yell in the background.

Blowing out a breath, she concentrated on Cooper and played her ace. "How will you face my mother if you send Pia and Revel home in pieces?"

A pause, then—"I'd tell her she birthed stupid pups."

Dark growls from the pups in question, but she knew the danger had passed. Cooper's response had been sharp, sarcastic. "Thank you," she whispered, because it was a gift he'd given her, this dominant wolf whose instinct it was to respond to any challenge with a show of violent force.

His next words were subvocal, for her ears only. "I like your claws. Next time, use them on my back while I'm inside you." Wrapping an arm around her waist after that wicked request, he tucked her to his side, ignoring her attempts to check what damage she'd done to his forearms.

"I should break every bone in your bodies for that display of insubordination," he said to Pia and Revel, his tone so coldly harsh that her siblings went quiet at last, a little of the color leaching from their skin. "But," he continued, "that would hurt Grace, so you get a single free pass."

Grace met her siblings' eyes. "You do it again, you deserve anything he dishes out." The hierarchy existed for a reason and could only be bent so far. Cooper had gone well beyond what might be expected of him, and she wouldn't ask it of him again.

"You're mad at us." Revel sounded lost.

Sighing, Grace went to walk toward him, found herself restrained. She looked up, asked another gift from Cooper, this man whose wolf was so close to his skin. "Let me go for a second. I need to say good-bye properly."

He released her, but she felt his eyes watching her every step of the way as she went into Revel's arms, squeezing him tight, then doing the same to Pia. Before she could speak, explain to them that her relationship with Cooper made her so, so happy, Revel jerked back, his eyes flicking to Cooper over her shoulder.

"Shit," he muttered, but not low enough that she missed the word. "Come on, Pia. We need to catch that shuttle."

Pia scowled. "What—"

But Revel was already dragging her away, waving good-bye to Grace as he went and calling out to say, "I apologize, Cooper. I didn't get things. Thanks for not shredding us."

When Pia squawked something, Revel hissed at her under his breath. Her sister stopped struggling, twisting her head around to stare at Grace and Cooper, her mouth falling open before an enormous grin crossed her face. "Bye, Grace! I'll tell Mom and Dad you're fine!"

Grace stared after them as they disappeared into the trees, a dark suspicion forming in her gut. There was pretty much only one thing that would've eliminated her siblings' protective worry with such absolute effectiveness. "Cooper, are we in the mating dance?" The male always knew when the dance began, and more than a few of them were less than inclined to tell the female half of the pair until said female was too committed to back away.

"If we are?" A challenge.

"Don't you think you should've told me?"

"No." The infuriating male kissed her. Unlike his coaxing kisses before, this one was a demand, a raw melding of mouths that swept away her foundations and left her floundering.

Then he grinned. "You're not afraid of the big, bad wolf anymore, Grace." Picking her up, he backed her into a tree, her legs going around his waist. "I want you." Clever fingers on the buttons of her shirt.

"Stop."

Hearing the panic, Cooper froze, realizing too late that he'd made a huge tactical error. Though Grace hadn't been frightened by his anger, that didn't mean she was ready to give him the kind of intimate trust he needed from her if they were to share a bed. During the fight, she'd been in that protective mode where a submissive could become oddly fierce, her body high on adrenaline.

But the fact was, she'd only offered him her throat last night. It was way too soon to expect more, any demand apt to push her into an instinctive submission that'd scar them both. "I'm sorry." He pressed his hands palms down on either side of her body. "Baby, I'm so—"

Fingers on his lips. "I'm *not* afraid of your anger," she whispered, eyes flicking up to meet his for a single, brilliant instant. "In fact"—a slow smile—"I'm proud I stood up to a lieutenant and forced him to listen."

He laughed at the adorable hint of smugness, tension snapping. "You also clawed him and he's keeping score."

A nuzzling kiss that told him she was utterly unrepentant, even as her hands stroked over the already healing cuts. "But deep inside," she continued, "the wolf already knew you're built to protect rather than hurt those like me. The other . . . the intimate skin privileges . . . that's new, unexpected, and the vulnerability it asks for . . . it frightens my wolf until it forgets what we've already shared and retreats into the rules of the hierarchy."

Fingers on his nape, petting gently before worried eyes met his for another fleeting moment. "You won't give up, will you?"

"Hell, no. You're mine and I'm keeping you." Conscious all at once that she'd softened around him, and made no protest to the fact he had her pinned against the tree, his hips nestled intimately against her, he brushed his lips over hers. She opened on a sigh, her hands sliding to grip his shoulders.

Much as he wanted to use his own hands, he kept them on the tree trunk, and in spite of the fact she wore his mark on her throat, he didn't attempt to move his mouth down to that sensitive area. Not today, when he'd inadvertently frightened her wolf in his impatience. Today, he'd just kiss her . . . and plan the next step in their dance of courtship.

COMING home after a midnight-to-six shift on the perimeter, Cooper crashed for a few hours. It felt as if the nightmare gripped him in its jaws the instant he closed his eyes and shook, until he woke screaming. Angry and frustrated, he punched the wall until his knuckles bled. It took teeth-gritting control to shake off the dark effects, and he kept his distance from Grace, not wanting her to see the emotional damage with those too-perceptive eyes of hers.

Instead, he sent her miniature peanut-butter tarts to have with her lunch, got a note in return saying he would make her fat . . . as well as a pink cupcake decorated with their initials in a frosting heart. Laughing when he hadn't thought he'd smile today, he bit into the cupcake and sent back a note saying he liked something to hold on to in bed.

When he finally dared go to her that afternoon, her eyes danced at him and he had to steal a kiss, squeezing her hips the entire time. Her touch warmed the ice-cold places deep inside him that no amount of hot water could reach, her fingers soft against his cheek. "You didn't sleep well." She brushed at the smudges under his eyes, a frown marring her brow.

"Yeah, I'll sack out early tonight . . . unless you want to crawl into bed with me? Then I'm sure I could be motivated to stay awake."

The frown didn't disappear. "You're doing it again."

"What?"

"Using sex to muddy up the waters." Cupping his face, she rose on tiptoe and kissed him until he was breathless. "Talk to me."

Chapter 11

HE ALMOST BROKE, but he couldn't, wouldn't, taint her with his pain, didn't want her to feel caged by his need. "Why don't you talk to me? I hear you're going out with your engineering crew."

"Yes, a dinner to celebrate our early completion of the section 4B rehaul." She petted his shoulders in that affectionate way she had of touching him. "Want to come?"

Yes. "No, you have fun. Shamus and I are planning to go shoot some pool." He would not monitor her life just because it drove him insane to not be certain if she was safe. "I'll come by and say good night if we get in at a reasonable hour."

Dark eyes watched him. "I haven't forgotten."

He knew she hadn't. He also knew this was his cross to bear. "There's nothing to worry about."

The night was excruciating. Returning from the bar, he and Shamus got stuck in a traffic jam caused by some kind of protest and didn't get back into the den till after eleven. Aware it was too late to wake Grace up, he nevertheless went past her quarters, hoping against hope to see light under the door. But she was asleep . . . or not in. And there was no one he could ask to confirm without betraying too much, so instead he waited for dawn and turned up to take her out to breakfast.

Where he held her for so long, she knew something was very wrong. He dodged her questions again, though he knew it couldn't go on this way forever. But today, he wanted only to bury himself in the wild joy of courting her. Because she was the bright light in the dark—his wolf swaggered around the den, so delighted with the woman who was his own that he didn't care who razzed him about being smitten.

"Word is she's got you wrapped around her finger," his alpha said to him two days later, an amused look in eyes so pale, they were those of a husky given human form. "They're taking bets on what you'll do next to court her. I heard about the violinist."

"This pack has far too much time on its hands," Cooper muttered, but even sleep deprived as he was, he was in too good a mood to be mad. Because Grace was letting him chase her—and his wolf did love a challenge.

He grinned, thinking of the surprise he'd left her.

GRACE had to physically fight a hot red blush when she walked into her office to see the black box tied with a pink ribbon sitting on her desk. That wasn't what had heat blazing over her skin. It was the discreet symbol on the bottom left corner of the side facing the door—of a high-end lingerie shop.

Vivienne whistled from beside her. "Oh, now the man is playing hardball."

Grace had heard about the male wolves' exhibitionist tendencies during the mating dance, but Cooper knew very well she was shy about certain things. "I'm going to kill him," she muttered, trying to avoid the chief's and Paul's eyes as they walked past her office for the third time, necks craning.

"Don't murder the man until you see what's inside."

"I am not opening this here."

"Come on, Grace." Vivienne nudged the door shut in the men's faces. "There, see? We're all private."

Someone knocked.

When Vivienne scowled and opened the door a peek, Emma poked her head inside, the glossy dark of her bob swinging across her cheek. "I had time before a class, and I heard . . ." Her eyes lighting up when she saw the box, she came in, shut the door, then hit the lock for good measure. "God, he really did do it. Even my guy wasn't this shameless."

Grace's stomach did a little flip. *My guy.* That sounded nice. She'd like to call Cooper her guy. After she killed him. "He could've had this delivered to my room."

"Please, Grace." Vivienne snorted. "The lingerie might be for you, but the message is for everyone else. Hands off sexy Grace. She's all miiiiiiiiine. Grr and snarl and grr some more."

Grace glared at her as Emma dissolved into giggles . . . but when Vivienne started beating her chest, her teeth bared, it was all over. It was some minutes later that she wiped the tears from her eyes and, giving in to their wheedling, tugged on the ribbon. "Breathe a word of what's inside and I'll make sure the lighting in your room gets stuck on bright noonday sun all week."

"Done."

Emma hesitated. "Can I tell Shamus? *Please*." She pressed her hands together. "It might, you know, give him ideas."

"Not a word."

"Okay, okay." Miming zipping her lips, the other woman said, "Open it before I explode."

They crowded around as she lifted the lid to reveal fine white tissue paper. Nestled within was a garment that made all three of them exhale in sheer pleasure. Rather than anything scandalous, Cooper had bought her a thigh-length nightgown in midnight blue, the straps ribbon-thin, the material cut so it would hug her body in all the right places, the fabric itself pure sin.

"Oh, this makes me want to purr." Emma rubbed the midnight blue between her fingertips. "I'm dragging Shamus to this store until he gets the hint."

Vivienne sighed again. "The man gets serious brownie points for taste."

Grace stroked her hand over the garment, in love. She'd never have bought it for herself, would've considered it too decadent, too expensive. "Maybe I won't kill him," she admitted in a dreamy voice, imagining Cooper's big, callused hands sliding the straps from her shoulders, his stubbled jaw rough against her skin, his lips possessive.

Vivienne nudged her shoulder, a knowing gleam in her eye. "Aren't you going to open the other packages?" She pointed inside the box.

"No." Cooper only had a limited store of good behavior, and she was dead certain he'd used it all up on the nightgown.

Her friends made disappointed sounds, begging pitifully,

but Grace held firm, ushering them out the door, and locking it behind the two before returning to the box and surrendering to her own wild curiosity. She'd been right to worry.

"I would," she muttered to him later that night, as she straddled him in the backseat of the SUV he'd signed out of the garage, "have to be in a very, very, *very* good mood to put on that teddy. It might as well be made of tissue." Instead of impossibly delicate red lace that would cup her breasts and glide over her abdomen with no intention of hiding anything.

Cooper, sprawled half naked and magnificent against the seat, grinned. "I liked the hooks."

"That's because they're on the back." Making it clear it wasn't a garment a woman was meant to either put on or take off by herself. "And what do you call that last piece?"

"Panties." Knuckles running down the naked line of her breastbone to her abdomen, exposed due to the fact the sexy male beneath her had talked her into unbuttoning her shirt for him. "Definitely panties."

Her thighs clenched. "What exactly is that teeny, tiny scrap of red meant to cover?"

"Hopefully not much." He tugged at the waistband of the floaty knee-length skirt she'd dressed in tonight in a conscious decision that made her feel naughty in the most adult way. "Tell me you're wearing them."

Arousal was liquid honey in her veins, thick and rich and oh-so-luscious "No," she said, playing with him. "I think I should punish you for how you've been tormenting me."

Teeth on her lower lip. "God, I love it when you're bad, Grace." His fingers went to the bottom edge of her skirt, his hand spreading on her thigh in a caress of rough heat. "Can I?"

Heartbeat jerky in her throat, she shook her head . . . and reached down to slowly, so slowly, bunch the skirt ever higher up her thighs. Cooper's breath was harsh, loud in the confines of the SUV, his eyes a wild yellow that traced every inch she bared. It was intoxicating, his raw desire made her feel like a sexual siren when she'd always thought her sensuality a gentle flame.

There was nothing gentle about her need or her possessiveness where Cooper was concerned. He could arouse her with a word, a look, and she hungered for him to complete his claim, her body in a constant state of readiness. It wouldn't be long, she thought, before her wolf took that final step into absolute, unremitting trust.

"Higher." A growled demand when she stopped near the top of her thighs. "I want to see."

Skin damp with perspiration, she kept the skirt where it was. "What's my incentive?"

Wild yellow blazing at her in the dark, the windows fogged up to enclose them in steamy intimacy. "I'll lick you until you come. Now, keep moving."

Whimpering, she obeyed the order, saw him jerk his head up and check that the whimper was one of passion. Satisfied, he returned his gaze to the miniscule red triangle that shielded her from his view, his hand clenching on her thigh. "Take them off."

Her legs quivered. Dropping her skirt, she leaned backward until she hit the back of the front seat, her chest rising and falling as she fought to suck in enough air to clear the haze in her mind.

Muscular thighs rock hard beneath her, Cooper's hands closed over her knees. "You're going to make me wait?"

She licked her lips, nodded. "You're being punished, remember?"

"Then let me plead my case." Holding her gaze, he cupped her.

She moaned at the proprietary hold, feeling herself grow more damp with every passing second.

A brush of his thumb across the taut nub at the apex of her thighs, the pleasure piercing her to the core. She arched into his touch, even as an acrid sensation she didn't want to feel began to eat away at the sumptuous wave of passion, the wildness in her sensing the acute vulnerability that awaited if the wave crashed. Gritting her teeth, she tried to ride it out, but Cooper knew.

Removing his hand, he tucked her against his body, one hand cupping the back of her head, the other on her lower back. She wrapped her arms around his neck and breathed in the rich earth and dark amber of his scent, her wolf rubbing up gently against his own in silent apology.

His response was a low rumble of a growl. "It's my own damn fault for buying you those panties."

Laying her head against his shoulder, she petted his beautiful chest. "Yes," she agreed, "it is."

That got her a growl . . . and, "When are you going to wear the teddy?"

ABLE to feel herself hovering on the brink of that final, ineffable trust, Grace got up the next morning wishing the hours away so she could play with her dominant lover when night fell, but the day ended up being unexpectedly, dangerously long.

"We have a serious problem at the hydro station," her boss, Barney, said around five that afternoon. "A computronic issue that only became apparent a couple of hours ago."

The timing, Grace thought, couldn't be worse. The region was heading into a severe new storm, forecast to hit tonight. It was meant to be so bad that a team had been dispatched to bring the wild wolves that shared their territory into the den for the night. "Are Elizabeth and Diego up there?" she asked, referring to the two senior station techs.

"Yeah, but they need someone from your team. The air system at the control station is acting glitchy, CO_2 alarms on the fritz, and they have to batten down the hatches, spend the night babying the computronics."

Dangerous, Grace thought, if the air filters failed and carbon dioxide built up in a contained area. Unlike the den, the below-ground control station had no natural airflow conduits to negate the risk, and the storm would make heading outside just as bad a choice. "Den's got generator backup," she said. "It'd be safer to recall them."

"I suggested that, but Elizabeth says if they leave the problem, it could end up crippling the station, take weeks to repair. That happens, den will be reliant on the backup battery units in the critical systems—generators are only meant to run for a few days at most." He rubbed his forehead. "We won't go dark, but things will function at minimal levels at best. If the solar panels hadn't been damaged. . . ."

Grace knew even with the pack's scientific manufacturing arm putting a rush on the specially calibrated panels, it would take at least another week to get everything in place. "Paul's our air expert," she said, hating the idea of sending any of her people out in this weather.

"I tried him, but he's not in his quarters and he didn't file a schedule. Figured you might know where he's working."

That was when Grace recalled why she hadn't seen Paul today. "Damn, I forgot. I gave him a couple of days off so he could go to his father's birthday party in L.A. He left this morning."

"How about Jenson?"

Grace shook her head. "Jenson's still apprentice level." He might panic under the kind of pressure at the station. "I'll go—air is my secondary specialization, and I have plenty of on-the-ground experience." She frowned. "Jenson should be able to deal with anything that comes up here, but call Paul in L.A. and have him provide remote backup and guidance. If you can't get hold of Paul, call Zang at the San Rafael den or Shae at the main den."

Ten minutes later, she threw an overnight bag in a truck and sent Cooper a message.

Heading to hydro station. Staying overnight.

Chapter 12

SHE WAS TWENTY minutes away when he called on the car's system.

"Are you driving up alone?"

His protectiveness warmed her. "Yes, but the winds are manageable." Though she could feel them buffeting the heavy all-wheel drive vehicle she'd signed out. "I'll be safe under shelter before the storm breaks."

"Call me when you get to the station."

"You stay safe, too." She knew he'd be the first one out in the fury if anything happened. "Have you got a satellite phone?" Proving the adage that trouble came in threes, the main comm tower had gone down forty minutes ago, leaving a huge dead zone as far as normal mobile reception. The only good news was that thanks to underground cabling, the den's hardwired lines remained functional.

"Yes. You?"

"No, but Elizabeth and Diego both do." Personnel who worked regularly in isolated areas were issued them as a matter of course after a packwide mandate.

"Take care, Grace. I'll be pissed off otherwise."

For some reason, that bad-tempered statement made her smile. "Same."

She reached the station as the wind was kicking up, and found the techs both outside, attempting to coax a wild wolf and her tiny pups out of a tree hollow that wouldn't protect them from the raging force of the storm. Aware the female would react better to her, Grace waved Elizabeth and Diego away and held out a hand. It took ten minutes in the driving

rain before the wolf gripped one of her pups in her teeth and
gave her to Grace. Grace cuddled the pup close and led the
mother—who gripped the second pup by the scruff of its
neck—into the station.

"Could I borrow one of your sat phones?" she asked after
they'd dried off and created a nest of blankets for the wild
wolves. "My cell's got no signal." She'd double-checked to be
certain.

Red hair in a halo around her face, Elizabeth glanced at
Diego with a distinctly guilty expression. "I forgot mine in the
rush to get up here, but Diego's way more organiz—"

Loud swearing from her partner. "I had it in my pocket,
must've lost it while we were outside."

Since it was their sole means of communication with the
den, they decided to go back out into the now-pitch-black night
to look for it—only to be shoved back inside by the gale force
wind that turned even the smallest object into a deadly projec-
tile. A heavy broken-off branch nearly took off Elizabeth's
head before Grace wrenched her out of the way.

"Hell!" Shoving the door shut with their help, Diego bolted
it, leaving the branch where it had crashed into the opposite
wall. "That's it, we're stuck here till the storm passes."

Grace thought of the concern in Cooper's voice and hoped
he wouldn't worry too much when he didn't hear from her, even
as her wolf fretted about him in turn. "I better get to work on
the air"—she picked up the wolf pup clawing at her work boot,
took it back to its exasperated mother—"or we'll have to open
a window."

The other two laughed but it was strained—built into the
side of a small hill, with only a doorway to reveal it was there,
the control station *had* no windows. All three of them knew
that with the unpredictable air glitches, there was no way of
knowing for certain how much breathable air was left in the
bowels of the facility, two levels below this one . . . the area
that housed the sophisticated computronics needed to run
the hydro station.

COOPER carried in the soldier who'd broken his leg when he
slipped in the muddy terrain and deposited him in the

infirmary. "Are they all in?" he asked Shamus, using a towel to wipe off the wet, a touch of blood saturating the fabric from a piece of debris that had whipped across his face.

"Yes. Or accounted for—few are bunkered down in the perimeter shelters, but they've called in and nobody's alone."

The words did nothing to ease the ugly knot in Cooper's abdomen. "Any word from the station?"

Shamus's expression turned grim. "No, but we've had no power fluctuations, so—" He stopped talking as the lights flickered. A second later, a low hum filled the air, the generators kicking in.

Bile coated the back of Cooper's throat, a cold sweat breaking out along his spine. "I'm going up there. You're in charge." He knew the senior soldier could handle anything that occurred in his absence.

"Jesus, Cooper. Be sensible."

"Would you be if it was Emma up there?"

"Shit." The other man shoved a hand through his hair. "Take the armored all-wheel drive. Thing's a tank."

Cooper shook his head, impatient to start moving. "I'll make better time in wolf form, be lower to the ground."

"If you need to bring someone back . . ."

Someone hurt . . . or dead.

He nodded, unable to voice the thought that was a razor in his throat.

Shamus walked with him to the garage. "Turn on the tracking signal so we can keep an eye on you."

"Done." As he drove, he tried to focus only on the weather and the track, in spite of the scrabbling panic that clawed at him, filling his mind with images of fire and melting flesh.

He knew that was stupid, that even if something had gone wrong at the station, it would've involved a slow suffocation as the air turned to poison, not an explosion. It didn't matter. Fire was his horror and it was what haunted him.

Crash!

Wrenching the wheel, he barely avoided the tree smashing to the earth, his wolf's eyes scouring the wind- and rain-lashed dark for signs of further danger.

Be safe, Grace. Be safe.

They were the most agonizing three hours of his adult life,

the journey taking twice the time it should have. When he pulled up in front of the door of the control station, it was to see the vehicle he knew Grace had checked out of the garage flipped over and smashed into a tree.

His heart turning to ice, he fought through the wind toward it, the rain knives against his skin.

GRACE sat in silence, fiddling with a conduit. Elizabeth and Diego had both bedded down in bedroom cubicles at the end of the corridor, and the rambunctious wolf pups had exhausted themselves at last, but she couldn't sleep. Her gut was all twisted up, as if something was horribly wrong. But when she checked the air systems indicator on the wall—set to sound a piercing audio alarm if it detected a problem—it was to see everything was as it should be. No abnormal CO_2 readings, the air breathable.

She'd repaired it, knew this one at least was functioning fine now. Regardless, she verified the readings with the small hand-held unit she'd brought up. Discovering no discrepancy, she walked over, ensured the wild wolves were okay. The mother raised her head when Grace petted one of her babies but didn't protest. Knowing she shouldn't wake the pup, she took her hand from his baby-soft fur and stood . . . just as a banging came on the door.

The mother wolf sat up, ears pricked.

"It's a branch," Grace murmured, but the sound came again, the rhythm too precise.

Was someone out there?

When she saw Cooper's face through the reinforced glass at the top of the door, she threw back the bolts so fast she tore off a nail, scenting the air with blood. "Cooper!" Her cry was lost in the howl of the wind as he came in, shoving the door shut again with the force of his body as she reengaged the bolts.

The mother wolf growled but a single violent snarl from Cooper and she backed down, wrapping herself protectively around her babies. Whipping back toward Grace, his eyes wolf-yellow and feral, Cooper grabbed her, burying his face against her hair, the water from his rain-drenched clothes seeping into her as she clung to him. He didn't say a word, just held her with raw ferocity.

Tears blurring her eyes, she hugged him as tight as she could. "You shouldn't have driven in this. You shouldn't." Fear for him had her heart stuttering, her wolf pushing at her skin to get closer to him.

Lips against her temple, on her cheek, her mouth, a hungry, desperate kiss.

When Cooper drew back, glanced around, his gaze still inhuman, she found the breath to say. "They're asleep." Dragging him to an unoccupied cubicle, she stepped out to grab towels from a nearby supplies cabinet, snagging the portable air gauge at the same time.

He watched her every move and when she returned, pulled her in and shut the door. The space was tiny, but putting the gauge on the shelf above the bed after turning up the volume on the audio alarm, she sat cross-legged on the mattress as he dried his face and hair, began to pull off his clothes. She removed her sweater and set it aside, the rest of her only a touch damp.

"The three of us talked about it," she said, speaking to fill the terrible silence, "and decided not to go down into the computronic center. If the station malfunctions and the den loses power, it won't be a total disaster—we're wolves, we'll handle it, and we can always jerry-rig something if necessary for places like the infirmary."

No one, Grace had pointed out to Elizabeth and Diego when the techs argued with her, would thank them for dying when it could've been avoided. "If there's a problem while we're on this level, we have the option of opening the door, even if it means dealing with the wind."

She tried not to stare as Cooper stripped down to the dark bronze of his skin, wrapped the towel around his hips, and came to sit beside her. Still not saying a word, he picked her up and put her in his lap. "You didn't call."

"I know. I'm sorry." Shaken by the tone of his voice, she told him what had happened, stroking his face, his shoulders in an attempt to pet, to comfort. "I'm okay. I'm fine."

It seemed to take forever before his skin warmed, the rigid

tension in his muscles melting away. "Are you going to tell me?" she asked, rubbing her cheek against his when he finally relaxed his hold on her.

He didn't speak for a long time, but she didn't shove at his defenses. Not now, not when he was so very vulnerable. Instead, she continued to touch him, soothe him. "It's okay," she murmured. "I can wait." Kisses on his temple, his cheek. "Let me make you some coffee."

He shook his head. "No . . . it's time." A rasp in his voice, his next words vibrating with old emotion. "When I was sixteen, my parents went out of state for a wedding. They told me no staying up late and gorging on pizza and burgers. Then my mom let it slip she'd made my favorite pizzas, frozen the packages, and my dad put double credits into my comm and games account, even though I hadn't earned them by doing extra chores."

Grace could hear his love for his parents in every word. "Lucky."

"I was." A quiet, somber agreement. "Normally, I'd have invited Riaz over for company, but he was grounded. Saturday, I ate, played games, watched X-rated movies after hacking into the comm's parental guidance controls—and sent Riaz a message to brag about my genius since he'd lost his entertainment privileges." A faint smile. "Mid-morning the next day, I went for a long run with him and our other friends, didn't come back in till around four, when it started to rain."

She knew something horrible was coming but didn't interrupt, knowing he needed her to listen, to understand.

"The wedding was on Saturday night. Mom and Dad left before dawn on Saturday morning, planned to drive back Sunday." He swallowed, the strong muscles of his throat moving. "My mom kissed me good-bye while I was still in bed. And my dad rubbed the top of my head in that way dads do."

She could almost see him, a juvenile young and lanky, his eyes sleepy as he said good-bye to his parents.

"Then they were gone." The words sounded terribly final. "I got a message from Mom around ten Sunday morning saying they were on their way. When they didn't arrive by seven p.m. as planned, I didn't worry. I figured they'd taken a detour that looked interesting. We always did that even when we went running in wolf form." A shuddering breath. "But when they weren't home by nine and hadn't called, I started to call them. Over and over.

"I told myself I was being stupid to be so worried, but there was this stone in my stomach that kept getting heavier. I'd contacted the seniors in the pack and they tried, too, even got in touch with Enforcement to see if my folks' car had been logged passing a tolling station, but . . . nothing."

Grace's heart ached for the frightened boy he'd been.

"I stayed up all night, waiting by the den entrance in wolf form as the pack rang friends, hospitals, restaurants, and diners along the way. It was raining and every time a vehicle appeared, I'd run out to see if it was them. It never was." His voice broke. "We managed to track them to a restaurant halfway home, but then it was as if they'd vanished. Eighteen hours." Stone-rough words. "That's how long I waited for them to come home before their vehicle was found at the bottom of a ravine."

Tears rolling down her cheeks, Grace hugged him tight. "I'm so sorry. I'm so sorry, Cooper." She understood what it was to lose her parents, understood what it was to wake up and not have them be there.

Damp against her neck, one of his hands fisted in her hair. "They'd taken that detour, along a rural road with hardly any traffic. Their car was up to safety specs, had all the anti-skid, anti-collision technology, but something made them swerve into the barrier—maybe an animal—and their car, it exploded as it hit the bottom of the ravine. *It shouldn't have.* A freak accident, the authorities said. They told me my parents must've died on impact, but I could see they couldn't be certain. The fire . . ."

"I know it hurts." She stroked her hand down his nape. "I know."

Cooper lifted his head, held her gaze with eyes gone night-glow. "I'm getting you a sat phone, and if you *ever* forget it, I will never forgive you."

"I won't forget, I promise."

For the first time, he was the one who broke the piercing eye contact. "No. I promised myself I wouldn't do this—I don't want to control you, Grace." He brushed his thumb across her cheeks, wiping away the remnants of her tears. "I know the problem is mine, so if you want to take off and leave the phone behind, or if you're pissed at me and don't want to talk, I'll deal."

She heard the taut thread in his voice, knew what her silence would cost him, knew, too that he'd never blame her for it. "It doesn't bother me, Cooper." Honest in her choice, she kissed him, his shoulders hot silk under her hands. "I like being cared for, like knowing that you watch out for me."

It made her wolf feel secure on the innermost level, and she had no quarrel with who she was, what made her happy—and one of those things was giving her man what he needed to feel the same. "Even if we're fighting, I'll send you bad-tempered text messages now and then. My way of caring for you." As integral to her personality as protecting her was to his. "Let me, okay? Don't do the proud dominant thing and get mad at me for it."

God, Cooper thought, she was beautiful. Taking something that had almost crushed him, threatened to shred his pride, and turning it around so that he was the one giving her a gift. "How did you get so strong, Grace?" Strong enough to not care about being perceived as weak by those who didn't know better, didn't understand the beauty of her spirit.

Her smile was slow and just for him. "I have to be—I plan to play bad-girl games with a lieutenant."

In her thrall, he ran his fingers under the edge of her T-shirt, touched soft, silky skin, the contact easing the agony of memory. "Any particular lieutenant?"

"Oh . . . I was thinking Matthias is quite a hun— Eek!" She landed on her back on the bed, with him braced over her, though he was careful to keep the majority of his weight off her.

"Take that back." He knew she was playing with him in an effort to lessen his hurt and loved her even more for it.

An impenitent glance. "Make me."

"Grr." He nipped at her neck, remembering too late that he had to be careful of that vulnerable spot . . . but she giggled, then slapped a hand over her mouth.

Chapter 13

"WE HAVE TO be quiet." A whisper. "Elizabeth and Diego are only two cubicles down."

Cooper ran his hand down her body, so delighted that he didn't care who heard them, the lingering shadow of pain eclipsed by searing joy. "What's my incentive?" he asked, luxuriating in the scent of her. Warm and luscious and pure woman. *His* woman.

A hand curling over his nape, fingers touching his lips. "Cooper."

That voice, that *tone*. "Nu-huh," he said, throat dry. "You are not seducing me on this tiny bed." He wanted to take his time with her, wanted her to feel free to scream.

She nuzzled at his throat in response, licking and sucking. And he knew he was a goner. Growling low in his throat, more a vibration than sound, he reached down and fisted his erection, his towel long since gone. It wasn't for pleasure but to force himself to slow the hell down. No wolf female would be impressed by a man who spilled all over her at her first touch.

"That's my job." A husky protest, her hand moving down his body.

Releasing himself, he halted her. "Wait, I want skin."

She raised her arms above her head at the blunt demand, let him tug the T-shirt over her body to expose lush breasts in a simple black sports bra, the neckline a deep vee. "I wanted to wear lace for you," she whispered, a touch of color on her cheeks.

"Next time." Since he'd all but swallowed his tongue, the words came out thick. "Shit, take it off or I'll rip it." Not the smoothest or most romantic of words, but Grace wiggled sexily under him as she pulled the stretchy material off over her head and threw it aside.

He already had his hand, his mouth on her ripe flesh, so creamy and plump and tantalizing. She jerked under him, her hand gripping his nape and a stifled cry escaping her mouth. Breath heavy, he rose up, demanded a kiss while he petted and fondled one of her breasts, received it.

Grace's fingers landed on his hips, dug in.

Breaking the kiss, his cock pushing into the silken skin of her abdomen, he looked down to see brown eyes gone hazy. Lush and curvy and all woman, Grace made him grit his teeth and bury his face in the curve of her neck.

Her hands stroked up over his shoulders. "What's wrong?"

"I'm about to come like a schoolboy," he ground out, and it might have been an embarrassing confession . . . if Grace hadn't softened impossibly further and reached down to curve her fingers around the hard evidence of his need. It wasn't brazen, but neither was it hesitant. No, it was the possessive grip of a woman who knew she could claim any and every skin privilege she wanted when it came to him.

"Christ, Grace. Sweetheart, stop or—"

His brain blanked as she began to move her hand.

"Like this." Closing his fingers over hers, he showed her how fast and almost rough he liked it. She followed his lead without argument, her confidence increasing with every stroke until he fisted one hand in her hair, levered himself up over her, and buried his face in the side of her neck again in an effort to muffle his growl as he came all over her hand and stomach.

The orgasm ripped over his spine, bowed his back, pulse after pulse punching through his body.

Breath harsh in the aftermath, he fought not to collapse on her. "I got you all sticky."

A nuzzling kiss to his throat from the generous, sensual woman in bed with him. "I like carrying your scent on my skin."

He thrust into her hand again, his erection near full-strength once more. And he had the thought that he could come all night for her, but he had other priorities. Forcing himself to get up, he used his still-damp T-shirt to clean off the evidence of his desire. Grace watched him with lazy eyes the entire time and when he threw the tee aside to move his hands to the button of her jeans, she sank her teeth into her lower lip and raised her hips off the sheet so he could tug the jeans off, throw them aside.

Her panties were black like her bra, but lace rather than cotton, hinting at the dark curls beneath. Shifting to the foot of the bed, he spread her thighs and settled himself between, breathing deep of her musk. "I want to eat you up, Grace," he murmured, pressing a kiss to her navel as he lifted her legs up around his shoulders, his gaze taking in those glorious breasts for which he had plans.

She ran the heels of her feet down his back in a gentle caress. "Cooper." It was a sexy complaint.

He smiled. "Am I talking too much and doing too little?" he murmured, using a claw to cut off the sides of her panties so he could tug them off. "Let me lick it better."

She sucked in a breath. "I like the things you say." A whispered admission that undid him.

"You're so pretty here, Grace." He nuzzled at her navel before lifting his head and sliding his hands under her buttocks to tilt her up to his mouth. Using his thumbs, he spread her for him. "So pink and wet and plump."

A feminine moan she blocked with her fist, her body arching toward his mouth in invitation. He took it, dropping his head to give her an openmouthed kiss that had her fingers fisting in the sheets, her body squirming as if she wanted to get away— except from the way she'd gone molten against his tongue, he knew she didn't. Changing his hold to below her knees, he spread her thighs even farther apart and feasted on the taste of Grace. When she began to come, using one hand to lift up the side of her pillow so she could bury her face against it, muffle her cries, he licked and sucked her through the pleasure, then inserted a single finger into her sheath.

Her muscles pulsed around the intrusion. "Grace, sweetheart," he said, his voice a rasp, "you're going to squeeze my cock so good and hard." He moved his finger out, pushed it back in to a gasping sound of pleasure, her face lifting from the pillow, eyes dazed. "Especially when I take you from behind."

Looking up, he made certain she was with him before he thrust again, and again. A fresh slickness coated his finger. He removed it and used his mouth on her once more, careful with her clit, which he knew had to be sensitive. But she didn't protest, her body undulating toward him. The complaint came when he stopped. "Cooper."

Blowing over the flesh he'd teased to creamy need, he said, "I want inside you."

A shudder rippled over her . . . and she spread her thighs for him, her feet flat on the bed. Biting back a primitive sound of pleasure, he rose up over her, stopping to suck a nipple into his mouth. "I'm saving these for later," he said when he released the hard nub to kiss his way to her lips. "For dessert." He nudged at her heat with his cock, his arm braced beside her head, his free hand on her hip. Urging her to wrap one leg around his waist, he began to push in, holding her gaze.

Her eyes fluttered shut after a few seconds, and he froze. "Grace, baby, are you with me?"

She ran her claws lightly down his back. "Yes. Oh, please don't stop, Cooper."

Sweat beaded along his forehead, but he locked his muscles in place. "I need to see your eyes, need to know you're really okay." That this wasn't primal submission, but an act of passion, of conscious surrender.

Swallowing, she lifted her lashes, the eyes that met his a shy wolf gold. No fear, human reason in her words. "I'm here. Every part of me." A nip at his throat, a quiet demand.

To have both sides of her nature dance with him, it was the most magnificent gift he'd ever received. Petting and kissing her, he continued to coax her to hold his gaze as he moved in her. "My pretty, sexy Grace," he said, and pushed in to the hilt, his balls slapping at her flesh.

Her nails scraped down his back in response.

His growl a heavy vibration in his chest, he pinned her in place and began to thrust slow and deep until she whimpered in a desperate effort to stifle her cries. They found a faster rhythm, were locked with one another when they fell, wild yellow looking into passion-drenched gold.

COOPER'S heart was still pounding like the rain outside when he fell onto his back, taking Grace with him so she ended up sprawled on his chest. Shifting one hand, he splayed it on her butt, stroked. She rubbed her foot over his shin in response, circling one of his nipples with a lazy fingertip. "I don't want to be quiet next time."

He tapped her butt playfully and drew in enough breath to say, "You wouldn't have had to be quiet this time if you'd waited."

Kisses on his chest, up his throat, along his jaw. "Are you sorry?"

"I just had an orgasm that almost killed me, and I have naked Grace for a blanket. Yeah, I'm real sorry."

Husky laughter, more kisses, eyes that shimmered with the wolf's amusement. And he had the thought that his choice to share his deepest vulnerability had shifted something between them, given her what she needed to trust him on this level. It embarrassed him to think how he'd fallen apart, but he could deal with it if this was the result. Still—"It wasn't a pity lay, was it?"

Pushing up so she could look down at his face, Grace glared at him, then slapped his chest. "Yes. Absolutely. That's me, a woman who goes around sharing skin privileges with anyone who looks sad. Did I tell you about the engineer who broke his favorite tool the other day? I had to strip right there and—"

He shut up her rant by the expedient of a laughing kiss that had feminine claws pricking his chest. "Sorry," he said when those claws dug a fraction deeper in warning. "I'm male. I had to ask."

A shake of her head but her lips curved . . . then she ducked her head. "I wanted to crawl all over you the first time we met."

His wolf preened. "I wouldn't have stopped you." He continued to pet her luscious body, his own very enthusiastic about the fact she was snuggled up so close. "God, it makes me feel good to have you here." A pause. "Where you belong."

Her gaze lifted to his again, a little shy, but not afraid in any sense. "I guess . . . I just needed to know you needed me on some level." It was a painfully honest statement. "You're so strong—my wolf understands a submissive's important role in the pack but couldn't comprehend what I could give *you*, how I could be your partner." A hand cupping his cheek. "Now I know it isn't about power, but about heart, about loving."

His hand shook as he brushed her hair off her face. "I will always need you—you're strong and brave and goddamn perfect, and you fucking *own* my heart." And he needed her inside that heart, needed her to accept the mating bond, couldn't understand why she hadn't already.

Especially when tears shimmered in her eyes, as she said, "I love you, Cooper."

His resistance broke. He tumbled them over, made love to her again, and this time, it was slow, full of whispered promises and caresses, a dance so beautiful it shattered his every remaining defense.

Maybe that was why he fell asleep curled around her afterward.

He'd never know what woke him, but he jerked into a sitting position to see it was just after four thirty a.m. Since Grace continued to sleep, he hadn't screamed, and he didn't have the foul aftertaste of nightmare in his mouth.

Thank God. Thank God.

Swallowing, he went to the door Grace had sleepily asked him to pull ajar as a safety precaution before they slept, and used the hallway light to check the portable air gauge, confirmed everything was fine on that point. Only then did he go into the tiny shower at the end of the corridor to wash and take a few deep breaths.

Diego's and Elizabeth's doors were ajar, too, and he heard snores from one as he walked back, the deep breathing of sleep from the other. He checked on the wild wolves as well, heard their sleepy *whuff*s as they resettled their bodies.

When he returned to the sleep cubicle, Grace had shifted to face the room rather than the wall, but her eyes remained closed. Moving with as much stealth as possible, he found his jeans, pulled them on, the material stiff but wearable. Though, he thought, he might as well run down in wolf form, since he was planning to leave both his phone and his vehicle behind for Grace.

"Cooper?" A drowsy question. "Is it morning?"

"Shh, go to sleep, darling." Taking a seat on the bed, he brushed tangled strands of hair off her face, then indulged himself in one last stroke of her curvy body, her skin marked from his caresses. Primitive as it was, the sight made him feel good. "Storm's past and even the rain's stopped. I better start my run down, help with the post-storm cleanup."

Instead of nodding and going back to sleep, Grace frowned and struggled up into a sitting position, pulling the sheet to her breasts. "You're leaving me while it's still dark? I thought you'd want to stay . . . a while longer, anyway."

Her hurt tone was an arrow to his heart. "The storm, sweetheart. It'll have made a mess of things. I'll stay tomorrow night."

Blinking, she stared at him for a long time, and he could almost see the wheels turning in her head. "You're always out in the dark, have far more night shifts than you should, and it's clear you don't get enough sleep. Why?"

His wolf paced, looking for a way out and finding only closed doors. "I take the shifts no one else wants." He shrugged and got up, then realized there was nowhere to go in this tiny space. "Just being a good lieutenant."

"That's not how a pack works." Grace got out of bed, the sheet wrapped around her like a toga, and pushed the door fully shut with a quiet *snick*. "We have to talk about this."

He turned with a snarl, going on the defensive. "Jesus, Grace, you're not that needy. I'm sure you can spend a few hours alone without breaking."

Chapter 14

EVEN A FEW weeks ago, those angry words delivered by a Cooper whose eyes were tinged wolf yellow, would've made Grace stumble back, lower her head and her eyes. That was before he'd played with her, courted her, taught her he'd never ever hurt her. "That's not the point," she argued, refusing to let this go any longer. Maybe she didn't like to push, to demand in the normal scheme of things, but she discovered her wolf was quite willing to do so when it was Cooper's happiness on the line. "I want to know why you avoid sleeping."

"I've told you," he snarled, quiet but adamant, his eyes slamming into hers, the fury in them a wild thing. "Just leave it." His dominance shoved at her.

If it had held the force of a command, she would've backed down, their relationship in splinters, her heart an agony of pain. But furious as he was, Cooper wasn't pulling rank. No, he was simply a pissed-off man who wasn't acting at all like the tough, strong, honest Cooper she knew and loved. "No," she said, holding that powerful gaze. "I won't leave it when I know something's hurting you deep inside."

When he would've opened his mouth to respond, she kept speaking, her words a taut whisper as she fought the urge to yell. "You think I don't know how sleep deprived you are? That I don't feel your wolf's exhaustion? I know you, and I know you're in pain, so you *will* talk to me."

He bared his teeth, went toe-to-toe with her. "Act like a damn submissive."

Tears pricked her eyes at those bad-tempered words, but they weren't tears of pain or of hurt. "I am. I'm acting like *your* submissive." The one who knew he'd die before he'd crush her spirit, no matter if such an act would win him the argument.

Growling deep in his chest, he picked her up and pressed her to the back of the door, the sheet falling to the floor as she grabbed reflexively at his shoulders, her legs going around his hips again. She found herself face-to-face with the wolf, his eyes pure feral yellow, his body pressed to the delicate, unprotected core of her, naked against the abrasive denim of his jeans.

Rather than flinching or pulling away, she touched her fingers to his face, stroking. "I see you," she whispered, her own wolf rising to the surface. "I see you, Cooper."

The affectionate whisper, that pale gold gaze devoid of fear, it destroyed him. Turning his face into her touch while never breaking the beauty of the eye contact, he reached down her body to stroke her, drank her sigh in a kiss. She didn't refuse him when he undid his jeans, taking him with a gasp of welcome, her lips seeking his in a delicate kiss that was inexpressibly feminine.

Shuddering, he let her take control, walking backward until the backs of his knees hit the bed. He sat down, his woman on his lap, and surrendered to her loving. Until he felt adored in the most tender of ways. Until he knew that if she ever left him, he'd break forever.

Later, after the pleasure, and knowing she would fight him again if need be, this woman with a spirit strong as steel, he admitted the horror that stalked him. "I don't want you to see me, hear me, like that, and it infuriates me that I can't escape it. I'm not that scared boy any longer, haven't been for a long time."

Grace brushed her hand over his scalp, understanding why he'd fought so bitterly against telling her. For a dominant to confess to such a weakness would feel like an unmanning—and he'd already been emotionally raw after last night. Even now, she could see him withdrawing, his wolf refusing to meet her gaze.

But there was something important in what he'd said, something he was too close to see. "You said the nightmares started up around the time you began to court me seriously."

A nod, jaw clenched.

"It's because I matter, Cooper." It made her heart hurt to

understand how much. "You worry about me in a way you haven't worried about anyone since you were a boy."

Cooper didn't say anything for a long time. "I'm always going to worry about you."

"Ditto." Pressing her fingers to his lips, she said, "But maybe the nightmares won't come when you know beyond any doubt that I'm safe and sound. I can't get much safer than in your arms."

He didn't look convinced, but he didn't fight her when she asked him to come to her bed again the next night. She knew he didn't sleep properly, determined to hold the darkness at bay, but by the third day, he was so exhausted he crashed. This time, it was Grace who didn't sleep. She knew what it would do to him to wake up screaming—so she'd kiss him at the first sign of trouble, seduce him until he forgot what had originally disturbed his sleep.

It was the only answer she had, and if it failed, she didn't know what they'd do. Cooper was so proud, it would savage him if he couldn't win the fight against the nightmares, because a fight was how his wolf saw it. He needed to beat this challenge, needed to protect the woman who was his own against the shadows in the dark.

To her endless relief, he slept like the dead.

And woke amorous.

Grace smiled as she wrapped her legs around his hips, met his sleepy-eyed kiss. Maybe she was wrong and the bad nights would return, but she didn't think so. Not when Cooper had spent the night with her tucked up tight against him, his arm locked around her waist. "Possessive beast," she murmured when he bit her throat hard enough that she'd wear the mark all day.

She felt his lips curve against her as he licked over the brand.

TWO weeks after their return from the station, and with the den's power supply back to full strength as of five days earlier, Grace came home to find a bath in the room she now shared with Cooper. An honest-to-goodness bath, clawed feet and all. Filled with steaming water that carried a heady floral scent, delicate pink petals scattered over its surface.

Grace stared. She had no idea how he'd even gotten the thing into the room, much less how he'd arranged it so the water would be the perfect temperature when she arrived home. Shucking off her clothes, she slipped into it with a groan of pure pleasure. No one could say her man didn't know how to court a woman— the entire pack was wondering why she was leading her lover on such a chase, even as they applauded his tactics.

The fact was, it had taken an agonizing level of self-control on her part not to surrender to the bond. She'd been teetering on the cusp of it the morning at the station, but after his confession about his nightmares, she'd known she had to wait, no matter if the hunger to bond with him was a constant ache inside her. Never did she want him to wonder why she'd accepted the bond, whether she'd done it only so he'd always know if she was safe.

He'd been a little shaky the first few days, his wolf waiting for the ax to fall. But as the nights continued to pass, dreamless and peaceful, he began to get aggravated by her resistance to the bond. She'd danced in joy when he restarted his relentless campaign, complete with deliveries of romantic handmade chocolates . . . inscribed with sexual favors on the backs; the sudden appearance of a coveted new tool in her toolbox; and daily love-song requests on the internal SnowDancer radio station that had every adult in the pack—and some clever juveniles—tuning in at 9 p.m. to see what he'd ask for next. And how.

Her favorite was the time he'd dedicated it to, "The obstinate she-wolf who thinks I should learn the meaning of patience." A pause before his growl turned silky. "Though last night, she threatened to murder me when I tried to demonstrate how good a student I've been."

Mortified by the intimate tease, she'd blushed her way through the next day . . . but secretly, she liked being an "obstinate she-wolf," loved that he never used the careful voice on her anymore, demonstrating his rock-solid belief in her emotional strength with every dirty trick he played as he attempted to wear down her resistance.

And Cooper had some *very* dirty tricks in his arsenal.

Moaning with remembered pleasure, she rose out of the bath, dried herself off, then shifted. Her wolf sniffed at itself, not too sure about the floral scent but deciding it was acceptable since Cooper's scent underlay it, embedded into her very skin. Jaw dropping in a wolfish grin, she padded to the door, pressed her paw to the special footpad to open it and slipped out, the door swinging shut behind her.

It took her no effort to track Cooper, his scent vivid to her every sense. He was outside, speaking to several of the senior soldiers. When she would've remained on the edge of the clearing, waiting for him to finish, he turned and smiled at her, angling his head in welcome.

She padded over to lean against his leg.

As she listened, Cooper finished working out some kind of a rotation schedule, and the soldiers began to break away one by one, the grins on their faces having nothing to do with work.

Cooper came down in a crouch after the last soldier left, stroking his hand down the slope of her back. "You're such a pretty wolf, Grace."

She yipped in a request for play.

Hand fisting in her fur, he said, "Okay, you convinced me. Give me a minute."

It took him less than that to strip and cache his clothes in the hollow created by the thick roots of a forest giant. A wonder of light and color, and she found herself faced with a heavy-boned wolf who had become a familiar playmate. He was at least a hand bigger than her, maybe twice her weight, his eyes shimmering yellow and his coat a luxuriant dark red.

She quivered as he pressed his body against hers, acting shy . . . before she pounced up to grip at his neck with her teeth. He snapped his own teeth in a pretend growl and nipped at her ear as she jumped back, making her release a startled squeak-bark.

A wolfish laugh.

Snarling, she attacked him and they rolled around on the grass, wrestling and whipping around one another. She knew he was letting her play—he was so much bigger and stronger that it would've taken him but a second to seize control. But she also knew he was having fun. So when a low-hanging branch distracted him, she took off.

Grace didn't like being chased as a rule—it was scary,

stressful . . . except when it was Cooper doing the chasing. Then it was *fun*.

Heart thudding, she scrambled up hills and across clearings, aware of him gaining on her—and then his paws were on her shoulders, taking her down. It was a classic demand for submission, but when the bigger wolf nuzzled at her and jumped off, she knew he was telling her he'd won the game, nothing more.

Grinning, she rose up to her full height and yawned in a gesture of impertinence.

Cooper bared his teeth at his mate—*if* the contrary female would just accept the bond—and stared into her eyes. She stared back, unafraid, her tail up, her gaze bright. Had anyone come upon them, they might have believed she challenged him, but that wasn't it at all. It felt as if she was adoring him.

All at once, her form dissolved in faceted sparks of color.

He shifted alongside her and let out an "oomph" as she pounced on him again, playful as a pup. "Hi, Cooper."

His cheeks creased where he lay on his back with her over him. "Hi, Grace."

"Guess what?" A very wolfish angle to her head.

"What?"

Leaning in close, she whispered. "I decided."

His spine bowed as the mating bond locked into place, as gentle and as fierce a thing as Grace herself. Throwing back his head, he howled his joy, heard the wild wolves howl back. And then he heard his Grace, her voice melding with his in a harmony that was their song of the heart.

—◆—

Texture of
Intimacy

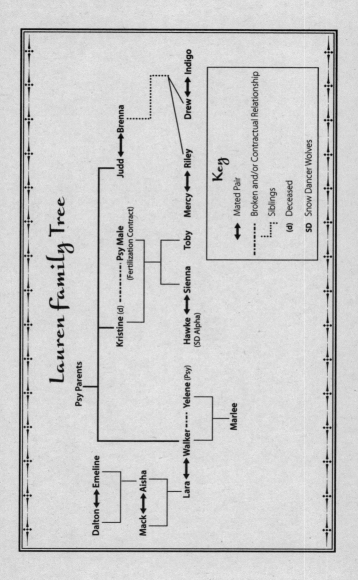

Lauren Family Tree

Psy Parents

Kristine (d) --------- Psy Male (Fertilization Contract)

Judd ↔ Brenna

Hawke ↔ Sienna (SD Alpha)

Toby

Mercy ↔ Riley

Drew ↔ Indigo

Walker ---- Yelene (Psy)

Marlee

Lara ↔ Aisha

Mack ↔ Aisha

Dalton ↔ Emeline

Key

↔ Mated Pair

Broken and/or Contractual Relationship

⋮ Siblings

(d) Deceased

SD Snow Dancer Wolves

Surcease

THE PURE PSY army, formed of militant Psy who believe the Silence Protocol is the salvation of their race, that emotion is the enemy, and that the changelings, with their wild hearts, represent all that is wrong in the world, has been defeated. Broken on the wings of an alliance that stretches across the three races that form the triumvirate that is the world.

Human.

Psy.

Changeling.

The lines have shifted forever.

Will shift further . . . but not just yet.

Now, *this*, is a moment free of violence, a timeless pause in which a Psy formed in Silence, and a SnowDancer wolf born to heal, discover the searing pleasures and startling textures of an intimacy luminous with hope.

Chapter 1

LARA WOKE SKIN-TO-SKIN with a long, hard male body, her head tucked under his chin, her hands against his chest, her legs intertwined with his. Lean muscle and a rough masculine heat, he surrounded her, possessed her.

As she did him.

Eyes still closed, she luxuriated in the scent of dark water and snow-dusted firs . . . and the exquisite tug of a bond that tied her inexorably to the quiet, powerful telepath who was the only man she had ever wanted to call her own.

Mine.

Opening her eyes on that primal thought, she flexed her hand on the tensile strength of Walker's chest, the firm surface covered with a sprinkling of dark blond that was an invitation to her senses. Her wolf rubbed up against the inside of her skin, unable to contain its delight, wanting only to touch, to pet.

"Unconditional skin privileges."

That's what her mate had given her. And she had every intention of taking advantage, her thirst for him endless. How could it be otherwise when he was such an intelligent, dangerous, beautiful man? The ease of sleep did nothing to hide the fact that he was built lean and strong. Wide shoulders, ridged abdomen, taut muscle, and a will akin to steel, this was a man who would stand unflinching against any wind. And he was *hers*, touched her with a devotion that was breathtaking in its passion, piercing in its honesty.

Shivering at the painful beauty of the bond that connected them, she shifted to look down into a face that was all clean angles and sun-golden skin, which betrayed how much time he spent out of doors. His lashes threw crescent shadows on his cheeks, his dark blond hair threaded with the finest sprinkling of silver.

Butterflies in her stomach.

He was, she thought, one of those men who would only become better looking with age, the determined force of his personality reflected on his face. Given that he was already the sexiest man she knew, she was going to be in serious trouble as the years passed—a single look, and she had the feeling she'd fold like cooked spaghetti.

The thought of growing old with him made her blood turn effervescent, the natural dark tan of her skin turn radiant with warmth. Unable to hold in the happiness, she pushed back her unruly curls and leaned down to brush her mouth over his, felt his lips curve the slightest fraction. "I knew you were awake." The wolf that was her other half scampered playfully inside her mind.

He ran his hand up and down her back. "Is it time to get up?"

Lara wouldn't have bothered checking the time if not for Marlee and Toby, pups who were under Walker's protection . . . and now her own. Her family. One was his daughter, the other his nephew, but he was father to them both, this man who had been willing to give up his life on the slim chance that the children would find sanctuary in SnowDancer.

"No," she said after a quick glance at the small comm unit on the bedside table. "It's been less than an hour." An hour of peace, the battle won, the enemy routed so decisively they'd prove only a lack of intelligence should they decide to return.

Lashes rising, irises of a striking light green meeting her own. Not soft. Walker would never be that. But his gaze was . . . open in a way it had never before been. Until she felt invited into him.

Body aligned with the dark heat of his, she ran her finger through his hair and asked, "Are the kids okay?"

He continued to stroke her back, the calluses on his palm creating sensual friction against her greedy skin.

So long she'd waited for Walker's touch.

It had torn her to pieces, made her bleed when he'd told her this could never be, his soul too scarred by the emotionless chill that was Silence. Now she knew that though the power-hungry Council had attempted to condition emotion out of him, they had never succeeded, his heart so powerful he'd managed to love even in the pitiless cage of the PsyNet.

His daughter.

His niece and nephew.

His lost sister.

His brother.

They had been, and were, a family *because* of Walker, because he'd refused to allow them to fragment, refused to give up on any one of them, whether cold-eyed assassin or heartbroken child.

"Yes, they're fine," he said in response to her question, no change in his expression to betray the fact he was in telepathic communication with the kids. "Toby and his friends are shooting hoops with Drew, and Marlee's with Ava."

"Ava's a good friend." Given the speed and accuracy of the pack grapevine, the other woman had likely heard that Walker Lauren was inside Lara's bedroom about two minutes after the event. Lara knew her best friend would ambush her later for a debriefing, but until then, Ava was doing her best to ensure they had some more private time.

"Marlee just told me Ben's snoring in wolf form, she made him so tired."

Laughter bubbled up in her throat, an image of an utterly exhausted wolf pup curled up nose to tail forming in her mind. "Poor Ben."

Ava's son adored Marlee, the unexpected friendship between the two innocent and joyful. Ben was five and a half, Marlee four years older, but in spite of the age gap, they made each other laugh until they ended up rolling around on the floor, holding onto their stomachs. Lara wasn't the only one in the pack who wondered if the friendship was an indicator of a far different relationship in the future, but they were babies yet.

Before she could give voice to her thoughts, Walker's eyes caught hers, held them. "I'm not likely to be an easy mate."

The stark statement was unexpected, but she knew her answer, "I think you're wonderful. My perfect mate."

"Remember that," he said, continuing to hold her gaze, the intensity of him a near physical touch. "When you ask yourself what you're doing with me."

A sudden fear gripped her, an amorphous, cold thing born of his certainty that their mating would be no simple dance. Shoving it away before it could take her hostage, her wolf's teeth bared in a snarl, she held on to the glory of a bond that came from a place beyond fear or doubt, a place untainted by the shadows of the past.

All she said, however, was, "All right," because she knew Walker. He'd been marked deep within by the life he'd lived, the choices he'd had to make. It would take him time to trust in happiness, in a forever where he no longer walked alone. "But make me a promise?"

Watchful attention, his hand stilling its caressing strokes.

"That you'll talk to me if there's a problem. Don't close up on me." It was what she feared most. She knew that while in the PsyNet, Walker had managed to maintain the fiction of total Silence, of unrelenting emotionlessness, icy and without heart, even as he fought to save his family. His fidelity to them had been unwavering, his dedication absolute. And throughout it all, no one had suspected that Walker Lauren was anything but loyal to the ruling order.

That kind of a will could turn into a stone wall.

Walker's answer was no simple agreement. "I'll try, Lara." His hand pressed her closer. "But the quiet, if not the Silence, is a part of me."

"I like your quiet." He was so centered, so solid that he'd become her anchor. "The only thing that'll hurt me is if you use that quiet as a weapon."

"That won't happen." A vow, simple and binding.

She smiled and knew it held everything of what she felt for him, her soul stripped bare. Some would say she was at a huge disadvantage in this relationship, her emotions naked while his were shielded behind a thousand layers of control, but she knew differently. Never would she forget the day he handed her his heart.

"It's fixed. As long as you don't mind more than a few scars."

Scarred and battered it might be, but Walker's heart was a gift beyond price.

"Marlee," she said, throat thick with emotion, "must have come as quite a surprise." Walker's daughter was a talker,

cheerful and with an infectious laugh. Her delight with the
world was so open, so innocent that she appeared younger than
her years, but Lara had seen Marlee's schoolwork—the girl
was blazingly intelligent. She simply loved life.

"I don't know where she gets it from." The faint smile on
his lips faded even as he spoke. "The Marlee you know, she
wasn't that girl in the Net."

Lara thought back to the day the Lauren family had walked
into the den, more than three years ago. Unconscious at the
time, Marlee had been in Sienna's arms, Toby in Walker's, the
boy much shorter and lighter than he was these days. Both
children had been hit hard by the backlash of separation from
the PsyNet, the psychic network that provided the Psy race with
the biofeedback necessary for life. It also kept them leashed,
at the mercy of the Council and of a protocol that forbade joy,
affection, and love. The only reason the Laurens had survived
was that they'd reconnected their minds in a tiny familial
network.

Judd was the first one she'd seen, his assassin's gaze never
moving off the grim-eyed SnowDancer soldiers who'd escorted
the family into the infirmary. She'd known at once that he'd
kill to protect the others. Then her eyes had connected with
those of lightest green; she'd seen the way the stranger held the
child in his arms, and she'd understood that this man might
well be the more dangerous one in spite of his outward calm.

Marlee, when she'd woken at last, had been a shell-shocked
waif, all huge eyes the same shade as her father's in a bone-
white face. It had taken months for her cheeky, vivacious personality to emerge. Walker, Lara realized, had had to watch
for years as his daughter was taught to be a well-mannered cog
in the PsyNet machine, her spirit crushed at every turn.

Cupping his face, she said, "You got her out, made sure
she'll never have to Silence her personality again."

An unexpected glint of humor. "I dare anyone to attempt to
Silence Marlee now."

Lara laughed, then gasped as his hand moved over her lower
curves. "I see you're fully awake."

"Hmm." It was a low, deep sound she'd become used to in
the hours since their mating, the sound her mate made when
he was far more interested in something else.

Initiating a kiss as he brought her over his body, her nipples rubbing against the crisp abrasion of his chest and one of his hands fisted in her hair, Lara was thinking this was a fine, *fine* way to wake up from a nap when the comm beeped.

She groaned, her body crying foul. "I have to get that." As SnowDancer's healer, she never ignored a comm alert.

Walker was already reaching out to press the audio-only answer key on the touchscreen. "It's not an emergency code."

"Doesn't mean anything. Some of the juveniles break a leg, then don't use the emergency code because they 'can take the pain.' " Shifting to lie flat on her back, she wrenched her frustrated body under some sort of control, as Walker said, "Yes?" into the comm.

A startled silence, followed by a hesitant young voice. "Um . . . can I talk to Lara?"

Recognizing it, Lara sat up. "Silvia?" The girl was one of the most stable teens in the pack, and she wouldn't be calling Lara now if it wasn't important. "What's happened?"

"I just got back on one of the evac transports."

Inside her, Lara's wolf raised its head in a howl, happy that more and more of the pack's young had begun to return to the den from the safe areas where they'd weathered the storm of battle. "Go on," she encouraged the girl when Silvia hesitated.

"I know you must be exhausted"—apology in every syllable—"but the pup I was buddied up with won't stop crying because his mom and dad aren't here. I would contact the nursery, but I know how much Mason likes you . . ."

"I'll be right there." Already up, she began to pull on her jeans, aware of Walker doing the same. "In the meantime, tell Mason his parents are fine. Your group came in a couple of hours early—his mom and dad are still out on the perimeter."

When she finished dressing and turned, it was to find Walker with a cell phone in hand. "I'll get in touch with them."

Promising herself she'd pet her way across that finely honed chest tonight, she blew him a kiss and jogged to the area just outside the den that was the drop-off zone.

"Lara!" Mason whimpered and clung to her like a little monkey the instant he saw her.

"Hush now, baby." Cuddling him, Lara pulled back enough that she was looking into his eyes. Unlike Silvia, she was an adult, the hierarchy crystal clear—Mason's wolf snapped to attention, even as his rich brown eyes swam huge and wet. "Your mom and dad are on their way," she said, certain Walker would've ensured that outcome. "They aren't hurt."

His lower lip quivered. "Coming?"

"Yes. They're so excited to see you again." Kissing his wet cheek, she lowered her voice to a conspiratorial whisper. "Now your bus has arrived super early and surprised them. Did it have wings?"

The boy shook his head. "No . . . I didn't see."

"Shall we go have a look?"

The three of them were walking around the armored evac vehicle, Mason engrossed with checking every nook and cranny for wings, when two out-of-breath adults burst into the clearing. "Mason!"

"Mommy! Daddy!"

Grinning as the pup, who'd spontaneously transformed into his furry brown wolf shape, was swallowed up in a four-armed embrace, Lara hugged Silvia to her side. "You did well, sweetheart." She'd used her head, hadn't lost her courage even when the comm had been answered by an unexpected male voice.

A relieved smile brought a glow to the rich brown of her skin. "Sorry for interrupting you and Walker."

"How do you know it was Walker?"

Smile turning into a grin, Silvia tapped her nose. "I'm a wolf." A short pause. "And I saw you two sneaking a kiss a while back."

Then the teenager was gone in a shimmer of delighted laughter, and Lara's wolf was turning at the scent of dark water that held a thousand secrets.

"I'm not likely to be an easy mate."

And though she knew their love was steel strong, would never bend or break, her heart ached as she wondered if he would one day tell her those secrets . . . or if part of him would remain forever closed, forever a mystery.

Chapter 2

DUCKING INTO HER quarters on their return, Lara glanced at Walker, a lingering trace of anxiety in her gut at the idea of never quite knowing this man who touched her deeper than anyone else ever had, or would again. "I could shower here," she said, feeling unsure for the first time that day, "and meet you afterward to go find the children."

He closed the distance between them, cupped her jaw, his gaze direct. "Do you want to?"

"No." It came out husky, neither part of her wanting to be separated from him. Not yet. Not when the bond was so new, so raw, shocking her senses each time she became consciously aware of it.

A quiet smile that shattered the anxiety, made her stomach clench, her toes curl. "I've never shared a shower before," he murmured.

She wasn't certain how she made it to his apartment after grabbing a change of clothing from hers. Because she knew that look in her mate's eyes. It was the same one she'd seen before he decided to "explore the concept of oral sex." Walker's version of "explore" had left her an incoherent, trembling, pleasured pile of Lara-shaped jelly.

The man had concentration down to an art.

As he proved once again in the shower, when he ran soap-slick hands over her body and murmured he wanted to "explore" the idea of having sex standing up. Not that Lara minded being pinned to the wet tile by her mate's hard body, her legs locked around his lean hips and hot water cascading over them both while they "explored" the hell out of the concept.

Unsurprisingly, it took her extra time to get dressed after they exited the shower, her body boneless. "For some reason," she said, pressing a kiss to the center of his naked back before he pulled on a fresh shirt, "I never expected you to be so physical." So very demanding in that quiet, determined Walker way that made every feminine cell in her body sing.

He ran a finger under her bra strap when she circled around to his front, an easy, affectionate caress. "I have a lifetime of sensation to catch up on." Tugging her closer with a pull on the strap, he ran his hand down her back. "With you."

Oh, man. She really stood no chance. "Stop that." It came out sounding less than firm. "Children, remember?"

Walker angled his head the slightest fraction, as if listening. "Yes, I think we'd better go collect them." He circled his palm over her back, warm and a little rough, and answered the question she'd been about to ask. "Neither is in distress, but they need to be back with family."

Lara's wolf was in full agreement, and it only took her a couple more minutes to pull on fresh jeans paired with a thin sweater in her favorite shade of green. "Let's go," she said after slipping on her sneakers.

Toby, who appeared to have grown an inch since the last time she'd seen him—there was no longer any question that he'd end up as tall as his uncles—hugged her with thin but strong arms when she found him kicking a ball around outside, his joy in their mating unhidden. "I'm really happy you're our family now," he said. "Even that first day in the infirmary, when I was so scared of everything, I was never scared of you." Words poignant with memory. "Your hands were gentle. Like my mom's."

Tears burned the backs of her eyes. "She loved you very much." Toby's mother had fought for him until the violent power of her telepathic gift had sucked her under. A gift her child had inherited, his eyes the night sky of a cardinal, white stars on velvet black. But Toby would never have to deal with his ability in isolation—physical or mental, his support structure a sprawling network of family, other Psy, wolves, and leopards. "I hope you'll let me love you, too."

Toby's smile was sweet . . . with a fine, fine hint of mischief that told her he might just turn into a hellion juvenile one of these days. "You already do—you love all the pups in the pack. I can sense it." He hugged her again, whispering, "But if you want to love me and Marlee especially, I won't tell."

"Deal." Laughing, she went to brush his hair out of his eyes when Marlee appeared around the corner with Walker and ran full-tilt to throw her arms around Lara.

"Dad says you're ours now!" Green-eyed and with a clean line to her features, she was her father's daughter, but her nature was her own. Uniquely Marlee. "Is it true?" Strawberry-blonde strands kissed her face, having escaped the elastic band at her nape. "Are you?"

Any worry Lara had entertained about Marlee resenting her fell away under the force of the enthusiastic questions. "Yes," she said, bending down to embrace Marlee's small body, the girl's arms wrapping around her in turn. "All yours."

"Yay!" Dancing away with that sound of uninhibited glee, Marlee caught Toby's hands, made her cousin spin her around in dizzying circles. "Faster, Toby!" She squealed as her hair went flying, her feet up off the ground. "Don't drop me!"

Toby laughed at her scream, but it was the good-natured laugh of an elder brother—and that's what he was, regardless of their actual relationship—his hands gripping hers tight. "Want me to stop?"

"No! Faster!"

Lara looked up with a laugh of her own, caught Walker watching the children, his expression shadowed. Walking to him, she slipped her hand into his, touching the fingers of her free hand to the smoothness of his shaven jaw until he met her eyes. "The Council will never again steal their right to be happy."

He said nothing, her mate. But she loved him, knew him . . . and sensed the violent depth of his emotions in the tightness of the arms he closed around her.

His mood seemed much lighter the next day, and when he left to do a rotation on the border that night, he said, "You're spoiling them." The brush of his knuckles against her cheek, his lips at her ear.

"I know," Lara admitted as she put together a tray of chocolate cookies and milk for the children—both currently sprawled on the floor in front of the large comm screen in the living room, hypnotized by a quiz show.

Fiddling with the buttons of his shirt, his chest wide and strong, she said, "It's okay, isn't it? For just a few days?" Though she'd taken care of plenty of pups, it had always been short-term, where it didn't matter if she was indulgent. "I thought after everything, they deserved a little extra pampering."

Walker wanted only to kiss that rueful smile off of her lips . . . then realized on a surge of bone-deep pleasure that he could. Anytime he pleased. She'd given him that right. "I can see I'll have to be the tough one here," he murmured after both their hearts had turned to thunder.

She scowled even as she smoothed her hands over his chest, affectionate and possessive both. "I can be tough. Just ask the juveniles."

Yes, she had an unflinching courage, his mate. His pride in her strength of heart and determination was absolute. But he also knew that she was inherently kind, that she forgave far easier and quicker than anyone else he'd ever met, and that she'd cut off her own arm if it would heal another's hurt. No doubt, she'd spoil the children more than a little . . . but that was what mothers did. What they *should* do. He would never stop her.

Because even Marlee, in spite of her chirpy, chatty personality, had an inward maturity he wished she didn't. His daughter had learned the harsh realities of the world at an age when her spirit should've been innocent, without a single bruise. Instead, she'd been kicked in the heart by the very person who should've protected her beyond all others.

Never would he forgive Yelene the broken look in his baby's eyes that ugly day months after their defection when Marlee had turned to him and said, "Daddy, did my mother not want to come with us?"

For the first time in his life, he'd lied to his child, telling her that Yelene hadn't been able to get out in time. He hadn't wanted to wound her by sharing the brutal truth—that Yelene had written her child out of her life the instant she became a hazardous inconvenience. But Marlee, his little girl with her wise soul, had shaken her head and hugged him. *"It's okay, Daddy. I know she didn't love us."*

"Walker?"

He swallowed the memory of the cold rage that had gripped him in its teeth that day as he held his daughter, not wanting the past to taint the wonder that was his family, his mate. "I better go or I'll be late."

"Take care of yourself," Lara said, her eyes seeming to see right through him, to places only she had ever reached.

That tawny gaze ignited a sense of acute and gnawing vulnerability within Walker, but regardless of his discomfort, he fought the urge to close himself off, to attempt to block the mating bond using his psychic abilities. That would hurt Lara on the innermost level, and the one thing Walker would never consciously do was hurt his mate.

"Be good for Lara," he said to the children as she walked him to the door.

Cookie crumbs wreathing their mouths, they nodded and waved.

"Bedtime in an hour."

"Dad!"

"Uncle Walker!"

"Forty-five minutes."

There were no more arguments. Turning to see Lara biting back a smile, he pointed a finger at her. "Early bedtime for you, too"—he dropped his voice—"so I don't feel guilty waking you when I return." He *hadn't* been a physical man before her, having learned to live with his touch-hunger until it was simply a part of him, but now he wanted to explore each and every sensation with her, then he wanted to do it all over again.

"That's one thing," she whispered, rising to press her mouth to his, "you never have to feel guilty about. I'll wait for my wake-up."

The taste of her—lush, addictive, exquisitely familiar—lingered on his lips as he went to take his position on the perimeter. While he didn't often do a security rotation, his assignment being to oversee the education and general development of the ten-to-thirteen-year-olds in the pack, he was on the backup roster. And with a significant percentage of his charges still in the safe zones where they'd been evacuated, it had made sense for him to step up.

However, Walker had also made certain to stay in touch with his group throughout, addressing their worries and questions. They were good kids, belonged to him as much as they did their parents. That was a truth it had taken him a long time to understand—that everyone parented the children in SnowDancer.

An integral aspect of Walker's job was to make certain no child—dominant or submissive, shy or aggressive—slipped through the cracks. He often had pups seated along the bench in his workshop, doing their homework and eating afternoon snacks. And he'd tucked a few into bed, too, when needed. Perhaps he wasn't as affectionate as a changeling parent, but the children seemed to feel safe with him, and that was what mattered.

"Part dean, part teacher, part trainer, part mother, part father."

That was how Hawke had explained the position to Walker when the alpha had first extended the offer.

"You'll be responsible for making sure each pup navigates this time of growth in a way that leaves him or her with the skills needed for the next stage of their development. If you're good at what you do, the pups will come to see you as another parent."

"Don't you occupy that role as alpha?"

"Yes, but there's only one of me. That's why we have people in charge of all the separate age groups—so a child or juvenile never feels lost or isolated, even if their parents have to be away from the den.

"You'll work closely with the maternals and the teachers, and while they're responsible for different aspects of the children's health and education, you're the one who coordinates everything and makes certain every child in your group gets what he or she needs to feel safe, happy, and challenged."

Drawing in the crisp night air as he considered possible issues that might arise on the children's return, he caught an acrid scent, identified it as ash. He was, he realized, about to pass the area that Sienna's power had denuded, the earth barren . . . though he saw that someone had been out here since the last time he'd checked, marked out what appeared to be a planting grid.

Good.

The sooner this land began to heal, the sooner Sienna would be able to come to terms with what she'd done. Because while his niece put on a good face, he knew it haunted her, the lives she'd taken. That they had been of the enemy made no difference—and that was why Sienna would retain her soul in the face of a power that could well have corrupted her from the inside out, turning her into a presence as malignant as that of the Councilor who'd taken her as a child and attempted to form her into a weapon.

When, ten minutes later, he saw a tall, dark-haired man standing on the small rise that provided the best vantage point over Walker's section of the outer border, he thought again of power and corruption and of the strength it took to fight the insidious rot. Arrow training was cold and inhuman, designed to create killers.

It had succeeded in Judd.

"The blood on my hands will always be there."

A brutal acceptance, made without excuse, though his younger brother had been a defenseless boy when their parents had given him up to the horrors of the squad's training rooms. Never once had Walker heard Judd attempt to justify his lethal actions as an Arrow. No, his brother took responsibility, carried the weight, and in so doing, found his redemption.

"Did Riley make an error," he asked, halting beside Judd, "and assign us both to the same section?" It would be unlike the organized senior lieutenant, but as Hawke's right hand, Riley had a lot on his plate at present.

"No—I'm actually the one handling security assignments right now. Frees Riley up for other duties." Judd glanced at him, the gold flecks in his dark brown eyes shimmering under the moonlight. "I wanted to speak to you." Dressed in a plain white T-shirt and jeans, his hair tumbled by the night winds, he looked young, as carefree as the novice soldiers in the pack.

It was an illusion, of course, but still . . . "Something's made you happy." Even now, it felt strange to say that, to acknowledge his brother had broken the icy Silence forged in him by the merciless application of pain and torture; that he was free to feel, free to love.

Walker's own Silence had never been as pristine, though he'd concealed the flaws using telepathic abilities so subtle, no one had considered him a threat. It was his very need to hide the fact that he would die for his brother and sister . . . and later, for his daughter, his niece, his nephew, that had led him to develop and hone his skills at the most delicate, most complex of telepathic deceptions.

Flawed conditioning or not, those years of unrelenting control had left their mark. In many ways, Judd had managed to come further than he had.

His brother chuckled, proving Walker's line of thought. "Brenna," he said, "made me sit through a show about finding the perfect wedding dress. Not only that, she insisted I have opinions about the gowns."

The image was an incongruous one, but then, this Judd was not the same Judd who had worked with cold-blooded calculation beside Walker to ensure their defection did not fail, ready to stop hearts, slit throats, seize hostages, whatever it took. His own life had been a negligible consideration to Judd, his eyes dead, devoid of hope.

Why would such a show interest Brenna? Walker asked, and it was a surreal conversation to be having with his assassin of a brother . . . and yet it felt strangely good. As if they were normal men with normal lives and loves. *Changelings don't tend to choose traditional wedding gowns for their mating or bonding ceremonies.* Brenna's, he recalled, had been an ice-blue silk sheath shot with silver that fascinated Marlee.

Judd's response was a shrug. *Brenna said I should just accept it and consider myself duty bound by our mating to keep her company.* A quick grin. *Every week.*

A slow curl of anticipation in his gut, Walker wondered what Lara would demand from him. He wanted to create such memories with her, add them one after the other until the darkness of the past was buried under the brilliance of the present. *And did you?*

What?

Have opinions?

Yes. Apparently I have no taste.

As Judd grinned again, Walker felt something deep inside him close its watchful eyes at last. Judd might be a deadly blade, but he'd been Walker's younger brother first, his to protect. Except Walker hadn't been strong enough, old enough to keep Judd from being taken away, from being hurt until he he was almost broken, the innocent boy Walker had once known buried under the angry loneliness of believing he'd been forsaken by his entire family.

Seeing his brother happy, centered, was a gift. "What did you want to discuss?"

"I've told you of my contacts with other Arrows," Judd said into the night-dark silence, "but do you personally remember Aden?"

Chapter 3

WALKER'S MIND RACED back over two decades to present him with an image of a small boy with slanted eyes of liquid brown and hair of silky black cut close to his skull in an effort to keep it tamed.

He'd appeared fragile, his bones sticking out against his skin, but that boy, he'd had a will akin to a Lauren and a mind that echoed Walker's own—a telepath dismissed as a power because his ability was so subtle, so very fine-tuned. Like Walker, Aden had been miscategorized, his power level far, *far* more danger-ous than indicated by his official classification.

Eyes widening a fraction as Aden realized Walker knew the truth. "Will you tell?" A child's voice, but an ancient's gaze.

"No." Never would he betray one of his children. "I'll teach you to hide the truth better, until no one will ever again find you out."

"Why?" A flat question.

"Because you deserve to live without fear or pain. I can't give you that—but I can give you a weapon, show you how to use it so that you can fight when the time comes."

"Yes, I remember Aden." As he remembered every single child he'd taught in the Arrow school; every single bruise and broken bone he'd witnessed; every complaint he'd made as a wet-behind-the-ears teacher to the "protective" branch of the training squad, to his superiors, even to the Council itself, before coming to understand that no one was listening.

It could've broken him, but Walker had refused to buckle . . . because he *did* have the ability to give his charges psychic weapons, and sometimes, he'd even been able to protect them, if only for a short while. He'd kept more than one student after school, ostensibly for detention or extra tutoring—only to tell that child to sleep, to rest, to heal as much as he or she could, safe in the knowledge that no one would drag them out of sleep to face some dark horror meant to turn a child into a perfect killing machine.

So many of the youngest, their emotions not yet crushed under the weight of Silence, had ended up sobbing in his arms at the small kindness. He could still feel the weight of their tiny bodies against him, their tears drenching his shirt, their nascent conditioning fracturing inside the telepathic wall of protection formed by his mind . . . freedom for a fleeting instant.

Aden, he remembered, had never cried, never broken . . . and never lost his soul. "He used to shake his head at me when I attempted to keep him back after school"—because the boy had bruises no child should have, his arm showing signs of having been broken and reset over and over—"and tell me to keep one of the younger children."

"I'm stronger. I'll survive. They need the rest more than I do."

Judd turned to face him, his expression intent. Walker rarely spoke of his time in the squad's schoolroom, and his brother had never pushed. He didn't tonight, either.

"Aden's doing the same still," he said instead. "Leading the squad, protecting the ones who are broken, watching over the children."

Walker felt a quiet burn of pride for the boy he'd known.

"He asked me to thank you," Judd continued, "and to tell you that what you taught him has helped save the life, and the mind, of more than one Arrow."

The words meant everything. "I'd like to speak to Aden when it's safe for him." See the man the child had become.

"I'll tell him." Reaching into a pocket, Judd pulled out a black data crystal, handed it to Walker. "The names and addresses of the children in the squad's training program. Should anything go wrong with the Arrows' plans for the future, we have to get them out."

Walker accepted the crystal and the weight of the trust Aden had placed in him, old anger twining with new hope. Looking out over the star-studded landscape in the quiet that followed, he spotted several wolves loping out to roughhouse in the clearing below. "Lake, Maria, Ebony, and Cadence," he said, identifying them by the subtle differences in their size, markings, and coloring.

Lake was the one who lifted his head, gave the two of them a nod.

Walker acknowledged the greeting with a raised hand as Judd said, "It's good to be home, isn't it?"

"Yes." The powers in the PsyNet no doubt considered his family even more of a threat after the revelation of Sienna's power, might yet attempt to harm them, but that was a fight that would wait. At this moment, everyone he loved was safe, and he was tied to the woman who was his heartbeat by a bond as strong and as tender as Lara herself.

He only hoped that as the days passed, Lara wouldn't begin to regret the choice she'd made to bond with a man who still carried the shadow of Silence in his every breath.

LARA woke to a kiss on her neck, slightly rough night-cool hands on her sleep-warmed skin. "You're home." Turning into Walker's embrace, she nuzzled at his throat, drawing in the intoxicating scent of dark water hiding a thousand mysteries. " . . . time is it?"

"Just after six." A kiss, hot and wet and carnal, his body shifting to cover her own, his hands pushing up her silky thigh-length nightgown, the color a shade of plum so dark it was almost black. "I like this."

"I know." Feeling lazy and sleepy and sexy, she lay boneless as he peeled off her panties and returned to his position above her, his body pressed intimately between her thighs. It made her moan, rise sinuously against him. "Come inside me."

He didn't argue, simply stroked her with his fingers to check her readiness before pushing into her slow and easy. Her gasp was swallowed up in a kiss, her nipples rubbing against the crisp hairs on his chest as he lifted himself up enough to tug off the nightgown before returning until they were skin to skin.

It was something she'd realized about her mate. Now that she'd broken through the barriers that kept him so remote, he loved skin contact, whether or not it was sexual. He'd never be comfortable with skin privileges when it came to the majority of people—but with her, he was both demanding and so giving it made her heart ache.

Playing her fingers through the hairs that brushed his nape, she locked her ankles at his back and moaned softly at the exquisite feel of him stretching her, filling her. When he dipped his head to lick at her nipples with languorous ease, her nails dug into his back. "More, darling."

The sense of a masculine murmur, though she heard nothing with her ears, and then he gave her what she wanted. She arched under the sensations, her fingers fisting in his hair. Tugging him up when the pleasure became too much, she kissed her way up his throat and along his jaw to that spot under his ear that always made him shudder. A wet flick of her tongue, a husky request, and slow and lazy turned slow and relentless.

Pleasure rippled over her—not in a crash, but in a languid wave, her orgasm endless. She felt him stiffen, shifted her mouth to his throat, kissing and petting him through his own orgasm until he collapsed on her, a delicious weight.

"That was some wake-up call," she murmured much later, when he roused enough to shift to his back, with her sprawled half on and half off his body.

He drew circles on her back with his fingers. "I'm glad you approve. As you know, I was a virgin not long ago."

She laughed at the teasing reminder of how she'd offered to be gentle with him. "You're a fast learner, Mr. Lauren." Yawning, she dragged up the sheet to cover them. "How was the watch?"

"Trouble free," was the concise answer, but then he said, "Judd was there for a while."

Sensing he meant more than he was saying, she spread her fingers over the taut heat of his chest. "Did he want to catch up?"

Walker was quiet for a long time. "We talked about a boy I once knew. A trainee Arrow."

And then, as the final vestiges of the night faded from the sky, her mate spoke to her about the schoolroom that had been his for so many years, told her things she understood without asking that he'd shared with no one else, not even his brother.

Tears clogged her throat at all that he had witnessed, the pain of the children . . . and the realization that her mate was inviting her into a part of his life she'd only glimpsed till now, sharing one of his secrets with her.

THAT morning marked the day the pack shifted into high gear, all of the remaining evacuees scheduled to return within the next forty-eight hours. While not needed to heal injuries, Lara was needed nonetheless, as was Walker. The week passed in a rush of helping the pups resettle into the den, soothing their worries, and—for Lara—talking privately with packmates who'd been so badly injured that in any other situation, they'd be dead.

Tai had been dodging her in true wolf style, but near the end of the week she finally cornered him by the waterfall closest the den. Crushed skull, catastrophic damage to internal organs, as well as a laser burn on half of his body, Tai had been so critical, she'd shut herself in her office and burst into tears for a single stolen minute during the aftermath of the battle, her heart breaking at the sense that he was slipping through her fingers.

Taking a seat beside him on the stony outcropping that overlooked the crashing thunder of water, their feet hanging over the edge, she drew in a deep breath of the crisp air. The sky was a stunning mountain blue, the fine spray from the waterfall cool against her skin, but her wolf was focused only on the young male beside her. "How are you, Tai?"

"Fine." Pure exasperation. "Seriously, Lara, do I look like I need counseling?"

No, he didn't. Vivid blue-green eyes uptilted at the edges and skin of golden brown, his shoulders broad, he looked strong and young and gloriously alive. But he was a dominant, and admitting weakness was a thing he'd fight with gritted teeth and clenched fists. So she kept her tone undemanding as she said, "Most changelings don't have to confront their mortality until they're good and ready." Male and female alike, they thought they were invulnerable at this age, and that was how it should be. "You were forced into it."

Tai stared at the waterfall, eyes unblinking. And she thought he'd simply refuse to speak. If he did, there was little she could do about it—yes, she outranked him, but an order would gain her nothing, not with a wolf as strong and as determined as Tai. He had to trust her.

"You know what bugged me the most when I took that blow to the head?" he said almost ten minutes later. "When I realized I probably wouldn't come out of it alive?"

Breathing out a silent sigh of relief, Lara shook her head. "What?"

"That I'd never have a stupid fight with Evie ever again." He gave her a lopsided smile, that handsome face suddenly beautiful. "Dumb, huh?"

It eased her worry to hear no bitterness in his tone. "Do you enjoy the fighting or what comes after?"

His grin grew deeper. "A gentleman never tells." His smile faded into an intensity of purpose that brought a memory into sharp focus; something Hawke had said to her over two years ago—that Tai held the potential to one day be a SnowDancer lieutenant. Now, the young male looked back out over the foaming crash of the water. "There are so many things I want to do with my life, but Evie? She's at the top of every list I've made since the first day I realized neither of us was a pup anymore."

Evie, too, Lara thought, looked at Tai with the same devotion. "You took your time making a move," she said, thinking of the man who loved her in the same unwavering way, steady and sure . . . but with a raw depth of passion that grew ever stronger.

"I had to grow balls big enough to stand up to Indigo," Tai muttered. "First time I even looked at Evie, I got the ice stare and everything shriveled up."

Laughing at his reference to the lieutenant who was Evie's older—and very protective—sister, she nudged his shoulder with her own. "Liar. I bet you were sneaking off with Evie before anyone knew you two were an item."

A very satisfied grin was her answer.

"I really am okay, Lara," he said when he spoke again. "I know most guys my age don't think about death and stuff, but my generation didn't have a choice. We were born either directly before or after the violence in the den."

That violence, incited by an ugly Psy "experiment," had devastated the pack. So many of their own had died, leaving behind pups who were suddenly motherless or fatherless, or in the worst cases, orphans. Tai hadn't lost his parents, but he'd been surrounded by loss all the same—his uncle, his best friend's father, his novice-soldier cousin, the list went on. *Of course* he understood death.

"Has it . . . your life . . ."

Wrapping an arm around her in a dominant's instinctive effort to comfort, Tai tucked her against the wild heat of his bigger body. "You know the shit me and the others pulled when we were younger." His grin coaxed one out of her. "We weren't traumatized or stunted. Hell, we grew up *proud,* and we grew up bold—we saw SnowDancer not only survive, but spit in the faces of our enemies by becoming so strong that they came to fear us."

Lara thought back to a teenage Tai, to the hair pulling he'd incited in the maternal females and felt the knot in her abdomen unravel. "Have you spoken to Evie about what happened?" Even accepting that he'd thought about death in the abstract, facing his own would have been a harsh slap, and he needed to acknowledge that to someone.

Tai snorted. "You think she gave me a choice? Submissive, my ass."

Lara's lips twitched at the affection-laced growl, the last of her concern subsiding. She knew Evie would ensure Tai was healthy both in body and mind. "She's only like that with you, you know." Evie *was* a true submissive, happy to allow Tai's wolf to take the lead. That didn't mean she didn't love him as fiercely as he loved her.

"I know—and I wouldn't have her any other way." Arm still slung around her shoulder, Tai nuzzled a kiss into her hair. "So, can I stop hiding from you now?"

Laughing, she cupped his face and kissed him on the mouth with the easy affection of a packmate who'd played with him when he was a babe and bound up his injuries during his terrible teens. "Smart aleck. You can walk me back to—" Breaking off, she smiled at the man who'd appeared out of the trees. "On second thought, shoo."

"I feel so unwanted." Waving a quick hello at Walker with that laughing statement, he rose and jogged off toward the den.

"This is a nice surprise," Lara said as her mate took Tai's

place beside her, his denim-covered thigh pressing against her own.

Quivering with happiness, her wolf tried to nuzzle at Walker, its fur rubbing against the inside of her skin.

"I only have five minutes." Closing his hand over hers, he brought her knuckles up to his mouth, the unexpected caress making her breath catch. "I saw you kiss Tai."

She angled her head at the edgy comment. "You've been in the pack for years. You know how affectionate we are."

"You didn't belong to me before."

Lara's first instinct was to laugh, tease him about his unwarranted jealousy, but something in his expression made her pause, think. Touch was a precious thing to Walker, not something he shared lightly. And a kiss on the mouth . . . it was an act he *only* ever did with her. "I didn't know it would hurt you," she said, kissing his knuckles in turn, "and I'm so sorry it did."

He curved his hand around her thigh when she released it, squeezed. "I'm reacting badly," he admitted. "You're the healer, and the pack has certain rights to you."

Wrapping her arm around his, she leaned into his body. "I could never withhold my affection," she said, hoping he would understand. "It would go against my every instinct to do so."

"I wouldn't ever ask that of you." It was a quiet promise, his hair lifting in the breeze as he looked down at her with those eyes the stunning shade of new leaves under sunlight. "I know who you are, Lara. It makes me proud to be your mate."

Tears threatened. "Ditto," she said a little shakily.

Reaching out with his free hand, he brushed his thumb over her cheek. "But . . . not on the mouth, if it's an adult male. I can't deal with that."

The naked honesty of his request hit her right in the heart. "Only you," she promised, and it was no sacrifice. Affection was affection. She'd find some other way to show it to adult males if needed. "Only ever you."

Cupping her cheek, he bent his head until their foreheads touched. "I'm sorry—I know I'm being difficult," he said, and it was a comment heavy with things unspoken.

She rubbed her nose playfully against his, refusing to allow the past to suck him under. "More than one changeling male has been known to go all growly over his mate touching another man—you're pretty reasonable in contrast."

A single raised eyebrow that told her he didn't particularly like that description. Proven a second later by the kiss he laid on her. "I plan to be very 'reasonable' tonight," he threatened when he broke the kiss so she could gasp in a breath.

The smoldering tone made every cell in her body sit up in attention. And as he took her mouth again, she realized her complex, fascinating, addicting mate had taken down another shield, opened another door . . . invited her deeper into him.

Chapter 4

FOUR DAYS LATER, Walker put down his end of the sofa in the family's new quarters and nodded at Judd to do the same. In spite of his brother's telekinetic power, he and the others helping with the move had done the heavy lifting manually so as to conserve Judd's psychic strength in case of an emergency.

Standing up to his full height, his brother looked around the room. "Nice. Roomier than your old quarters."

It was, to a significant extent. Had Lara been any other woman in the pack, they could've remained in the family quarters he'd previously shared with the children, but she needed to be close to the infirmary. It was as a result of that necessity that their new quarters had been organized with such speed—a construction team had torn down the walls between Lara's original spacious apartment and two other units, converting it into a place suitable for a family. A big one.

Lara had told him the entire section had been designed to be transformed in that way when the time came. "Healers always have children around them," she'd said when he commented on the increase in square footage. "Our own, adopted, packmates . . . it's a good thing you're used to that already." She gave him a smile that came from the heart of her. "We'll probably also have the odd packmate sleeping over. You won't mind, will you?"

"No." He knew she healed as much with her gentleness and affection as she did her abilities. It would be no hardship to have his home be a place where the pack felt welcome and loved. "Family is important to me, too." And pack was family.

Right now, the youngest member of their immediate family

was happily setting up her dollhouse in her room, while Toby was hanging some posters in his, both children being "supervised" by their new great-grandparents. Lara's mother, Aisha, had also been popping in and out as her duties permitted, always with a snack for them in hand.

Walker had never truly had a maternal figure in his life, had been the patriarch of his family since he was a young man; so at times, he found himself startled by the way Aisha related to him, treating him as he imagined she might a son. It was a strange sensation but not unwelcome, especially since Aisha never forgot he was an adult male.

Funnily enough, it was his assassin of a brother whom she treated as much younger.

"You'll make us fat," Judd commented when she appeared at the door, even as he took two peanut butter cookies from the plate she held.

Snorting, Aisha pinched at the hard muscle of Judd's biceps. "Then I'll put you on a diet. For now . . ." She gave him two more cookies before handing a couple to Walker and heading off toward the kitchen section of the open-plan living/dining area. "Toby! Marlee! Cookies on the counter."

Judd grinned as the kids called out their delighted thanks. "Can I adopt you as my grandmother, too?"

That got him a slap on the back of the head as Aisha walked out of the apartment. "Call me old and live to regret it, boyo."

Laughing, his brother rubbed at his head. Walker felt his cheeks crease.

Lara and Brenna entered the apartment seconds after Aisha's departure, both carrying boxes filled with the last of the clothing from the old apartment. Walker's heart ached at the sight of Lara's smile, her curls—tied with a fine silk scarf in emerald green—shining under the simulated sunlight of the den. *His* mate. Who seemed not to care that he wasn't like the changeling males she'd grown up with, would never be like them, no matter how long he lived out of the PsyNet.

Yet . . . part of him remained wary, watchful for any sign that she was unhappy in this relationship. He knew that part had been born in the decades in which joy had been a mirage, survival his only focus, but he couldn't erase it, couldn't reform himself into some other, better man.

Lara's eyes met his at that instant, a frown between her brows. Crossing the room, she rose up on tiptoe to brush her lips against his, saying, "I adore who you are, Walker Lauren," as if she'd heard his thoughts.

Cupping the side of her neck, he slanted his lips over her own, drenched himself in the taste of her, this woman who saw pieces of him he'd long forgotten existed.

"Hold that thought." A husky command from his mate before she disappeared into the master bedroom with Brenna.

Turning, Walker found himself being watched by eyes of gold-flecked brown. "Mating's good for you," Judd said, his expression shifting to betray a deep vein of emotion. *I'm alive to love Brenna because of you. And it always seemed grossly unfair that you didn't have the same kind of love in your life.*

Walker had never known his brother felt that way. *Until Lara, I didn't comprehend the lack.* The safety of his family had been his sole concern.

Judd's clear telepathic voice appeared once again in his mind. *Aden says knowing we made it, have lives, gives him hope, though he doesn't use that word. I don't know if he even understands it.* Judd went silent until they'd finished repositioning the dining table. *It may sound cruel, but I'm glad he doesn't understand what it's like to have what I have with Brenna, you with Lara.*

Walker thought of the life Aden lived, a life that had once been Judd's. *You think the knowledge would drive him mad?*

Wouldn't it have done that to us? To know exactly how much we could never touch?

Walker shook his head. *The point is moot. To experience it is the only way to know.* The glory, the raw punch of emotion, no words could ever do it justice.

"Put it down on the left," he said aloud, seeing Drew and Hawke arrive with the second sofa, followed by Indigo—six cushions in her arms, her head peeking around the side.

The lieutenant's dramatic eyes, the reason for her name, locked with his. "Gotta say, Walker," she drawled with a grin, "I never took you for a throw-pillow kind of a guy."

"I bought them," Sienna said from behind Indigo, a duffel bag in hand. "Marlee and I chose the design." Her gaze shifted to Walker, and in her eyes was the memory of the piercing happiness she'd felt at being in charge of her own environment for the first time in her life. He recalled how she and Marlee had pored over the catalogue, how excited they'd been to get the cushions, put them in place precisely how they wanted.

A tiny thing, but it had *mattered*.

"All done?" he asked, running his hand over the distinctive dark ruby of her hair when she came to stand beside him. *Kristine's hair.*

She leaned into his body, cardinal eyes brilliant with stars as she spoke. "I gave the place a final sweep, picked up any odds and ends. It's clean, but Evie, the kids, and I will give it another polish tomorrow to make certain it's ready for the next occupants."

"Thanks, sweetheart," Lara said, coming out of the bed-room sans box. "But for now . . ." Walking to the cooler, she pulled out a bottle of champagne and one of sparkling grape juice. "A thank you from us."

That simple drink turned into an impromptu dinner, com-plete with takeout brought up by Riley and Mercy when they finished a security run in San Francisco, and special desserts prepared by Lara's mom. Having returned from the tutorial he'd been running for his junior engineers up at the hydro sta-tion, Lara's father, Mack, was also able to join them.

As Walker sat and listened to the ebb and flow of the voices—the laughter—around the table, an unexpected vocal music, he realized his family had grown by a factor of multiples in a few short years. Each Lauren mate had brought a cascade of family and friends into the mix, adding to the bonds he, Judd, Sienna, and the children had formed, and those connections would only continue to grow, lives entangling and intertwining.

It was an extraordinary network, beautiful and steel strong. Never again would any member of his family have to fight alone, hurt alone.

His eyes lingered on the wild curls of the woman who had banished the agonizing, endless loneliness that had lived in him for so long, he'd believed it part of his psyche. Even now, though she was laughing at something Indigo had said, her hand was a gentle heat on his thigh, the intimacy already famil-iar. He'd placed his own arm along the back of her chair, his fingers brushing her hair.

Regardless of what the future held, one thing he knew: He could never go back to the way he'd been, his body nothing but a tool he maintained because it was useful. It had become so much more, a source of pleasure for him and for his mate.

Fox-brown eyes meeting his own. "Happy?"

He twined a curl around his finger, his answer instinctive. "Yes."

Lara's smile was slow, deep, for him . . . as it was that night when she pressed him to his back and tasted him with unhidden passion and a sweet feminine possessiveness, until his nerves overloaded with sensation, his spine locking in a pleasure so intense, it was thunder through his blood.

A couple of nights after the move, Lara growled as she tore the shirt she was taking off, her claws having escaped to prick the fine cotton.

Walker dropped his hands from the buttons of his own shirt, looking at her in that way he had of doing—as if he could see through her very skin. "Do you need to hunt?"

"Healers have trouble hunting," she muttered, suddenly angry at him for seeing her so clearly when so much of him remained a mystery to her. "It goes against our instinct to heal. But"—she took a deep breath in an effort to clear the fog in her head—"I could do with a long run."

Her wolf clawed at the insides of her skin, ready to race through the forest, the wind in its fur, the scents of the night sharp and bright in its nose. She could almost taste the cold slice of the air cutting through her nostrils, almost feel the crackle of leaves beneath the pads of her paws, her skin shimmering with the need to shift.

Walker redid the buttons he'd opened, eliminating a view she'd been enjoying in spite of her temper. "I'll ask Judd to keep an eye on the kids."

"No, you stay here," she said, kicking off her shoes and wiggling out of her skirt. "I'll be back in an hour." After she'd run off the frustration that gnawed at her, vicious and relentless.

A dangerous pause, before her mate spoke again, his voice flat, calm . . . lethal. "You really think I'm going to let you out alone at night when the enemy was on the pack's doorstep less than two weeks ago?"

Lara wasn't about to be intimidated. "And you think I'll let you insult my intelligence?" It came out a snarl, her body and mind both ready for a fight. "I'm not a child. I know enough to stay in the safe zones."

Walker didn't yell, didn't get angry, which only increased her aggravation. Instead, he crossed over and tugged her stiff body into his arms, her near-naked skin flush against his fully clothed body. The rasp of the fabric was too much for her over-sensitized flesh, and she pushed at him. "I can't handle that right now."

He released her, but the set of his jaw made it crystal clear she would not be going out on her own. Fine, she thought, and not bothering to remove her underwear, shifted, her body turning into a million particles of light before coalescing into the wolf who was her other half.

Hackles raised, she padded out of the apartment and the den. Then she ran, daring her mate to keep up with her. He wasn't as fast as she was, but he was clever. He kept tracking her down, even when she raced away. The wolf liked his cleverness, liked his determination even more. It stopped trying to evade this strong, dangerous male who was its own, and they ran side by side under the diamond-studded Sierra sky, the night alive with the rustling of nocturnal creatures that froze when the wolf and her mate passed by, before going about their business again.

EVERY hair on Walker's body stood up at the haunting sound of the howl that rose on the night currents as he and Lara halted at the top of a hill, hearts thudding from the run, a silvery vista of towering pines and waving grasses in front of them.

Lara, her wolf stunning in silhouette against a heavy moon, went motionless for an instant before throwing back her head and joining in. The wild music was the most beautiful harmony he'd ever heard, so *alive* it made him want to add his own voice, so untamed it stripped away the civilized veneer to leave only the primal heart behind.

Only when the song had ended, the night quiet but with a complex depth to it that told him he didn't hear everything she did, did he run his hand down the proud line of her back, her fur thick and soft under his palm beneath the protective guard hairs. "Something is wrong, and you need to tell me."

A cock of her head that he didn't need to be a wolf to read.

"Yes, it's an order." He hated seeing her unhappy. "You asked me not to close up on you. Don't do it to me." She could hurt him in ways no one else could on this earth, savage him from the inside out, but the one thing that would hurt worse than any other was being shut out from the loving warmth that had become integral to his existence.

The wolf looked away . . . and suddenly, the air fractured under his palm, her body dissolving into a million particles of light. He froze, his heart a drum. Her trust in him cut him off at the knees, told him all over again what he was to her. *I will never, ever let you down.* It was a renewal of the vow he'd made the instant he claimed her.

A heartbeat . . . an eon later, he was touching night-cooled skin, a woman with eyes of fox brown kneeling in front of him, her hands cupping his face. "It's not you, not us. You're my everything."

He felt something in him break at the fierce honesty of her, didn't quite understand what it was, his emotions stuck in his throat. "Come here," he said, his voice a rasp.

Once she was in his lap, he petted her without further demands until she curled into him, her hand on his heart. He knew she had a high tolerance for cold, but he took off the shirt he wore and made her shrug into it.

She did so without argument, then put her head back against his shoulder, her legs silky under his touch. "No one"—a long, appreciative sigh—"will ever convince me that there is a more beautiful place on this earth."

Walker couldn't deny her words, the Sierra night a thing of near-painful beauty, but his attention was on his mate, on what might have caused her to snap at him in such an uncharacteristic way. There was only one possible answer.

Chapter 5

"ALICE?" THE HUMAN scientist had been put into cryonic suspension by unnamed parties over a hundred years ago, and now lay in a coma in SnowDancer's infirmary. Inside her mind were secrets that might further help Sienna understand her abilities, but whether that mind would ever wake, ever function as it should, was an unanswered question.

Lara fisted her hand on his chest, shuddered. "I can't reach her, no matter what I try." Not only frustration, but pain. "She doesn't deserve to die without ever living. I found out today that she was *my* age when they took her—she never had a chance to complete her work, fall in love, have children. The bastards stole that from her." Tears rolled down her cheeks. "I want to give her life back to her, but I can't!"

He gathered her closer to his warmth. "You know what was done to Alice was a high-risk, experimental process—the fact you've managed to keep her alive is an indication of your skill."

"Logic won't help, not when my wolf just wants to heal her."

Helpless, he realized, that's how she felt. And for a woman as strong and as dedicated to healing as Lara, that would be a terrible blow. Alice was likely never far from her thoughts, and source of intense stress though it was for her, that was nothing he could or would change about Lara—because her ability to care was at the very core of who she was as a person.

"Tell me," he said, and then he simply held her and listened.

Much later, after they'd made their way back to the den and to bed, she nuzzled a kiss into his throat. "Thank you for listening." Another soft kiss, her fingers petting his chest, her legs intertwined with his. "I'm here anytime you need the same."

He'd never shared his day-to-day worries with anyone—he was the head of the family, used to being looked to for advice, and it wasn't a role he resented. No, it fit him. But that wasn't the role he occupied in Lara's life, wasn't the role he *wanted* to occupy.

"I'm meeting with Sienna tomorrow," he said, and it felt as if he'd taken an irrevocable step on this new road he walked with a woman who had never accepted that he was forever broken. She'd taken him scars and all, and in so doing, taught him he could be far more than he'd ever believed. "I worry about her."

HIS conversation with Lara was still vivid in his mind early afternoon the next day, when he took a seat across from Sienna in a small, isolated clearing. The two of them had discovered this spot—complete with the stumps they used as seats—six months after they first joined SnowDancer. Over the years, it had become an unofficial meeting place for family discussions.

A polite mental knock broke into his thoughts.

Answering it, he heard Judd's voice in his mind. *Running late. Be there in fifteen.*

"I'm surprised Hawke isn't with you," he said after answering his brother. "Especially considering the subject matter." So soon after Sienna's brush with death, the wolf alpha was violently protective of her.

Eyes pensive, Sienna fixed the tie at the end of her braid. "He can't disappear from the den right now, with how unsettled everyone's still feeling."

Hawke's presence, Walker realized, was helping to soothe their packmates on the most primal level. "You two won't have had much time alone together." It concerned him—the alpha and Sienna both needed an opportunity to decompress, take a breath.

Sienna's gaze met his, and he knew she recognized his worry, even before she said, "It's okay. Hawke is certain it'll only be another week or so before things return to normal."

Conscious of Hawke's instinctive ability to read the pulse of the pack, he nodded. "How are you?"

"Stable." Teeth biting down on her lower lip. "As far as I can tell."

Walker knew why she couldn't give him an absolute answer. Sienna had lived her whole life fearing the rage of power that lived inside her—the fact it was no longer wholly uncontrollable would take time to sink in. Looking into the mental network that connected them, he focused on Sienna's mind. It glowed crimson gold with a beautiful, deadly power that then shot down the familial bond to Walker, feeding into the twisting vortex at the center of his own mind.

Until the battle, none of them had understood the reason for the formation of the vortex. Now it was clear it acted as a filter for Sienna's power, stripping her energy of its destructive potential. "There are no signs of a hazardous buildup." Of the deadly synergy that could turn her into a bomb of catastrophic potential.

"I initiated a massive discharge of power not long ago," Sienna said in so quiet a tone that he had to concentrate to hear her, her eyes midnight with tautly held emotion. "According to my estimates, we can't do a proper analysis until at least the six-week mark post-release."

"Agreed."

"And I'll have to continue to monitor the cold fire long-term."

"Of course." He captured her startled gaze when she jerked up her head, this girl who was as much daughter to him as Marlee. "Any Psy with a high-Gradient ability has to do the same—you know Judd is always aware of the exact level of his telekinetic strength." The act was no longer a conscious one for his brother, but a near-autonomic response. "It negates the risk that he'll cause an inadvertent injury.

"A Ps-Psy," he continued, seeing he had her attention, "has to learn to block his psychometry on a day-to-day basis to ensure he doesn't drown under the influx of other people's memories and emotions." Ps-Psy had diverse specialties within their designation, but the foundation of their power was the ability to pick up "memory echoes" left on physical objects, from a doorknob to a button.

He switched from verbal to mental speech for his next example. *A telepath maintains a shield against extraneous "noise" every instant of his or her existence—you learned to do it as a child.*

Sienna blew out a breath, her eyes no longer solid black. "That makes it sound so . . . normal." When her X ability had never been in any way normal. "I'll have to maintain a conscious watch until my mind learns to do so automatically."

"It already is automatic." The cold fire had branded her from the day the X marker first went active, becoming the central fact of her existence. "What you need to learn is how to push that awareness into the background, so it doesn't dominate your thoughts except when necessary." She deserved a life free of fear, and he would do everything in his power to make certain she reached for it.

Never again did he want to see the girl he'd seen after her mother, Kristine's death. Sienna had been taken for "training" by Councilor Ming LeBon at age five and allowed no familial contact except for limited time with her mother. After his sister's suicide, the only way Walker had been able to get in to see Sienna had been by using the most cold-blooded and mercenary of rationales—that the young girl was genetically a Lauren and her abilities belonged to the family unit. As the executor of Kristine's estate, which included her genetic legacy, Walker had rights of access.

For Ming to deny his claim would've breached laws that lay at the bedrock of Psy society. And at that point, the Councilor had still worn his mask of civility; Walker had been granted permission to meet with Sienna, albeit under tightly controlled circumstances, but the girl who attended their first meeting was a twisted shadow of the vibrant, mischievous infant he remembered.

Her gaze had been cold, flat, her voice toneless . . . without hope.

If it hadn't been for Judd's ability to teleport in for far more clandestine visits, paired with Walker's skill at creating telepathic vaults that allowed Sienna's mind privacy from Ming's constant surveillance—a skill Judd had learned, then passed on to Sienna—they might never have reached beyond the dull shell she showed the world.

"The cold fire," he said now, wrenching his mind back from the past and the icy rage it continued to incite in him, "is a part of you but no longer the most important facet of your existence."

"No," she whispered, a dawning wonder in her expression, "it isn't, is it?" Her mouth curved, a burst of delighted laughter escaping her throat . . . and his mind filled once more with images of the infant she'd been, a sparkle to her eye that had captured him from the instant he first met her, mere days after her birth.

"If anything happens to me"—Kristine's fingers so gentle as she tucked the blanket around the tiny body in Walker's arms, a silent indication of her imperfect Silence—"you will watch over her?"

"To my last breath."

When Sienna, her smile lingering in her gaze, stood and took a step toward him, he rose, opened his arms, and held her close as he once had the babe his sister had borne. *You'll fly, Sienna,* he said, his heart aching that Kristine wasn't here to see the incredible woman her daughter was becoming. *Higher and stronger than those who would've caged you could ever imagine.*

LARA'S wolf was padding happily around her skin after a quiet pulse along the mating bond that was Walker's touch, when her eye fell on the glass spiral of blue and green he'd repaired for her after it shattered.

"It's fixed. As long as you don't mind more than a few scars."

Her chest grew tight as it always did at the memory. That was the thing with Walker—he didn't say a lot, didn't make big gestures, but when he did speak . . . "I am so in love with you," she whispered, thinking of the way he'd held her, listened to her, spoken to her in the intimate dark of their bed.

Her quiet, strong, intensely private mate was coming to her, one step at a time.

If only patience would reap the same rewards with Alice. The human scientist lay unresponsive under Lara's hands as she checked the woman's vitals, her flesh pallid, her bones far too close to her skin. Lara continued to seek answers for the other woman, but having been able to unload her frustration had helped put her back on an even keel, and she was able to nudge Alice from her consciousness once she left the patient room.

She and her nurse, Lucy, had decided to use the respite provided by the current healthy state of the pack to tackle a number of practical tasks, with Lucy volunteering to set the storeroom to rights. The chaos of battle had left little time for niceties like neatness and logging supplies, and the pre-battle inventory was woefully out of date.

Lara, by contrast, was in the process of updating patient records. The fact was, she didn't *have* to record anything. She had the encyclopedic memory of most healers, could recite every injury or illness that had ever befallen one of her patients. But, she had to think of the future, of the person who would take her place were she incapacitated or otherwise out of the picture.

Two hours into it, eyes dry and fighting a jaw-cracking yawn, she looked up to find Riordan hovering in the doorway of her office. The young male was cradling his arm in a very familiar way. Boredom vanished under concern. "Broken?" she asked, already around the desk.

Deep red under his skin. "Not really."

"Not really?" Having reached him, she could see significant swelling and bruising. "So your arm is just kind of broken?"

He ducked his head.

Surprised—Riordan had the usual youthful cockiness—she shepherded him into the infirmary proper and had him take a seat on a treatment bed. "You want to tell me about it?" she asked, ignoring the technical equipment to run her hands over his injury. As a novice soldier, Riordan needed to be fully functional as soon as possible.

"No."

Her abilities told her it was a bad break. Frowning at the jagged edges she could sense, she bade him to lie down flat on his back. He resisted until she raised an eyebrow in a silent threat. They both knew she outranked him.

"I'm going to have to straighten this," Lara said once he was in the position she'd requested, then punched in a strong pain-killer through his skin before he could argue against it. The dominants—young or old—were always the worst. The last time Indigo had been injured, Lara had had to threaten to bring the lieutenant's mother into it before the long-legged woman would cooperate.

Riordan winced at even the slight pressure of the dermal injection, which told her exactly how badly he was hurting. Conscious of his pride, she used her abilities to further dampen the lingering pain. Only when the tension leached out of his body did she run her hands over the arm again, confirming the position and seriousness of the break.

"Is it like seeing a scan inside your mind?" Riordan asked, sounding more like his normal self.

"Hmm?" This was an unusual injury—almost as if the bone had been crushed. Had Riordan not been changeling, with their race's greater bone density, she'd likely have been dealing with a mass of splinters instead of pieces of solid bone.

"I always wondered, when you do your healer thing, what do you see?"

"It's not like a scan," she murmured, fixing the damage points in her mind, "not that visual." M-Psy, by contrast, *did* see things in that fashion—Lara knew because she'd had the chance to have long discussions with a number of them in med school.

It was largely as a result of those interactions that she'd had a more nuanced view of the Psy even before the Lauren family defected to SnowDancer. The Psy students she'd known might have used strictly technical language rather than emotive terms, but they'd all had a dedication to helping the sick and the hurt, a dedication that meant the M designation was the most well-known and accepted of all designations among non-Psy.

"It's more a 'sense,' I suppose," she continued. "Hard to describe, but it's almost as if I become part of your body for an instant, able to pinpoint every fragment of hurt."

Riordan looked down as she straightened his arm. "Whoa, that is so weird," he said, happily buzzed from the meds, "how it doesn't hurt, even though I know that's my arm."

She kept a constant eye on his veins and fine blood vessels as she performed the maneuver, not wanting to nick or otherwise cause further damage. "This is a very severe break, Rory."

He made a face. "Shh." His voice dropped to a whisper. "My friends have forgotten that baby name. Mostly."

Lips twitching, she said, "I won't remind them if you tell

me how on Earth you managed this." Riordan wasn't one of the more accident-prone people in the den.

Color kissed his cheekbones, his gaze darting to the door-way. Lara went over and shut it before returning to work on him. As she did so, she counteracted the more heady effects of the medication, so he could think clearly but without pain.

It took him almost five minutes to speak.

"It was a dumb mistake," he muttered. "Nothing spectacu-lar. I was in the smaller gym, doing some weights. Strength training."

She kept her tone easy, nonjudgmental. "Okay." Larger bone pieces in alignment, she worked at repairing the worst of the damage, which included removing any bone chips so that the shards wouldn't turn into shrapnel in his bloodstream. Her ability allowed her to coax those chips to the surface, but she had to use fine surgical tweezers to pluck them out.

Riordan groaned.

"Don't look."

"I can't help it." It sounded like he was gritting his teeth. "So will I be missing pieces of bone now?"

"No, I'll stimulate your body into fixing itself." Not quite correct, as she was the primary source of energy, but close enough. "It's why you'll be hungry after. Make sure you eat a high-calorie meal."

"Okay."

Satisfied every tiny, dangerous fragment was out, she moved on to the task of healing the most severe breaks. "You were telling me how you did this."

Another heavy silence before he finally said, "I decided to up the weights a level, except I must've pressed the wrong but-ton and suddenly the thing weighed a ton. It tilted sideways at a really bad angle—I had the choice of letting it crush my chest or my arm."

Lara frowned as she realized he was talking about the bench press. "Why were you working out alone?" Spotters were man-datory on the bench press, and Riordan had more sense than to flout that rule.

"I needed to think." Tight words.

Chapter 6

FOCUSED ON KNITTING the bone back together, Lara held her response. When she looked up after what the digital clock at the head of the bed told her was over forty minutes of concentration, it was to see Riordan lying there with his lashes closed, a half smile on his face. "Rory?" she whispered.

"I'm awake." Lashes lifting, the smile warm in those gorgeous brown eyes that had made him a heartbreaker as a little boy. "When you heal . . . it feels like sunshine. It's nice."

The words made her own lips curve. She kissed his cheek, ran a hand over his chocolate-dark curls, as she rose back to her full height. Rubbing away the ache in her back, she said, "What's got you so stressed out, hmm?" She'd babysat him when she'd been a teenager, been charmed by his sweetness and sense of mischief—he'd grown up, become a responsible member of the pack, but he'd always maintained his joie de vivre. Never had she seen him so tense.

"It's nothing."

"You know what you say to me in private will stay between us." Human physicians took an oath of confidentiality. Things worked slightly differently in a pack, as there were situations where the hierarchy meant Lara was permitted and expected to share information, but regardless of that, she *never* divulged information a packmate had asked her to keep confidential.

A long, steady look. "Even now that you're mated?"

"Walker understands who I am," she said, turning her attention to the muscle, ligaments, and blood vessels he'd bruised or torn. "He doesn't expect me to betray confidences."

It was a subject important enough to Lara that she'd brought it up during their courtship. "*I will keep some secrets from you,*" she'd said, aware how crucial honesty was to Walker after his experience with Yelene. "*But those secrets are given to me in trust, not to be shared. You do understand?*"

Walker had brushed her hair off her face in that way he had, held her gaze. "*The secrets you hold are a tribute to your packmates' faith in you. They're not for me to know.*"

The memory shimmered as Riordan's chest rose in a deep breath, fell in a long exhale. "You remember that time Hawke busted up our group at Wild?" he asked, referring to the bar/club not far from SnowDancer territory frequented by younger members of the pack—though as far as Lara knew, no one had been there since the battle.

Right now, it was about being with Pack.

"That incident is legend." The news that Hawke had carried Sienna out over his shoulder had spread through the pack with the rampant fury of a wildfire. "Never to be forgotten so long as we all should live."

Riordan's lips kicked up in a wicked smile. "That was some night." His smile faded as quickly as it had appeared, an unexpected maturity taking its place.

And she thought—*this* is the man he's going to be. Quick to laugh, big of heart, but with a depth that would surprise people who saw only the surface.

"I met someone," he told her. "From DarkRiver."

"Ah." She started checking each fine blood vessel, noting with a corner of her mind that she wasn't feeling as depleted as she normally would after a complex operation of this kind. "Is your girl leading you a dance?"

"No, I mean, that's not it. I don't mind playing with her." Another grin, that of the wolf he was. "I think this has the potential to be serious."

"Okay. So what's the problem?" Catching his look, she said, "I know she's a leopard, but a leopard/wolf relationship is hardly taboo these days. Not after the success of Mercy and Riley's mating."

"Yes, but they're sentinel and lieutenant," Riordan pointed out. "Hawke's talked to us about the subtle differences between the two packs, and how we should be careful to make sure both parties are on the same page during any kind of a courtship."

"But?"

"But I don't know if we're supposed to inform our alphas when a relationship turns serious, whether there are rules we're meant to follow to make sure we don't inadvertently hurt the alliance if something goes wrong. Riley and Mercy had direct access to that information—and the standing to fix any problems before word ever reached Hawke or Lucas."

Lara saw his point. Though the DarkRiver-SnowDancer alliance was rock solid, the two packs were still learning how to navigate these particular waters. "If I know Hawke, he's already aware of the issue." The alpha was nothing if not plugged in to the beat of the pack. "But I'll drop a word in his ear anyway—not about you and your girl specifically, but about the whole inter-pack dating situation."

Riordan reached up with his good hand to touch hers. "Thanks, Lara. I'd do it myself," he said, and she knew it for the truth, "but I don't want him or Lucas paying too much attention to us yet. It's . . . new."

"I understand." She'd appreciated the fact that her courtship with Walker had been a private matter for the most part, and could understand the need Riordan had for the same. "But will you tell me about her?"

His lush brown eyes warmed from the inside out. "Her name's Noelle."

"Zach's sister?" The other male was a DarkRiver soldier.

"Yeah. He's *real* protective of her and Lissa," Riordan muttered in the way of young males trying to court other men's baby sisters the world over. "Lissa is Noelle's twin."

"That's right." Lara's mind filled with the image of two identical girls, both with long black hair, vivid aqua-colored eyes, and skin the shade of sun-kissed copper. "They're lovely." Had grown into their coltish bodies over the past two years. "How old are they now? Eighteen?"

Riordan nodded. "Only a year younger than me." A pause. "Lissa's this wild, chatty tornado"—an affectionate grin—"while Noelle's gentle, quiet. It's like she's a peaceful spot in the world, but she holds her own." His wolf prowled to the surface of his eyes. "First time you meet the two, you might think Lissa runs the show, but I've seen how Lissa always asks Noelle for advice anytime it's anything important."

He was, Lara thought, falling very much in love with Noelle. "Does Zach know you two are dating?"

"No, but Lissa does—I don't think Noelle's ever kept a secret from her."

"Does that bother you?"

He took a moment to think about his answer, which made her believe him when he said, "No. I knew how close they were from the start." He held out his arm for the scanner, waited while Lara did a double-check to confirm all was as it should be.

"I hate sneaking around," he bit out after she put down the device, "and that's part of why we need clear guidance on the situation from Hawke and Lucas. As things stand, Noelle doesn't want to cause Zach any extra stress."

Lara frowned. "Why? Zach's as tough as any soldier."

"Yeah, but he's a bit crazy right now, with Annie being pregnant and everything."

"*What?* As of when?" While Lara didn't know Zach particularly well, she did know his mate. The other woman was a teacher at a school that drew from changeling territory, and ever since the DarkRiver-SnowDancer alliance, enough wolves had moved into the area that there were more than a few pups who attended the school.

Lara had met Annie at a parent-teacher conference she'd gone to on behalf of a couple who'd been out of town at the time, and stayed in touch with her ever since.

"They just found out a week ago," Riordan said with a grin.

"Well, I'm delighted for them both."

She was still smiling over the news an hour later when she met Walker for lunch, the two of them choosing a spot on the slope overlooking the lake.

The sun was out and so was the first-grade class of the internal SnowDancer elementary school, the pups having the time of their lives on the pebbled shore of the lake while their teachers stood indulgent watch. Deeply content, she opened the container that held the lunch Walker had brought for her and laughed. "You've been in cahoots with my mother again."

. . .

WALKER shook his head when Lara offered him a forkful of her mushroom and herb risotto, which he'd picked up for her from the kitchens—Aisha and he were in perfect agreement when it came to looking after Lara, though his mate didn't always appreciate their partnership. "I prefer my boring chicken and bacon sandwich."

She snuggled closer to him, her hip pressing against his, the warm feminine scent of her in his every breath. "Are you ever going to let me forget I said that?"

He finished half a sandwich, picked up the second half after taking a swig of the coffee Lara had taken responsibility for bringing. "No." It felt strange and yet perfect to tease her, to know that he had the ability to play in this way.

Wrinkling her nose at him, she ate another forkful before saying, "Can you look into the web for me?"

"Anything you ask."

Pausing in her meal, she pinned him with eyes gone wolf. "I adore you."

Her love stunned him, as it always did . . . but he thought he might be becoming used to it deep within. Never would he take it for granted, but he might just come to expect it, and that was an agonizingly beautiful gift she'd given him, that expectation of love, of tenderness. "What do you want to know?"

"I did a fairly complex healing earlier," she said, sipping from the coffee when he lifted the cup to her lips, "but I don't feel drained at all."

Interest spiked. "You think the neosentience in the web is feeding you Sienna's excess power." Every psychic network had a "mind." The one in the SnowDancer Web, which now included his entire family, was but a speck, nothing like the vast NetMind that was the guardian and librarian of the PsyNet. But it *did* exist, and as they'd seen in the aftermath of the battle, it could influence the web.

Lara chewed and swallowed before answering. "It crossed my mind."

Opening his psychic eye, Walker looked at the energy currents that rippled along the familial and blood bonds, saw the rerouting that must've taken place this morning. "You have priority," he murmured, closing one of his hands over her raised knee. "When you need the energy, it goes directly and only to you."

"That's good to know. If I'm ever in a triage situation, I'll be better able to judge what I can or can't do." Having finished her risotto, Lara put the container neatly in the thermal carry case.

"Here," she said, handing him his second sandwich. "I hope you brought more food for yourself. You're way too tall and muscular to survive on two sandwiches, non-boring or not."

Her frown as she dug into the carry case made parts of him he'd believed long buried stretch to enthusiastic life. No one had ever worried over him, not the way Lara did. If he'd considered the idea of it before they'd become a couple, he would've probably predicted an annoyed reaction to any such care—but he wasn't the least annoyed by his mate's desire to look after him.

Not when he felt the same piercing need to care for her.

"Here we go." Having discovered a closed container, she opened it to reveal two more thick sandwiches. "Seriously?" A laughing look. "Oh wait, this one's ham with cheese and tomato. You wild man, you."

Tugging her to him with his hand on the back of her nape, he kissed her laughter into his mouth. "Eat your fruit," he murmured afterward, nipping at her lower lip . . . and suckling at it when that wasn't enough.

He wasn't sure how the food got pushed aside, Lara stretched out on the grass beneath him, but they were tangled in a hot, wet kiss, his hand splayed on the silken skin of her abdomen when someone sprayed water all over his back and nape.

Jerking up, he found himself looking into the innocent eyes of a wolf pup who'd just shaken himself dry after jumping into the lake and racing up the slope to them. Recognizing the scamp, Walker gripped him by the scruff of his neck and brought that furry little face close to his own. "You are in big trouble."

Ben growled at him, batting at his chin with tiny claws that did no damage.

Husky laughter intertwined with the baby growls.

Turning, he found Lara sitting back up, having fixed the pretty spring green cardigan she wore as a top. "Give him to me." She shook her head at the teacher who'd started to clamber up the slope after the runaway.

Grinning his thanks, the older male went back down to the shore. "You," Lara continued, "finish your lunch before time runs out."

Realizing they only had about twenty more minutes, he obeyed the order as Lara gave Ben a smacking kiss before putting the pup down in the sunshine. "Dry off first, then I'll cuddle you."

Ben gave a huge sigh, but sat down on his haunches, muzzle turned toward Walker and ears pricked so hard they might as well have been frozen. Wanting to laugh, Walker broke off half his sandwich and held it out for the pup to grip in his teeth.

Lara leaned into him as Ben put the sandwich on the grass and sprawled down to nibble at it with surprising neatness. "They are so adorable at this age." Affection in every syllable.

"Want one of your own?"

Her fingers, having curved around his biceps, squeezed. "Walker . . . are you serious?" Huge eyes. "I wasn't sure— After— I took care that I wouldn't accidentally fall pregnant."

Cupping her cheek, he shook his head, humbled once again by the depth and generosity of her love. "There is no comparison." His painful experience at Yelene's hand, when he'd lost his unborn child to her mercenary desire to protect her own "uncontaminated genetic line," didn't blind him to the truth that Lara would fight to the death to protect their children. "I want to have more children, and I want to have them with you."

Her eyes shone wet, her voice shaky when she spoke. "Changelings are less fertile than Psy or humans, so it might take time, but I hope not." Throwing her arms around his neck, she rained kisses on his face, her happiness a luminous warmth. "Marlee and Toby will be such good older siblings. I don't want too big an age gap."

Throat thick, he held her tight. No one would've blamed her for forgetting Toby and Marlee at this moment, but she hadn't, her heart huge.

A cold nose poked between them, followed by a wiggling body, Ben excited to join in their fun, though his curious eyes said he didn't understand what had just occurred. Chuckling, Walker brought the pup into their embrace.

"Yes," Lara said, laving more affection on the boy, "I want one just like him . . . with his daddy's green eyes."

Chapter 7

LARA ENSURED SHE was fertile again the second she returned to the infirmary, every cell in her body humming with anticipation at the thought of nurturing a life in her womb, a life created out of the shattering beauty of the love she felt for her mate. Healers didn't have an advantage over the rest of the population when it came to conception, but she hoped with all her might that it wouldn't be too long.

Even if it did take time, the delay mattered less than the fact the terrible wound in Walker's heart was, if not healed, then at least no longer debilitating. Slowly but surely, her fascinating, complex, wonderful mate was throwing off the lingering shackles of Silence and showing her the parts of himself he'd had to bury to survive.

She thought of his chuckle over Ben, his slow kiss good-bye, and felt her lips curve in a silly smile.

"My God," Ava groaned, sinking into the chair on the other side of her desk, "you're smitten. It's so sweet I think I just got a cavity."

Lara threw a soft toy a patient had gifted her at her best friend's head. "I am newly mated," she pointed out. "Entitled to be smitten, thank you very much."

Sighing, Ava pushed her hand through the silky dark of her shoulder-length hair. "True, you're not a cynical old broad like me."

"*Please*. I saw you coming out of your office looking distinctly disheveled yesterday afternoon, accompanied by a certain Mr. Stone—who had a suspicious bruise on his neck and a shirt that was buttoned up crooked."

Ava grinned, unabashed. "Hey, we have a baby and a five-and-a-half-year-old with the world's worst case of curiosity. We have to get creative."

Having fallen foul of Ben's curious streak less than an hour ago, Lara grinned. "Lucky you mated a creative type."

Spencer "Spence" Stone was the pack's official photographer—not simply of joy, but of pain and war and loss. He'd been out on the battlefield, had captured the only known terrestrial images of Sienna's X-fire, taking photograph after photograph and transmitting them simultaneously to the den until the flames licked over his body. Even then, once he realized he wasn't burning, he'd somehow managed to get his arm up over the fire, capture a single shot of the column of flame that had encased Hawke and Sienna.

"Yes." Ava sighed, expression dreamy. "The man is supremely blessed in the creativity department."

Lara didn't think her best friend was talking about Spence's prowess with a camera. "He ever take photographs when you, you know?"

Ava waggled her eyebrows, eyes the same dark brown as her son's filled with unrepentant wickedness. "Not telling. But wait till you have a newborn *and* a teenager to deal with—I figure sweet as he is, Toby's gonna go crazy on you any day now. Then I will laugh."

The idea of a baby with Walker made butterflies break out in a manic jig in her abdomen. "I am *so* smitten."

"Told ya," Ava said, checking an incoming message on her phone. Her expression was suddenly one of pure delight. "Sorry, I'm going to ditch you. Mr. Stone is back in the den, the baby's with her aunt, Ben's in school, and I've completed my work for the day. Adios."

Lara was still grinning over the speed of Ava's disappearance ten minutes later when Riley caught her coming out of the storeroom after a quick chat with Lucy.

The senior lieutenant held up a small datapad. "You and Walker settle on a date for your mating ceremony yet? It'd be nice to give the pack the heads-up—there are a lot of folks who want to make certain they're in the den for the celebration."

His words made her wolf want to throw back its head, sing

in joy. "We had a chat about it last night," she said, inputting a date into the calendar on the datapad. "How's that work?"

"It'll be just over two weeks after Hawke and Sienna's ceremony," Riley said. "Fine with you?"

"Sounds perfect." Walker needed to see Sienna embraced into her new position in SnowDancer and would enjoy his and Lara's own night far more once he had. And as healer, Lara knew Hawke's mating and the attendant celebration was critical for the health of the pack. Everyone needed a chance to dance, to forget the blood and pain of battle, and to howl their joy at the mating of an alpha who'd bled for the pack since he was little more than a boy.

"Any plans in terms of the celebration itself?" Riley's eyes, steady and calm, met her own. "I've already got a laundry list of volunteers who want to help."

Warmth spread through every inch of her body at his words. "I'll have a preliminary sketch for you in a week or so." In this, Walker was being the typical male—he accepted everything she suggested. Frustrated, she'd slipped oiled male dancers into the plan, complete with whipped cream and a strategically placed tassel or two. That had received a response—a very firm "No."

Sliding the datapad into his pants pocket, Riley nodded. "Sounds good." His expression softened. "I'm very happy for you, Lara. He's a good man."

"I know," she said with a smile she knew shouted her delight in her mate, and returned Riley's affectionate hug, his body solid as a wall. "Where are you heading now?"

"Down to do some digging in the section being replanted."

Lara scowled, jealous. "Enjoy. I'm off to slave away at more patient reports."

The paperwork kept her busy till ten after five, interrupted only by a fifteen-minute break when Toby and Marlee returned home to change and eat a snack before leaving for their after-school activities. Though Toby was old enough to supervise his cousin, Lara enjoyed spending that time with them.

And, she thought with a smile, recalling the kisses on the cheek as they'd left in the same rush they'd arrived, the children had started to expect to see her—to the point that if she was busy in the infirmary, they came searching. It was nice in the best sense of the word. However, she'd been hard at work since sending them off, and now decided she'd done enough to assuage her guilt.

"Lucy, go home!" she called out to her nurse, closing the file she'd been working on at the same time.

The younger woman appeared out of the storage room a minute later, tugging off her hairtie to redo her sadly drooping ponytail. "Time flies when I'm cataloguing supplies," she said, tone dry as dust. "I'm a third of the way through. Want me to do the reorders as I go or at the end?"

"As you go. Better if we're out of some things than if we're low on everything."

"I'll break out my secret-recipe chocolate brownies and bribe someone from operations to process the orders, speed things up."

"I already asked." She'd figured Lucy would appreciate the help. "No luck—operations has its hands full to overflowing." SnowDancer had won the battle, but the violence had left the pack with broken or destroyed equipment, part of a forest to replant, packmates in the city who'd suffered damage to their homes, disrupted comm lines, debris from the enemy's ships to clear . . . the list went on.

"Damn. We really need that dedicated admin person." Putting her hands on her lower back, Lucy bent over backward to stretch her muscles.

Lara nodded. "I had a chat with Ava about it." With a degree in managing Living Resources, Ava was the one who oversaw the arm of operations that had to do with finding the right people for internal Pack jobs. "She's making up a shortlist for us to go over, but I think we'd better wait till things settle down a little more before doing interviews."

"I hope Ava's list includes lots of smokin' hot males from other sectors."

Lara laughed at the plaintive wish. "Dry spell?"

"You have no idea—everyone *likes* me, but I want to be ravished! Nice Lucy wants a gorgeous hunk of man to see and devour Sexy Lucy." Shaking her head, she left the infirmary with Lara, her own quarters just across the hallway. "I had a couple of soldiers drop in today. They helped me with the supplies. We talked."

That was why Lucy was such an exceptional nurse—she understood that not all healing happened in the infirmary and that Lara needed to be kept updated with the health of the pack.

"Younger males," the other woman added as Lara indicated for her to come into the family apartment.

It was empty, the children's activities scheduled to run late today, but it held the imprint of the family. Scattered school backpacks, textbook and game datapads on the coffee table, Walker's jacket hanging next to her own on the coat hook to the left of the doorway, the quiet, deep scent of dark water and snow-dusted firs underlying the brighter, brasher scents of the children.

Wolf and woman, every part of her felt a simple, deep happiness at being home.

"Grab a seat," she told Lucy. "I'll put on some herbal tea—we've both overdosed on coffee today."

"Do you have that peppermint and chocolate one we had last time?" The blonde woman beamed when Lara held up the tin, before pulling out a seat at the kitchen table and continuing with their earlier subject. "I think the guys felt more comfortable with me, since we're friends, grew up together."

"And because you're very good at what you do." Lucy had an inherent kindness of heart that could put anyone at ease, young or old. "How are they doing?"

"Fine, generally speaking, but they're having the issues we discussed—both were taken out by the sonic weapon, made helpless against the Psy. The experience haunts them."

Changelings termed the Psy arrogant, but Lara was well aware her race had its own arrogance, especially when it came to physical strength. It had been a hard lesson to realize that one of those strengths—acute hearing—could be turned into an agonizing weakness. "How did you handle it?"

"I listened. Like we talked about, most people just need to get it out." She accepted the tea Lara held out, breathed deep of the decadent aroma. "And, I pointed out that now they're aware of the weakness, they can guard against it, take countermeasures."

Lara slid into a seat across from the nurse, luxuriating in

the scent of her own cup of tea. "Good. That returns control into their hands." Critical when it came to dominant wolves.

"I think it worked, but I made sure they know I'm there anytime they want to talk."

"Thank God you decided to work for the pack." Lara adored the young nurse. "As for the dating situation—have you tried the cats? I don't want you being ravished by someone out of the territory and stolen away."

The front door opened before Lucy could reply, the whirlwind that was Marlee running in to throw her arms around Lara in wild affection. "I'm starving! Can I have cake?"

Laughing, Lara hugged her tight. "Fruit bowl will tide you over till dinner."

Not the least abashed, Marlee grabbed an apple on her way to hug Lucy. "Hi, Lucy! Are you staying for dinner? Want to see my art project?"

"Yes, stay, Lucy," Lara said. "I'm in the mood to cook—you can be my sous-chef."

It ended up being a dinner party of seven. One of Toby's friends had permission to eat with them, and Walker brought home a twelve-year-old female pup whose parents were running late getting back from their work outside den territory.

As they sat down to eat, her mate reached over and ran his knuckles down her cheek, the affectionate gesture making her wolf rub against her skin. "Hey, you," she whispered.

He tipped up her chin, kissed her to the delight of the children and Lucy, before turning back to the table. It wasn't until after everyone had filled their plates that she saw him watching Toby and Marlee. Marlee was currently giggling with the pup who'd come home with Walker, while the boys chatted to Lucy about the effectiveness of a twist in a recent movie. All the children were clearly in good spirits, but there was something in Walker's eyes, the same shadow of pain she'd seen the day of their mating, as Toby spun Marlee. She *knew* in that moment that there were gaps in her knowledge of what had taken place in his life immediately before his defection.

"Walker?" She touched her fingers to his thigh. "Sweetheart, what is it?"

He closed his hand over hers. "Sometimes, I see Marlee laugh," he said in a rough tone so low, it reached her ears alone, "and I remember a time when my daughter didn't understand what it was to be happy. Only what it was to be hurt." His gaze shifted to a grinning Toby, the memories a quiet ache in his voice as he spoke. "And Toby, he was in so much pain after Kristine's suicide, I was terrified we'd lose him, too, my sister's cherished baby boy."

The poignant sadness of his words wrenched at her. Tangling their fingers together, she "spoke" to him through the visceral connection of the mating bond, showering him in her love, in the joy she felt at being his mate, in the cheerful contentment her wolf sensed in the children. His gaze sharpened, the shadows fading to be replaced by a deep happiness that made her entire body sing.

And she knew she wouldn't ask him about the shadows, not tonight. No, she would love him, counteract any lingering whispers of sadness with affection, pleasure, and touch. He would tell her when he was ready—she had faith in the trust that linked them to one another, was no longer afraid she'd never know the heart of this incredible man who was her own.

Perhaps it would take a little more time, a little more patience . . . but they had a lifetime.

WALKER woke around midnight, Lara curled up against him, and he realized he couldn't imagine ever again spending the night without her at his side. Even the idea of it caused an agony of pain inside his chest. It was a startling sensation for a man who had always come to a cold bed, believed himself wholly self-sufficient, but one he had no will to fight. He wanted a forever tinged with the warmth of her against his skin, her hand on his heart, her curls tickling the bottom of his jaw.

Shifting with care so he could look down at her sleeping face, he ran his finger along the delicate shell of her ear. His mate was so lovely, and so gentle. So very *good*. That was what made her a healer. She might be a SnowDancer, but should he bring her the broken body of a Psy Councilor, she'd do her best to heal the enemy, regardless of the fact that enemy might one day strike her dead.

That was who she was.

It was also why she needed him. Because Walker wasn't

that good. He'd do whatever it took to protect her from harm, spill blood without blinking. He knew Lara saw that ability to kill in him, understood his moral compass wasn't like her own, but she loved him just the same.

He didn't know what he'd done to deserve her, deserve this life where he was so passionately loved that it was an incandescent glow against his heart, but he knew he'd fight to the death to hold on to her. *Lara was his.*

Chapter 8

QUIETLY MOVING ASIDE a curl that was tickling her in her sleep, he felt his lips curve when she wrinkled up her nose before falling asleep again. It was something she did every time he cleared away a curl—and he loved that he knew that. As he knew that if he ran a finger down her throat, she'd sigh and turn into the touch, her hand flexing on his skin. It made his entire body tighten, his flesh hungry for her though he'd shared skin privileges passionate and exquisite with her a mere two hours ago.

Shifting his focus, he played with the thin strap on her left shoulder, his callused fingertip scraping against her skin. He didn't pull back—Lara had made it clear she loved his hands. Instead, he smoothed the strap down her arm and leaned over to press his lips to the silky hot skin he'd bared, the taste of her an addiction he intended to indulge in for the rest of his life.

Making a sleepy sound, she tunneled one hand into his hair, holding him to her as he slid his own hand up over her thigh and to her hip, pushing up the satiny fabric of her short nightgown at the same time. He'd experienced sensation, so many layers of it since leaving the Net, but each time he touched Lara, he found there was more to feel, to explore.

Kisses along her throat, her pulse thudding against his tongue, her breast taut and perfect in his palm.

"Oh." A hitch in her breath, followed by a husky, "Don't stop."

He ran his thumb over her nipple. "Before," he murmured against her mouth, "I comprehended the mechanics of this act, but I never understood." That it could be lighthearted or intense, smoldering or wild . . . any of a thousand different moods, playing off his own and hers to create a new alchemy of pleasure every single time.

Today, it was slow, lazy, a touch playful.

Fisting her hand in his hair, she brushed her lips, soft and lush, across his cheekbone. "You know what I find sexy? These pajama bottoms you wear to bed." She ran her foot over the fine blue cotton striped with black.

He knew when he was being teased, nipped at her lower lip in sensual punishment. "Those," he said, her unrepentant laugh tangling him up, "are so as not to shock our youngest child if she walks in after a bad dream." Unlike after they first defected, Marlee rarely had nightmares these days, but she wasn't totally free of the scars the PsyNet had left on her psyche. When the dreams did hit, she still ran immediately for Walker. Which was why their bedroom door stayed unlocked at night—except if he flipped the remote switch as he'd done a few minutes ago.

Lara suckled kisses along his neck, spreading her thighs to better cradle his body. "She's growing up in a changeling pack." A graze of teeth. "I bet you it wouldn't faze her."

He had the feeling she was right. Changelings were very respectful of one another's personal space, never assuming even casual skin privileges with people they didn't know, but nakedness was accepted as a natural state of being, a logical outcome of the fact that every changeling young and old, came out of the shift naked.

"Well," he muttered, "it'd faze *me*."

Lara laughed, breath hot against his skin. "So shy, my poor darling."

Tugging her up from his throat to claim her mouth, drink of her laughter, he moved his hand down past her navel to cup her over the lace of her panties, kissing her slow and deep until she grew damp against his palm, the scent of her an invitation. In no hurry, he continued the lazy seduction until she began to move restlessly against him, her delicate flesh plump against the lace.

His mate was more than happy to cooperate when he tugged off the silky shred of cloth, sighed as she realized he'd stripped off his pajama bottoms before returning to her. Rubbing her partially bared breasts against his chest when he bent to her mouth once again, kissing her one of his favorite pleasures, she wrapped her legs around his hips, her nightgown bunched up at her waist.

Silky and feminine and soft, she surrounded him, claimed him.

Moving one hand between their bodies to grip his erection, position himself at the tight heat of her entrance, he said, "Yes?"

"Please." A sultry invitation, her body rising to welcome his.

He shuddered as he pushed home. Bracing himself on one arm and controlling the urge to thrust, he used the fingers of his free hand to tug the straps of her nightgown all the way off and brush his fingertips over the bare mounds of her breasts. She moaned, drawing her nails up along his back in a light caress as her internal muscles fluttered around him, her flesh molten honey with welcome. "You feel so good inside me."

Her words were a caress as intoxicating as the possessive clasp of her body.

Lowering his mouth to her throat, he kissed his way down to her breasts, teased her with his teeth, his lips . . . while rocking into her, slow and easy. They had only been mated a short period, but he knew how to listen to his mate's body, never forgot a single detail of what pleasured her.

"You're thinking," she accused.

He tugged a sensitive nipple between his teeth, released it to her gasp. "For the moment." He knew from experience he'd soon succumb to an overload of pure sensation.

"You know this"—a soft moan as he drew back at leisure, pushed in as deliberately—"drives me crazy."

"Hmm." Reaching down, he insinuated his hand between their bodies once more to touch her exactly where and how she loved it the most; knowledge he possessed because she'd whispered it to him when he'd asked her to teach him her pleasure points, his wild sensual mate who denied him nothing. "Is this better?"

Her body tightened then broke in a shocked ripple of ecstasy, her muscles clamping down on him. He gritted his teeth to hold back the urge to rush—he wasn't in a rushing kind of a mood tonight—and then, when she softened beneath him, he kissed her with languorous sensuality, petting her down from the peak.

Heavy lids lifted to reveal eyes gone nightglow. "I guess," she murmured, kissing his throat, "this patience is a side effect of the control you had to maintain in the PsyNet."

He held her to his throat, sucking in a breath as she licked out at a particularly sensitive spot. "Possibly."

A smile against his skin. "Lucky me."

Looking down into her pleasure-drenched expression, he whispered, "No. I'm the lucky one."

He held her gaze for every long, deep stroke, luxuriated in the touch of her hands down his back as she tried to bring him impossibly closer, gloried in the secondary wave of pleasure that turned those wolf-bright eyes hazy . . . and took him under in a passionate storm that short-circuited his every nerve.

HE came to, collapsed beside his mate's body, his thigh pinning both of hers and his arm over her breasts, his face turned toward her own on a single shared pillow. Breathing was an effort, but since Lara seemed to be having the same problem, he was content to lie there, hot and sweaty and happy.

Happy.

It was the wrong word to think tonight, the wrong key to turn after the flash of memory at the dinner table.

Fingers against his nape, rubbing at the sudden rigid tension. "Walker?"

The past shoved at his defenses, and it took all of his strength to fight the urge to let it spill out. "I don't want to taint us with what was."

Lara nudged at him until he shifted his body enough to allow her to turn to face him. "We're stronger than memories, stronger than hurt." A luminous smile. "We're a mated pair, a family."

So simple, so powerful, her words smashed the dam inside him. But it took him time to speak, time to think past the violent crimson haze incited by this particular fragment of the past. Lara didn't shove, didn't attempt to force. No, his mate simply nuzzled close and held him, as if she knew he needed her touch at this instant more than ever before.

"The day the rehabilitation order was authorized," he began at last, his voice a harsh rasp, "when I came home to find Yelene packing because she didn't intend to let her genes die out with mine"—the reason she'd aborted their unborn child with cold-blooded callousness—"I discovered she'd put in a call to pull Marlee and Toby out of school." Jagged, brutal, the words cut at his throat, made him bleed.

"It's okay," Lara said, her distress open. "You don't have to tell me if it hurts."

He fisted his hand in her hair, anchoring himself in the warmth and heart and wildness of her. "No, I need to tell you." Needed her to accept him in spite of the terrible mistakes he'd made and the pain those mistakes had caused. "Yelene had every intention of telling both children to pack up their belongings for donation to charity, because they'd be vegetables after the brainwipe of rehabilitation, with no use for any of it."

Horror colored Lara's eyes. "That's not Silence, Walker, that's cruelty."

Walker stroked his hand down her side, felt the rage that vibrated through her. "It was as if she had never been their guardian," he said, the insight making no more sense now than it had then, "never vowed to care for the children."

A growl came out of Lara's throat. "Healers might have trouble with killing, but if that woman ever ends up in front of me, I will carve out her heart without anesthetic."

Shifting his position so that he was braced over her, he rubbed his cheek against her own and spoke the worst truth of all. "*I* was the one who chose Yelene to be my co-parent." He'd been so careful, had read through multiple PsyMed reports on each candidate, done a deep background and personality check before he settled on Yelene.

And still he'd failed to protect the vulnerable lives under his care.

"I will never forgive myself for that." Regret spun razor-sharp blades in his gut. "The way Marlee looked when she realized her mother had abandoned her—so small and broken; the way Toby went rigid and silent when he understood he'd lost another maternal figure, it's on me and it always will be."

"Don't you let her evil eat away at you," his mate said, her hands cupping his cheeks, forcing him to hold eyes of wolf amber grim with purpose. "You aren't superhuman—and you aren't a foreseer, that you could predict the future. You made the best choice in the situation you were in."

Claws pricked his face as her wolf rose closer to the surface. "Yelene's cowardice belongs to her alone. When she was asked to take a stand, she broke, while you put your life on the line and did everything in your power to protect your family. Remember *that*, not a woman who saved her skin and lost everything else."

When he would've spoken, Lara shook her head, voice steely as she continued. "You *will* forgive yourself." It was a command. "Because if you don't, your unnecessary guilt will taint your happiness—and Walker? The children take their cues from you. If you don't step fully into the light, neither will they."

Trembling because he knew she was right, he pressed his forehead to hers. "I want them to misbehave," he whispered. "I want them to talk back to us and throw tantrums." The children were both so good that he worried some part of them feared another terrible rejection. "When they do, I might just start to believe they'll be okay."

Lara's lips curved, the emotion in her smile a punch to the gut. "It'll happen. Have faith in their strength and our love." Claws retreating, she patted his cheek. "They do have Sienna as an example, after all."

And his niece had been a "devil child," according to Aisha (who had a soft spot for said devil child after all the dishwashing Sienna had done in the kitchens in recompense for her misdeeds). "They'll have to work hard to beat her record of punishments." He'd never admit it to Sienna, but some of her now infamous stunts had made him want to grin with pride.

"I put my money on Marlee," Lara said. "There's a bit of 'devil child' in her, too, according to my mother, bubbling under the surface."

Walker rubbed his jaw. "I've heard it's the quiet ones you have to watch out for." Lara had murmured that to him in a voice hoarse from screaming her pleasure not long ago. "I'm backing Toby."

"You're on, Mr. Lauren." Claws running lightly over his back, her smile softening and gentling. "It's all right, Walker. Let go of the past. It has no claim on you anymore."

He knew he was too heavy for her, but he shuddered and covered her body with his own, her arms and legs coming around him, one of her hands stroking through his hair. "It's all right, darling," she said again. "It's all right."

Embraced by her on every level, the warmth of her within his very heart, Walker did what his mate had ordered and broke the final rusty chain that tied him to the life he'd lived before defection . . . taking the first steps on the road to forgiveness.

Chapter 9

BUOYED BY A bone-deep feeling of rightness, Walker finished a phone conversation with the mate of the leopard healer the following day, then went to supervise an outdoor exercise. It was a half hour into it that Hawke appeared beside him. The alpha's eyebrow rose when he spotted the three pups, two male and one female, sitting cross-legged on the grass, faces set and arms folded. "Why aren't those three participating?"

"It's a punishment." Walker had learned very quickly that changeling kids *hated* missing out on a physical activity. "I've had some problems since the evacuees returned to the den." It had disturbed the children to be shuttled off, to worry in safety while their families and packmates fought, were hurt. "A few of the pups think they should've stayed behind and helped."

Shoving a hand through hair the same unique silver-gold as his fur in wolf form, Hawke blew out a breath. "Future dominants, I'm guessing. Hard for them to accept being protected in a situation where they know their packmates are standing in the line of fire."

Walker understood in a way the pups couldn't comprehend. It had been brutal for him to leave the den when Lara, Sienna, and Judd remained behind. But it had been necessary, his strength needed to provide a shield for their most vulnerable. "Do you want to speak to them?"

"You're their handler; your call."

"Leave it to me." He planned to have a quiet talk with each child.

Hawke nodded, the pale strands of his hair vivid in the sunlight. "You're not the only one who's had issues. The worst have been with the older teens, the ones on the cusp of adulthood."

"Did you knock sense into their heads?"

"No." A slashing smile. "Left that to Sienna and the other novices. Nothing bites worse than being chewed out by those immediately above you in the hierarchy, the people you want to emulate."

Walker called over and gave some instructions to two of the boys, before returning to his conversation with Hawke. "I don't think this"—a subtle nod to the three pups—"is serious. They just need the stability and discipline of pack to settle."

"What about Marlee and Toby? Any problems?"

Walker couldn't have pinpointed why, but right then, he had the distinct sense of talking to an alpha inquiring about his pack rather than Hawke the man. That alpha had looked out for the Lauren children from the instant he'd accepted them into SnowDancer, regardless of his suspicions of the adults, and Walker respected him for it.

"Marlee's young enough to have taken it in her stride"— though his daughter felt far deeper and with more subtlety than most people understood—"but Toby's having difficulty." It was Lara who'd noticed his nephew seemed oddly subdued at times. "I've spoken to him about it, and I think he'll be fine."

"There's so much heightened emotion everywhere," the boy had said, "happiness and relief and worry for what's coming. It's hard for me to block it all out, but I'm getting better at shielding."

"Sienna," Walker said, shifting focus. "She's happy." A statement, not a question, because he'd seen her this morning, felt her increasing steadiness.

And that quickly, he was talking to Hawke the man again, rather than the alpha. "I'm her mate, Walker." It was a growl. "I'd never consciously do anything to make her unhappy, you know that."

Yes, he knew. But— "You realize I'm not going to be rational about this." She was under his protection, and that protection didn't end simply because she'd mated. It was forever.

"Yeah, yeah," the other man muttered. "I won't take it as an insult since I know logic has nothing to do with the instinct to protect."

No, it didn't. It never had.

"There are more like me." A truth he'd understood the first time he'd seen a parent brush the tears off a child's face. "In the PsyNet. People whose Silence is outwardly perfect, but who'll fight to the death to protect their young." Not because those children were a genetic legacy but because of instinct ruled by a far more visceral need.

"I know." Hawke, this alpha who'd seen the worst of the Psy race as a child, folded his arms, wolf-blue eyes looking into a future that was spiraling closer with each moment that passed. "Their dawn is coming. Can't you feel it?"

"Yes." In the trickle of fractured Psy heading into San Francisco, in the words of Arrows unbroken, in the increasing desperation of the corrupt to hold onto their power.

Change was a force that had the world in its ruthless grip.

For some, the consequences would be devastating. For others, it would be a welcome freedom. Some would fight it, some would embrace it, but no one would escape it. Walker hadn't expected the painful joy the crashing wave of change had brought into his life, but he intended to hold on to it with an iron grip.

AS the days turned into weeks, Lara's contentment only grew deeper. Walker's smile was no longer such a rare occurrence, the bond between them a thing of complex and ever-growing beauty, her mate's voice one she was used to hearing in the warm quiet of the apartment as they talked after the children were in bed.

She'd convinced herself her earlier fears had been for naught when it happened.

Two days before Hawke and Sienna's mating ceremony, she was in the midst of a detailed workup on Alice when she felt a . . . stutter in the mating bond.

An instant later, the bond was so calm, it was frigid.

Shocked into a pained gasp by the sudden absence of emotion, she ran to the small comm unit on her desk and put through a call to Walker's sat phone. It rang, then went to a message prompt without being picked up, which did nothing to negate her worry. She thought of what he'd told her of his schedule for this afternoon—a simple walk with a small group of children under his authority, the aim to work out the parameters of a new project in a stress-free environment.

He'd never risk the children by taking them into a section that hadn't been cleared by SnowDancer security, and she'd heard no alarms that indicated an attack of some kind. Yet Walker had all but disappeared under the brutal force of an iron control that made her feel like the mating bond was being strangled to death.

Forcing herself to breathe, to think, she decided to walk outside and follow the tug of the bond until she found him. It might end up being nothing but—"No, don't go there." With that shaky admonition, she managed to tell Lucy she was heading out, and left.

She'd barely reached the middle of the White Zone, the safe play area for the youngest SnowDancers, when Walker exploded out of the trees, a child's limp body held in his arms. Healer instinct slammed into force, and she was running full-tilt toward him before she'd consciously decided to act.

"What happened?" It was Tyler in his arms, the boy's dark brown skin sheened with a thin layer of perspiration that smelled "wrong" to her senses.

"Far as I can figure," Walker said, chest heaving from the speed of his own run, "he's had an allergic reaction. An insect bite, maybe a plant. He collapsed after complaining of shortness of breath and dizziness—it was a rapid reaction, less than thirty seconds from complaint to collapse."

An allergic reaction triggered by a pack's long-term natural environment was so rare in the changeling population as to be negligible, but there was nothing to say this pup might not be one of the outliers. "Place him flat on the grass." Ignoring everything else, she put her hands around the boy's throat, worked to open air passages that had all but closed up. If Walker hadn't reacted as he had by bringing the pup to her, instead of calling for assistance, they could've lost Tyler.

"I've managed to open his airway for the time being." Having bought a temporary reprieve, she checked the boy's body for any clue as to what had provoked the near-lethal reaction. The presence of a toxin or venom would require a different treatment from a response incited by a plant.

"There." It was on his ankle, just above his sock. "A sting of some kind."

Working on him again to ensure his airway remained open and his heart continued to beat, she asked Walker to carry him into the infirmary. "Where's Judd?" She knew that if at all possible, Walker would've alerted his telekinetic brother at the first sign that Tyler was in danger and requested an emergency teleport.

"Other side of the country till eight tonight. With the psychic energy he's already used over the past couple of days, teleporting back to the den would've wiped him out, left him with nothing to help Tyler."

"I don't think even a Tk could've gotten Tyler to me as quickly as you did." Lara grabbed a scanner as Walker placed Tyler on a bed inside the infirmary.

Turning to face her, he said, "I have to go. I left the other pups alone and they're in shock."

Lara nodded, her concentration on what was happening inside her patient's body. "Go. I'll tell you the instant he's out of the woods."

Lucy was there to assist after Walker left—with a brush of his hand over Tyler's tight black curls and a touch of his knuckles to Lara's cheek. When the boy's parents arrived, Lucy made sure the distraught couple didn't disrupt Lara.

Much as Lara understood their worry and fear, she needed to focus. The scanners confirmed what she'd suspected: The venom had provoked an overwhelming negative reaction in the pup's body, the worst she'd ever seen. The average changeling, child or adult, would've perhaps felt a tingling, maybe had to deal with an itchy red bump for an hour or so, but that was it.

Tyler's entire body was threatening to shut down.

"I've got you now. You'll be okay," she murmured, injecting him with a drug designed to counteract the worst of the effects, before using her abilities to stabilize the systems of his body. She not only soothed the ragged edges, she worked to make sure he'd never again respond in the same dangerous way to the same type of sting.

If an M-Psy or a human physician had asked her how she did what she did, she couldn't have explained it except to say that she could sense an imbalance, one at the source of the reaction. All she had to do was nudge Tyler's body back into the correct equilibrium.

The task took over three hours.

"I've eliminated the risk of another extreme reaction," she said to his parents afterward, rubbing the cramp from the back of her neck. "It should protect him against other allergens as well, but I'm going to keep him in the infirmary, run a battery of tests to make certain."

"As long as you want." Hugging Lara, the couple left to sit with their sleeping son.

"Did you call Walker?" Lara asked Lucy once they were alone, having given the instruction the instant she knew Tyler would pull through.

"Yes," the nurse replied. "He's still with the other kids, wanted to make sure they were okay."

Lara had expected nothing less from her mate. "Hawke?"

"He's not in the den, but I contacted him with an update." Lucy blocked her when Lara would've headed for her office. "You need to sit down, rest. There's fresh coffee and sandwiches in the break room. I'll handle anything Tyler and his parents need."

Exhausted, Lara didn't argue . . . but no matter how hard she tried, she couldn't relax. Not when the bond remained so icily calm on Walker's end. The remoteness of it made her want to scream, her wolf clawing at the insides of her skin. She'd looked into his eyes, glimpsed the intense, protective worry ripping him apart, and yet if she were to judge from the bond, she'd say he was unmoved by the near tragedy.

A sob burst out of her throat.

God, she was so *angry* with him.

WALKER had just escorted the last of his charges home and was about to head into the infirmary to look in on Tyler when he glimpsed Marlee and Toby in the White Zone. They were both involved in their own activities and didn't see him, for which he was thankful. Leaning against the outer wall of the den, the stone covered with a fine fern that meant it was invisible to aerial surveillance, he drew in a long, deep breath and fought the urge to wrench both children into his arms.

So quickly, he could've lost Tyler today.

Releasing the breath he'd taken, he turned to look at the woman who walked toward him, frowning when he realized he hadn't sensed her until she was almost to him.

"Tyler's awake." She joined him against the stone of the den. "He doesn't remember what happened, which is a blessing, I think."

Reaching down, he closed his fingers over hers, found them chilled. "How are you?" Her face was drawn, lines of strain around her mouth. "Sienna's power didn't replenish you?"

"I didn't need it. This was more about unmitigated concentration." She broke their handclasp to wave at Marlee when their daughter looked over.

"And you?" Lara asked softly once Marlee had returned to her conversation with her friends. "It must've been terrifying to see Tyler collapse, begin to suffocate."

The fact was, Walker's mind had slid into a hyper-calm phase the instant he realized what was happening, his emotions under lockdown. He'd made sure the boy's airway wasn't totally closed, given orders for the two oldest in his group to take care of the others, and then he'd gone to Lara. All the while, a fierce protective fury had raged beneath the calm. He *would not* lose any more children under his command.

Not as he'd lost so many of the child Arrows, their bodies and minds breaking under the pitiless regime of training, no matter what Walker did to alleviate their suffering. He remembered each and every face, each and every name. They haunted him. He refused to add another ghost to their number.

When he opened his mouth, however, what came out was, "I'm fine," and it was a response fed by the decades he'd lived in the cage of Silence, his mind still on autopilot. "I'd like to see him." He reached for her hand again, needing her on a visceral level.

Lara folded her arms.

Every muscle in his body froze, and he barely heard her say, "Tyler would enjoy a visit," through the rush of blood in his ears.

"What's wrong?" Only once before—during their turbulent courtship—had Lara pulled away from him. That day, he'd drowned in bleak despair; today, a hot flame of anger licked at him. Because he knew she'd only do something like that if she was hurting. And still she didn't speak, didn't tell him what had wounded her. *"Lara."*

"You're doing it again," she whispered at last, the simmering anger in her tone seeded with a fine vein of pain that cut like a razor. "I *know* you're angry, and yet here"—she thumped a fist against her chest—"I feel *nothing.* Just this mirage of peace that you throw at me to block me from seeing you." A single tear rolled down her cheek. "Why would you do that, Walker?"

He'd gone motionless at her first words, welcomed the *whack* of the errant soccer ball that bounced against his leg. Jerking, he kicked it back and gripped Lara's forearm when she would've turned and walked away. "You knew who I was when you accepted my courtship." If she couldn't take him as he was, the fractures inside him would be permanent and irreversible.

"And you knew who I was." Wolf amber brilliant against the lush hue of her skin. "I'm not fragile. I won't break if you let me see your pain, your fury, your worry."

It felt as if she'd kicked him in the heart. "I've told you things I've told no one else on this earth." He wanted to yell, but his voice came out deadly calm.

"Yes." Tears shone wet in the amber, her voice dropping to a whisper, "It means everything that you invited me into your secrets. Everything."

The panic struggled to recede under her passionate vow, hit a snag. "Then why?" Why was she walking away from him, ripping him to pieces?

"It's not enough to allow me into your past if you shut me out of your present. *Our* present," she said softly. "I need to walk beside you, to be your shield as you're mine. I can't handle being shut out, being cut off when I know you're in pain."

His heart thudded in his mouth, his skin going hot then cold. "If I can't be that open?" He'd learned too young how to keep his mind contained, his emotions hidden, especially in high-stress situations.

"No, Walker." Her voice was fierce, the curls that had escaped the clip at the back of her head catching the fading red-orange sunlight as she shook her head. "You don't get an easy pass, don't get to give in without even trying. I know the strength of your will better than anyone!"

Chapter 10

WALKER WASN'T CERTAIN what to expect from Lara when he came home that night after a scheduled meeting with pack-mates whose responsibilities in the den were either similar to or aligned with his own. Maternals, teachers, coaches, other "wranglers," they got together regularly to ensure no pup missed out on the attention he or she needed to thrive. His head hadn't been in the game, the need for solitude beating at him, but he'd leashed his chaotic emotions because such meetings were even more important now than they had been before the battle.

As a result of all they'd had to discuss, the meeting had run late, and the apartment was silent when he entered. Looking into Marlee's room, he saw her sprawled out in sleep, her arms and legs thrown every which way. It made him want to smile. She'd been like that since she was a babe. Silence hadn't man-aged to "fix" her before the family defected.

He tugged up her blanket, kissed a soft, sleep-warm cheek, then gave a light knock on Toby's door, entering only when Toby called out. The boy was now of an age where he needed his privacy, something Walker had to make a conscious effort to remember—to him, Toby would always be his sister's baby boy, given to him in trust.

"Hi." His nephew put down the spy novel he'd been reading, the digital cover displayed on his reader a garish orange with black silhouettes.

Walker took a seat on the edge of the bed. "Are you sure you're old enough to be reading that?"

Toby's response was a grin.

They talked for a few minutes, with Toby telling him of being put in charge of a junior soccer team. "Pups think rules are suggestions." He rolled his eyes, but Walker could tell he was pleased by the responsibility.

Ruffling the boy's hair, Walker rose. "You'll do well." The words said so much less than what he felt, his pride in Toby a huge thing.

A steady look. "I know, I just copy the things I see you doing. I want to be like you."

Heart twisting, he bent down to hug that gangly body, felt Toby's arms lock around him. And he knew he had much to learn from this boy who was his blood. Toby's openness of heart was a courage not many possessed. "Don't stay up too late," was all he said when he drew back, but Toby smiled the smile of a child who had no doubts about his place in his family's heart.

"Goodnight, Uncle Walker."

"Goodnight, Toby."

Lara was also propped up in bed reading when he entered their bedroom.

He'd never been a man who hesitated, but he did so tonight, unsure how to read her silence. Lara always talked to him, even when she was angry. Walking to the shower without breaking that silence, he shrugged off his clothing and stepped under the heated spray. Once there, he focused not on the way she'd left him this afternoon, striding off without a backward look, but on how she felt inside him, her love unshaken.

Shuddering, he pressed his palms to the tile, head bent under the spray.

His grip on the simple, inexorable truth of her love a bloodless one, he wiped himself off, and hitching the towel around his hips, he walked back into the bedroom. Lara had put down her reader, turned off the light on her side, and lay on her back with one arm above her head . . . and he saw what he hadn't earlier.

She was wearing the nightgown he liked best.

Everything came to vibrant life inside him as he realized she *had* spoken to him. He simply hadn't listened well enough. Not a mistake he'd make again.

Throwing the towel over a chair, he slid in under the sheet, switched off his own light, and reached for her. She came, warm and soft, and *his*. He shifted to enclose her with his body, his forearms on either side of her head. "Did we," he whispered, "just have our first fight as a mated couple?"

Lara felt every ounce of tension leach out of her at that quiet question. When he'd gone into the shower without saying a word, she'd almost burst into tears. Now, she nuzzled at his throat, taking the clean, male scent of him inside, her wolf's fur rubbing up against her skin. "Yes. This is the making-up part."

He shifted his weight to settle more intimately between her legs. "In that case, I'm already looking forward to our next fight."

He was playing with her, she realized, this man who hadn't believed he had the capacity for such lightness of heart. Throat thick with emotion, she curved one leg over his hip, stroking her hands across the slightly damp skin of his shoulders—he never dried them properly and she usually had to finish the task.

"I'm sorry I yelled at you then took off," she said, feeling terrible about how she'd avoided his touch. It had been an unconscious effort to protect herself from pain, but the instant she'd cooled down enough to think, she'd realized she'd hurt him, hurt her mate. It had killed her. "I didn't mean to deny you skin privileges."

He nuzzled back at her, kissing the side of her temple. "I know. It's okay." His jaw, rough with stubble, rasped over her hair. "Will you forgive me, too?"

Her eyes burned at the unvarnished request. "Always."

Lips closing over her own, his kiss a reclaiming, the heat and weight of his body a tactile caress. She gave herself up to it, up to him, loved him as he loved her, their limbs tangled so completely at the end that she didn't know where she began and Walker ended. And then the pleasure crashed over them, their bodies locked together as they fell.

LARA'S cheek was against her mate's chest when she rose out of the languid haze of desire, his arm around her and her leg thrown over his body, both of them slick with sweat, hearts thudding. "You'll have to shower again."

It took him so long to answer, she was half-asleep when his voice cut through the lingering scent of the pleasure they'd found in one another.

"The shielding, it's instinctive at this point." A quiet confession. "I had to learn how to create and maintain it as a young male, when I realized my Silence was problematic."

Because, she understood, fully awake, he'd loved his siblings—and later the children—enough to fight for them, enough that he'd gotten through to an Arrow and a young girl trained by a Councilor. "You had to hide even the faintest trace of an emotional response." It was a truth she'd realized the instant she'd broken the stranglehold of her own overwhelming response.

A nod she saw in the dark, her wolf's night-vision acute. "After defection, I knew I had to give the children, Sienna included, the emotional support they needed to thrive, but the fact is, while I can function with that shield lowered during the normal course of events, I'm not always aware of it snapping up in a high-stress situation."

"I know—I realized." Had remembered that her strong, quiet, beautiful mate had scars that didn't show on the outside, that he made certain didn't show, in order to provide a stable home for the children. "The way I reacted, struck out . . . I panicked," she admitted, shifting to look down into his face. "It was the first time you'd gone so remote, to the point where I could barely sense you, and the shock made my wolf so afraid."

"I'm sorry." He tugged her down, kissed the corner of her mouth.

Sensing his distress at causing her pain, she petted his chest. "You didn't know. I understand the shield now, so I won't panic." She'd worry, but she'd hold it together, hold him when he came to her. Because he would always reach for her. As he had today. "Just don't ever do it on purpose, okay?" She brushed long strands of dark blond off his forehead. "I promise I won't ever again pull away like I did today."

Walker's silence was deep, his eyes holding her own until

she felt lost in the translucent green. "Why are you so patient with me?" he asked at last, his tone raw. "It must frustrate you that I'm so unlike changeling males." Men who wore their emotions on their face and made no bones about their adoration of the women who were their own.

Lara laughed, her delight infectious. "I love you *because* of who you are, not in spite of it, you wonderful man." A passionate kiss that marked him as hers, made him want to stretch in pleasure like one of the felines.

"I like everything about you"—she continued kiss by kiss—"your integrity, your ability to love so deep and true, your courage, even the fact that you have a limit on how many words per day you intend to speak—" Giggles erupted as he flipped them, reversing their positions.

"Teasing me again?"

"Maybe."

Tasting her smile, he rubbed his stubbled jaw against her cheek in punishment. She cried foul, tried to push him away, even as her legs tightened around him . . . the same instant a knock came on the bedroom door.

Lara went quiet, listening with sharp wolf ears.

Reaching out with his telepathic senses, he found his daughter outside.

"A nightmare?" Lara asked, already out of bed and pulling on her robe.

"No, but something similar." Having rolled off on the other side, he pulled on the pajama bottoms he'd earlier ignored.

They reached the door at the same time. Pulling it open, he picked Marlee up in his arms. Though his daughter always protested she was too big now, Marlee didn't do so tonight.

Lara made soothing sounds. "What's the matter, baby?" she asked as they all took a seat on the bed.

Marlee, who never cried, grabbed hold of Lara's hand as if to a lifeline, sobbing too hard to speak.

"We're here, sweetheart." Lara leaned in to brush Marlee's sleep-tangled hair out of her eyes. "Tell us what's wrong." Her gaze met his, the worry in the tawny depths unhidden.

Wrapping one arm around his mate, he brought her close as he tried to speak to their daughter on the telepathic plane. *Marlee?*

I'm so sc-scared, was all he got out before tears took over again.

Walker wasn't surprised when a wild-haired Toby appeared in the doorway. The boy always woke when Marlee was in distress. "I went to get her some milk when I saw you had her," he said, holding up the warmed-up glass.

Walker nodded at him to come in. Putting the milk on the bedside table, Toby took a seat beside Lara and leaned over to tug on Marlee's hair. "Don't cry, Marlee-Barley, you'll turn into a turnip."

Marlee smiled through her tears at that ridiculous statement and began to sniff, the sobs abating in slow gasps. She remained locked around Walker, however, and her grip on Lara's hand was white knuckled. "What happened?" Walker asked as Lara brought Toby into their embrace with her free arm.

"I had bad thoughts," was the unadorned answer. "I woke up and I couldn't sleep and I started having bad thoughts and they wouldn't stop." Anguish in every word as she described what appeared to have been a severe anxiety attack. "I couldn't make them stop."

"Will you tell us about those thoughts?" Lara asked softly.

"I thought what if the Council came and took us away again? We couldn't be a family anymore."

His eyes met Lara's—it didn't take a PsyMed specialist to unravel the roots of his daughter's fear. Deep within, Marlee was scared of her happiness. Walker understood. He still woke without warning some nights, certain his new life was a dream, that he slept in a sterile cot rather than beside Lara's warmth, his family safe from harm.

"That's not going to happen," he said firmly as Lara raised her free arm from around Toby long enough to wipe away the remnants of Marlee's tears and smooth back her hair. "We're part of SnowDancer now, and our pack stands with us." No one would ever hurt any child in SnowDancer and get away with it.

"Yeah," Toby said, leaning into Lara's embrace once more, "plus Uncle Walker and Uncle Judd and Sienna and Hawke are way too scary for the Council."

Walker's eyes narrowed when a true Marlee smile peeked out, the storm passing far quicker than he'd expected. *What are you doing, Toby?* He knew even a slight empath like Toby could draw away some negative emotion.

I just helped her a little. Took the really bad fear away so she could think.

How are you? Experiencing the darkness he'd taken from another was the price an empath paid for his gift.

Fine. I'm conscious of the possible impact of Marlee's fear, so the panic can't grab me like it did her.

Making a note to share the details of the telepathic conversation with Lara later, Walker watched his mate pick up the milk Toby had brought. "Marlee? Why don't you have this, sweetheart."

Releasing Lara's hand at last, their daughter scrambled off his lap. "I'm too big," she said, a flush of red on her cheekbones.

But she accepted Lara's cuddle and kiss despite her embarrassment, then leaned her back against Lara's legs while she drank the milk. "I acted like a baby," she said after downing half the glass.

Toby poked her in the side. "You *are* the baby of the family, Marlee-Barley."

"Am not." A glare directed at her cousin, she finished the milk and put the glass back on the bedside table. "And you're babier than Sienna."

"Babier isn't even a word." Toby grabbed her body in his arms when she whirled toward him, both of them laughing as Toby pretended to defend himself from Marlee's "claws."

Lara smiled and leaned her back against Walker. Wrapping his arms around her, he propped his chin on the springy silk of her curls and watched the children, his lips kicking up at their innocent joy. Then Lara laughed as Marlee let out a perfect imitation of a wolfish growl, sending Toby into a fit of uncontrollable laughter that made his nephew easy prey, and his smile turned into a grin.

My family. My mate.

A fox-bright gaze met his as Lara twisted around to look at him, almost as if she'd heard his thoughts. "It's nice, isn't it?" A smiling kiss pressed to his jaw. "Our own little pack."

"Yes."

Epilogue

LARA COULDN'T BELIEVE it was already the night of their mating ceremony. Held in the arms of her mate as they swayed to the music from the live jazz band, she looked around the Pack Circle, the dance area in the center surrounded by wooden picnic tables. Those tables held an array of delicacies that had the children and adults both in raptures—her mother, Lara thought with a smile, had no doubt been planning the menu since the day Lara mated Walker.

Giant painted butterflies decorated several trees; Marlee's contribution to the plan. The wooden creatures had been cut out and glued together by Toby and his friends before being painted by Marlee, Sienna, Evie, Brenna, and a number of the younger members of the pack, including a rambunctious but wildly talented Ben.

"Look at what my baby did," Ava had said with delight earlier that day, pointing to a butterfly painted with a joyful enthusiasm that made the creature seem alive. "The Stone artistic talent clearly runs true."

Now, that butterfly and the others shimmered in the fairy lights that lit up the early evening darkness, the sound of their packmates voices and the children's laughter intertwining with the music to create a harmony unique to this moment.

"Happy?" Walker's breath brushed her temple, the masculine heat of him making her wolf rub up against her skin, as it had against his hand when she'd shifted for their early morning run.

"So happy."

The pack's pleasure in their match had been clear since the

day word got out about Walker's courtship, but Lara hadn't realized the full extent of it until tonight. Kisses on the cheek, hugs, whispered congratulations accompanied by thoughtful gifts, they kept coming. Walker had found himself shaking hands with people throughout the night, been hugged by countless children.

"Are you having fun?" she asked, aware he preferred to stay out of the limelight.

"I get to celebrate you." A slow curve of his lips. "It's a perfect night."

"Walker."

Bending his head and sliding one hand around her nape, he kissed her slow and with exquisite patience . . . so long and deep that howls went up around them. But her mate didn't release her until he was good and ready. Flustered and pleasured, her hands fisted on the fine cotton of his white shirt, she drew in a trembling breath. "Just when I thought I could predict what you'd do next . . ."

Walker ran his thumb across her lip, his other hand splayed on her lower back to hold her close. "I love you more than I'll ever be able to say, ever be able to describe. You're my starlight on a dark night."

Eyes burning at the stark beauty and romance of his declaration, she whispered, "You just did."

He went motionless. "Lara, did you hear that?"

"Yes, of course," she said, sniffing away the happy tears. "It's not that noisy."

Walker's lips curved, and then he was grinning in a way he hardly ever did outside the privacy of their home. *Can you hear this, too?*

"Yes, I—" Her eyes went wide as she realized she hadn't seen his mouth shape the words. "This is impossible." She knew of two changeling/Psy couples who had a level of true telepathic communication between them, but there were unusual circumstances in both cases. "I don't have any Psy genes."

Walker cupped her face, bending his knees so they were eye to eye. "Yes, but you have an ability that may as well be a Psy one. It makes rational sense that there is a connection, even if changeling healing is no longer recognized as a true psychic gift."

Lara tried to think, lost the thread, her mind a place of delirious chaos. "Let's talk about the logic of it later." Bubbling with excitement, she was the one who kissed him this time, nipping at his lower lip, suckling the sensual hurt, her wolf all but bursting out of her skin. "Can you hear me, if I think hard?"

Walker cocked his head, frowned. "No. But it may develop in time."

Knowing that the telepathy only went one way for now didn't diminish her excitement in the least, not when she'd just been given the greatest of gifts, the ability to hear the beautiful things her Walker thought about her. "Talk to me," she whispered, snuggling close. "I like hearing you inside my mind."

His cheeks creased. *Did I tell you how very, very much I like your dress?*

"No." She linked her hands around his neck, his own on the waist of her flirty red halter-neck dress. "And I didn't tell you how sexy you look in this suit." The steel gray was perfect on him. "It makes me want to grip this tie and haul you off to our bedroom."

You won't hear a protest from me.

Reaching down to fiddle with one of the buttons on his shirt as they continued to sway to the music, she said, "Your starlight?" her voice soft with wonder.

My everything.

**THE NEXT BREATHTAKING NOVEL IN THE
PSY-CHANGELING SERIES!**

From New York Times *Bestselling Author*
NALINI SINGH

Tangle of Need

A Psy-Changeling Novel

Adria, wolf changeling and resilient soldier, has made a break with the past—a past as unpredictable in love as it was in war. Now comes a new territory, and a devastating new complication: Riaz, a SnowDancer lieutenant already sworn to a desperate woman who belongs to another.

For Riaz, the primal attraction he feels for Adria is a staggering betrayal. For Adria, his dangerous lone-wolf appeal is beyond sexual. It consumes her. It terrifies her. It threatens to undermine everything she has built of her new life.

Too late, they realize that they have more to lose than they ever imagined. Drawn into a cataclysmic Psy war that may alter the fate of the world itself, they must make a decision that might just break them both.

"The alpha author of paranormal romance."
—*Booklist* **(starred review)**

penguin.com
facebook.com/AuthorNaliniSingh
facebook.com/ProjectParanormalBooks
nalinisingh.com

M1091T0412